THE COVE
SHIVERING CLUB

Michael Curtin is the author of four previous comic novels: *The Self-Made Men*, *The Replay*, *The League Against Christmas* and *The Plastic Tomato Cutter*, published by Fourth Estate. He lives in Limerick.

MICHAEL CURTIN

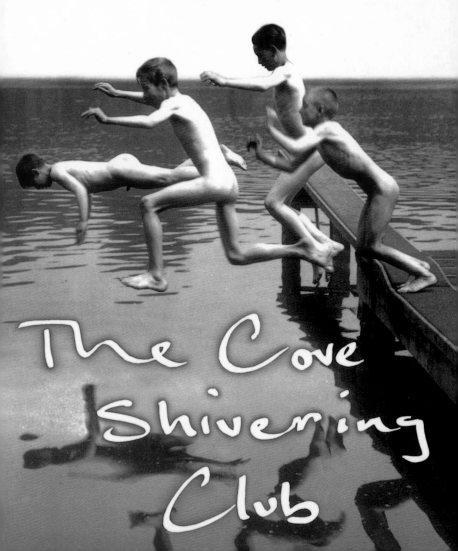

The Cove Shivering Club

THE COVE
SHIVERING CLUB

MICHAEL CURTIN

FOURTH ESTATE • London

For
Jason, Michael, Sarah and Andrew

First published in Great Britain in 1996 by
Fourth Estate Limited
6 Salem Road
London W2 4BU
Copyright © 1996 by Michael Curtin

ISBN 1-85702-473-7

Phototypeset by Intype London Ltd
Printed in Great Britain by
Clays Ltd, St Ives plc

PART 1

CHAPTER 1

THE DUST JACKETS of my books proclaim the usual codswallop: clerk, bus conductor, factory hand, builder's labourer, barman, burden on the state. Yet if the midnight knock ever comes to my door and I blink awake into the truncheons and the barrels of the guns and hear the bark: What are you?, Junior Nash is likely to come back with: I'm a swimmer.

We were all swimmers once but most grew up and out of the practice, seeing it as having been an appurtenant of poverty. Sure, they swim abroad in the Canaries and Majorca and at home in the heated pools twelve months of the year, the type of swimming that constitutes a bauble of success. I would give that lot room, consider them outside the freemasonry of those who still swim as we did as children, in cold water – though many of the faithful are now grey or bald, survivors of bypasses, artificially hipped. But we retain the ecstasy of swimming as kids by never changing the style of stroke or of life.

The city river was long, broad and accessible. We were brought up to swim and were hunted out to the sunshine and fresh air that, with spoonfuls of cod liver oil, inoculated us against the TB-riddled winters that sniped our elders –

including both my parents. Today there are few enough around who will swim in the river, because the old beauty spots are littered with municipal notices warning that the river is polluted, notices signed BY ORDER OF THE CORPORATION. Those who do still plunge in are idealists – the sunshine and fresh air and cod liver oil having built up our immunity against reality.

We were also brought up to be men: to open a door for a woman, not to swear in female company, to walk on the outside of the footpath, to carry the umbrella, give up the seat on the bus and – at a stately age – to raise the hat when passing the church or a lady. Manhood, as we aspired to the condition, embraced respect for women as well as learning to smoke and drink and a lot of other guidelines that are not fashionable today. Nobody then went around with a baby strapped to his neck or doing the washing-up or both.

My uncle, Budge Griffin, was a swimmer. He lived with us. Though the house was as much his as my mother's, Budge was unobtrusive, using his room and the pub. He was a season retired from the rugby front row. An uneducated man, he was set to enjoy as much drink as a bachelor's wages could afford. He was of the breed who would never marry – too much the sporting man, the drinker, maybe too gentle for the trappings of courtship and marriage. They are in every generation, their own times too coarse for them, belonging to an earlier graciousness.

Once both my parents were removed to the sanatorium, Budge Griffin burnt rashers and sausages for the tea. He sat by the fire and listened to the wireless while I did my exercise. He washed my hands and face and knees, and carried me on his back upstairs and listened to my prayers. He kissed me and then dragged a hand through his own hair before leaving the bedroom. His world was out there on the building site by day and in the pub at night; at the rugby

4

match on Saturday and in the pub for the post-mortem; at mass on Sunday and in the pub Sunday morning, Sunday afternoon and Sunday night. Downstairs, sitting by the fire and listening to the wireless, Budge Griffin gave up his world for me. He didn't even drink at any of the funerals.

The first fruit of his abstinence was a Raleigh three-speed. At weekends and during the builders' August fortnight Budge carried me to every swimming spot on the river: the Lagoon, the Point, Sandy – idylls baptised by children. The philanthropist Sir Sylvester Barriscale had built our houses – homes for the poor – in 1913 and let them accordingly. Ours was a stratum of society that did not go on holiday unless subjected to a freak spasm of affluence. Thanks to the oddity of Budge on the dry, I saw the Seaside for the first time on Good Friday, 1955. Budge put a foam-rubber saddle on the bar to cushion the sixty-mile cycle. We had a boiled egg each at five in the morning and set off with egg sandwiches, a flask of tea and the towel tied with twine to the carrier. Budge's old drinking crony and fellow labourer, the next-door neighbour Tom Tucker, was some way behind, with my pal Dunstan on the bar of a borrowed crock. We didn't travel together because Budge said, 'He won't get up on time.'

The cars began to overtake us about ten miles from the Seaside: a Morris Minor with Mr Dennison, the photographer, and his son, Dessie; Father Ab Sheehan, SJ; Mr Butler, the manager of the Provincial Bank; the mayor. They were some of the cars Budge recognised but most were unknown to him, out of his class, the legal mob, the merchant princes, the well-off in general. Those he could identify he knew only from seeing their photographs in the paper.

After six hours and four stops it was there in front of me for the first time: the horseshoe bay, tide in, village deserted out of season except for the Good Friday fanatics come sixty miles for the ritual. Budge turned right at the prom and slowly navigated the climb past the boathouse and golf club and on out to the Cove. We stretched our legs walking along the cliff path until we came to the steps. Most of the crowd were below before us and we were given a big cheer. It was a camaraderie thing, a swimmer's warmth, all in it together. I cheered and clapped with the best of them when Tom Tucker and Dunstan paused at the top of the steps – with only twenty minutes to spare.

We went along the rocks to look at the distance from ladder to ladder. Dessie Dennison, whom we met for the first time, said, 'It's easy.' At ten to twelve Mr Dennison called out, 'Gentlemen, if you please, all those not in the water by twelve are ineligible to vote.' At that time kids would do anything to be a man. We were quickly stripped and ready to show off. Easter is a movable feast that has never moved as far as August, when the sea warms up. The water was fresh, that was the Cove word. For us kids swimming in the nude for the first time, the water was all the fresher.

We swam across and back. Mr Dennison wrote our names on the certificates. When we had dried and dressed and the men had had their token dip, Mr Dennison called on the outgoing president to make the presentation. My certificate read:

Having attained the age of ten years
and having completed the crossing of the Cove
JUNIOR NASH
is thereby deemed a member of
THE COVE SHIVERING CLUB
and entitled to vote in the
PRESIDENTIAL ELECTION.

The Cove swimming fraternity could be traced back over a century, but the first president of the Good Friday Shivering Club was not inaugurated until 1950. It was part of the kick in the arse to post-war austerity that drove the city nobs sixty miles down the road, away from the closed pubs, cinemas and dance halls and sacred music on the wireless. After a few years they saw themselves as an élite and elected a president. The mortification was to endure until 1957, when a consensus emerged that they would all be better off holding the election in July. A few diehards continued to go down on Good Friday, philosophers from the 'when-I-was-a-young-fella' school of reminiscence.

The 1955 election was a shoo-in. Father Ab Sheehan was opposed by Mr Butler of the Provincial just to observe the decorum. 'Those for Father Sheehan,' Mr Dennison announced, 'this side. Those for Ronnie Butler, that side.' Disbarred from voting for himself, the priest crossed over, shanghaiing two others to bolster the vote for Ronnie Butler. There was another big cheer for the election of the Jesuit. Then we assembled for the photograph. Myself and Dunstan with Dessie Dennison on one knee in the front; the new president in the second row between his predecessor and the mayor; the rest fell in as suited them, except for those jocosely pretending they were joking in not wanting to stand beside an undertaker. Ronnie Butler had his arm around Tom Tucker's shoulder. Since everyone would buy a framed print, it was a fair bit of business for a photographer at the Seaside on Good Friday.

Father Ab Sheehan left immediately to officiate back home at the Good Friday ceremonies. We had as much of our egg sandwiches as the fast allowed and then went to the local church for the three hours' agony. Afterwards in the yard Mr Dennison came over to us and said, 'Would you like to fit the bikes in the back and come home with us? The boys could sit on your laps.'

Tom Tucker looked at Budge.

'Ah, it's OK, Mr Dennison, I'd miss my exercise. But thanks anyway.'

'Or I can take the boys in the car. Then you won't have to carry anyone.'

Budge put his hand on my shoulder. 'Well, young man, how would you like a lift home in a car?'

I could read his face. 'I'd prefer to go with Budge, Mr Dennison. Thanks.'

'We'll all go with Budge,' Tom Tucker caved in. They had lost a lot of what they had in common – drink – but Tom Tucker could not endure the comfort of the car while Budge enjoyed the heroics of a sore arse. Dessie Dennison looked at me for the first time as if I was some sort of individualist. And as we walked to the bikes Dunstan hissed at me, 'You little bollix.'

That summer I had my first holiday at the Seaside during the August fortnight, staying at the Seaview Guest House. Budge got the letter confirming the booking in June but he didn't tell me until the last Thursday in July. Maybe it was a form of Budge's independence since he had gone on the dry that he kept his business to himself. Maybe he knew something. I didn't tell Dunstan until we were almost home coming from the Lagoon. Because I knew something. I knew I had a penny for sweets going to school when Dunstan sometimes didn't. We shared the sweets. I waited until we were a few doors from the house. 'Hey, I forgot to tell you, Budge is bringing me to the Seaside for a fortnight on Saturday. Only told me this morning.' Dunstan was hurt. He thumped me on the shoulder. He just said, 'Poxy.'

We played soccer on the road but Dunstan sat on the footpath, watching. 'Too soon after my tea.' Because we lived next door, we hung around the gate after the other kids were called in. Dunstan said, 'Junior, how much does it cost to stay in that Seaview place?'

I didn't know.

'Couldn't you ask Budge?'

I knew I couldn't ask Budge: I would get a box on the ear. But I knew something: I knew I had to ask Budge. He was listening to the wireless. 'What do you want to know for?'

'Dunstan asked me to ask you.'

'If Tom Tucker wants to know what I pay for my holidays, tell him come straight out and ask me.' Dunstan waited in the passage, Dunstan who would follow me into the house as though it was his own home. 'It's six pounds fifteen and a fiver for you a week. Twenty-three ten – if anybody must know.' Almost three weeks' wages.

'Junior, come down with me to my father.'

I waited outside the pub. They came out after about ten minutes, raspberry on Dunstan's lips. Tom Tucker had his hand on Dunstan's shoulder. He tousled my hair. 'The terrible twins, here, here's a tanner between ye, buy crisps for yereselves.' But Dunstan was almost crying. 'Please, Dad.'

'You don't know what you're asking. Hold on, I hope Budge didn't put ye up to this?'

'Budge doesn't know anything, Dad. Junior only asked him how much it was.'

Tom Tucker put both his hands on Dunstan's shoulders. 'Look, I explained it to you inside. Even if Mammy said the two of us could go, even if we could persuade the girls – I mean, could you leave Mammy and the girls at home? And anyway we don't have the money!'

'Just this year, Dad. Mam could go next year with the girls and we'd stay at home.'

'But we don't have the money! My pint is goin' flat. Don't you understand, Dunstan? Explain it to him, Junior, you can't get blood from a stone!'

'If you asked Mr Butler – '

'*Who?*'

'Mr Butler . . . if you got a loan off him . . .'

'What's he sayin'? What Mr Butler? I don't know any Mr Butler . . .'

'Mr Butler in the Provincial. You know him, Dad. He's his arm around you in the photograph.'

Dunstan was blond but Tom Tucker had a full head of black hair combed back to his neck with Brylcreem. He got a fit of laughing, a drunken splutter, a cigarette cough. Trying to get his breath, strands came loose on top of his forehead. But the more he laughed, the more Dunstan persisted. 'Go on Dad, please, just for this year, you could try him, he's his arm around you . . .'

Tom Tucker put his arms around Dunstan and me and pulled us into his chest. 'Ah, boys. Boys, boys, boys . . . Go on now, go on up home. Be good now, off with ye.'

'Please, please, Dad. I'm begging you, Dad, please . . .'

'Now, Dunstan, don't start, that's enough now, don't get me angry.'

'Please, Dad. Oh, God, Dad, please, please, Dad . . .'

'My pint . . . Look, hop it, go on, hop it . . . Christ . . . wait . . . look, go up and tell Budge, tell Budge to have the kettle on, tell him I'll call up at closing time. Now, scoot!'

Although Budge left for work at a quarter to eight, I stayed in bed until ten during the holidays. Dunstan was banging on the door at nine. Tom Tucker's suit was to be pressed, his shirt ironed and he didn't want to have to waste two seconds looking for a stud.

And a new Mac Smile blade . . . having to shave in the middle of the day. No dinner. He came home at ten past one and before half-past we were outside the bank. 'Wait here.' We could see through the glass panel of the main door. We saw him go to the counter and speak to a lady. She pointed to a seat, knocked on a door and went into a room. She came out again and spoke to Tom and again knocked and went into the room. When she came out, Mr Butler was with her. Mr Butler was smiling. He shook hands with Tom, put his hand on Tom's back, indicated the office. When they came out Mr Butler had his hand around Tom Tucker's shoulder.

Walking back up the town, Tom Tucker explained, 'He didn't know who I was at first until I explained to the woman about the Cove. He was all about me then. He said he'll look upon it favourably. The only problem is he'll have to get on to head office. He could have word at around four, but the bank will be closed then. But someone can collect a letter if they knock at the side door. I told him 'twas tomorrow we wanted to go, but things don't happen that fast. Monday is the earliest if it's granted . . . The forms . . .'

Tom Tucker changed into his duds and went back to work. Mrs Tucker collected the letter that Tom would open at half-six. We went swimming at Sandy. Dunstan said, 'We'll go in three times a day. Even if it's raining. Junior, you on?' Stretched out on the grass after the swim, Dunstan said, 'We'll try and get a colour so's we won't be white going down.'

I was helping Budge with the dinner. Budge did the washing and I did the drying and then we packed and I said it during the dinner and while we were washing and drying and packing, I said, 'I'll go out and see how Mr Tucker got on.'

During the dinner Budge said, 'Wait till you finish your dinner.' And, 'We'll do the washing-up first.' And, 'We'll get the packing out of the way.' And, 'Wait another few minutes. Tom might be shaving.' I said, 'He shaved at dinnertime.' And, 'Can't you wait until Dunstan calls for you?' Until at last to my, 'Can I go out now?' Budge gave up and turned on his wireless, having done his best.

The front door was locked – in summer. Mrs Tucker answered. Mrs Tucker who fondled me, clipped me on the ear, looked out for me always as though I was her own son.

The half-open door and Mrs Tucker's body blocked the hall as she told me, 'Dunstan's gone to bed, he's a cold.' Through the crook of her elbow as she held the door latch, I could see Tom Tucker sitting at the kitchen table with his chin in his hands.

Tom Tucker was at the gate the next morning when we came out with the suitcase. 'Have a nice holiday, Budge,' Tom Tucker said and wrapped my fingers around a three-penny bit. 'Now, Junior, don't spend all that in the one shop.'

We walked to the station for the bus and Dunstan had his last hour on his mother's lap, her arms around him, letting him cry.

Young wounds heal quickly, especially when they're someone else's. I got over Dunstan's disappointment. It was a brilliant summer. Every morning after breakfast we swam in the Cove. We were there after dinner. At night I went in off the beach while Budge sat on the prom wall eating peri-winkles. I knocked around with Dessie Dennison and other kids whom I didn't know at home and would meet only on holiday. Mr Dennison took a house for July and August every year. We swam at the boathouse pier, dived from the rocks at Gilligan Point. We played soccer on the beach until dark or went to the pictures. But above all we swam and basked and got a colour. In the Seaview porch at night the sober Budge taught us to play cards.

One afternoon in the middle of the first week, while I was basking, I heard Budge's voice cut into a crowd who were having a rare old time. 'That's enough of it. Bring it up again and I'll put your head through that cliff.' The Cove wasn't used to fighting talk. The chat all round faded away. Men sat up. Heads turned. There was an atmosphere for the rest of the afternoon, Budge, with a red face, not moving until everyone else had left the Cove. At the end of the holiday while Budge was packing and paying the bill at the Seaview, I had a last dip in the Cove and overheard a version that featured two men in white coats arriving at the bank seconds after Tom Tucker left.

Tom Tucker haunted our house in November and Lent while the Seaside fund accumulated in the post office. Budge told him he was looking well and must be feeling the good of being on the dry, but Tom Tucker was a wreck without the booze. He belonged in a public house, swarthy, jovial, laughing, going home foolish, giving his wife a squeeze in front of the children. He saved enough to rent a flat at the Seaside so that he could bring all the family. I introduced Dunstan to the routine of the Cove, the beach, the boat-house pier, Gilligan Point, the soccer after tea, the picture house, the cards in the Seaview porch. Tom Tucker would never be let forget his visit to the bank but he had the drinking man's humour and told the story against himself. And just like Tom, it seemed that Dunstan didn't have a glass jaw either . . .

Brother Chuckey stood at the top of the class. We were twelve years old. Not one of us blinked. Brother Chuckey said, 'Hmmm, slouchers.' We were the cream of the school. Brother Chuckey said, 'Nash. Who's Nash?' I put my hand up. Brother Chuckey sat on my desk. 'I dislike backsliders. What are you, Nash?'

'I don't understand, Brother.'

Brother Chuckey hit me. Just a few knuckles on the side of the head. 'Backslider. What are you, Nash?'

'A backslider, Brother.'

'Second in the Christmas exam and third in the summer. Backslider. Young scut. You're a scut, Nash. What are you?'

'I'm a scut.'

Brother Chuckey grabbed a fistful of hair, twisted it,

lifting my head, my backside leaving the seat. 'What are you?'

'I'm a scut!' Brother Chuckey let go of my hair so that he could give me the back of his hand across my lips. 'You're a scut . . . *What*?'

'I'm a scut . . . *Brother*.'

I was a celebrity for a day. Within a week Brother Chuckey taught a class full of celebrities.

' . . . Hmmm . . . you look like you need shaking up. You're asleep, what are you?'

'I'm asleep, Brother.'

'Hmmm, impertinence. You're not asleep, impertinent scut. What are you?'

'I'm awake, Brother.'

'Impertinent scut. What are you?'

'Aaagh, I'm asleep, *aaagh*, I'm an impertinent scut, I'm asleep, I mean I'm awake . . . I'm a scut . . . I'm a scut, Brother.'

It was the way then, beaten into being good at school. Budge or Tom Tucker or any other parent never met our teachers. There weren't any parent-teacher associations. We were never sent home with a note saying we were giddy. It was the *belle époque* of corporal punishment. We were too afraid of our fucking lives to be giddy. At that time elderly adults were allowed to address strange young boys who went home from school through the park. The old men dabbed at winter tears with snuff-stained handkerchiefs and pontificated: the happiest days of your lives, always remember that boys, the happiest days of your lives.

Brother Chuckey terrorised us into knowing now long forgotten and no longer taught esoterica: the rivers of Russia, the coalfields of Europe, the heavy industries of Britain, every lake, river, puddle, hillock, hamlet, mountain, market town and railway siding in Ireland, roods, perches, long division, date of birth and execution of every patriot, the grammatical structure of English, Irish and Latin, the Old Testament, the Gospels, the Catechism, the Acts of the Apostles, poetry . . .

When we went into secondary, Brother Chuckey was promoted with us. Towards the end of the third year in his charge we learned that he was being transferred. There were backsliders and scuts all over the country. And after three years he didn't need to chastise so often a class that had grown with him. Except when it was necessary . . .

It was the first week in June. Brother Chuckey looked out of the window while we had the heads down, writing compositions. We knew he had eyes in the back of his head – he'd told us – but I was still surprised when he shattered the squeaking of the fountain pens: 'Tucker! Tucker? Why are you crying, Tucker?' Dunstan's forehead rested on the fork of his thumb and forefinger as he crouched over the foolscap. He held the pen in his hand but he wasn't writing. '*Tucker*, are you *deaf*? Why are you crying, Tucker?' Brother Chuckey stood over Dunstan and said, gently for Brother Chuckey, 'What is it? What's wrong with you, Tucker?' Then he tried the tried and trusty, 'Tucker! You scut, Tucker, what are you? *Answer me!*' Then he had to hit Dunstan with the fist half-closed and knock him on to the floor. Dunstan sat slumped against the desk, his eyes closed, the tears running down his face. Brother Chuckey kicked Dunstan's thigh. 'Stop crying, Tucker, you scut. What are you? *Answer me!*' Brother Chuckey lifted him by the hair, dragged him to the top of the class, shook him. 'Why – are – you – crying, Tucker? Hmmm? No answer for us, is that right?' He hopped Dunstan's head off the blackboard. 'Nash, take him out to the yard.'

I linked Dunstan out of the class and along the corridor, asking him all the time, 'What's wrong, Dunstan?' But he just kept slobbering, and when we got out to the yard he shook me off. He leaned his hands against the railings for a minute and then he wiped his eyes with his knuckles. He said, 'That fucker . . .'

'We only have him another three weeks.'

He laughed. A snot laugh. 'Chuckey? Not Chuckey the bollix. Jesus, a hundred Chuckeys . . . it came at me from nowhere . . .'

Even after five years I didn't have to ask. I said, 'You'll have to tell him something when we go back.'

'Well, I can't tell him the truth, can I?'

'You'll have to tell him something. He'll beat us all up if you don't tell him some fucking thing. He'll keep us in, give us an extra one of those We Must Not Keep Secrets comps. Tell him some fucking thing, will you?'

We stood inside the door because Brother Chuckey had a who-told-you-to-sit-down itch in his toe inside his black leather shoe. He was looking out of the window again with his back to us and he let us stand there for a very long minute and then, still with his back to us, said, 'Why were we crying, Tucker?'

'Because . . .'

'Yes, Tucker?'

'Because . . .'

'Go on. No one will bite you.'

'Because you're leaving, Brother.'

Even the cowards tittered. I moved a step away from Dunstan before Brother Chuckey turned round. Brother Chuckey looked at the class first, so that even the bravest shut up. He studied Dunstan from across the room. 'Sit down, Nash.' Brother Chuckey took a hand out of the pocket of his soutane, flicked the finger at Dunstan. When they were toe to toe, Brother Chuckey looked down at Dunstan, who was looking down at the floor. Brother Chuckey raised Dunstan's chin. 'You'll miss me, Tucker?'

'Yes, Brother.'

'I'll miss you, Tucker. We'll all miss each other some day. Sit down.'

When we gave Brother Chuckey the Conway Stewart pen and pencil set, the class elected Dunstan to make the presentation.

Those years and the Seaside holidays quickly passed until at eighteen nobody wanted to go to the Seaside any more. What was there to do after a swim? At night? The place was full of kids. Nobody would want to go there again until married and burdened with young children themselves. That was how it had always been.

So we swam in the river and at the Seaside in summer and then went indoors to read, to study, to sit by the fire listening to the wireless. We were the first generation of our class who could take a secondary education for granted and the last for whom a secondary education would be enough. We were welcomed into the civil service and semi-state bodies and the clerical arm of industry. Now, without a university degree, the lot is selling insurance on a commission-only basis. The last to receive religious instruction, we were the first to lose the faith almost *en masse*. Today's unbelievers have no knowledge of what they are sceptical about. They do not know what feast day it is that they are not keeping holy.

A fly-blown lament? The caterwaul of everyone with a bald patch groping in the dark for yesterday's standards? Maybe. Yet we cold water swimmers did have something, if it was only cold water swimming, morality, reading, music from the wireless uncomplicated by technology, respect for women. Ours was an enclosed and impractical preparation for a world impatient to dance around the golden calf. We were unsteady on our feet and lucky in our innocence that we couldn't anticipate the collapse of the certainties. We didn't know that our morality was merely the product of the sheltered age and bound to wither from the blast of enlightenment; that reading was a sitting duck for the first pot shot from television; that we would acquiesce as the piss, shit, slurry and poison sneaked into our sacred Ganges. We weren't prescient, but when the future came we learned to live with it, though with our heads down.

Chapter 2

I'M BALD BUT I have a black and grey beard. Dessie Dennison's crew cut is steel-grey.

'How is he, Dessie?'

We were in the Dew Drop Inn, off the Chalk Farm Road, one of Dessie's fifteen pubs in London. Mr Dennison had sent him to the Jesuits to learn rugby and get a good job. We would not have known him only for the Seaside. He went into banking through the pull of Father Ab Sheehan and Ronnie Butler. He played for Lansdowne in Dublin. I heard people say Dessie could have been an international but he was too fond of telling phoney alickadoos to fuck off. During one of the bank strikes, Dessie did his picket working in a London bar. The bar business seduced him. He stayed on and joined London Irish, where he was encouraged to find employment more appropriate to a Sunbury club representative – snobbery being relative. The club found the job for him, selling photocopiers. All his calls were made to those with whom he drank in the pavilions after the rugby games. He won the top salesman's prize of a trip to Majorca three years in a row, but always settled for cash and the Cove. He didn't mix with eighteen-year-olds exclusively when he was eighteen, didn't lose faith in the Cove. The progression was to his own office equipment business, where he put in even longer hours drinking in the pavilions after the rugby matches. He flogged the business just in time, before the oil crisis and also because he could not get it out of his head that the whole world drinks something, even if it is only bottled water, and the government wasn't invented that knew how to tax soup and sandwiches.

Dessie first bought a ramshackle establishment in Stoke Newington called the Pig and Whistle, closed it down for renovations to building and custom, renamed it the Angling Cot and brought in a crowd of heavies from the Sunbury club to oversee the barring of the hardchaws. His first manager had once owned a large pub in Dublin's southside and a bit of a mansion in the Wicklow hills, but lost the lot gambling. His wife had dumped him. He was on the dole, living in a northside one-bedroom council kip, when Dessie offered him a new start. Dessie had known him through the bank. The manager joined Gamblers Anonymous. He did so well for Dessie that after four years he went back to open his own pub in Dublin. Dessie was so proud of his initial recruitment policy that ever after, be it for barman or manager, cleaner, potman or enforcer, he hired only those in need of a second chance. All his bars are run by creative accountants, gamblers, alcoholics, all of whom have done time in jail or in the mind. He was rarely let down and only by those who couldn't help themselves helping themselves. Big Dave who had just served us a couple of pints and gone to bed was an ex-Bristol second row – watches and money missing from the dressing rooms.

'*How is he?* You think I care? They laughed at me when I built the houses at the Seaside after four bad summers when they had envelopes in the windows for the entire three months and couldn't give the flats away except for the Shivering Club. But I knew there was value there, the Blue Flag, fresh air, clean water, the Cove. How is he? You think I give a shit? I have fifteen pubs. I had eleven when I wanted to build the houses. I was stretched. How many houses? the banker said – the banks were wary of bad weather, what's new? How many houses? I said the site would hold twelve. The banker told me that was an unlucky number, why didn't I think of building thirteen? That's the real world: there's a banker staying in my thirteenth house buckshee. The deeds are in his mother-in-law's name. And you're asking me about Dunstan the dreamer, who's wasted his life trying to steal from these people . . .'

We had started work on the same day in the cement factory two miles outside the city. I was in the general office, Dunstan across the yard in the stores. We worked Saturday mornings but most Saturdays the accountant would look into the general office at around twelve and suggest that we go home. I would wave my hankie to Dunstan.

Come summer we had our first holiday away from the Seaside, camping in the north-west, a place alive with musical pubs and dance halls. Budge was angry. Budge said, 'Are you telling me the Seaside isn't good enough for you?' But Budge was now a throwback, a manacle impeding my prance. Dunstan's sisters went to Scotland. Tom and Dunstan's mother boarded with Budge at the Seaview. After tea Budge sat on the prom wall and watched the kids swimming from the beach. On his way to the pub, Tom Tucker sat with Budge for a while. They looked out at the children who were gone. With Tom in the pub, Budge was alone, teaching the children of strangers to play cards in the porch.

We had that first holiday away from the Seaside in May. On a Saturday in June there wasn't even the pretence of work. The accountant left his office at eleven and joked, 'Time to get ready for the racecourse.' I waved the hankie. Dunstan came over and we drank coffee and smoked and played poker. The rear entrance to the racecourse was a mile back on the road to the city. Even though we were there at half-twelve, the stands were already full and there was hardly room to sit down on the grass. We were there an hour before the start. When all the speeches were finished, the president broke from his secret service men and moved along the inside of the rails. In the Down Memory Lane column of our local newspaper we are lost in the photograph of the crowd's outstretched hands. Every time the photograph appears Dunstan says, 'Fuck that photographer,' because, as I can testify, Dunstan pleaded, 'Mr President, here, Mr President.' And JFK did shake his hand, smiled the famous smile and said, 'How are you, young man?'

On the way home Dunstan held out his hand, the hand that shook the president's hand. He said, 'I won't wash that hand for a week. One up on you there, Junior. That's quits for the time you got to the Seaside before me.'

On the Saturday in November I waved the hankie as usual. By the time I got out to the yard, Dunstan still hadn't come from the stores. I went inside. Dunstan was in the stores office. He was shaken, as was the rest of the world, and he was crying. I put my hand on his shoulder. He said, 'That bollox!'

'Fuck Oswald is right.'

But he looked at me in a way that made me feel guilty.

'Oswald? Butler! Fuck the banks! Bastards. They have to pay. I'll get them. *They have to pay me back, the cunts!*'

After seven years in the factory – without leaving my desk – I was moved from invoices in to invoices out, to shipping, accident officer, to wages analysis. I was content with the cosy evolution, not knowing that the well-rounded clerk was destined for the knacker's yard. Dunstan was then assistant stores controller, two increments above me. I had just started to chase Peggy O'Neill in the Stella ballroom.

She was a neighbour's child. I danced with her, brought her into the mineral bar and bought her an orange and club milk. I had the next dance when we came out. But when it was ladies' choice, she didn't get up. Still, when the band announced the last dance I rushed her. She let me bring her home. I tried to get a kiss, but her head moved and I tasted the privet hedge. I was bad at this. I said, 'What's wrong?' Peggy said, 'Junior, it's better to tell you the truth. I like you, I like you a lot, but I don't love you.' She wasn't the only woman at the Stella who liked me a lot. Dunstan refused to recognise that she was beautiful. He said, 'I suppose she's all right.' Every Saturday I asked her up at the Stella and she danced with me but declined the mineral bar and the last dance. Then one night I was standing next to Dunstan when she came across the hall for ladies' choice. I was practically hawing my fingernails. But she stood in front of Dunstan and said, 'I'm sorry for what I said to you once.' Dunstan nodded his absolution. Peggy went on, 'So would you like to dance?'

He took her home and next day at work he explained. It was when they were thirteen or fourteen, an argument when they were playing hopscotch: he pinched her ear and she said, 'Go away and get your oul fella to borrow money from a bank.' I asked him how he got on. He said, 'I courted the fuck out of her.' I said, 'That bollix!' Dunstan had thought I meant Peggy. He grabbed my arm. He said, 'Who?' I yanked my arm free. 'Ronnie Butler, *that* bollix.'

They were already saving to get married when the Gestetner man called to the factory. The Gestetner model was state of the art at that time – so much so that the union Luddites wouldn't let the machine in the factory gate, to take away the bread and butter of their printing brethren. The Gestetner man worked on Dunstan and invited him to see the machine demonstrated in a hotel. Dunstan brought me along because the Gestetner man was buying lunch.

Dunstan was a financial innocent. Paid weekly, he didn't even have a bank account. I was at the lunch as his adviser. I had never been in a bank myself. But the Gestetner man was enthusing, '. . . recommend only five thousand an hour until it's run in . . . My brother in Dublin, only last week I was in his place, I watched it, he did fifteen thousand two-colour in three hours. Now, Dunstan, from your own buying, you know what you can charge for that. Fifteen thousand two-colour in *three* hours – the letterpress people, you can blow them all out of the water . . .'

Dunstan would have almost a thousand pounds coming out of the pension fund? 'There you are, I can bring you to Mr Bowman, you'll have no problem. What you're talking about here is literally a licence to print money.' By half-past two the Gestetner man, myself and Dunstan were sitting with Billy Bowman, the manager of the Provincial, drinking tea and eating chocolate biscuits. The Gestetner man and Billy Bowman considered the figures: the lease of the printing machine, camera, printing down frame, purchase of light box, guillotine, rent of premises, initial stock, prospective income.

Billy Bowman nodded yes. 'I'll back Dunstan's thousand with an overdraft of two to fund stock and the gestation period. As to premises, I may be able to point you in the right direction there. The insurance we can handle here ourselves.'

It was all no more than showing Dunstan that no man is an island in the business world.

The Gestetner man's initial stock comprised paper, board, envelopes, plates, dark-room supplies, numbering machines, inks, fountain solution, blankets, cleaning pads. Dunstan was loaded up like any nun or county council buying a duplicator.

'So?' Dessie barked at me.

'I saw it. I was there. Dunstan was gobbled up. He didn't go into business. He was sold into business.'

'The Gestetner man was only taking the money off Dunstan and it was Dunstan's job to take the money off the people. All business is taking the money off the people.'

'The premises was a room on the top floor of a three-storey building. I helped carry the stuff up. There were seventy-eight steps on the stairs. I counted them after I felt my stomach was so hard King Kong could have jumped on it and broken his leg.'

'That's why the rent was economical.'

'The auctioneer was a buddy of Billy Bowman.'

'That's how the auctioneer got Dunstan for a client. It's known as business.'

'Dunstan didn't have buddies, not business buddies. The only printing he ever got was from loner freaks like himself.'

'So? Is that the bank's fault?'

'They knew he was carrying top weight, they put the lead in the saddle. When he didn't win, they wouldn't give him another mount.'

'Save that shite for your books. Dunstan got the same second chance as everyone else. He wanted every horse in the stable yard.'

Dunstan got three days' rudimentary training from the Gestetner man and then he had to learn the machine for himself. The guillotine was manual. Dunstan's first time using it he lost most of the flesh of his left thumb. We were still decent people then, so Dunstan didn't have the brains to claim against his own insurance. I was lonely in the factory without Dunstan. I was lonelier without Peggy O'Neill. Looking out of the window down the yard, I saw the black finger of the chimney stack poking the blue belly of the sky. I wrote it down on the back of a time sheet. 'The black finger of the chimney stack poking the blue belly of the sky.' It was my literary call! I didn't tell Dunstan. I didn't even tell Budge. I told the factory accountant that I wanted to keep it quiet, no farewell presentation. I sneaked out early in the morning after Budge went to work, past Dunstan's door, carrying the black finger of the chimney stack poking the blue belly of the sky, a leg-iron that would take me years to unfetter.

I started out a nice fellow. The spirit of the sixties lingered. Young, energetic, I found romance in the London bed-sit and the variety of jobs, accumulating the CV for the dust jacket. London buzzed and it would be only a short time before I could go home, cock of the walk, with money and a reputation and discover that Peggy only liked Dunstan a lot after all. I didn't hate anyone then, certainly not my own. How could I? They were the people whose applause was just around the corner. But the bed-sit turned cold and my clothes became shabby and all the time when I sat down to write, I had nothing to say. So I felt sorry for myself, a condition in which I had no time to feel sorry for anyone else. When I couldn't think warmly of others, I slid into hating them just to keep going. I would look back later – hatred, what a warped position from which to be detached about the world.

When the lingering sixties grew threadbare and the arse was out of everything I owned, including my soul, I went to town with the scorn. I hated hearing of someone's marriage or having a kid, getting on in a job. Pygmies with their ideal homes, settled people. UNSECURED PERSONAL LOANS, I read in the window, from £1,000 to £5,000. All I wanted was a hundred, but they threw me out because all I wanted was a hundred and didn't have life assurance. I looked homeward and hated all those in pension schemes. Lonely, I loathed the very idea of neighbours, the molasses of familiarity.

After too long farting around with the black finger of the chimney stack poking the blue belly of the sky, I got the letter from Dunstan with the usual bank troubles and the news that Peggy was pregnant. It was a day when I hadn't the price of a drink. I had fags and tea and two slices of bread. I ate and sat down and lit up and set in to hating Dunstan, and learned before I was half-way down the fag that all along it had only been hot and cold hatred, the fly-off-the-handle variety of the tempestuous years, because how could I hate Dunstan? Instead I was forced to get to know myself, and the knowledge was not uplifting. That hatred could comfort me was little comfort to any noble idea of myself. So I forgave myself for all the spite with which I had girded my frailty. I drew my hand along the bald head and decided to grow a beard. I read Dunstan's letter again, read Dunstan's delight, and remembered what it was to smile in the sunshine, felt the warmth, started to look at the loneliness through the right end of the telescope and recognised the boon of solitude.

At peace I opened my writer's notebook. I began to obliterate the curiosities in the stale collection. I drew a line through the black finger of the chimney stack poking the blue belly of the sky. I tore the pages out altogether and threw them in the bin. Hatred!!! All I needed was a beard. I hadn't money to go out so I hadn't shaved, I already had a bit of a beard. I started *Hand Me Down* that night because at last I had the calm to write about what I knew – loneliness, from the hindsight of solitude. My protagonists would work at dead-end jobs and live in bed-sits and be lonely and well read. Their real-life counterparts were great readers too, but they could afford only books borrowed from the library. No matter.

I came home the first Christmas and Dunstan was already bollixed by then. Trying to get in orders from his flyers and cold-calling, he was all the time running at a loss meeting the monthly repayments. By that Christmas he was sixteen hundred into the overdraft and had received a 'call into the office to discuss your account' letter from Billy Bowman. Dunstan dragged me in with him. Billy Bowman gave me a look when I was reintroduced as Dunstan's adviser. They went over the creditors and debtors. Tax provision. Stock. There was fuck-all tea or chocolate biscuits. Dunstan had plenty of stock thanks to the Gestetner man. Billy Bowman identified the problem: Dunstan didn't have enough of business. 'You don't golf, Mr Tucker?' Billy Bowman asked Dunstan. It was 'Mr Tucker' now. Dunstan said no, he didn't golf. Billy Bowman didn't pursue it, didn't have to. Then he said, 'I'll tell you what I'll do. I'll convert the sixteen hundred into a term loan.' Dunstan didn't know what a term loan was. Neither did I. We couldn't believe Dunstan's luck when Billy Bowman explained what a term loan was. To Dunstan it was a comparatively measly amount of quids a week over a few years to pay off the sixteen hundred. Dunstan said to Billy Bowman, 'Thank you very much, Mr Bowman, you're a gentleman.'

I said, 'Dunstan did his best, Dessie. He tried,' but I said it lamely. 'Dunstan printed up flyers. CALL TO DT OFFSET for all your printing requirements. Flyers! Picked businesses out of the Golden Pages and sent them flyers. Call. *Call!* Call to DT Offset! That's trying? And another thing. I knew Billy Bowman. He *was* a gentleman. He was one of the first to be promoted sideways when they needed to bring in thugs like the cunt in my thirteenth house.'

Dunstan carried me that Christmas, thinking he was flush again. He made me stay an extra week. The day before I was going back I was in DT Offset in when the call came to drop round immediately. Billy Bowman gave me his look again, as though with advisers like me who needed enemies, but he was glad I was there at the finish. He had a few cheques on his desk amounting to a hundred and thirty-odd quid. Had Dunstan a lodgement to cover them? 'Not at the moment,' said Dunstan, 'but I'm only barely into the overdraft.' Billy Bowman raised his eyes at me: 'I didn't grant an overdraft, as no doubt Mr Nash will recall.' Dunstan jumped in: 'What about the two thousand?' And I nodded. 'No, no, no, no, no – ' Billy Bowman almost laughed at our ignorance. When we had to accept that the two thousand had melted into the maw of the term loan, that there was no overdraft, I felt exposed as an adviser and Dunstan copped on that he was fucked without the two grand. He explained to Billy Bowman that it was Christmas, that he'd treated his girl-friend to a week in the Canaries and that he would never have gone if he thought the two-thousand overdraft didn't still apply. Billy Bowman observed that he didn't think it was in the best interests of the business to have taken a holiday that year. Dunstan hadn't been near the Canaries, but all he could hear was a banker denying him a holiday. Billy Bowman had a high chair behind a big desk and all Dunstan had was a low seat to cringe in. I was sitting in a sort of half-way house chair probably reserved for advisers. Dunstan started sweating, looking up at Billy Bowman. And then he began to beg, 'If you could give me a chance to build up the order book, let me keep the overdraft until – ' but Billy Bowman cut in, 'I'll fund stock but I won't fund leis-ure.' Then Billy Bowman's financial paternalism suddenly hit a brick wall: Dunstan started crying. He was crying like a kid, a kid on his mother's lap. My experience of banks was limited to being Dunstan's adviser, so I don't know how many crooks or honest wheelers Billy Bowman had ever had in his office, but I doubt if he'd ever had a grown man shaking with pain and crying like a child. He was out from behind the high desk in a sweat, his arms around Dunstan: There, there, now, Mr Tucker, pull yourself together now, come now, we'll see if we can't work something out. And he was giving me the look, as much as to say: When the fuck do you do your advising? What I did was, and it amazed me that it worked, I raised the palm of my hand and Billy Bowman withdrew behind his throne and I put a finger to my lips and the two of us just sat there until Dunstan recovered, and then I said to Dunstan, 'Dunstan, listen to Mr Bowman.' The sweat is dripping off the bold Billy while he's trying to retain his power of reprimand. He croaked out the offer of a two hundred and fifty overdraft, strict adherence – looking at me, me nodding: suggest broaden circle of acquaintances, understand golf not necessarily everyone's cup of tea, squash, tennis or perhaps Junior Chamber of Commerce?

' . . . you'll notice he didn't suggest jogging . . .'

Peggy was a clerk in the corporation but she would have to resign when they married next summer. Dunstan did get some of the business that is based on price, but even when he was busy he wasn't making money – all the non-golfing printers cut each other's throats with their prices. I got a job handling baggage for Aer Lingus at Heathrow and at Easter came home again on a stand-by flight. I called in to Dunstan while he was doing his books. He was owed something like two grand and his creditors amounted to seventeen hundred, the overdraft was up to two hundred. Dunstan wrote his wages cheque for forty and I toddled round with him to the bank. The teller pressed buttons, asked Dunstan to excuse her. Next minute there's a gentleman – to wit Billy Bowman – giving us the finger. In under the naked bulb department. Definitely no tea or chocolate biscuits. Not even a chair for either of us this time, high or low. Billy Bowman is like a dog. The overdraft is gone to more than the two hundred Dunstan had calculated, it's two hundred and thirty-nine – something about a cheque or leasing payment

Dunstan hadn't taken into account, so if the wages cheque for forty was cashed Dunstan would be over the limit. Dunstan said, 'I'm sorry about that, Mr Bowman, I hadn't realised.' Billy Bowman asks Dunstan his figures. How long is he owed the two thousand, a month? Two? Three months? To make it look good Dunstan says most of it is two months out, in any day now. Get in your money, Billy Bowman orders, I'll fund stock but I won't fund debtors. Dunstan says, 'I'll get cracking first thing in the morning.' Good man, Billy Bowman nods but adds, 'Bring in a lodgement tomorrow and we'll clear your cheque immediately.' The bad news dawns on Dunstan. 'But can't I cash it now, it's my wages cheque?' Sorry, no authorisation to go above the limit. 'But my mother is waiting for her grocery money,' Dunstan beseeches him. I can't even look at Dunstan, because I can guess what's happening – it was even getting to me, grocery money being turned down. Without looking at Dunstan I know I'm right, because Billy Bowman is saying, 'Now, Mr Tucker, we made an agreement . . . Please don't cause a scene . . . You're well aware, Mr Nash will testify . . . No acting the martyr, please now, there's a good man . . .' Dunstan is crying again, he's standing in the middle of the office, hands by his sides, his head jerking with almost silent sobs . . . 'I must ask you, I must insist,' Billy Bowman says, and he looks at me, and to give me my due, I know how to respond. I said, 'Dunstan, out.' I caught him by the arm and pulled him and pushed him out of the door and around the corner into the pub.

' . . . you mean you weren't head-hunted by Coopers and Lybrand on the way out of the bank?'

Dunstan had put a back-in-ten-minutes note on the door before we went to the bank. In the pub Dunstan started feeding himself propaganda: 'I'll fund this but I won't fund that, drawerful of fucking sayings.' Just then the Kodak traveller who supplied Dunstan with film came into the pub for a coffee. He flashed his smile at Dunstan and ribbed, 'Long ten minutes, Dunstan.' But then he noticed Dunstan's face was longer than the long ten minutes. The Kodak man adjusted immediately in case there had been a bereavement. He said, 'Nothing wrong, I hope?' And with our permission he joined us, full of banking stories. He had a brother in Dublin just like the Gestetner man. Selling film and squee-gees and dark-room odds and ends and with his brother in business in Dublin, the Kodak man had no more time for bankers than anyone else who didn't actually work in a bank. Grocery money, he echoed Dunstan, they're some bas-tards, you should hear my brother on about them.

The Kodak man asked Dunstan the same questions that bank managers ask, but the answers that displease bank managers encouraged the Kodak man to beam and nod: Good, good, good. When he discovered Dunstan didn't own his house, the Kodak man said, 'Bingo! Walk away.' It would take the Provincial at least two years fucking around with letters and courts and judgements and putting Dunstan in Stubbs, and if they couldn't shame Dunstan, they couldn't get him when they hadn't collateral. Once Dunstan got the idea that he could actually catch a bank for money, he insisted on buying the Kodak man a drink. All we had to do – I was accepted immediately as an adviser – all we had to do was walk away and go to another bank, but to stay with the truth – as much as we could. To go in confidently with the line that we didn't want all our eggs in one basket. They were the two commandments of his brother in Dublin. The truth and confidence except where it was necessary to tell a white lie, or where a white lie wouldn't do to tell a black one or – if necessary – lie through the teeth. Because the most important thing in dealing with banks was to get the money first without giving them guarantees and then to fuck them afterwards.

Going over Dunstan's figures, the Kodak man was satisfied that Dunstan didn't have the money to pay anybody anything. If they were coming after him at that very moment, they would stop short of an examination order and sign off with Stubbs. Could Dunstan handle the commercial shame of Stubbs? Dunstan could, and I could nod at that because I could see that Dunstan was bursting with pride at the idea of catching a bank.

The next day Dunstan got in almost fourteen hundred pounds out of what he was owed, with me running all over town collecting while he was on the phone. We went down town with the money and the white lies to see Roger Egleston in the Munster Bank.

Mr Egleston had silvery hair, charm, a mauve handkerchief in the breast pocket matching his mauve tie. Dunstan's confidence was based on the fact that whatever happened in the Munster, he had fourteen hundred in his pocket and he could walk away from Billy Bowman. Introducing me as his adviser, Dunstan was cool enough to say, 'Junior Nash, the writer.' Roger Egleston said, 'Ah, literature, and what have we written?' The first white lie of the day, or barefaced lie, was my claiming to be three-quarters through the third and final draft of my first novel. Good stuff, he was a C. P. Snow man himself. We had gone in with the plan of having fourteen hundred to lodge immediately and looking for a two and a half thousand overdraft. When Dunstan saw us talking literature, he had a go for three grand. Mr Egleston suggested two thousand until we saw how business developed. Done. Out with the forms.

' . . . Roger didn't deserve what happened to him. His decency was catching up on him. Joe the Boss would have taken Roger out eventually, but Dunstan was the last straw . . .'

'I didn't know people like Joe the Boss existed.'

'They didn't. Until cunts like the Kodak man's brother entered the scene. Gentlemen like Billy Bowman and Roger Egleston were raped by fucking liars like Dunstan who had no shame and held parties when they were put in Stubbs. Banks fought back and produced the likes of Joe the Boss . . .'

The Kodak man was right: it did take the Provincial over two years before Dunstan made Stubbs the first time, but by then Dunstan was so far gone that he was ashamed to think a day might pass during which he hadn't caught a bank. He was able to hang on with the scraps of business and Peggy's wages – and the bank overdraft – until after the wedding, and then he opened a third front. The Kodak man's brother sent down a newly minted third commandment: Don't wait until you're in the shits again. By now banks were losing the old aura and becoming demystified and the dogs in the roads knew that any manager had the OK for five grand without going to head office if you had any sort of an in with him. My book was with the publishers. Dunstan was living with Peggy's mother. While he was only half-way into the overdraft, Dunstan produced the dormer windows lark and pitched Roger for four and a half grand to convert the attic and install a bathroom. It was all there in the bank brochures: HOME IMPROVEMENT. And Dunstan told Roger about my book and how I would like to send Roger an inscribed copy when it came out.

Out of the four and a half thousand that Dunstan got from Roger, he lobbed three thousand into the Southern Bank – without any adviser – where he got an overdraft of another three, and he put fifteen hundred into a merchant bank. Before he even put a toe into the Southern overdraft, he got five thousand term loan from them to convert the attic. Before he even made Stubbs the first time, he'd also got three grand from the Merchant, two and a half to buy a car and five hundred to go to Cheltenham.

Joe the Boss was twenty-seven or twenty-eight. Mr Egleston was just over sixty. It was a bit of a fluke that I was there. After the funeral, Budge even went into the pub with Tom to mind him. Dunstan had to go into work to get his cheque book, pay for rounds for the neighbours in the pub. I went with him. He had taken his mother's death as most do, badly, wept as she was brought to the church the night before and through mass that morning and all through the graveside prayers. I cried even though I'm not the crying type, like Dunstan was. We were alone in the office, just the two of us, for the first time since I had arrived. He could let himself go. He sat at his table and said, 'Junior, I always loved her.' I said, 'I loved her myself, Dunstan, she was a second mother to me.' Dunstan said, 'The day you went to the Seaside, what was she going through? Having to hold a child while he's crying, can you imagine what was happening inside her? Bastards!' Dunstan had a CLOSED UNTIL TOMORROW sign on the door but we hadn't locked the door, and the footsteps we heard on the stairs were those of Joe the Boss and Roger Egleston.

'This is where the shares in Kleenex go through the roof?'

Roger did the introductions. Mr Tucker, this is our Mr Joe Murray from head office. Dunstan hadn't worn a black tie for his mother's funeral and black triangles on the elbow of the jacket had gone out of fashion, so there was no evidence to guide Roger. Roger introduced me as 'the writer'. What kind of books did I write? Joe the Boss asked, but I know when that question is perfunctory, I know a non-literary man when I see one. Roger stepped in: 'Mr Nash writes literature.' And for a moment I was almost on Roger's side. Joe the Boss nodded away as though he had the remotest interest. But he quickly asked Dunstan, 'How's business?' Dunstan answered, 'Times are tough.' But Joe the Boss wasn't listening. Joe the Boss would not have been there in the first place, only Dunstan had the Munster on the ropes, had ignored every effort of Roger's, and it was now a Greek meets Greek situation. Joe the Boss let Roger make the running and I could see it was to humiliate Roger, who wouldn't have had to have Joe the Boss there if Roger knew how to get the money back from Dunstan. To put up a show in front of Joe the Boss, Roger tried to act tough. Cleared the throat: granted you extreme latitude . . . despite numerous letters and phone calls . . . account dormant . . . insist mutually satisfactory arrangement . . . must address situation . . . otherwise necessary steps.

All this to Dunstan after burying the mother who had held him on her lap. I wanted to step in, but Dunstan's cool disarmed me. 'When you say mutually satisfactory arrangements, Mr Egleston, what do you have in mind?' Dunstan asks Roger, but Joe the Boss is impatient to bounce across the stage. He pulls out a notebook that's carrying a list of names and drags his finger down the page. Something like two hundred a month for five years to conquer the six and a half grand plus the interest that Dunstan was into them for. Dunstan ignores Joe the Boss and answers Roger, 'I can't promise that, Mr Egleston. I buried my mother this afternoon. With funeral expenses I don't even know how I'm going to eat next week.' Roger: 'My dear fellow – ' grabbed Dunstan's hand, shook it, squeezed Dunstan's shoulder – 'I'm so sorry for your trouble, I had no idea.' Roger looked at Joe the Boss with a patrician eyebrow that I vulgarly translated into let's get the fuck out of here. But Joe the Boss stepped in front of Roger and emphasised with a stabbing finger, 'Can – you – pay – us two hundred a month?'

'No,' Dunstan said, 'I wish I could pay myself that these days.'

Dunstan's cool was unnatural. I lost my temper here myself. I snatched the newspaper off Dunstan's desk and shoved the death notice in the face of Joe the Boss. 'Can't you read?' I snapped at him. But Joe the Boss just stared me off. He pulled at his cheeks and did a three-pace walk, turned back, having for our benefit contained his patience. He said, wearily, but with a touch of finality, 'Can you let me have a voluntary judgement on your house?' This was easy for Dunstan, they were playing in his own backyard. 'I don't own the house, we live with my wife's mother.' 'Then will your mother-in-law give us a voluntary judgement?' At this stage I had the impression that Roger was standing with us, three outraged against one. 'I don't know,' said Dunstan. 'I'll ask her, but what's the point? We'd never sell, it's where we were brought up, it's our roots.' 'You think that now,' Joe the Boss claimed, 'but in ten, fifteen, twenty years' time, your family grown up, you might decide to move then.'

Dunstan began calmly enough: 'Twenty years' time? Twenty years?' And then upped the stakes: 'Are you telling me you'll be after me in twenty years? In twenty fucking years? My mother isn't cold in the grave and you'll be with me in twenty years? You cunt, you,' Dunstan roars at him, and because of the great advantage Dunstan had of being a smoker and able to get the phlegm up, Joe the Boss has a big dirty green spit running out of his eye, down his face and into his lip. Roger whipped out the mauve breast-pocket hankie and tried to wipe down Joe the Boss. But Dunstan was already pointing at the door: '*Out*, get that scum *out*, get that scum off my premises.'

Roger's handkerchief was purely decorative. I could see the spit glistening against the mauve.

*

' . . . Roger was wearing a mauve handkerchief when he was laid out, and the tie to match . . .'

I thought at the time that Dunstan did the right thing. If I had been advising him, he would have spat earlier and oftener. But once I had returned to London and enjoyed the contemplation between bouts of writing I began to worry. This Joe the Boss who had the venerable Roger by the short hairs, Joe the Boss would surely go for Dunstan, have spies counting the number of Dunstan's pints in the pub, tally the amount of Kentucky chicken boxes Dunstan brought home. My insight as an adviser was corroborated by no less an authority than the Kodak man's brother in Dublin. Dunstan wrote me the news. When the Kodak man next called and he heard the story, mother half an hour in grave, he asked Dunstan would Dunstan mind if he mentioned it to the brother in Dublin and he would report back in a week. The intelligence from Dublin confirmed that the only thing open to Joe the Boss was an examination order, but that they didn't normally use that because they knew all about you anyway. But anyone with spit on his face would do it just to humiliate you in court. The pre-emptive strike called for in Dunstan's case was for Dunstan to get in ahead of Joe the Boss and at the same time grab the chance to take out the Provincial, the Southern and the Merchant. And the way to do it was through St Vincent de Paul. St Vincent de Paul had indebtedness officers to advise on such matters. The Southern and the Merchant were actually being paid up to date until then. With interest Dunstan owed the four banks over twenty-five thousand and not one of them had a slate of security. On the basis of Dunstan's figures – true figures (outside of the jobs for which he was paid cash) – the indebtedness officer calculated that the most, the outside most Dunstan could manage to discharge his obligations was twenty pounds a week. Dunstan was advised to write to the four banks and offer it to them pro rata: two pounds to the Provincial, seven to Roger in the Munster, eight to the Southern and three to the Merchant, and all were to be informed of what he owed to the rest of them. And it was all done on Vinnie de Paul notepaper.

'... Roger was allowed to retire on full pension. Some people thought that Roger did well there. Other managers got shifted to sheep-shaggin' villages to serve out the time, so taking the spit and the seven miserable quid Dunstan got them down to, it might appear Roger did OK. But I was talking to Roger's wife after the funeral. Like everyone else, I was consoling her that Roger had died so peacefully from the brain haemorrhage. Roger was a good banker. He would never have told his wife anything about business. She was upstairs getting ready, they were going out to dinner. She came down and found Roger sitting in the armchair dead. He was clutching the mauve handkerchief in his hand. She said to me, "Dessie, I'll always remember Roger that way, his beloved mauve handkerchief, that's how I'll think of him." The poor woman, if she only knew what Roger must have been thinking ... that Dunstan, he's a fucking murderer as well as a thief. How is he? Who cares?'

'How is he, Dessie?'

'Gone. He put his wife on the streets.'

Dessie thought he had me there and he was right. I nearly threw up my pint. My Peggy.

'That's what we call it in banking circles.'

'We?'

'The only person not in banking circles is Dunstan.'

'What are you talking about, the streets?'

'His last gasp was the credit union through Peggy. That's the streets. He has to pay his paper supplier up front, the last crowd put him in Stubbs. It's his fucking family album now – here's me when I was with the Provincial. And this is me with the Munster. I know a guy who went to him for a thousand letterheads on cream laid. Dunstan said everybody was using white bond these days. That's all he stocks. Jesus, copying paper. Printers are tinkers, their motto is Put the Good One on Top. But at least they have materials to fuck up. My houses are a flat two hundred and fifty a week, he takes it July, August and September, depending. So he has to come up with two grand minimum. I usually throw in September, pretending I can't get anyone else to take it. I'd give him July and August too, I'd give him the fucking house, but no, he insists the banks must pay, his whole existence is down to that, the banks must pay for his Seaside holiday . . .'

'You're a decent man and you won't admit it.'

'Shut up. Keep the crap for your books. OK, he's managed it every year, but he won't manage it any more. Two grand rent! Any banker will throw himself in front of your car to lend you money to buy a mobile home rather than let you pay two grand rent, that's if your name isn't Dunstan Tucker. He's now down to the credit union but next year he won't get a bob. From anyone. The guy is sick. Doesn't he know what a bank is? A bank lends you money to find a cure for cancer or to develop a plague. You think it gives a fuck? A bank wants its money back. What kind of a prick is he he doesn't understand that?'

'Can't he get a toppy up from the credit union?'

'No. There are circumstances but not in this case. Even doing it through Peggy. How I know is I was drinking with Johnny O'Donnell, the loans' director with the credit union. I had a game of golf with Johnny . . .'

'Golf?'

'Yes, golf. If that prick Dunstan played golf, he wouldn't be where he is now. Johnny's a smiling guy, but I can see something's bothering him. We have a jar. He says he can't tell me. He says they have only two rules in the credit union: you must be a member three months before you can tap and there's total confidentiality. They don't run a credit check or ask why or tell you to live in a smaller house – which, of course, I know. But I can see he's itching to tell me, so I say, "Johnny, what the fuck is confidential?" So he tells me. Johnny discovers there's a Peggy O'Neill has an appointment to see him. Johnny doesn't go to the Seaside – he's a pervert in that respect, drives around France for his holidays. He doesn't know Peggy Tucker, let alone her maiden name. Before he sees Peggy he looks up her form. She's saved the bones of a grand, twenty a week operating out of her cousin's address. She wants to borrow three grand. Guess for what? Converting the attic. OK, we both know the attic was converted by Tom Tucker on the dry and Budge and a couple of volunteer carpenters and stolen materials. Where Johnny's concerned it's statutory stuff, a woman has one in, borrows three. Peggy fills in the bit of a form and Johnny lobs out the cheque. A month later Johnny is pushing the grocery trolley out of a supermarket and sees this Peggy O'Neill outside lifting her messages into the boot of the rust bucket and who's helping her but Dunstan. So I say to Johnny, "What's the problem?" Johnny admits there are actually *three* rules in the credit union: you must be a member three months, there is total confidentiality and the third rule is that everyone from the trustees down to the cleaning woman is sworn to keep their eyes open in case Dunstan Tucker even puts his foot in the street. "I know," Johnny says, "that I'm only going to be caught for two grand because of the deposit, but I've a clean record and I hate the thought of facing the credit committee, because even though we don't run checks, Dunstan Tucker's reputation came seeping in under the door. I mean," Johnny tells me, "he even took five hundred off the Thrift Cheque Company."'

'The Thrift? Don't they charge thirty-nine per cent or something?'

'Not to Dunstan they don't. How he got it was he did a

bit of printing for them and casually asked the guy what kind of money they do, and the poor fucker was blind – his usual clients are those birds in jeans and white high heels that you see hanging around the labour exchange trying to drag a few bob out of their common-law husbands. To him Dunstan was blue chip. They don't have access, the banks would even lead the Thrift astray. Anyway, the guy apologised to Dunstan that they only did up to five hundred. Dunstan told him, "I'll tell you what I'll do, I'll take the five hundred. It's my wife's birthday coming up and I owe her a treat, but the way I'll pay you is I'll send it to you monthly. I want to surprise her because, you see, we have a joint account and if I take it out of the bank she'll know about it, so I'll pay you out of the petty cash I get in here." The poor bollix nodding: I understand, Mr Tucker, have to keep the little woman happy.'

'I'm not going to cry for the Thrift Cheque Company.'

'Who is? Dunstan sent fuck all. After the first month the guy called in and Dunstan explained it had been a bad month and he'd do it on the double next month. That's all right, Mr Tucker, I understand. This is a guy who's used to dogs biting him in the leg and the wing mirrors being torn off his car while he's knocking at council houses. The next time he called, Dunstan gave it to him straight, because Dunstan's disease is at the galloping stage. He told your man to fuck off. I got it from Johnny, who got it through the grapevine, to wit, banking circles.'

'Banking shits. Don't they have professional etiquette, honour, and what about the confidentiality?'

'This is money we're talking about.'

While Dessie put on another pair of pints I looked into the old mirror showing twenty Gold Flake for a shilling and a bald head and a writer's beard. I had what I wanted but I couldn't be at peace until Dunstan came into his own.

'How is he with the credit union?'

'Johnny called into the Dennison Arms on his way to France. I said, "How's the account?" Johnny says, "I may have misjudged your friend. Peggy got the money at the end of May, paid in advance for the holiday, as they always do, and on the first of July paid the credit union two months in advance, explaining she would be taking a house at the Seaside." I didn't wise Johnny up. I let him go off to enjoy his holiday. I didn't tell him that this is classic Dunstan form, on time, for a while, so that when he defaults it will be because of some calamity. Now just suppose Dunstan fell on his head and decided to keep up the payments – the best toppy up he could get next year would be a grand, because he's only paying back at twenty a week plus interest, so next year he'd only have it down to two grand. A grand won't cover next year's holiday. But even if it did, that's not the point. The credit union isn't a bank. The credit union is your neighbours giving up their free time to sit on committees, trying to put decent bankers out of business. Dunstan couldn't do it this year. It's over. The banks won. They always win because they can't lose. But you talk to Dunstan, he'll tell you he has them all by the balls. Let them stay awake at night. That kind of shite. No banker stays awake at night. Dunstan stays awake, probably stressed out of his mind. He might look young, still have his blond hair, but look at his eyes . . .'

'So Dunstan's fine.'

'He should be fine. He'd be fine if he minded his own business. Is he the secretary of his Residents' Association? No. He's still living in a house built for the poor. Does he play golf? No. Is he on a festival committee? A rugby club? You name me an organisation and Dunstan isn't in it. What does he do? He jogs. Now there's a business contact for you, jogging. The only people you meet in jogging circles are your local doctor who refers you to a specialist and when the specialist can't find the cure you trek half-way up a mountain to some mystic to fix your bollixed knee. What about you, you skint?'

'No. I work for a guy on a bookstall, but he lets me go for August when he brings his kids in. It keeps me going. And I got a royalty cheque for five hundred and thirty-four pounds.'

'Hmm. Then what's to stop you going to the Seaside?'

'Nothing. I'm flying out in the morning.'

'I'm on the evening flight. You missed the election: Joe O'Connor. They shouldn't have been allowed to move it to July. Easter was my Christmas with what my father made on Good Friday. People worry about you, not back in two years. So you're winning? You writing?'

'Start again September.'

'Bed-sit-land?'

'*The Second-hand Wardrobe*.'

'Sounds like fair warning. The tin of beans?'

'Yep.'

'One-bar electric?'

'Yep.'

'Wonky immersion takes four hours to heat?'

'Yep.'

' "No thanks, Mr Dennison, I'll go with Budge." How else could you have turned out? But you're winning. Budge is winning. Tom Tucker is winning. If my father was alive he'd still be winning. I'll be over tomorrow night, we'll all be in the Cove, winners, except for bollicky. How can he look only twenty-five and still have blond hair? You've proved you're doing your business, hardly a hair. I have mine but at least it's grey, it shows I'm not a wanker. Bollicky's like a film star because he neglects his business. Except you can see into him now. You haven't seen it in two years – think of it as cancer, it's galloped. I'm telling you, we're talking about a desperate man.'

Chapter 3

I was so flush from the royalty cheque that I tried to get a taxi from the airport to the Seaside. The first in the rank had it in his blood, out of the car and ready to take my bag before I could ask how much. The cab was fetid with air-freshener. The radio was tuned to Station Two, the second channel in any country representing esperanto-fashion the cave-in to rock music. It was a free world. But the dashboard and windows were desecrated with NO SMOKING signs. I produced the coward's 'I just remembered' and walked off to hitchhike.

Or walked off to walk.

Of the welcomes? My arse! STAY OUT OF IT! When I couldn't kid myself any more that I was gathering material, I turned up at the publishers where I was let use the basement for three months, eight hours a day, seven days a week. Before I started I looked up at the sign. It wasn't a hiker's optimistic piece of cardboard. I had paid a fiver to a printer and twelve quid to have it framed. STAY OUT OF IT! The command looked down on me and I tried to obey. I tried too to carry the admonition into my private life, a writer supposedly never off duty. I remembered Dan Dennison offering to take two bicycles, two adults and two kids with himself and his son in a Morris Minor. But my sign helped me to avoid a dissertation on motorists. I won't count them, I told myself, I won't count them, I could observe dispassionately after nearly an hour at the side of the road, I won't count the number of miserable motherfuckers of unhung cunts who pass me by.

STAY OUT OF IT!

I was just over the hour and four fags waiting before Dunstan came over the crest of the road pounding the horn with his fist. An eleven-year-old banger, the body gaping with rust holes. We hugged each other.

'Hop in this side, that door's wonky. Dessie rang. I thought I'd make the airport but I got a cash job in.'

It was an hospitable jalopy, cigarettes and matches in the groove beside the gear lever. We were no sooner puffing and letting the ash fall on the floor when I said, 'Dessie says you're finished. You won't get your holiday money next year. You're so beaten you had to deal with the credit union. All the bankers sleep at night but Dessie bets you don't. You can't. You're stressed.'

I STAYED OUT OF IT, watching him. He had no answer except to mutter in small print 'fuck Dessie.' And then he tried to bluff me. 'Hey, you know when we do it upside . . .'

'You told me before. I don't want to hear it again.'

'No, no. We have a new bit. We have it perfect now . . .'

'Dunstan, don't do this to me. Please!'

' . . . last time we did it was July, a scorching night, we drove out past the head and walked about two miles until it was dark. Peggy had on this white blouse and shorts and black und – '

'I don't want to hear it!'

'She understands I like to take off her . . .'

'I know!'

'I stripped her and just like we do it in bed, but out there we could really shout. We got the timing perfect. And just before we're both coming, we come up for air and roar: FUCK THE BANKS!'

I was entitled to sulk. He knew I couldn't get a woman. I wouldn't talk to him. I looked out the window. He said, 'Hey, come on, hey . . .' But I pulled on my fag and stared out at the fields. Until he said, 'I'm bollixed, Junior.'

I listened.

'I'm going to go back to the Provincial with a proposal.'

'The Provincial? With the attic?'

'A business proposal. The Kodak man called in for old times' sake. He's retired a few years and doing bits and pieces for his brother. His brother knows of people who went back where they were in the bad books with new ideas and there were cases of let bygones be bygones. As long as the banks can get detailed business proposals. Facts. Figures. Forecasts. Now, my problem is the same as it always was: not enough business. So my business proposal must be based on business development. Here's my plan. Warren's old enough to do part-time and I could train Peggy to work the machine. All the brochures show women operating the machines, the women and the machines spotless, not covered from head to fucking toe with ink and bits of fingers missing. Peggy and Warren could be in the job holding the fort while I'm out drumming up business. In no time we could be flying it. And when I get the business in, I could start at seven in the morning until one o'clock. Peggy could come in until six and then I'd come back until nine or ten. Fourteen or fifteen hours' solid production. I can prove it in black and white that we'd make money and all I'm going to be looking for is a miserable three grand until we're on our feet. Right?'

'That's a good idea. But, Dunstan, why do you need three grand? You can carry out your plan without any bank. You could join things.'

Dunstan took his left hand off the wheel and thumped

me on the shoulder. 'I need three grand to spend on next year's holiday! I need it just to take it off them! You think I'd have Peggy inside the door of that kip? Getting ink under her nails?'

'Who the fuck do you think you're thumping?'

'Look. You be the banker. I come to you with my proposal. I want to develop my business. It's a good plan. Extra hands and no extra wages. Me getting in the business. I just need the cushion of the three grand so that I'll be confident getting in the business, so I won't be sweating. What's wrong with that? You come with me as my adviser, you've a bit of a name now . . .'

I could blush with pride or I could tell him the truth: 'I will in my bollix come with you. As your adviser I'm telling you to forget it. They've a black spot against you. Dessie knows it. If you were a golden oldie they wouldn't give you a balloon. Forget banks,' I trailed off, watching his jaw, 'you don't need them, Dunstan. Develop your business and fuck 'em.'

Dunstan slowed down and pulled into the lay-by. 'Get out of the car.' I had to haul my arse across the gears to get out the driver's side. Dunstan stood me against the bonnet, held my shoulders, his hands dangerously near my neck. 'I can't ask for business. I can't take the rejection! When I try, some secretary says we deal with someone else or asks me for quotations and they never come back to me. They can smell my fear of hearing a no. A no means only one thing to me: I'm a child again and the no means I can't go to the Seaside. I'm sitting on the wall outside the door for two weeks thinking of you swimming in the Seaside, and I'm burned from city sunshine while you come back with a brown tan from the sea. I'm a fucked person. Thanks to banks, I can't ask anybody for anything except banks for money because they owe me, they owe me every penny in the whole world that's in any bank. *Fuck the cunts*! Do you understand?'

I pushed him away and climbed back into the passenger seat and pussed while he drove on. He drove on in a sulk of his own, an aureole of martyrdom around him, the whole world mad except himself. I could see that and agree with it because he was my pal.

The Dessie Dennison dozen houses, plus one, are in the west end directly across the bay from the Cove. We shared a salad and read the note: 'Gone to the hot rocks. Warren in Cove. Love, Peggy.' Dunstan gave me a Cove Shivering Club T-shirt and a pair of shorts. We drove back in by the prom and out past the boathouse and golf club. In front of us on the cliff were two girls giggling and hesitating at the MEN ONLY sign. 'Hop it. Go on, hop it,' Dunstan ordered, but he didn't say it with much authority. Too much of a ladies' man. He led the way down the steps to the Cove.

Big, bulky crew-cutted Budge blushed and gave me an awkward hug. 'What you stay away so long for?' Budge gave out to me, but Tom Tucker was on his feet, all the black hair white now. Tom said, 'Where is he? President, Mr President, what about a welcome for the stranger?' Tom was comfortable embracing me, while Joe O'Connor came forward in his tanned nudity. 'Nephew of Budge,' and pro-longing the handshake and projecting the voice, 'writer of dirty books,' to chuckles, such good fellowship, the harm-less ribbing enshrined in the manly Cove. I went along with it, tomorrow I would have the laugh on whoever it might be. 'A warm welcome – hold on – as long as he doesn't piss in the water or bring a woman down.' Guffaws all over the Cove. I fought back: 'Fuck ye all, let me have a swim,' kicking off the runners, dropping the shorts, pulling the T-shirt over my head. A large patch of blue had stowed away among the clouds. The Cove was cut off from the wind. In bollock-naked warmth I did the pathfinding.

I hit the water, swam across to the far ladder, climbed out, plunged in again, swam out the Cove, crawled, did the breaststroke, floated and tried a few other disportments peculiar to swimmers who were never formally trained.

I lay on the Atlantic bed and felt the sun shine down.

' . . . Warren, hold on, Warren, wait for Junior . . .'

I swam back in to be a friendly witness as Warren Tucker dived in naked from the far ladder and went across under water.

Challenged, we would have answered, puzzled: Where's the harm in all of us? Kids trying to be men and men hanging on to childhood.

But there was a time when none of us knew what it was to be challenged. For instance, togs in the water, once the dispensation of those self-conscious of disfigurement or anatomy scars, had crept in and were now worn by as many as a third of the swimmers. That was a challenge, apostasy from within, from the new men of the computer generation, young captains in the financial services miasma, the podium élite of natural selection as they saw themselves – in a word, bollixes – they would have been too young for a Good Friday baptism or ever to have heard the old command: You want to wear togs in the water, fuck off to the beach with the women.

Togs optional for sunbathing had never been a contentious issue. A man might want to give rein to a furtive erection or his dick might be small or he might have a potbelly that needed all the camouflage it could get, though the Cove was understanding of potbellies and we were all self-trained not to look at another man's dick unless somebody had an almighty dong altogether and even then that would not be mentioned except behind his back.

Out of the water I pulled on my shorts and produced the

fags. Cut off from the breeze and with the sun pelting down, we stretched out to grab the best of a fitful summer. My eyes closed and I heard someone say, 'Let's go find mammy.' Must be one of the togs in the water crowd, dressing their kids and not hanging around. Under orders.

A place in the Cove sun hadn't come to all at the same time. Some were born to it. But more typical now of the democratic membership was the long haul beginning with the first child and a booking at the Seaview for two weeks' full board. An addition to the family led to a flat and self-catering. Then it might rain for fourteen days, the novelty shop doing business with snakes and ladders and the sun coming out on the last day of the holiday. Inflation made the millstone building society repayment seem like a pebble. Bankers swam in the cove. It was pushing an open door to tap one of them for the price of a mobile home – if your name wasn't Dunstan Tucker. The logistics of mobile-home ownership demand a car. Topping up a loan after six months is no problem but just in case – to keep them happy in head office – all is covered by a second mortgage.

There was the old money, the old houses. Bar a spectacular collapse, the holiday home stayed in the family for generations. They could not flog the house and explain it away airily by claiming to have discovered the Canaries or Corfu or the South of France, because they all knew – and everyone knew that they knew it – that there was no place in the world on a fine day like their own Seaside, on their doorsteps, only sixty miles from home. A man who gave up a house at the Seaside just had to be on such a slope that could only end with his trying to effect a discreet visit to the Community Welfare Officer, a breed of official inclined to rejoice: It's easy talk to them now.

And there was Dunstan the bank robber.

Come early, come Johnny-Come-Lately, they were all equal under the Cove sun as long as they didn't piss in the water or bring a woman down. There are no medals on a nude.

There we were, basking in our Men Only Cove. ' . . . a fucking woman!' The alarm came from someone with his back to the sea. The Cove blinked alert. She was at the top of the steps, jeans torn at mid-thigh to make hot pants, long tanned legs down to the runners, a denim halter and a terrific pair of diddies. A real beauty – in the words of the Cove, would put a stalk on a dead Dominican – shoulder bag, paperback in hand. Some could not resist the view – four thousand miles of a calm sea sparkling. It was a compliment to our Cove.

' . . . fuckit, she's coming down. Cover up, lads.'

Of course, we had had women who came down to the foot of the steps before – foreigners, short-sighted, absent-minded – only to halt with the four fingers to the lips and give a titter of embarrassment that the Cove accepted with the courtesy endemic to our little colony.

' . . . Jesus, is she blind?'

Somebody stretched out a leg to prod Joe O'Connor in the arse. 'President, what are we paying you for?'

Joe O'Connor knotted the towel around his belly and stumbled barefoot on the stones to greet her. 'Excuse me, madam. I'm afraid this is, it's Men Only here, we swim in the . . .' But she walked around our president and kept going. Some of the men giggled, not manly laughter. Budge spoke for the old consensus, 'She can see the small print in her book and she can't see the foot-high letters of the MEN ONLY sign.' She stepped up on to the rocks on the far side. Those awake and sitting up threw towels over the recumbent sun-worshippers. She sat down with her back to the cliff and opened her book.

The Cove were old hands in this situation. She wasn't blind, not with the paperback, and when Joe O'Connor spoke to her she made no sign that she was deaf. No. This was the brazen bitch department. For a minute the Cove enjoyed the lads in the water who couldn't come out because they were naked. And there was the murmur of fairly coarse talk on the lines of 'I'd give my right hand' and 'Would you go down on that?' But there was also a hefty silence from others who might have been thinking: We could do with more of her nibs here and less of the Dark Ages, disgusting fat fuckers flaunting their bollix.

The president dropped his towel. 'Enough is enough. C'mon, lads. Off with the togs. Fall in.'

He led the way down to the ladder, myself, Dunstan, Budge, Tom Tucker and the rest joining the handful already in the water. We swam across to the far side and climbed out and stood with our backs to her, presenting the lady with a grand view of our arses. We looked over our shoulders. It wasn't working. We turned around to dangle our dicks. No good. Or else it was a great book. It was an unpleasant duty. Far from getting any pleasure out of harassing the lady, we were irritated to have our basking siesta interrupted on a beautiful day during a temperamental summer. But we owed it to her and to all women everywhere to exclude them from the company of men engaged in the coarse business of being men – rough talk, unexpurgated farts, sexual speculation – not to mention rugby, about which all women are ignorant. Unedifying, but true. The lady might have been a brazen bitch, but even she did not deserve to have her femininity sandpapered by lax access to our Cove.

Frustrated, our president tried again. 'Young lady, this is embarrassing. Why don't you be a good girl now and off with you?'

She continued to stare at the book. The pity of it was that she was so attractive. We might have been forgiven for producing a collective horn. The Cove was fully awake now and most of the crowd were standing and wearing togs and towels, except for those of us in the capacity of the task force. Some of the men were amused, some outraged by her presence and some of the new men, I could sense it, on her side – on her side if she never had the pair of magnificent knockers, on her side against our side. I heard a shout: 'They should fuck her into the water.' And a laugh: 'Look at Joe, he doesn't know what to do.'

But the Cove president did know what to do. He had to behave like a gentleman and he had to get her out of the Cove or there would be no more Cove for anyone any more. We would be invaded and might as well move to the Canaries and come home with one of those shit grey colours that fades in a week. What constituted gentlemanly behaviour in such circumstances? She wasn't put off by our arses or dicks. Back at home with a recalcitrant daughter, Joe O'Connor might have sent her to bed supperless or slapped her. But corporal punishment had drifted out of all houses of correction and in the Cove our president was not *in loco parentis* vis-à-vis the lady, deluded bitch that she was proving herself to be.

'Come on now, you've had your sport. Be a good girl now.'

She turned a page and folded the paperback, her impression of reading. In so far as I could be representative of the plenipotentiaries I felt we were being made to look foolish.

'All right', our president decided, 'we'll entertain her. Lads, the cancan.'

About eight or nine of us linked arms and kicked our legs. We accompanied ourselves: da-da-dadadadadada-da-da . . . I had personally never been in the Cove before when it was necessary to produce the cancan and the weapon was only ever issued to the troops when a gang of scrapes came down together carrying a ghetto blaster. They weren't long hopping it. But this time it was a very short dance. I'm not sure how it collapsed. The Shivering Club was getting old and most of the men were a bit ancient for that type of lark and the rocks were awkward and our feet were wet – whatever, the ensemble slipped. We all unbalanced each other and somebody was brought down, causing his kicking foot to hit the hand holding the paperback, the book's edge ramming her nose, drawing blood. And her head reared back against the cliff, earning a cut on the back of the pole.

'*Jee-zuss!*' she screamed, clutching her hair, looking at the blood on her hand and the blood from her nose pumping on to her halter. '*Jee-zuss!* Fucking *animals*!' While I was still sitting on the rocks, feeling a painful bone in the arse, everybody else was around her asking if she was all right. 'Somebody get a hankie,' our president commanded, 'or a towel or something.' All sorts of offers of towels were proffered. Our president grabbed one. 'You'll be all right, love. It's not as bad as you think. Here, let me wipe you.' But she was on her feet. She pushed our president and made a swipe at him with the paperback. She roared, 'CUNTS!' and stumbled away, carrying the scalps of blood and tears with her along the rocks and on to the stones and up the steps out of the Cove.

Those who had been about to go in when the lady arrived took their dip now. The rest of us slouched back to our basking spots. The Cove tried to settle down again, but the lady had taken the good out of the afternoon. We did our best in the spirit of the poet Paddy McCormack's lines from 'Ode to the Head':

> Most noble profile
> In whose proud shadow
> Bare-bottom'd bathers
> Do bask and chat

with our president suddenly pointing, 'Quick, two right-looking cows up on the cliff.' We looked up. There were two cows grazing at the cliff's edge. We chorused, 'You bollix, Joe.' The old joke should have restored our harmless fun. But not today. I felt sorry for us.

CHAPTER 4

I LEFT WITH Budge and Tom Tucker. Up out of the Cove we could see the horseshoe bay necklaced with caravans. We weren't the only slobs at the Seaside. As we passed the golf course on our left, Budge or Tom were saluted by some of those playing the first to the third holes. They would have been mostly self-confessed shysters driving the ball to sell aluminium windows, insurance, accountancy, *printing*. From the boathouse we watched those who had spent their childhood racing inner city lollipop sticks in gutters towards shoreholes now sporting in motley craft. The working class had risen but the old crowd had their own citadels: the solid Victorian lodges that protected the seashore from the march of the caravans.

We walked along the prom past the lodges and half-way Tom Tucker continued over to the Dessie Dennison house for his tea while I went with Budge to the Seaview Guest House where it was some sort of tradition that I should eat with Budge on my first day down.

We had the bacon, egg, sausage, liver, black and white pudding. Most of the people at the other tables were elderly, one of the men having lost his emancipation: 'You know the fry isn't good for you, you'll have the salad.' There were only two young couples with a kid each, starting out, taking their places in the cycle. One of the husbands was spoon-feeding the baby. The sky cleared again but the view of the bay from the Seaview porch just didn't compare with the enchantment of looking at it through drooped eyelids on the packed London underground. Maybe that was because in the tube I didn't see buggies passing by and most of them pushed by men.

Who am I to preach? When women were all that I was brought up to expect of them I couldn't cope. Giving myself the best of it, I had always been over the top, adored women. They were on a pedestal since I was a kid. I was inclined to worship. I craved an ideal and so I missed out, just couldn't grab one before the vintage evaporated and there would never be such a year again. Giving myself the truth though, I wasn't good-looking, not in Dunstan's class. I managed to avoid remaining a virgin, but I had always to be grateful for whatever fuck came my way. Like myself, they were women for whom things hadn't worked out. But they were women. They didn't want me to make the scrambled eggs. I could boast that I never tasted plonk.

I don't go round talking like this from the back of a lorry. If there is one place today where you don't put your head above the parapet, it is no man's land. The building site whistling is muted.

'Well, young man, what did you stay away so long for?'

'It's not that long.'

'You missed two elections.'

'But only one summer, Budge. I had to run the bookstall all last year. The boss was away.' I lied. I was too broke to come. So broke that I reverted. I picked any old face from the Cove and told myself: Imagine that prick floating under the sun and me sweltering in this oven of a city. It showed that all of the hatred muck could not be cleansed with the swipe of a feather duster. But I was OK now. I said to Budge,

'I got a royalty cheque for five hundred and thirty-four pounds.'

'Did you? That's good.'

A widower without heirs, Sir Sylvester Barriscale died in Kenya. By then the rents of the homes he built for the poor were a nugatory thirty bob a week that he neglected to mention in his bequest to the Society for Distressed Gentlefolk. The yield from our entire street was less than sixteen hundred a year, collected weekly by personal visits by the estate agents to the eighteen houses. Any claim by the Society for Distressed Gentlefolk would have been costly to prove and if successful more burdensome to administrate. After the obligatory search, the houses reverted to the tenants by virtue of adverse possession. So Budge had a free house. He had always saved half his wages. He had the old age pension and an insurance policy that came to a total of two hundred and seventy pounds a week.

Budge wasn't impressed by the royalty cheque.

Tom Tucker didn't have an insurance policy but he had his free house, the pension, what Dunstan slipped him and occasional dollars from Dunstan's married sisters in the States. Tom stayed buckshee in Dunstan's Dessie Dennison house, sponsored up to now by the banks. Dunstan's house was free and in Peggy's name and he let it stay in Peggy's name, because by the time Sir Sylvester died Dunstan was already boasting: You don't own your own house, fuck 'em. Dunstan's crusade aside, the poor for whom the houses were built were well off now but getting old and all they had to live for was all that they ever wanted – the Seaside and the Cove.

'I see what's his name – got a million pounds for a book before he wrote a word of it.'

Budge wanted to see me in that class. So did I. But having to stand outside the door wasn't as hard on me as it was on Budge. He didn't understand.

'Budge, I'm on holidays. No talk about books.'

He would find a way to stuff a couple of hundred into a sock of mine and warn Dunstan to tell me at the airport not to send socks to the cleaners without checking. I washed mine in the sink.

I'd see him later. In the Dessie Dennison house I had my hug, kiss and squeeze from Peggy. After the usual god-fatherly inquisition of Warren, I defeated his protestations and lumbered him with a fiver to go to the amusements. The four of us sat in the bay window and smoked. Tom Tucker had first crack at the bathroom. I said to Dunstan, 'Dunstan, go across the road and have a sit on the wall for yourself.' You're looking terrific/How is Dunstan, Peggy?/How's Tom?/Warren's shot up/Budge OK? Nothing wrong with him that he's not telling me about? I had it all ready as usual. And Peggy would look at my pale face and ask if there was any air in London, did I feed myself. But she looked out of the bay window after Dunstan and nibbled at a fingernail so much that my first question broke through the queue and it was, 'Peggy, is he going to do the credit union?'

She took a pull of her tipped and blew the smoke out of her round lips.

'A week ago I left my note saying I was gone to the hot rocks. I got too much of it. I thought I was getting sunstroke so I came back and lay down on the bed. When Dunstan came in from the Cove he thought he was alone. I heard him talking. First I thought there was someone with him. I went to the landing. He was in the hall talking to the mirror. It was like the mirror was a girl, like we had a daughter. He was wagging his finger at the mirror. He said, "Some day you'll bring a guy to this house, he'll have half his head shaved and the other half standing up painted green and he'll be wearing a jacket made of razor blades and Doc Marten boots and he'll have a ring on his nose and a med-allion round his neck with The Pope is a Wanker printed on it and what will I say? You'll say get rid of him, Dad. No, I won't. Or some day you'll bring a guy to the door and you'll say, Dad, this is John, and I'll say, how are you, John? And it turns out he's a traffic warden. What will I do? You'll throw him out the window, Dad. I won't. I'll say to both of them, Come in and make yourself at home. But by Jesus you come to the door and you have a fella wearing a suit and tie and a neat haircut and it turns out he works in a bank, then I'll tell you this, I'll never look on my daughter's face again as long as she lives." '

I reached across the table and held her hand. Myself and Dunstan were like that – I'm holding up two fingers stuck together – and he hadn't told me about talking to mirrors. As his adviser for so long, and possessed of the wisdom accreting to such a position, I understood it to be perfectly normal for Dunstan to talk to his mirror. But doing so behind my back rendered it likely that I would be surprised when he stole a gun and shot half the customers in the bank and then pointed the finger at the bank manager during his speech from the dock. I said, 'I'll talk to him.'

'I didn't tell you he was talking to his daughter in the mirror.'

'Peggy, what do you take me for?'

When I came down from the bathroom Dunstan was slapping Peggy on the bottom and saying, 'I'll help you with the washing-up,' which was a private joke between Peggy and Dunstan and between Dunstan and me, because I knew from what Dunstan had told me that it meant, Get 'em off you. Tom Tucker said, 'Come on, Junior, let's walk in and talk literature.'

Good man, Tom. When my first book came out, Tom used Lent to convert the four alcoves of his parlour into bookshelves and he labelled them CRIME, BIOGRAPHY, HISTORY, FICTION and LITERATURE. The recess dividing fiction and literature was according to Tom's autodidactic taste and I was on the top shelf of literature out of all alphabetical order. Like Budge, Tom read about the lives of writers, but Tom was more interested in the authors on the upturned crates living on the half-empty cold tin of beans. I was almost ashamed to mention my royalty cheque of five hundred and thirty-four pounds. But Tom said, 'Great stuff. You know the bit I thought was terrific . . .'

Tom knew how to shorten a walk. Praise!!! We were in Scotts. While the sunburnt gorged on greasy fries, the old money used Scotts as an aperitif to the evening dinner cooked by domestics. They drank spirits from half-six to half-eight. Wearing white cardigans on brown shoulders, their wives joined them for just the one or two – or three – or four. They were OK, good old diehards, some of the husbands swam in the Cove.

The dinner-crowd men were on high stools in a circle at one end of the counter, while their women sat at tables in the dog-leg section of the bar. I got Tom a large one to settle his stomach while we were waiting for the pints. The body of the bar was choked with the pullovers around the necks mob, and because of their proximity they roared at one another. It was a form of confidence. At the counter inside the door sat two locals. We stood by the wall near them with our pints on the wooden shelf while Tom was saying, 'You had one marvellous expression . . .'

When half-way down the pints Tom stood out in front of me to get Scott's attention and signal two fingers for reinforcements, I caught from the babble: ' . . . baldy guy with the beard . . .'

I had learned my logic at Brother Chuckey's knee and from his toe in my hole, so how did I deduce that I had been identified in my capacity as a writer? Well, say, yesterday I'm in London, dripping sweat so much from travelling on the tube that I have to take a cold bath in my kip before I can tackle making a pot of tea. Next day I have a royalty cheque for five hundred and thirty-four quid, my body and my bollix have lolloped in an invigorating ocean, I've had a taste of the sun, the fry in the Seaview, have held Peggy's hand, am about to plunge into the second pint, Tom Tucker is drenching me with praise.

I inhaled the praise and digested it all the way down to my ankles and let it ooze back up again so that I could lick it. I heard 'baldy guy with the beard' and, festooned with money and drink and good company and praise, I heard 'more praise'. Of course, I did not know who he was, but big Ingy Casey had come in. And it is from Big Ingy himself – through Dessie – that I am enlightened as to the basis of my misconstruction. Big Ingy bought himself a pint. The only person in the bar that Big Ingy might have known would have been Dessie. But Big Ingy did not have the patience to wait for Dessie. It happened that it was a togs-in-the-water-gobshite whom Big Ingy tapped on the shoulder. 'Tell me, is there a Men Only swimming cove in the Seaside?'

'Sure,' said bollix.

'You swim there yourself?'

'Yeah. All the time.'

'Were you there today?'

'I was. Why do you ask?'

'Were you sticking your prick in my sister's face by any chance?'

Togs-in-the-water did not need to be the cutest hoor in Christendom to cop on pronto. He sang. Not only was he not waving Sergeant McDangler in the face of a giant's sister, he thought the carry-on had been disgusting and had left the Cove immediately in protest and further did not approve of nude bathing in the first place or for that matter a Men Only Cove as such, but if Big Ingy was looking for a lead, there was your man over there with his back to the door, the 'baldy guy with the beard'. Looking around to find the source of the hosannas, I saw a finger pointing at me, a finger attached to a shovel of a fist of a big man – I'm holding my two arms out now, way out, to frame my shoulders – that wide a guy and about a foot taller than Dessie Dennison himself, the big man was pointing the finger as though saying, 'Him?' and his companion nodded.

Big Ingy approached, smiling.

I smiled back, modestly.

'You might be able to help me.'

My bet was that he wanted an autograph for his wife. He didn't look the type who wanted me to read his short story. 'People who swim in the Cove,' he went on, 'they big?'

'Well,' I said, 'they'd be – ' and suddenly I knew but didn't want to admit it to myself, didn't want the praise to melt away – 'I suppose they'd be different sizes.' Big Ingy nodded with understanding as though I had said something profound and I was willing to settle for his having written a short story about people of different sizes.

'You swim there yourself? Would you be the biggest guy who swims there?'

'Me?' I grasped at the straw of truth as a way out, because he had jettisoned the smile. 'If anything I'd say I'm the smallest.'

'Sure?' Big Ingy retrieved his grin.

'Practically certain.'

Tom Tucker turned from the counter, his hands full with two pints. Big Ingy grabbed me by the shirt and gave me the head and a knee in the bollix just as in the mirror at the end of the bar I saw the door behind me open and Dessie and Dunstan come in together and I heard Dessie shout, 'Ingy! What are you doing?' I thought I saw one of the old stock begin to topple off his stool at the end of the bar, but the stool stayed attached to his arse and the floor stayed stuck to the stool and over his head the ceiling tilted with him. Dessie caught me before I could hit the floor and then laid me on my back and put his business suit jacket under my head.

When I woke up, Dessie was dabbing with a bloody hankie under my left eye and he was saying, 'He won't need stitches, he's coming to.' I was conscious that Dessie was crouched and talking up to the big man, this Ingy. The women had come out of the dog-leg and the men from the back of the bar and all around they were on their tiptoes, trying to look down on me. The next practical step taken came from the resourceful Tom Tucker, who, conscious of his hands full of two pints, nudged Dunstan with his elbow and said, 'Take one of them.' Dunstan brought his mouth down to the cream of the pint as though it was he who needed the restorative. I noticed this in the absence of Dunstan leaping on Big Ingy to avenge his pal and I heard John Scott's voice command, 'Let me through there, please. What's happened?' And at last I realised Dessie was talking to me.

'How many fingers have I up?' He was holding out two fingers in a V sign.

'Two,' I said.

'What's the name of your next book?'

'*The Second-hand Wardrobe.*'

'He's OK.' Dessie dabbed at the cut under my eye again as he spoke up to Ingy and Ingy said, 'His voice is a bit squeaky.' Dessie nodded and said to me, 'How are you there?' tapping my crotch, and when I said, 'Jesus,' and tried to get up as Big Ingy stooped over me, Dessie held my shoulders down while Ingy pulled the zip and put his hand inside the jeans and retrieved my balls. Then Ingy went behind my head and lifted me under the arms and did a bit of symbolic dusting down of my back. At the edge of the crowd Tom Tucker took three large rapid swallows from his pint, put the glass on the ledge and said to Dunstan, 'I'll get Budge.' And John Scott came through and looked up at Ingy and said, 'You'll oblige me, sir, by leaving my premises,' but Dessie caught his arm, respected as Dessie is, being the son of Mr Dennison, a great butty of Scott's in the old days, and Dessie said, 'It's all right, John, he's a friend,' and then Dessie said to Ingy, quietly, 'Ingy, what the fuck is going on?' and at the same time said to me, 'What did you do?' To provoke poor Ingy, he meant. And looked around and continued, 'Tom, where's Tom?' and Dunstan made his contribution: 'He's gone to get Budge.'

'Ingy, quick. Quick. Out of here. You stay here,' he ordered Dunstan and fingered my chest, 'Mind him, Dunstan. Ingy, out.'

Dessie pushed Big Ingy out of the door in front of him. Some of the dinner brigade began to move, so we found room to sit down while Dunstan minded me. The rest of the bar went cross-eyed trying to pretend they weren't looking at us. The only person who was not looking at us was the guilty cunt who had shopped me. The pain in my balls so contradicted the ache in my head that I didn't know how to hurt properly. I held Dessie's hankie under my eye and when I took it away the bleeding seemed to be about to stop and that made me feel cheated. Then I realised I missed something more than the bleeding. I missed being minded. Dunstan was sitting beside me doing fuck all. I said, 'Dunstan, get me a pint.' 'Sorry,' Dunstan said and did all of standing up and waving a finger at Scott and holding his palms apart the length of a pint. And then Dunstan began his minding by inquiring solicitously, 'Junior, will you come with me?' For once off his wavelength, I said, 'What? Where?'

'I told you. The bank.'

And for the first time I got angry with him, thinking of myself for a change. I said, 'I'm sitting here with a screaming bollix and a throbbing fucking head and you don't even ask me how I am, all you think about is your fucking war against banks.'

'Are you all right?'

'You don't even ask me what happened, why the guy did it.'

'Why did he do it?'

'I don't know. It must be something to do with the bird in the Cove. It's something to do with the Cove. That prick at the counter, he put him on to me. Dessie will find out, he seems to know this Ingy. Dunstan?'

'Yeh?'

'What are you talking to daughters in mirrors for, Dunstan?'

Just as Dunstan blushed and I thought that there was some hope, that he could be embarrassed in his derangement, Budge came in, the doors swinging behind him in Tom Tucker's face.

'Who did it? Where is he?' Budge swooped his head around the bar even as he was examining my eye. 'Where's Dessie?'

'I'm OK, Budge,' I said, not wanting to be mothered in public. 'It's a guy Dessie knows, Dessie'll be back in a minute. It's probably all some mistake. Sit down for a minute. Dunstan, get Budge an orange.' I didn't say anything about the bollicky at the counter, not wanting Budge to commit murder in public, and not yet having figured it all out. Dunstan brought my drink and got one for himself and Tom, and Budge's orange, and drinking my pint nothing seemed to matter as much as the pint, which is the way it usually is. And I hadn't more than a couple of sups when Dessie did come in, alone.

CHAPTER 5

INGY CASEY WAS actually one of our own, Dessie explained to us, in that Ingy was a great man for the Forty-Foot – as befitted a Dubliner who had never read James Joyce. Ingy had been a plod horse in the second row with Lansdowne in Dessie's day but there had been something about a dispute with a referee continuing long after the match, with the referee's head being hopped off the bonnet of his car.

So Ingy graduated to London Irish and Dessie and was now the general factotum in Dessie's pub in Belgravia, Dessie's Rolls-Royce of a pub, named after himself, the Dennison Arms. Ingy did a lot of other jobs for Dessie, like accompanying Dessie when Dessie toured all his pubs, jobs Dessie did himself anyway but felt it was necessary to have Ingy along because Dessie was the softest touch in the business. Dessie managed the Dennison Arms personally, yet had Ingy installed as manager there. But the one job Ingy had to do all by himself in the Dennison Arms was bounce. And all Ingy ever had to do in that department was look crooked at putative messers and they would scrape their arses off the walls, slinking out.

When at home in Dublin Ingy had always been a Forty-Foot man, swam there all the year round. There had been no better man than Ingy to bare his arse when the Forty-Foot was invaded by lesbians and assorted crazed libbers when the Dublin newspapers needed copy during the August silly season. Dessie and Ingy had often compared the Forty-Foot and the Cove, with the Forty-Foot losing hands down because Dessie had swum in both and knew the difference between four thousand miles of unpolluted ocean and the Forty-Foot, where to piss in it would have been to purify the water.

Dessie stopped telling us about Ingy for a moment and nudged me and nodded towards Judas at the counter and said, 'That him?' I said it was and Dessie said, 'That figures.' Then he went on to explain about Ingy. The incidence of crime in Dublin was at the unacceptably high level that it always was and always will be when Ingy's sister had her handbag snatched at eleven o'clock on a Saturday morning while she was window-shopping in Grafton Street two years ago. On a fine day in August. Then came September, when the rain settles in all over the country for eight months and people are driven to all sorts of night classes, women who have reared seven children go to domestic science, back-to-the-workforce former Woolworths floor walkers to computer classes, clerks to woodwork and so on and the rest commit suicide. Ingy's sister went to a Self-Assertive Course for Women. She went innocently enough, under the delusion that she might learn karate, but it was one of those courses that train women to notice that their husbands are snoring in front of the television while they are doing the washing up and other allied observations and also incorporated the right to multiple orgasms, as though being fucked by film stars and the rest of the seditious shite that has birds not knowing what to think or how to behave any more from reading the woman's page in the newspapers.

There isn't much point in having parchment without knowing what to do with it and the following Christmas morning Ingy's sister turned up as part of the invasion at the Forty-Foot, having threatened to do so and having been told by Ingy, 'Do and I'll tan your arse.' Which is exactly what Ingy did do when he got her home. He put her across his knees and walloped her affectionately for her own good with Ingy's parents agreeing: It serves you bloody well right. Like most people at all the other courses, Ingy's sister did not go back to the Self-Assertive lark in January. People see the sunshine holiday ads on television and they shake off the old September depression.

She went back to being a fine normal bird, but just like me when I caught the hatred malaise, she carried with her a sediment of insurgent bullshit that remained dormant for two years.

Ingy was on a week's holiday at home in Dublin and due to fly back tomorrow to manage the Dennison Arms, as Dessie was arriving tonight for his usual summer long week-end. Ingy was suffering the normal end of holiday edginess when he got the figairy to see this Cove Dessie was always on about and so he switched his return flight from Dublin to our airport and enlisted his sister to drive him down, where they intended to do B&B overnight and she would drop him at the airport in the morning and carry on back to Dublin herself.

They arrived about half-three and decided to see to the little matter of the B&B. The first place they tried was Plunkett House, on the left as you see the bay. Ingy got out of the car and trotted in and confidently slapped his palm on the bell at reception. Mrs Plunkett herself came out and Ingy said would you have two singles for myself and my sister please. Mrs Plunkett, a veteran at the game, looked out past Ingy at the 'sister' with the hot pants and the knockers at the wheel of the car. She was sorry. She had only doubles. Ingy crossed the road to the Stella Maris, where a little girl of nine or ten answered his ring and when Ingy gave his order said I'll ask my mother. While Ingy was waiting, he looked at the open registration book with the day's date on the top of the page and five names entered. The little girl came back to say sorry we're full. Ingy came out and looked at the building and calculated that the five guests must have been given a wing each. Ingy tried the Seaview, where Budge stayed, but the Seaview was nowadays genuinely booked out in January for August. Outside the Seaview Ingy told his sister, 'You fuck off to the beach for yourself and meet me back here in an hour.' He tried the two hotels, the Albert and Gilligan's, and was told in both that they were bursting from the presence of a Düsseldorf sub-aqua club, which Ingy was obliged to believe since the lawns of the front gardens were carpeted with wetsuits laid out to dry. Ingy got the inspiration to go back to Mrs Plunkett. He would hire a double for his sister and sleep in the car himself after getting properly pissed. Mrs Plunkett said, 'Double for yourself, and your sister?' Ingy explained a double for his sister and he would sleep in the car. Mrs Plunkett said, 'And my name is Shirley Temple. Good day to you.'

Ingy had become accustomed to reception desks in London and Dublin, where he could be tickling a fanny with one hand while signing the book with the other and nothing said other than that will be one night in advance. He was so rusty of the wiles necessary to commit sin in the countryside that his innocence was judged guilty on sight, and so in a few minutes he landed on automatic pilot in Mick O'Mara's bar down the street. With the pint plonked in front of him and the fag lighting, Ingy sussed out the proprietor. Ingy asked Mick O'Mara did he know Dessie. Sure, good God man, doesn't everyone know Dessie? Mick said, doing his own sussing. But when it was on the table that Ingy was a buddy of Dessie's from London Irish, Mick O'Mara wouldn't take for the pint and reminisced about his days in London in the fifties and a gang of pubs that were all gone now and with McAlpine in the grave. Ingy moved on to the Cove and was it the great spot as made out by Dessie? Sure, good God man, where would you find better? He swam in the Forty-Foot himself, Ingy told Mick O'Mara by way of establishing his bona fides. What? Sure, good God man, haven't I a grand cesspit beyond in the farm? What need have you to go to Forty-Foots. Ingy ordered another pint and Mick O'Mara had one with him, all on the house, because Mick O'Mara was a great man to want to talk about London in the fifties, the golden days of the navvy, but Ingy got in first with the accommodation problem. Sure, good God man, you're landed, Mick O'Mara assured Ingy, aren't the two boys on the land day and night and can't Siobhan doss with her pal down the road. Hold on, Mary? Mary, make up Eugene and Michael's room and Siobhan's bed, we've guests and they'll be wanting big breakfasts. Where were we? The Crown, did you ever drink in the Crown . . . So they set in and Ingy accepted he would not have his dip in the nip in the Cove until first thing next morning, as no true swimmer would go near the water with as much as a drop in him. By the time Ingy did look at his watch it was a half-hour after the time he was to meet his sister outside the Seaview.

She had driven out to the Cove just to see could she see the Cove and without intending to strike a lib blow any further than that. But when she looked down into the Cove from the top of the steps, she saw what she took to be a harmless collection of latchikoes. She was emboldened by her origins, a metropolitan, a Dub for whom anybody beyond the Naas Road was a hick. Dammit, she had breached the Forty-Foot, where every married nude was probably a veteran wife-beater, and all she had suffered were a few slaps on the arse from Ingy. The bunch of country mugs below her in the Cove, they didn't own the place and she wasn't going for a dip. She saw where she could walk through them and go and sit on the rocks for a few minutes and turn the pages of her book and then drive back and boast to Ingy that she had been there. It was all too, too late when she discovered what she had always known in her Dub heart, that the rustics might be a pack of goms but, without the polish of the big city, they were after all no more than savages.

She drove back in to meet Ingy and sat on the seat outside the Seaview porch and looked out at the bay and was assaulted by the same emotion of uncleanliness that she had experienced the day her handbag was robbed in Grafton Street. Some of the people who passed by gave her one look – a bird with blood on her halter – but some others stopped to say: Are you all right, girl? She discouraged the solicitude because she hated everyone in the accursed place, but one old lady and her husband sat beside her to try and comfort her distress. They were with her when Ingy came up the street and Ingy could not have been more tender, thinking she had been in a crash, looking around for the remains of the car.

She told her story and the old couple said: A disgrace. They had heard of that place, those people, if they were in her shoes they would go to the guards. And as soon as they were gone, shaking their heads, Ingy said, 'You stupid bitch.' Then Ingy told her about his problems with the accommodation and how they were fixed up with Mick O'Mara, and brought her down to the pub, telling her not to open her mouth about the Cove, she had slipped on the rocks near the bay. She said, 'You wouldn't stand up for your own sister?' Ingy said, 'I'll look after that, don't you worry, even though you don't deserve it.'

Ingy brought her down the road to the pub and when Mick O'Mara heard she had slipped on the rocks, he said, sure, good God man, them rocks are dangerous bastards, and called out, Mary, we've a casualty, look after the poor creature and flog on a mixed grill, the poor people must be famished. After the tea Ingy asked Mick O'Mara what were Dessie's haunts and Mick O'Mara said, sure, good God man, that boyo could be anywhere but he always starts in Scott's and finishes where it's last to close, the golf club or the Albert or the Seaview or in here when they make me sing. Ingy left his sister with Mick and Mary O'Mara and crossed the road to Scott's.

Dessie told us the bare bones of the story and I got the trimmings later from Ingy himself in the Dennison Arms after Ingy had decided to become my buddy.

'Where's this Ingy now?' Budge said.

'He's gone, Budge. He's well on the way to the airport by now. Forget about him. With Junior it wasn't personal, just the old scrum-half syndrome.'

They had a job escaping from Mick O'Mara's. Ordered by Dessie to evacuate the Seaside, Ingy charged into Mick O'Mara's with the news that Dessie had a phone call and their mother had had a stroke. Sure, good God man, no one can drive in the state ye must be in, sure I'll drive ye myself, Mary will whip up a few sandwiches and . . . But Ingy was able to persuade him that Ingy had driven in many an emergency even with police after him and he scuttered. Still, Mick O'Mara saw them to the car and gave the boot a slap like it was a horse as they drove away.

'What do you mean it wasn't personal?' I demanded.

Dessie said it was an old forward's trick. Budge had taught Dessie some things that kept him alive on the rugby field. And it was Dessie himself who inducted Ingy into the scrum-half syndrome, which was simply that to show you were an evil gouger altogether and get the respect of the opposing pack, you took the ear off the little scrum-half. Budge, Tom and even Dunstan all nodding away at this perfectly satisfactory explanation. Then Dessie said, 'Now for bollix.'

Dessie led the delegation over to the counter and we followed, carrying our drinks. Dessie said in his old-worldly way, 'Who are you?' And the answer came with a bit of a laugh, 'Come on, Dessie, stop messing, you know me better than an old penny.' Tommy Ryan-O'Brien was his name, a most unlikely double barrel and worthy of suspicion in itself. His mother had been Ryan and to perpetuate her memory he had incorporated her name on the day he qualified as a solicitor. 'I mean,' said Dessie, 'who are you to speak about the Cove, to speak about it like a fucking rat?'

'I don't have to take that kind of talk from people like you.' He lifted his voice and that brought in John Scott with, 'Now, gentlemen.' And that brought in the rest of the bar, so that a subsequent whisper sounded like a bark.

'You're in the Cove, when? Fine days. You're a foreign holiday cunt.'

'Dessie!!'

'Sorry, John.'

'No language. No language, please.'

'I swam in the Cove when I was ten years of age.'

'Yeah. In July.'

'No. Good Friday 1957. I'm as much a member of the Shivering Club as anybody – and I've my cert and my photograph to prove it.'

'Then you know the rules.'

'Rules? Come on, Dessie.'

'You don't piss in the water and you don't bring a woman down.'

'Jesus!'

'Sir!'

'Look, Dessie, back off. You want to live in the Dark Ages? OK. Don't bother me with it. Your friend got what he deserved. Their behaviour was disgusting today . . .'

Budge pulled Dessie out of the way like he used to do to one of his own men when he wanted to get at the opposition in his rugby days. But hyphen was as quick to lift the stool and hold it between himself and Budge and call out, 'Go on. Go on, assault me. Attack me in front of witnesses.'

And John Scott was out from behind the counter. 'That's it. Bar is closing, gentlemen. Everybody out. Settle your business in the Cove, don't bring it in here. Time now, gentlemen. Thank you.'

Dessie said, 'We didn't bring it in here. We'll settle this in the Cove in the morning.'

'. . . you come to the Cove again, I'll jump in on top of you and drown you,' Budge promised.

'I'll swim in the Cove any time I like – and I'll bring my wife down and any other woman I feel like . . .'

'. . . everybody, everybody now, please . . .'

'We're going, John,' Dessie said and began to herd us towards the door. He turned back and pointed his finger. 'You. The Cove. Tomorrow morning.'

Outside the door Dessie looked at his watch. 'Up to the square, the bingo bus is just due to go.'

Our president, Joe O'Connor, did not even drink. It was the sport of the lads to sit on the prom wall with their backs to the sea and look up towards the square at Joe getting on the bingo bus with his wife and all the other women. The few men on the bus were henpecked or old locals wearing wigs in search of widows. It was well known that on the eight-mile journey back to the Seaside Joe sang sober 'Red Sails in the Sunset' as his contribution to the entertainment on the demented bus. On non-bingo nights he brought his wife to the Victorian singsong in the Albert Hotel and most mornings he crawled around the nine-hole golf course with her and often did not make the morning swim until we were breaking for dinner. Our president was a couple of years retired from his job as manager of our block-length department store, a satellite of Harrods. He had been a well-known bottom pincher and at his retirement party all his female staff wept. That was Joe O'Connor, our president, the woman-basher.

The bus driver was already flashing his left indicator when we got there. Dessie had to run in front of the bus and wave his arms. When the door was opened, Dessie hopped on and called down the bus, 'Joe. Emergency.' Our poor president, followed by his wife, squeezed up the aisle, both their faces pale. 'What is it, Dessie? Is it the grandchildren? Which one? What happened?' And Mrs O'Connor clutched the buttons of her blouse and pleaded, 'It's not Audrey, is Audrey all right?' We had piled on after Dessie and most of the passengers from the back were on their feet. I noticed a few, though, looking at their watches. 'Relax, Joe. Everybody's fine, Mrs O'Connor, it's nothing to do with anything like that. It's just the Cove. We've a problem in the Cove. We need to talk about it. Joe, that bird that was there today, that problem.' A man with an old face and a young head shouted up, 'Driver, look at the time please.' Mrs O'Connor said, 'The what? The blasted Cove? Are you gone mad, Dessie? We're late for bingo. Sit down, Joe.' But Dessie persisted, 'Sorry to frighten you, Mrs O'Connor. We just need Joe, that's all . . .'

' . . . driver . . .'

'You'll have to wait until we come back then, Dessie. Get off the bus. Driver, drive on . . . you sit still, Joe.'

CHAPTER 6

WE LEFT BUDGE in the Seaview porch, where he liked to sit
and have a cup of tea and chat with the lady guests. It wasn't
as easy now to round up a collection of children to instruct
in the art of forty-five, not with the 'amusements' down the
road. And it was Budge's job to watch out for the return of
the bingo bus and bring our president to Mick O'Mara's.
Dunstan went back to the house to spare Peggy looking for
us in Scott's. I followed Tom and Dessie into Mick O'Mara's
and as Tom pushed in the door I heard: God save ye, ah tis
Dessie, we heard about poor Ingy's mother, the blessings of
God on her, good God man, Junior Nash, is it an argument
with a rake you had?

Dessie explained about the Cove and the provenance of
my black eye, while Mick O'Mara was filling the porter and
Mick O'Mara said: Sure, I knew that Ingy was a mad bastard the minute I clapped eyes on him, but his mother is
grand, thank God, I must tell Mary. He shouted down into
the kitchen: Mary, Mary, Ingy's mother is fine, there's
nothing wrong with her, 'twas all an invention. And then he
came back and said: I don't know did she hear me, she's
watching *Coronation Street*, 'tis the only rest she gets and
Eugene and Michael in any minute now to ate the cross off

an ass's back. Sure, good God, that reminds me, Mary, Mary, toss those boys' rooms again not to be giving them bad habits . . .

There was a smell of steak and onions coming from the kitchen. Mick O'Mara began to top off the pints: Are ye fed, lads? Would ye like something? Ingy the blackguard, and we having such a good time about the old days, Dessie, Ingy doesn't remember the Crown . . .

'Mick,' Dessie said, 'all the people who remember the Crown are dead from falling off scaffolds.'

'The Lord have mercy on them, Dessie. But Ingy's one of our own you say. There's good stuff in Ingy, I knew it the minute I saw him. And what about this mad bastard of a law man that says he's going to invade yere Cove, do I know him, Dessie?'

'He doesn't come in here. Drinks in Scott's.'

'I know. Sure, there's no one comes in here, only yere-selves and a few more, sure, why would they and Batsy over there in the corner with the tea cosy on his head and he not washed for a month with a whole ocean outside his door, isn't that right, Batsy, and the rest that do come in all have the shakes and they shagged up with rheumatics from the good old days on the buildings and the better nights in the Crown, sure, if I don't look after them no one will and sure, good God man, who'd want to come in here and have to listen to myself talkin' non-stop mornin', noon and night, will I get you a T-bone to slap on that eye, Junior?'

I managed to convince him I was all right even though he insisted: Are you sure, we've plenty, the pan won't be lonely with one less. At a polite juncture we succeeded in with-drawing to a corner of the bar – as we usually did – to have our old friends reunited chat. But outside of Mick O'Mara's the bad word was spreading.

There are about three thousand mobile homes encircling the

bay. Throw in the hundred-odd houses owned by the old money and the hotels and guest houses and flats, and taking the average number of children per family at the present low of three point one, there is a floating population from our town at the Seaside of twelve to thirteen thousand. But they don't all float in the Cove. On a normal summer's day – during which someone might suddenly sit up in the Cove and exclaim: Hold it, I think I see a patch of blue out there – our Cove hard core varies from half a dozen to twenty. But when a heat wave breaks through our natural defences and the meteorologists are scratching their heads, our numbers are sometimes swelled by the intrepid to fifty or sixty. Generally we are left alone and what happens in the Cove stays in the Cove. Most people think they prefer to sit on the beach because they are brainwashed into thinking they enjoy sitting on the beach. Then you have the many who secretly pray for rain so that they can be in the pub all day as a refuge from having paid good money to look out of another man's window. There are those who play golf – stay out of it. Quite right. I won't start. You have boat people, sub-aqua merchants, cliff walk fetishists, the hot rocks sun-worshippers, squash up against the prom wall fitness fanatics, tennis ponces – *Stay out* . . . All right, all right, all right, and a recent addition, or should that be subtraction, a basketball court. *Stay* . . . Comparatively few people swim in any of the swimming spots or the beach, so we in the Cove are a minority of a minority. Nobody outside ourselves should have known anything about our little incident but TROUBLE AT SCOTT'S had the tocsin clanging all over the village. SCOTT'S CLOSES EARLY was written on the foreheads of all who were turfed out.

When Dunstan came in with Peggy and she sat beside me and examined my blackening eye, I felt like a hero again until she held my hand and said, 'Junior, you will do it for

him, won't you? I know you will, you'd never let him down.'
We were back to normal – I didn't have to ask what.

I said, 'Peggy, for you . . .' but I was interrupted, 'Sure, good God man, 'tis dead in here. Tom Tucker give us a song, let ye.'

My voice does not sound dulcet to me unless I have had the first seven pints. Tom Tucker has no such inhibition, yet he still needed the ritual, sure, good God man, what are you sayin', you haven't enough taken, aren't the eyes rollin' around in your head from the drink you had last night and sure won't we all join in? So Tom sang 'The Moon Hath Raised Her Lamp' and even through my by now slit of an eye I could see that the world was again a fine place to be in. Before Tom finished a party from the Düsseldorf sub-aqua club poked heads around the door and Mick O'Mara put one finger to his lips and waved them in with the other hand. They stood attentively and then clapped with the rest of us and said *Ja* or something, and their pathfinder consulted a phrase book and asked Mick O'Mara: Do – you – put – on – Irish – tra – ditional? Sure, good God man, aren't you just after listenin' to the very boyo, come in and sit yereselves down, Batsy get up out of that and move down wind of the visitors – what'll I get ye all, are ye hungry? Ye're not? Ye're sure? I suppose 'tis lager ye want? Who? Geyness?

While Mick O'Mara filled the drinks, he shouted hospitable questions across the floor at the Germans, when did ye come and how long are ye staying, that class of inquiry and with the help of Mick O'Mara translating his own language into English they were able to struggle out the information that they would be a week at the Seaside and were then going on to Scotland, having already done London in four days. Did ye drop into the Crown at all by any chance? Mick O'Mara asked without too much hope, but after a gander at the phrasebook they all nodded and said *Ja*, the Crown? *Ja*. Ye did? By Jasus tell me, is Monty Gleeson still drinkin' there, we soldiered together – Monty Gleeson was the man who taught me everything during the great days on the buildings – Monty'd be in his sixties now, he's a bit of a stoop I heard, but Jasus I knew him when he could do eighteen hundred bricks in a day. They collogued on that one with many frowns and another look at the book but could not agree, as some nodded and others shook their heads so that Mick O'Mara nearly knocked down the counter coming out to clarify the position. Ye met Monty? he begged. But then it emerged all too quickly and sadly for Mick O'Mara that they had mistaken Gleeson for Queen's son and the Crown for what they saw standing on the pavement looking through the railings at Buckingham Palace.

Mick O'Mara said, 'Who'll sing next, lads? They didn't meet Monty at all, they weren't in the Crown, 'twas the palace they were lookin' at. Will you sing, Junior, or will we have Peggy or what about yourself, Dunstan?'

'Mick,' Dessie said, 'give us "South of the Border".'

'Already. Sure, good God man, the night is young. 'Twas Monty's song, he learned it after watchin' Jack Doyle, 'twas Monty taught it to me. Will I sing it so? In honour of Monty?'

He went behind the counter and clutched the beer pump, as that was his customary singing stance, closed his eyes and sang 'South of the Border, *up* Mexico Way'. He had been singing it for years before some thick who couldn't keep the laugh in enlightened him about the finer points of the compass. But Mick O'Mara said: But sure the man that taught me sang *up*.

When he finished he was less sad than when he started and came out with a grin for the Germans: And ye never met Monty, a pity, will ye sing yereselves? They looked up the book and said: But we are shy. That was acceptable. Mick O'Mara said: I know, wasn't I like that myself till I met Monty. What about yourself, Dunstan? Dunstan sang the drinking song from *The Student Prince* and the Germans weren't shy after all, joining in and banging their glasses on the table. Batsy sang 'My Darlin' Girl from Clare' and Mick O'Mara gave him a free pint. The pub began to fill with people who heard the singing as they were about to pass by the door. Peggy sang 'I Dreamt I Dwelt in Marble Halls' and called on me to sing next, so I had a go and was awful and this was corroborated by the over-zealous applause. But still the night grew older and we were having a great time and then Budge came in by himself.

Sure, good God man, here's a rare sight now, we're honoured Budge, you're welcome, what can I get you, are you hungry? But Budge gave him a pooh-pooh wave and sat down straight away at our table with the bad news. He was intimate with Mick O'Mara from meeting Mick on the prom and sitting on the wall listening to Mick's tales of the Crown. There's something urgent up if Budge is here Mick went on. Budge, I hit the crossbar: our five friends from Germany, I thought they met Monty but they didn't meet him at all.

'She won't let him come down,' Budge began. 'Joe's wife. I was sitting in the porch when I saw the first crowd off the bus, so I hopped out and this woman who always gave me a great salute nearly bit the face off me. I was just saying something like "Joe the lads are waiting in Mick O'Mara's" when she cut in and said they can wait, you disgusting individual. She'd met Mrs McGuigan at the bingo. Mrs McGuigan got it from Donal Brock's wife even though Donal Brock was never near the Cove in his life, Mrs McGuigan was driving up the road on her way to bingo when Brock's wife came out of Scott's after we left and she had it all about what happened in the Cove, so it was all over the bingo. One other thing. The two Miss Shines, they've been sitting in the porch with me for fifteen years now for their fortnight, they came out tonight and the minute they saw me, Chrissie said, "Mags, we'll sit some-where where it's decent." They moved around the corner where they couldn't even see the bay.'

'I don't understand,' Peggy said. 'Budge, why would Mrs O'Connor call you a disgusting individual?' Budge looked at Dunstan and then at the floor. 'Dad?' Peggy tried Tom, who said, 'I've to go out the back.' Peggy went on, 'Junior? A girl went to the Cove and ye told her it was Men Only and because of that her brother – Dessie's pal – lost his head in Scott's and hit you? So why would Mrs O'Connor say Budge is disgusting? Junior? That's what you told me, Dunstan? Isn't it?'

I had to look at the floor myself. I imagined a helicopter hovering above the Cove, a lady emerging at the top of the steps with her clothes smathered in blood and below, say, Budge. Lolling around after a swim Budge favoured his underpants, white Y-fronts that accentuated his bulging bol-locks under a billowing belly and having only put on his clerical grey socks he was the image of a Cove set in its ways. Bad ways, looking out from the chopper.

'It's nothing you need to know about, Peggy,' Dunstan said, putting his hand on her thigh, but it didn't work. She slapped his hand and insisted, 'I want to know.'

'Tell her, Dunstan,' Dessie decided, 'or do you want her to hear it from Donal Brock's wife or Mrs O'Connor or Mrs McGuigan or the million more who must know it by now?'

Dunstan gave a better performance than he ever did in a bank. He took Peggy's hand and leaned forward and kissed her. 'Of course you're entitled to know. Have I ever hid anything from you? Now – ' Dunstan flashed his best smile – 'Ingy's sister invaded the Cove. Right? Joe O'Connor explained to her that it was Men Only, but she walked past him and sat down on the rocks. So then we all swam across to where she was sitting reading a book and got out and stood with our backsides to her. You with me?' Tom Tucker came back from the jacks and stayed standing, listening. Dunstan never lost the smile and when Peggy nodded and looked at the rest of us, we all nodded too in the same spirit with which Dunstan was investing the tale. 'You see we thought that would be enough and that she would leave, but our backsides didn't bother Ingy's sister. So then we all turned round so that she could see our, you know. And when that didn't work we did the cancan. Right?'

'Can what? What does that mean?'

'You know, the dance? The Moulin Rouge thing?'

Peggy said, 'Dunstan, that's not fair. Come on, tell me what happened.'

'I'm telling you. We were dancing the cancan naked in front of her all linked together and kicking our legs with our whatyoucallums swinging and even at that she ignored us, so then someone lost his temper and kicked her in the nose and her head hit the cliff and she was spouting blood all over the place. That was all, nothing unusual.'

The way Dunstan managed a straight face was to keep smiling and when Peggy looked around our table we must have seemed like a chorus saying cheese, but it worked as it does in photographs because Peggy said, 'I should have known better than to ask.'

'Honest,' Dunstan said, and Mick O'Mara was out on top of us again with, 'Budge, are you all right there, Budge, do you want a mineral or a cup of tea and a sandwich or will you come into the kitchen and have something proper, sure, good God man, we can't have you sittin' there with nothin' in your hands, do you want Mary to kill me?'

'I'm grand, Michael, thank you. It's back to the Seaview for my cocoa and bed. Pubs aren't for non-drinkers.'

'Sure, isn't that what Monty used to say? He wouldn't go into the Crown at all when he was off it. Monty said he'd feel like an atheist goin' into a church out of the rain disturbin' people at their prayers. But who'll sing next, lads?

Batsy, Batsy sing that other thing you sing, that dreadful dirge you have, sure, 'twill cheer us all up.'

Eugene and Michael came in from the land while Batsy was singing 'You'll never miss a mother's love till she's buried beneath the clay' and Mick O'Mara held up his hand to halt the two boys and whisper: Batsy's singin', lads. But the two boys said in the manner of their father: God save ye, and continued towards the kitchen with the older Eugene barely breathing – from my humble deduction as a lip-reader – Fuck Batsy. And again before Batsy finished his song Siobhan came in. She was about fourteen and a half made up to look fifteen and three-quarters, wearing high heels, a miniskirt, a mouthful of lipstick, Frisbee earrings and there was a smell of brown vinegar perfume off her that drowned out Batsy's pong. Her hair was streaked a few shades of blonde. Mick O'Mara said: Batsy's singin', Siobhan. I hope you weren't hangin' around them amusements. Siobhan said: Hi, Dad, hi, Batsy, hi everyone, and continued down to the kitchen.

It was very much a normal night in Mick O'Mara's, even with – and more accurately because of – a party of Germans who had not met Monty Gleeson in the Crown. But Mick O'Mara opened the front door to let out the singing and entice custom, irregulars who had to wait for drink until Batsy had performed, while Mick O'Mara looked across the road and down the lane towards the bay and gave the weather forecast: There's some dirty bastards of clouds comin' in there now, lads.

Batsy finished his lament and Mick O'Mara called down to the kitchen: Mary. Mary will you come up and give us a song, the crowd want you. And then Mick O'Mara said to himself: She didn't hear me. But he persuaded a group out of our sight in the corner behind the door, who all sang together, the pits in any singsong but what can you do? And inevitably out of the influx came a couple of women who were gossip pals of Peggy's and though they sat away from us with their husbands, soon enough one of them needed to go to the ladies' and as is the way with women, when one goes they all go. When Peggy came back, Dunstan swung his knees to let her pass in to her seat so he was doubly surprised when Peggy let him have it with her open hand right across the mouth. She said, 'You bastard,' and then lifted Dunstan's pint and turned around and threw it in my face.

Even though Mick O'Mara was saying, 'Whist, lads, we have a row. Peggy, do you want a weapon or anything?' Peggy hit for the door and shouted back, 'Ye can all starve.' Dunstan was feeling his mouth and I had the porter running down my neck to distract me from my black eye, and the only one with a bit of a smile on his face in our company was Dessie Dennison.

Since we hadn't gone to the same school as Dessie or lived in the same part of town and only knew him through the Seaside holidays, there was nothing unusual in that we barely knew his wife. She had been a rugby groupie, a sheep-skin chaser, and caught Dessie when he had a lazy horn after twenty pints. At the Seaside Desiree – honest – liked to stretch out under a sponsored umbrella in the front garden of their house facing the hot rocks. In the same exclusive way she would not go into Mick O'Mara's. The golf club was her local, where she played bridge. Back at home she was a coffee morning chinwagger, a fashion show enthusi-ast, member of the Soroptimists and on the committee of some such fuckology as Women for Peace in the North. Desiree spent a lot of money on costly clothes and the one night Dessie lured her into Mick O'Mara's she sat stiffly and ran her finger along the seat beside her to see how much dirt she could mine. And when Mick O'Mara greeted her: 'Tis Mrs Dessie, you're welcome, can I get you somethin' to ate? Desiree did not warm to him. Desiree had two daughters of fifteen and sixteen and they were sent for most of the summer to an island run by nuns off the west coast to learn exam Irish and to France in pursuit of the notion that they would be all the better for it. When we did meet Desiree in the golf club, she was cold to me. As Dessie said, 'Desiree tried to read your book, she gave up after forty pages.' He told me that at a time when I had the hand out, yet I was brave enough to come back, 'Can I put that on the blurb for the paperback?' When Dunstan was with us in the golf club he smiled at Desiree, the way he does at all women, and while all the women melt Desiree was rude to Dunstan even while she blushed. But outside of the company of Dunstan and myself and Dessie's other charity cases, Desiree and Dessie were very happy and united and Dessie was smiling now, because if Desiree ever hit him across the mouth or threw a pint over him Dessie would ring the bank and soon Desiree would not have as much as Batsy's tea cosy to cover her fanny going into Mick O'Mara's.

Mick O'Mara came out with a towel and the traditional: Porter doesn't stain – not when it's added to all the other accumulated stains. Would ye get crack like that in Germany, lads? I wiped my neck and Dunstan said, 'Sorry about that, Junior,' just about the oddest thing I had ever heard him say. Tom Tucker flicked his fingers and pointed at the door: 'Dunstan. Go after her and make it up.' Dunstan nodded and leaned over to me. 'Junior, will you come with me?'

'You don't need Junior.'

'I'm talking about something else, Dad, something else we have to do.'

'No problem, Dunstan,' I said. Dunstan left and then Dessie said he had to go, but Tom Tucker insisted we have one more and while he was at the counter Dessie said to me, 'Go with him where?'

'Guess.'

'Jesus.'

So we sat on over the last pint and then decided to have another last pint to give Dunstan time to make up with Peggy. But Dessie had to go to his golf club and was adamant: 'No. There's a guy here who's had a knee in the bollix, got the head, and a pint thrown over him in a couple of hours, it's dangerous to be near him.'

It was one of the few times I had seen Dessie wear his happiness nakedly. I said, 'Fuck you too.' The bar was now crowded enough for us to be left to our anonymity, except for Mick O'Mara finding time between orders to come out and say: Isn't it gas, lads, hasn't Peggy a great wallop, I never thought she had it in her, I remember Mary years ago, ah sure, and won't our visitors have somethin' to remember when they go back to Germany, although 'tis an awful pity they didn't meet Monty.

We didn't have any more last ones because Tom said, 'Junior, we'll go back in case he needs reinforcements.' It took us a couple of minutes to let the door close behind us while Mick O'Mara was shouting good luck and God speed and sure tomorrow is another day, and managed once more to infiltrate his choice litany with another reference to the sainted Monty Gleeson, whom no one had ever met but everyone had heard about.

Mick O'Mara's forecast met us at the end of the street and we were pelted all the way out. Tom rang the bell and we were answered by Dunstan with his arm around Peggy's waist. Peggy said, 'Fools. Get those clothes off.' Upstairs, changed and drying what's left of the hair in the bathroom, I said to Tom, 'They made up.'

'Of course they did. I taught him.'

We went down to hot tea and ham sandwiches. Warren came home from the amusements. Tom and I sat by the bay window looking out at the rain. Dunstan was in the middle of the sofa with Peggy on his left, with his right arm around Warren's shoulder, the boy snuggled into Dunstan.

Of such heartbreaking moments is a bachelor's life composed.

Warren kissed us all goodnight and Tom yawned his way upstairs with him. While Peggy washed up in the kitchen Dunstan sat with me at the bay window. I said, 'The Cove is forgiven?'

'Well, I've been forgiven.'

I introduced the bank for a change. 'You want me to go with you?'

'Please.'

'When?'

'Tomorrow's Friday. Do it tomorrow?'

'We have to go to the Cove in the morning to see what happens if bollix turns up. The afternoon?'

'Thanks.'

'Suppose I go in on my own? Make a detached pitch? I won't be sweating.'

'Would you, Junior? Christ, I get sick at the thought of going in there. I'll never forget you for it.'

'Oh, fuck off.'

'I'll rehearse you. I'll tell you what to say.'

'My life is devoted to words, I can do it in my own way, do you mind?'

'OK, OK. Of course. How's the writing going, Junior?'

Chapter 7

I thought I was staying awake listening to the rain. I love rain but have no idea why – unless it is because rain is made of water and I'm a swimmer. I don't eat fish because they're swimming pals and I don't like the taste of fish and Budge was always a red meat man, and I don't remember what that led to because Dunstan was standing by the bed, dripping. 'Wake up.' His T-shirt and shorts and runners were saturated after his regular pound across the beach and up the head. 'It's half-eight.' We went across the road to Gilligan Point with just togs and a towel each. It was a get it over with job, the cure, more so in the rain. Dunstan dived and I jumped from the lower board and we swam out twenty yards and back in a few times and added our cigarette spits and piss to the ocean as it was not the Cove. We wore togs because Gilligan Point is not forbidden to women.

We went back to the house, where Peggy had a bit of a fry on, and we got Tom Tucker up. We had the after-breakfast fag and used the jacks. Dessie came pulluped and hooded in rain gear and hauled me with him for company and had everything in the boot, oilskins for me and a couple of alickadoo umbrellas. We went on and left Dunstan and Tom to collect Budge.

The Cove shelter has a doorless entrance and two glass-less or anythingelseless windows that look out on the rocks and the stones leading to the ladders and that let the storm come in and wet the wooden seat the length of the wall on which the clothes hooks are always wet. We were the first two and waited, walking up and down in our wellies.

'This is rubbing it in,' Dessie said, standing at the entrance.

'What?' I had backed into a corner to have a dry smoke.

'Ryan-O'Brien and the cunt Timmie Frawley from *my* thirteenth house – all cunt buddies together. And I know that other guy, he's a barrister, Coleman, Francis Coleman. I've never seen either of the two of them swim here.'

The banker came in first, Timmie Frawley, his half-open, waist-held company brolly leading him in. Ryan-O'Brien had ICI and Coleman a prosaic lager. 'Morning men,' Frawley said, a solecism. The shelter had its own protocol. We never used the shelter unless the rain was cold and could not be gainsaid by togging off on the rocks and putting the towel over the clothes. Our more accurate benediction was, 'Jesus, lads, we must be all off our fucking game.' Francis Coleman's stab was nearer the heart: 'Well, Dessie, what I have to do for those who send me briefs.' Dessie stood with his arms folded and his back to the open window, the rain blowing in over his shoulders. He said: 'Howryou,' with an Et Tu Brute lack of enthusiasm. Ryan-O'Brien, sharp, said, 'Cheer up, Dessie, it might never happen.'

'Outside of yourself,' Dessie said, 'and your present company excluded, where are the women?'

'That's verbal assault in front of witnesses.'

'You read that in a book to get your exams? It's not. Not in the real world. Not in this Cove. Shitface.'

'Lads, lads – ' Francis Coleman held up his hand – 'look who's coming. Speaking of assault, Father Ab used to give me six of the best. Gaga now.'

Under his black stalwart umbrella, still sponsored by the Society of Jesus, Father Ab gingerly tasted every step down to the Cove with both feet and wobbled across the stones to the shelter.

'Boys, I thought . . . dentures, do not fail me now – I thought I taught you sense. Do you not observe it has a propensity to be fluvial?'

Father Ab often missed fine days but he never missed wet days and the three of them advertised their Cove gaucherie by applauding the old mot that we had heard a thousand times. Father Ab said to Dessie, 'Hello, Dessie,' and Dessie just said, 'Ab.' And then Father Ab stepped nearer to me, wagging his finger: 'Mind you keep up the good work. My oculist cannot get glasses to accommodate me. But I have been told, I have been told, you are respected.'

'Budge,' Dessie said.

In our umbrella camp Budge had a magnificent weapon, a Bus Eireann with the Red Setter logo. Tom and Dunstan had one pound-shop job between them, skirts lifting like Marilyn Monroe's in the *Seven Year Itch* poster, if you could imagine Marilyn Monroe's legs as spokes.

Father Ab hung up his clerical collar. He wore black pants, black shoes, black shirt, black short coat, black long coat and a see-through mac. He was dressed like a priest used to be dressed for most of Ab's life as a priest. The rest of us started to strip. Father Ab was the last surviving adult snapshot from our Good Friday photograph. He inched his way in flip-flops along the stones to wade in, retired from diving, crabid in the nude, skinny, all bone. He let the water come only just above his knees, splashed his face and shoulders, did a couple of strokes and came out again while we were still queuing on the rocks leading to the ladder.

'For fuck's sake hurry on,' Dessie said to Ryan-O'Brien and Coleman, who stalled in front of him baptising their heads and shoulders with handfuls of ocean. So they dived in and shouted: Jesus, it's fucking freezing, when they should have come up on their backs and insisted: It's grand. After we were all in and swimming around for a few minutes it was grand and while we were all treading water between the ladders the ball-hopping began. Budge kicked off with, 'No sign of the women,' and Dessie upped the stakes by suggesting, 'They're probably lying in after being served breakfast in bed by their menfolk, I beg your pardon, husbands.' The old Cove had an archive of such witticisms into which we had dipped only when Ryan-O'Brien swam to the ladder and walked up the rocks in his togs, up the steps and along the cliff to where the cars were parked, our guffaws battling against the wind to keep him company.

Dessie said to Francis Coleman, 'Where's he going, Francis?'

'To get Kerr the Cop.'

'You're joking?'

'I'm not.'

Kerr Clery had been the Seaside sergeant for over thirty years. His visibility to the holidaymakers was that of the guard who sat at his desk to receive the watches, wallets and keys found on the beach. The pubs stayed open until three or four in the morning or until whenever the customers allowed them to close, except for the last weekend in August when the pubs were granted an extension to one o'clock, when Kerr the Cop toured the town enforcing the extension to prove that his Seaside was not entirely lawless. He would have never seen the Cove other than the occasions when he had to orchestrate the removal of an injured cow that had slid down the cliff. But he was here now, preceded by Ryan-O'Brien in his togs and Ryan-O'Brien's wife in track suit and umbrella sponsored by the American piss that is apparently beloved of rodeo cowboys. Kerr the Cop wore a cape.

The procession entered the shelter and before Dessie

could finish saying 'What the fuck?' Kerr the Cop came out again and took a long time coming down the slippery rocks to us, carrying our seven towels.

Kerr the Cop said, 'Will ye wrap these around ye and come out and get me away from this pissin' rain and sort out yere business without botherin' me.'

We swam to the ladder and Francis Coleman and the banker Frawley identified their voluminous swaddle, stolen from New York and Dublin hotels respectively. Budge was next on the rocks, but he said, 'I'm wearing no towel.'

'Please, Budge,' Kerr the Cop said, 'just this once. For me.'

'No.'

'Ah, go on, Budge. Look, when the extension is on and I'm raidin', I'll leave the Seaview alone. You can tell them 'tis cos of you, you might get somethin' off the bill.'

'No.'

But he took the towel.

As we walked up the rocks two more arrived down the steps, old hands, and they reached the shelter before us. We could hear one of them say, 'Jasus, that's one cunt of a day – I beg your pardon, Father, I didn't see you there. Oh . . . Is that . . . is that a . . .'

' . . . with all due respects to you,' the previous conversation continued in tandem, 'that Men Only sign is painted by the people who swim here, it's not put there by the county council, it has no validity in law . . .'

' . . . here's Kerr the Cop, the very man, Kerr there's a woman sitting there . . .'

' . . . my dear boy,' Father Ab was saying. He had a hand behind his neck affixing the collar. The rest of us tried to get our underwear on while wearing the towels, but Budge undraped and used his as the Cove intended. Ryan-O'Brien's wife sat on the wet seat just inside the entrance, staring with determination everywhere but at Budge, as though she had agreed to something the night before in the golf club, when she was half steamed. ' . . . my dear boy . . .'

'Ab – ' Dessie took charge – 'it's OK.' And to Ryan-O'Brien: 'You've made your point. You win, all right? You brought a woman down. I don't know whether you pissed in the water and I don't care. You brought a woman down and no one bothered her and Kerr's a witness, so you can go and boast about it and tell everyone you got the better of Dessie Dennison et cetera, but right now I'm getting wetter just standing here and we all want to get dressed, so if your wife would leave we'll all live happily ever after. Fair?'

Kerr the Cop nodded at that, shaking his shoulders inside the cape with the cold. But Ryan-O'Brien laughed, skitted. 'You guys don't understand. I'll bring my wife here any time I like. She'd swim today only it's too wet. I'll bring my sister down. I'll bring any woman I like down . . .'

Budge, hampered with one leg in his trousers, tried to make a go for Ryan-O'Brien but Kerr the Cop said, 'Budge, please. Please.' Dessie let his towel fall: 'I have no intention of getting pneumonia,' pulled his shorts up on to his wet arse, began to dry himself with a jumper, as we all started to do, as Father Ab came in: 'Boys. I have a suggestion. Francis, we believe in democracy, Francis?'

'We do, Father Ab.'

'But not necessarily Brussels. We are not enamoured of Brussels, Francis?'

'No need for Brussels.'

'We vote, Francis. *We* vote. We settle this *our*selves. The Cove, Francis?'

'Certain parties are outnumbered at the moment.'

'Well observed. Ab can see that. Ab is *not* gaga. Let Ab ponder. I have an old head . . .' Ab did a bit of his old school-masterly pacing, which was just for show, he told Dessie later. He had, he said, put on his thinking cap the night before when the word came through to Ab's poker game upstairs in the Albert. Ab and his school – a fellow Jesuit, a retired banker, a judge, a publican and a doctor, none of them Covites apart from Ab – musing on the Armageddon tentacles of Brussels eventually reaching the Cove via the pub – we would all, the school agreed, sooner rather than later, be obliged to wear seat belts while sitting on the high stool lest we fall off inebriated and claim against the publican's insurance. It was part of the process of 'being brought into line' and 'harmonisation'. In cruder words Ab's poker school had degenerated into just another Fuck Europe night, as regularly befell less salubrious assemblies, such as possibly six messenger boys playing pontoon down a lane mulling the diktat ordaining the saddle to be raised or lowered an inch or its metric equivalent. But Ab, as he told Dessie, had put on his thinking cap and now ceased pacing and held his finger up.

'I have it,' Ab said, as though it had been blown in the wet window. 'Let the president decide,' Ab teased us, naked scepticism snorted by Ryan-O'Brien, Francis Coleman shaking his head Ab-is-gagawise. 'But – ' Ab shot forward a second finger – 'let the boys decide the president. And when I say boys, I mean boys,' Ab beamed. 'Good Friday boys only. Who have the certificates to prove they were Good Friday boys. Not July boys, Good Friday boys.'

Ab's subject was history, he reminded Dessie later. And he had done his thesis on the foot-in-the-door pattern of emancipation. When Ab heard I was clobbered by Ingy, Ab looked back only to look forward. Consulting the runes of his learning, Ab foresaw another Ingy's sister – Ryan-O'Brien's wife, for instance, there today – and another can-can or its equivalent and another retribution. Violence, Ab saw, until heads cooled and the inevitable democratic process ensued – at a time *when we would not have the high ground*!

We were already dying out, Ab elucidated to Dessie, and the gerontocracy was tottering, witness, Ab was able to corroborate his theory that afternoon, Joe O'Connor, whose wife did not give a shite about Ingy's sister but would not accept our president dancing in the nude while she made the dinner. The way to fight hot blood was with hot blood, from our own loins, and the time to fight was now.

'Thomas – ' Ab held out his palm towards Ryan-O'Brien – 'you will stand for president on the reform ticket.' Just then Ryan-O'Brien would have fought the election on a bring-back-the-yashmak manifesto. His face blushed with the same humility of every politician who ever craved office. He actually nodded sagely, when the thick cunt could hardly have understood Ab's machinations. You could see him trying it on: President Ryan-O'Brien, adjusting it: the president, Thomas Ryan-O'Brien. 'And Dessie, I appoint you to represent the diehards. I will formally accept nominations this afternoon and the election will take place, not July, but next Good Friday. And will be contested by and voted by bona fide certificate-holders exclusively.'

Ab told Dessie that he had identified where our flank was strongest. The Good Friday civilisation lasted from 1950 to 1957. It was certainly monolithic in its resistance to the Hun up to 1955, our year. Ryan-O'Brien was '57 and even if a form of rot had set in in '56 the odds were very much in our favour.

'Thus Spake Zarathustra,' Ab signed off. And thus we were in danger that Zarathustra had landed us in the shit.

CHAPTER 8

WE SQUELCHED BACK to the cars in pairs, Tom and Budge, Dunstan with me, Dunstan animated, on the ball: 'Junior, remember, go in confident. They can smell fear.' We might have been limping out of Hiroshima and Dunstan would not have noticed. Dessie trailed behind with Father Ab. 'Dessie can drive Tom and Budge back and we'll go straight away.' Having conducted Father Ab to his car and digested Ab's philosophy, which he now passed on to us, and also having half listened to Dunstan's alternative travelling arrangements, Dessie said to me, 'What do you think?'

'I'll do my best,' I said, humbly.

'What?'

'I'll give it my best shot. Maybe on my own I can pull it off.'

'You fucking ape. I'm talking about the Cove, you prick. Two dickheads. And I'm up against a solicitor and a barrister and the cunt in my thirteenth house and all I have is dickheads and a gaga Ab. Be back here in time this afternoon.'

'Where will you be?' I asked Dunstan. He had been in great form driving back to the city. I tried to get him to remember

Ryan-O'Brien's face when Ab announced his candidacy but I don't think Dunstan even remembered being in the Cove that morning. All he talked about the whole way was the Kodak man and the Kodak man's brother's commandments and precepts, reminding me of everything we should have learned in our years jousting with the banks.

'I'll be out here walking up and down.'

'You can go someplace for a pint if you like.'

'No, no. You won't be long.'

Banks have changed. The oak, the solidity is gone. I'm not saying the counters are made of Formica, but there's a fragility about them that would not inspire me as a depositor. They're like new churches compared to old churches, except in so far as they're not empty. The Provincial was crowded. It was all open-plan with snakes of queues roped into obedience. On the day Tom Tucker made his pitch he was better dressed than the tellers in the Provincial now. The material in their suits didn't last pissing time, rumpled, after a month, like the ten-year-old suit of a teacher who had a large family. Distributed about the bank floor were seven functional desks manned by seven bank chaps, all of them busy, the picture of officials processing immigrants. Whatever their business, I thought the supplicants deserved a more formal hearing. I could hear without trying as I walked to inquiries: And how much per month do you calculate you can afford to repay? Some of the people in some of the queues were close enough to the desks to sit on them. But whatever was going on it was none of my business. At inquiries I exchanged good morning for good afternoon with the girl and we had a bit of a giggle about that. Good start. Could I see the manager. Had I an appointment? No. What is it in connection with, Mr . . . Nash. Junior Nash. Business finance.

I see.

So. Forty minutes later I was still sitting in a queue to

see one of the seven assistant managers. I had my ticket in my hand, number ninety-eight and the contraption on the wall read eighty-seven.

My man had his jacket off, collar loosened, tie dangling and sleeves rolled up a little. We shook hands standing and then he spoke: 'Please sit down. Now what can I do for you?' You could not ask for a more mannerly chap. 'Junior Nash,' I said, 'actually I'm here representing someone else. You see, I'm a writer and I want to take the opportunity to try and kill two birds with the one stone.'

He nodded, impressed. 'What do you write, Mr Nash?'

'Books. Fiction.'

'Good man. I don't get the chance to read as much as I should. I'd love to write a book. Have you had something published?'

I mentioned *Hand Me Down*. 'That seems to ring a bell, I know I heard something or read something someplace. Can that be got in the shops?'

'Not at the moment, but you'd probably get it in the library.'

'I'll do that. So you're here about someone else?'

'It's a friend of mine. You see, I'm based in London and I really haven't that much experience of banks here, but you know there's been a lot of hubbub about the banks being supposed to be impersonal and heartless and all that rubbish, I personally have always found my own bank perfectly civilised and accommodating, although I'm not in business and it's the business, the small business people, who seem to be kicking up over. It's just a figairy, I said to my friend, let me go in and represent you so that I can prove to myself that we're just as understanding and civilised here and, you know, I hope you don't mind, I mean is it all right if I just put the case, the same as if I was, as if I was in business, and I was looking for accommodation, for myself . . .'

He seemed to understand, although I hadn't a fucking

clue what I was after saying. I hadn't yet started to beg but my hand was shaking as I took out the fags and pleaded, 'Is it all right if I smoke?'

'Of course. I'll get an ashtray.' It took him five minutes to disappear down a corridor and come back with a plastic yoke the size of the bed of a bun.

'Your friend that you're representing, is he a customer here?'

'Yes. But let me explain. He's a customer but he is not a good customer – no, what I mean is he's a customer but he's had problems in the past that, what's the best way to put it, say, that militated against his prosperity. You see he has a one-man business, it's a good business but he hasn't enough of the business, he hasn't enough of the market share and that's because he can't get out to sell himself properly, because while he'd be out someone might come in . . .' I was not convincing myself as much as Dunstan had convinced me earlier when I was listening to him with a raised eyebrow. The man across the table was rubbing his eye with the back of his hand and almost yawning and that inspired me to remember my own black eye. 'You must be wondering how I got this?'

'Hmm? Oh. You walked into a door?'

'No. Rugby. I play a bit of thirds with Harlequins,' hoping to see him sit up. I didn't bother with thirds for London Irish because it is not a distinction, everyone bar maybe Monty Gleeson having had a go sometime. 'Harlequins?' I repeated.

'They're in England?' he chanced. I may as well have been Monty Gleeson. He didn't wonder how I could be playing rugby in August. 'London. But where was I?' not wanting to boast any further of my association with Harlequins, seeing as the unlettered prick had never heard of them. 'Yes. You see my friend is, repentant is the word I want, sorry that he can't just right now pay his way, which is his one great ambition, but he talked the whole thing over with his wife and what their plan is is this. He wants to bring his wife into the business to start at eight in the morning and keep it going while he is full-time on the road to get the customers until lunchtime, when he'll then take over production and work on until ten at night. That's how hard he wants to work to get his head above water again, and also his young son is now old enough to come in after school and maybe do a bit on Saturdays and Sundays, the whole point being that he will have extra staff but won't have extra overheads. There's only one way that he can go and that's up.'

'Sounds fair enough to me.'

'I said that to him. I said the bank would understand. Now what he wants is a loan, what I would call it now is a confidence loan . . .'

'What kind of business is he in?'

'Printing. What I mean by confidence loan is the order book is thin at the moment but if he had a loan it would bide him over until the order book was bursting and he'd be a customer that any bank would be proud to have helped . . .'

'How much – sorry, what's his name, his business?'

'DT Offset, dunstantucker,' I whispered. He didn't ring the alarm. Maybe it was so long ago they might have forgotten. Before his time. 'Would five thousand be a reasonable amount? He has said to me that he could probably wing it on three but five would be a comfortable cushion.' I didn't blink as his fingers played the keyboard. I plotted the whole map of his face for a sign.

'What did you say, five thousand?' I tried not to let the air out of my mouth too quickly. 'Yes, five, I'd say,' I said with a casual gesticulation of the palm.

'Well, the only problem is.' Only? 'With a customer whose credit rating isn't a hundred per cent, we may have to look for a guarantee.'

'A guarantee?'

'Insurance policies. Or a guarantor.'

'I'm not sure, no, I'm almost certain there was something about those having lapsed, the insurance policies, when trade was very bad, I'd be nearly sure there, that those policies would have lapsed. Now when you say a guarantor, you mean a person who will go guarantee . . .'

'A person of substance. Not a man of straw. Someone – I bet you have all sorts of people coming up to you saying, I'm not being nosy now but how much do your books make, that sort of thing. I'm not asking that, but would you be in a position to act as guarantor, would you be willing?'

I couldn't believe it. He was going to part. Would I guarantee it? I'd guarantee it and fuck 'em.

'Of course I'd be very willing. I wouldn't present the case if I wasn't a hundred per cent willing.'

'Good. Because you understand it has to be a hundred per cent in this type of case. And only over three years, which is all the better where you personally are concerned. I may as well be honest with you, your friend is lucky to have someone like you, not everyone will do it, I know fathers who won't do it for their sons. His, Dunstan, it is Dunstan, isn't it? Yes, Dunstan's repayments will be –' the calculator in action this time, he told me a figure and then said, 'And for you, I can give you, can I, I can, the extra quarter, yeah, eight and three-quarter per cent?'

'You were a long time,' Dunstan said, the hope hanging out of his face – hope founded on the fact that I was a long time.

'It was packed in there. I had to queue for the best part of an hour.'

'So how did we do?'

'I'm not sure I understand it. Let's get in the car and head straight back. I'll tell you on the way.' I was trying to filibuster until we at least got out of town on to the straight road where the road did the driving.

'Well? Get me out of my agony.'

'Give me a chance to light a fag, will you?'

I made two miles.

'For fuck's sake, Junior, is it yes or no?'

'It's yes and no.'

'What does that mean?'

I told him about my approach to inquiries, the queues, the seven desks and the seven assistant managers. I told him my pitch, my writer's curiosity, about Harlequins . . .

I made another three miles.

' . . . I said five even though you'd be willing to scrape by on three . . .'

'Yeh.'

' . . . then he asked me who it was, I said DT Offset, Dunstan Tucker, and he didn't say anything, just fucked around with his computer and said he'd need a guarantee, like insurance policies . . .'

'I don't have any insurance policies.'

'I know. I told him you had but that they'd lapsed, so we started talking about a guarantor, a personal guarantee. He asked me would I guarantee it. I said I would. I'd be delighted to.' I couldn't keep it up any more. 'Dunstan, if I give him five thousand pounds that he can hold for three years, he'll give you five thousand that you pay back in three years and if you don't pay it back he'll take my five thousand and put it in the bank's pocket.'

I didn't mind having to go over it again and again because it helped to leave the miles behind. No, that was the only way the Provincial would part. Yes, I did try him and he said he had absolute confidence in a man of my stature whose word alone he personally would be satisfied to take but his hands in certain cases were tied with red tape. I left him, needing time, as he perfectly understood, to return to

London and visit my own bank and building society and talk it over with my accountant to decide which funds were best transferred to meet the needs of the case. I left him with the circumference of his loosened tie a tug larger than when I met him.

Bastards and so on got us within twenty miles of the Seaside and from there on we enjoyed the comfortable silence that can endure between old friends, one looking out the left window to avoid seeing the fixed grip of humiliation on the steering wheel.

Tom and Peggy were sitting at the bay window watching the rain. Peggy let us in, held the door open and looked at Dunstan. Dunstan just shook his head and walked on. Peggy said to me, 'No go?'

'Sorry.'

'Dessie was here. You're to call up the minute you get back.'

Leaving Dunstan, I found Dessie, who had his swimming rainclothes on, ready to go. He had the eight framed photographs laid out in chronological order on the dining-room table and his father's journal opened at the 1952 page.

'You know a guy called Harry Lamb?'

'No.'

'How did you get on?'

He cut me short. Did I get it? No. The five-grand guarantor, he waved that away, just said, 'For slime.' And then did not hide the fact that he was looking at me, measuring me: 'Harlequins?'

'It didn't matter, he never heard of them I think. What d'you mean for slime?'

'Dunstan. I was expecting that but I let you off. When shit comes up on that computer screen that's the way they do it. Say your bank man tried to forward a proposal for slime – it's the in-house off-the-record name for guys like

Dunstan – he put forward a proposal, he'd be promoted assways where sheep wouldn't be safe, but let's say he could get five grand in on Dunstan's behalf, OK, they'd lose because the interest on the deposit wouldn't cover the interest on the loan when Dunstan tells them to go and fuck, but Dunstan would have caught his guarantor, his friend. They can take losing that few bob just to have Dunstan spread his mucky name among his own. Now fuck Dunstan, you never heard of Harry Lamb, neither did I. Maybe Dunstan did. Or Tom or Budge.'

Dessie handed me the 1952 photograph. 'That's him on your left as you look at it.' Dessie turned the '50, '53 and '55 photographs face down. 'Ring a bell?' No more than the name Harry Lamb, the ten-year-old boy in the photograph was definitely unknown to me. But there was something familiar about the boy beside him. I said, 'No. But this fella, I know him from someplace.'

'Rugby. Charlie Anka.'

'Of course. Well that's one up for us.'

'No. Someone must have kicked the fucking head off him too often. His wife's in the Soroptomists with Desiree. They stopped coming to the Seaside years ago. They have some time-share kip in Spain. When he was captain of the golf club he broke new ground. For the first time, under Charlie Anka's captaincy, the wives were allowed go to the captain's dinner. People had to go into the jacks to tell jokes. Now if I could get Desiree to work on his wife to work on him, it would be something. But the way it is, I got to work on Desiree to keep her from getting too contaminated by Charlie's wife. Stupid cunt, Charlie.'

'You'd write him off?'

'I'll write no one off. Maybe he can be bought. But I doubt it. OK, we will write him off. Francis Coleman was here an hour ago. Francis is OK. I said, "Francis, what are you doing on the side of that gobshite?" but he was straight up. He said, "It's the compensation cases: Tommy Ryan-O'Brien is the best collar man in town." Anyway Francis wanted our evidence so we went through the photographs together and he immediately lamped Charlie Anka as one for them. Now, 1950 is a non-runner, only one that year, Phil Quigley, if he was alive he'd be ours. '55 just you, me and Dunstan. '57 Tommy bollix-prick himself and Shamey Flynn, who's his brother-in-law, we write them off. '53 there was no one at all, so that leaves us with '51, '54 and '56, and there's just two in each, in all the years our year had three, which was the highest, a headstart there. Look at '51, '54 and '56 what do you think, know anyone?'

'I know him,' I said, putting my finger on the head of a little blond boy in the '51 photograph, 'he was doing his leaving when I went into secondary, right? That's Maxie McManus, the aluminium guy, isn't it?'

'Bang on.'

'Then that's one for us. Didn't he put in the windows in your houses?'

'Yeah, Maxie did my windows.'

'And he swims in the thud. And he fucks and blinds. He'll be sound, right? Can't place any of the rest of them though.'

'You weren't ever out in the rain, were you?'

'Where do you think I've been all day.'

'You never had to hustle. You never had to tender, I'm talking about tender when the bank is half-way up your hole. Maxie plays golf . . .'

'. . . there you are . . .'

'Maxie plays golf but he hates golf. He goes to all the big GA games and Maxie hates hurling and Gaelic football. When these parent-teacher fucking larks are on and any man worth his balls is looking at his watch with his eye on closing time, Maxie is there with questions. Suggestions. Volunteering. Once a month he collects outside the church for Vinnie de Paul. He's in the Chamber, Rotary. He wears his dicky bow to the licensed vintners' do every year and laughs his head off at every stupid dirty joke that those thick cunts of publicans tell . . .'

' . . . you do that kind of stuff yourself . . .'

'Of course I do. When I have to. But Maxie – Maxie's obvious. He has no style. He gives arse-licking a bad name. What I'm telling you is this, and I know because I put him through the fucking wringer when he wanted my business, what I'm saying is I wouldn't trust that cunt. Put him down as a don't know.'

I looked at the other boy in '51 and the two each in '54 and '56. I said, 'I can't place any of the rest of them.'

'How could you? You came down on the bar of a bicycle. People who drove to the Seaside on Good Fridays were well off. All their kids went to the Jays. Dan Dennison was well off, that's how I know them. The only guy who came down in a car from that kip of a school you went to was Maxie and he came down in a van 'cos his father was a barrow boy and he taught Maxie everything he knew and which he summed up in one word: rob. OK, kid long side Maxie is Dollars Mulcahy, ever hear of him?'

'No.'

'You heard of half a dollar?'

'She was some kind of a bicycle when I was a kid. But I never even saw her.'

'Dollars was expelled for fucking her when he was fourteen. She made him use a hankie as a johnnie and next day at school he was showing the coagulated bit to the guy next to him, Ab was teaching them, Ab lamped them anyway, did the usual separate interviews, got two different stories and eventually the truth from the guy sitting next to Dollars. The thing about Dollars was he was a fucking altar boy, real holy, he even had a vocation. He was whisked out of town and sent to St Kieran's in Kilkenny and then Maynooth and then the American mission, where he still is, in Oregon. He was actually here last year when you weren't around, swam with Ab every day.'

'So we have him through Ab?'

'No. Maybe. The Jays expelled him mind. But we have him because – it must run in the family – the guy who shopped him was Tommy Ryan-O'Brien's older brother.'

'Great stuff.'

'That leaves two each in '54 and '56 and they were a year behind me and a year in front of me at school so I know them. Benny Bobinizer and Staff Cox . . .'

'The insurance brokers Bobinizer and Cox? They were there yesterday. Bobinizer was in the cancan . . .'

'Good. But we have them anyway. They're my brokers, for everything. Outside of that they're friends of mine and they're OK. That's '56 but we're bollixed with '54.'

'Why? Who are they?'

'The Fennessys. Fennessy's Pharmacy.'

'The chemist twins? I haven't seen either of them here in years. What's the problem with them?'

'I used to bully them at school.'

'That was years ago. What do you mean bully them? How? Why?'

'I don't know. They used to come in dressed the same. Their noses were shining like they were polished. They had the same trousers and jumpers and blazers and shoes. And they both had the same cow's lick, combed the same way. There was something goody about them, you know? I couldn't stand the fuckers.'

'What way did you bully them? They've probably forgotten.'

'When we'd go out at eleven to the jacks I'd kind of whirl around and piss on their shoes or up the leg. They had a way of taking their mickeys out that was the same, there were buttons in their trousers and they seemed to open the same button and just let him barely peep out. Going home from school then I might grab their bags and throw them down a basement where there was spiked railings. When they hit eighteen, even though I only bullied them for a couple of years when they were thirteen and fourteen, once they left school they never came to the Seaside again. If I see them in town I salute them, they say hello to me, as far as I'm concerned it's forgotten, but if I were in their boots . . .'

'So how many have we got?'

'We have six definitely out of thirteen. There's this Harry Lamb, Francis never heard of him either and Francis is like myself, he knows everyone. He only comes to the Cove once in the blue moon but barristers, they know everyone. I'll probably be able to figure out a way to get Maxie, when I get into some kind of training at his level, the sewers. And Charlie Anka, fuck, we're both rugby, there must be something there. Let's go. You run in and get Tom out, he might know Harry Lamb, and tell Dunstan to ask Budge when they're collecting him.'

I nipped up the steps in the rain. Tom saw me coming, let me in. To a scene. I know I was away mostly, but I never even got the hint of impatience from Dunstan's domestic life before. Peggy looked ugly, not just angry as she was the night before when she heard of Dunstan flashing his dick, but ugly angry, with her hands on Warren's shoulders, shaking the kid. ' . . . I want the truth! Don't tell me again you gave two pound to a poor man you met, there are no poor men here . . .' Warren was crying. He said, 'Honest, Mam . . .' 'Liar!' Peggy slapped his face. Tom stood beside me in all his uselessness, knowing about marriage, not interfering. Where was Dunstan? But as a bachelor I could act. I went in and caught Warren, put my arms around him, held his face to my chest. I said, 'Peggy! Peggy?'

She put her hands to the sides of her head. 'Oh, God!' and went out to the kitchen.

Dunstan had gone to the bedroom. Peggy heard Warren go up and try to tap him for fifty pence, heard Dunstan snap at Warren, 'Leave me alone. Just leave me alone.' Dunstan, who would give Warren the world. I got all that later. But now I said to Warren, 'What's going on?'

'Mam doesn't believe me, she thinks I lost all the money on the machines, but I bought a burger and chips and gave two pounds to a poor man.'

I brought Warren over to the bay window, sat him down and held his elbows. 'I want you to do something for me, kid. Listen to me, I'm not giving out to you, OK? But we have to do this quickly. First – ' I took out a fiver and stuffed it into his T-shirt pocket – 'first thing you got to do is – here – dry your eyes. Now I want you to go into your mother and say: Sorry, Mam. Say: I'm sorry I told you lies but I was afraid. That's all you have to do. What you went through, I went through that myself, so did your father and I know that 'cos I grew up with him, and your grandfather went through it, right, Tom? Just go in and say: Mam, I'm sorry, and take my word for it, Warren, everything will be fine.'

Good kid, he did it. I told Tom to go out to Dessie. I had a well-earned fag. I looked into the kitchen. Peggy was hugging him. ' . . . Warren, Warren, Warren, I'm sorry. Sorry, sorry, sorry I hit you. My lovely boy . . .' When she saw me, Peggy said, 'Warren, go and call for someone, I have to talk to your Dad.'

The ugliness and the anger were gone and she was sad. She said, 'Thanks, Junior.' And then, 'He's not going swimming this afternoon, he said to tell you.'

With Tom in the car, all I could say to Dessie was, 'He has a cold.' Dessie got out of the car, made me get out. I explained in so far as I understood. Dessie said, 'I'll put up the five-grand guarantee. Go in and tell him.'

'This will take time.'

'So take time. The Cove will survive without you for one afternoon.'

I poked the bell and had to wait a few minutes before Peggy answered. She was wearing jeans and a denim shirt that was now not fully tucked in. 'Back again?' She put on a breezy smile.

'I'm going up to him. I think I've good news.'

'Dunstan?' I said, with two little taps of the knuckle.

'Shit. Come in.'

'Dessie will guarantee the five grand.' He was in bed, sat up, naked at least as far as the waist.

He thought about it. I could hear him thinking about it. 'But they'll keep his five grand? They'll hang on to it if I don't pay?'

'That's what the man told me.'

'And Dessie knows that?'

'Of course.'

'So what good is it? I can't rob Dessie of five grand. Or can I? I can't.'

'No you can't. But you can do what you said you'd do. Work. Get the business. Pay the fuckers back.'

'But the whole point is to take it off them. For the holiday.'

'Dunstan, you have to stop. You have to stop sometime. You've run out of banks. If you haven't you'll run out of them sometime. Stop now. You had a good run. Get on your own feet and fuck 'em.'

He thought about it. 'I know. I've more or less decided that myself. But I just want one last chance. Give them one last kick in the bollix. That's all I ask for. One last go. Then I'll retire.'

'Promise me one thing, Dunstan. Give it till teatime. Think about letting Dessie guarantee the loan and you pay it back. Just think about it until teatime. Think. That's all I'm asking. To think about it. If you paid it back, in three years' time your name might be good with them again. You might get a loan then without a guarantor, then catch the cunts.'

'Do me a favour.'

'What?'

'Take a walk for an hour.'

'It's pissin'.'

'Take a walk in the pissing rain then. I want to talk it over with Peggy.'

I did the cliff walk. Half-way round I sat in a shelter and had a few fags. Sitting there reality crept in beside me. The dank fuckology going on in the Cove just then, Dunstan bollixed and at the same time Dunstan back there under the sheets 'talking it over with Peggy' and me here with a horn. Sure, good God man, what state is that for a man to be in? It was the pre-creative depression, the only way out to go back and start *The Second-hand Wardrobe*, get away from another week swimming in the rain. Getting older. My one true pal Dunstan a hopeless case and the next best thing Dessie nuts with gaga Ab playing elections in the Cove. Just lonely willy-nilly thoughts . . . sunlight, the rain was thinning, nothing to distract a depression like a bit of sunshine coming out. By the time I was back on the road I was carrying the rain gear over my arm and people were out of the houses, leaning on the wall looking out at the sparkling ocean. Even Dunstan was across the road sitting with his feet dangling, Warren beside him, Dunstan with his arm around Warren, giving the boy a tickle, both of them laughing while Peggy was packing stuff into the car.

'Warren,' Dunstan said just as I landed, 'bring out the cases for Mammy.'

'What's happening, Dunstan?'

'We're going home.'

'Why? For what?'

'Had enough of it. Pissin' rain. Peggy wants to organise Warren's books for school . . .'

'This is Friday, it's the weekend . . .'

'That's our story, lots of people do it, there's only a week left anyway. This is for you, no need to broadcast it but we're starting work tomorrow. Me, Peggy, Warren. Like you said, I'm beaten, so it's probably all that's left to do. Work. Get in the business.'

'Great. But why not start Monday?'

'Tell Dessie thanks anyway. But I don't need it. Explain to Tom, but say fuck all about banks, he's never known about that. We'll come back down next weekend to tidy up. Meanwhile make yourself at home.'

'Dunstan, come on. What am I supposed to do with myself here for a week?'

'. . . ready, Dunstan . . .'

'See you, Junior.'

I walked after him to the car. He got in first. Peggy kissed me and sat in the driver's seat. I leaned on the bonnet and put my face to the open window. Warren stretched from the back seat to give me his kiss. I said, 'Peggy . . .' but she started the engine. She said, 'Bye, Junior.' I backed off and they drove away, waving.

I sat on the wall, smoking and waiting. The Seaside was empty without them. I sat there for almost an hour until Dessie drove back with Tom. I told them. Dessie said, 'When's your flight?'

'Next Friday.'

'Harry Lamb's an English guy. You have to find him and find him fast, any expenses or any other shillings you need I'll fund it. What are you doing for dinner, Tom? Come up to the house?'

'No, no, I'm grand, Dessie.'

'Suit yourself. Junior, you come, we'll go over it.'

I didn't say it in front of Tom but I said it: 'I can't sit down to dinner with Desiree, she doesn't like me.'

'Desiree's gone home for the day to see if the house is still there. Otherwise I wouldn't be allowed to bring to you in.'

'How come you never got a maid? I mean, I can see Desiree with a maid.'

'She suggested it. I agreed with her. I said it was a terrific idea. I said I had the exact person. I said our cook in the Dennison Arms was homesick and that she'd last because she was young and had big tits. Desiree didn't mention a maid again.'

I was given a mug and a tea-bag and had the breadbin and the door of the fridge identified for me, as happens in houses where they don't have a maid. 'One last hit and he'll retire? The banks will fight with each other to see who'll give him the gold watch. Fuck Dunstan. Harry Lamb, Ab remembers him. At least he remembers he had an English accent. He remembers talking to the boy, asking him where he was from, but he can't remember where now, just that he was English. Apart from the accent, how Ab remembers at all is that just before twelve, man, woman and child are passing on a walk up the head when they see the Men Only sign and child comes down to investigate, asks can he go in too, sent back up to his parents, who send him back down with is it safe? Ab and the rest wave up at them and nod that it's safe. The only other thing Ab remembers is, after hopping in the car to go home for the three hours' agony, he sees them going into the Seaview. Which is where I've just come from, where they let me go through the books in the attic and where I found the entry: John Lamb, Winifred Lamb, Harry Lamb, and the address: 30 Colehill Lane, Fulham, London SW6, England. On the door of which establishment you'll be knocking on Sunday, having cut short your stay and flown back tomorrow on whatever flight I can arrange.'

*

Tom and I had a quiet night in Mick O'Mara's. When we went in Mick O'Mara called me aside to whisper with professional discretion after Dunstan and Peggy. And then he shouted down to the kitchen: Mary, Dunstan and Peggy made it up. After four pints Tom decided that he was going home to see if he could help Dunstan and when Budge came in for a few minutes – the two Miss Shines again did not sit with him in the porch – Budge said, 'I'm not staying down here all by myself.' Somehow, I heard later, word went round that we were all run out of the Seaside.

PART 2

CHAPTER 9

I HAVE MY own bedroom, a toilet and shower next door. Down the hall there are two other bedrooms, Bill, in his seventies, a retired civil servant and George, an uncle of our landlord's wife. Our landlord owns the pub downstairs, where Bill sits most of the day doing *The Times* crossword and his few bets. Down the hall we have a living/television room with a kitchen off and a bathroom that Bill and George share. I use the kitchen only for the odd cup of tea since I discovered Arthur's Caff up the road in Kensal Rise. Arthur does the best bacon, egg and sausage in London. He uses a frying pan. George gets whatever few bob it is from the landlord for watching the television a lot and not coming downstairs too often to help out in the pub. We don't see each other unless I have a pint in the pub or we coincide at the electric kettle or there's a black and white movie on the television. But we have a pay phone on the landing and Bill or George take messages for me.

Dessie got me on the Saturday night seven o'clock flight that was late getting in and with a couple of changes on the underground I arrived after ten o'clock. I went downstairs to the bar and had a few drinks with Bill, who had taken a message that I was to phone Dunstan.

I rang him: 'Junior, started this morning going around with Peggy. Started at eight o'clock, first place we went to that was open was Pat O'Connor, the butcher's. He's nothing to Joe. We got an order for five thousand labels. We got thirteen orders altogether and I'm working until now setting them up to print tomorrow. Warren was in cleaning the machine. I'd go for a well-earned pint but I'm now on the dry – have to go, bye.'

There was a brass shingle on the red-brick wall beside the front door:

HARRY LAMB, IMPRESARIO

I rang the bell. His hair was black and combed back with oil exactly like Tom Tucker's used to be and the growth was luxuriant enough to camouflage any suggestion of high fore-head. He wore a mustard-flecked dark green tweed jacket and a check shirt, floral tie, Fair Isle pullover, cavalry twill trousers and solid brown brogues. He gave me the friendliest smile, flashing well-attended teeth, a hybrid of dog-show judge, spiv and squire.

He said, 'Baptista and the Blessed Virgins?' holding the front door wide and welcoming, not a bit afraid of me.

I said, 'Pardon?'

'Not Baptista? Thought it might be early. The Daltons?'

'The what? Mr Harry Lamb? My name is Junior Nash . . .'

'Come right in, Junior. We'll use the parlour, not to disturb mother.'

I stood respectfully in the hall as he closed the door. 'After you, Junior, a good name. You believe in the live act? Make yourself comfortable, Junior. Tea? But do you agree, I insist on asking you first, am I right: England was diagnosed

as having cancer of the tabloid and with admirable coward-
ice blew its brains out with the TV?'

'You could have something there, Mr Lamb.'

'Damn right I have. Harry. Call me Harry. Now, tea?'

Only a month before I rang his door bell Harry Lamb had
found Baptista and the Blessed Virgins at the Annual Convention of the British Barbershop Singers, staged this year in
Fulham. They were entered as Four from Finsbury in the
heats of the ladies' quartet.

As a young lad in the late fifties, Harry Lamb had gigged
in a skiffle group, playing the washboard and doing the solo
'Does Your Chewing Gum Lose Its Flavour on the Bedpost
Overnight?'. Skiffle then was a phase to go through, like
having pimples or supporting Fulham Football Club. Harry
Lamb did not dream seriously of stardom. He was happy as
an enthusiast on the fringe until a new fad came along and
nobody wanted to be the next Lonnie Donegan any more.
But having been in the business in however peripheral a
prominence, Harry was hooked and drifted out of his clerical job with the West London Gas Board into small-time
management.

He was ambling along, not really knowing why he was
doing what he was doing, but then the disco came and smote
him with a vocation. Though unconscious that skiffle was
the foot in the door that sold the big band dancing days
down the Swanee, Harry saw the birth of the disco as the
death of all decency and fought to espouse the live act all his
life. He was a Bing Crosby man because he could hear Bing's
words and sing Bing's songs himself. But then the music
industry evolved and since nobody could be sure what was
bad and what was worse any more, the artifice of gimmicry
all but took over.

No more than he had as a performer, Harry Lamb did
not aspire to gluttonous riches as a manager. He just liked to

keep a show on the road. He specialised in a scissors-and-paste con of letting talent flower out of its setting – sending a Cockney version of the Beatles across the water for THEIR FIRST TIME IN IRELAND and bringing them home again DIRECT FROM THEIR SUCCESSFUL TOUR OF IRELAND. There was his recent canny development of Pat and Mick Dalton, the fiddlers from West Clare – Harry would not let them appear in an Irish pub, at least not in an Irish pub patronised exclusively by Paddies.

Harry Lamb remained a small-time impresario operating from his home in Colehill Lane, a posters and leaflet provender of a modest stable of support groups for the big concerts and turns for the London pubs and the ingenuous Irish circuit. Before his curiosity was aroused by the bits of leg going into the Annual Convention of British Barbershop Singers, Harry Lamb, after over twenty years in the business, averaged a thousand a week for himself after paying tax on an income of two hundred.

Out of the eleven entrants in the ladies' heats, Harry picked Four from Finsbury as the winners by a mile. They sang 'By the Light of the Silvery Moon' and 'On the Banks of the Wabash'. For Harry it was an innocent and delightful Saturday morning's entertainment, reminiscent of an age that even preceded skiffle, brought back memories of Bing. But not the stuff to beat the disco, not any more. What could he do with them? The live act needed so much help.

But I didn't get Baptista that Sunday afternoon. I was fed the Daltons, the fiddlers from West Clare. Mother brought us tea and biscuits, mother, to whom I was introduced as 'My friend Junior, mother.' With the parlour door open, I could hear from the kitchen Bing and Grace singing 'True Love'. She was a lovely old lady, a mother like I certainly would have wanted myself, a Katie Johnson style from *The Lady-killers*. 'Hello, Junior,' she said. 'Now, Harry, you're not to go on to the young man about the television sets. We don't have one, Junior, but that is not to say other people . . .'

'Thank you, mother,' Harry stood up and kissed her forehead and aimed her back out the door. 'Mustn't leave Bing on his ownio.'

I said, 'She seems a very nice lady, Harry. My parents died of TB when I was a kid. I really didn't have a mother. I would have liked a mother like your mother.'

'Mother is a darling, Junior, thank you. You didn't have a mother? Mother is now your mother. But first, shall I be mother? Say when. We almost lost Dad once from TB. When I was ten . . .'

'And you swam in the Seaside on Good Friday . . .'

'Well, hotdiggity! I would not be so abrupt as to ask a chap his business until we were at least on the cigarettes – you do smoke, I hope?'

'Yes.'

' . . . but you know about me and the Seaside?'

I told my story.

'I have my certificate and the photograph hanging upstairs in the den, with all of my stable, and I'll show you my latest, the Daltons. But of course I'll vote for your friend if we can arrange mother and everything. How did I happen to be there, you say? Dad's cough. We feared it was TB, but it can't have been. You see, Herne Bay did the trick after all. We've just been, mother and I, staying with Aunt Sookie. That's where mother is from. We go every year. That's where I learned to swim. But Dad's cough. Our GP down the road, I think it was O'Dwyer, that was his name. He said keep your old Switzerland, the west coast of Ireland will kill the best of TB. He recommended the Seaside. I'm not saying the chap wasn't right and maybe the journey – we had to go to Euston to Holyhead to Dublin and down the country by train and then on to another train that ran out of fuel and we had to get out with the other passengers and go into the fields collecting firewood – it may be that Dad was fatigued, but he did declare that though the air might kill the TB, he was very much afraid that it would kill the carrier first. Six months in Herne Bay, that softened the cough. Stay in your own backyard. And after all those years, here you are. We'll smoke to that. Mother will be delighted when I tell her. And what do you do yourself, Junior? And your friend Dessie, our candidate?'

'Dessie's in London too, he owns a chain of pubs, and I'm a . . .'

'What did you say? A chain? How many? How many is in a chain?'

'I think it's fifteen. I'm a . . .'

'Fift – come upstairs, Junior. I must show you my stable. Especially my Daltons . . .'

Dessie never did believe me when I swore that Harry agreed to vote for our side before Harry heard that Dessie had fifteen pubs.

The walls of Harry's bedroom were covered with photographs of his live acts. I had heard of most of his Irish showbands, many of whom had a Hank as the lead singer. And, hey, there was the Bedouin Showband.

I said, 'They're from our town, Harry. That's Butch Frawley, he owes me five bob.'

'They come together only on special occasions now.'

There was a Chris the Cap wearing a suit too small for him with the buttons bursting. Even though Chris was English, from Birmingham, Chris told English jokes, that is Polish or Irish or Kerry jokes, but where the thick was an Englishman. Harry tried Chris the Cap on the homogeneous English scene but the customers hadn't laughed, so Harry had to confine him to the ethnic circuit where the Poles, the Irish and the Kerrymen were mad about him. Many of the photographs were of troupers who were getting on in the calendar stakes, female impersonators and buskers Harry had brought in out of the rain, reflecting what I understood was a trait of loyalty in Harry. And true enough in a central setting of main-altar status there was the certificate and the ten-year-old Harry 'Johnny Weissmuller' Lamb just pipping the Daltons for pre-eminence.

One of the Daltons – Pat – wore a polka-dotted bandage around his forehead and had a large pirate's earring and a Mexican moustache. Mick had dirty, scraggy grey hair down to his shoulders, a pinstriped waistcoat, blue jeans and brown boots. I have to admit that they did look like traditional Irish fiddlers from County Clare.

'But,' Dessie said, 'I don't have music in my pubs. You've been to them all, have you ever seen music in my pubs?'

'I told him. That's what made him happy.'

'I haven't heard of any Daltons. Have you?'

'No, but I'm not as well up as you are.'

'Fuck. When do I have to look at them?'

'Wednesday.'

'I haven't a bar in Kilburn. I hate going near Kilburn. Fucking kips.'

'It's not Kilburn.'

'No? Where? Camden? Acton?'

'The Fulham Arts Club.'

'Piss off.'

'Straight up. It's like I'm saying, that's Harry for you.'

'Arts! Look, this Harry, is he queer?'

'No.'

'How do you know? He lives with his mother.'

'I wish I had her to live with. No. I'm in the publishing world, I've met the people. From the book business I know a gay just by being able to identify the guys who aren't gay. Harry just loves his mother. Full stop.'

'And he had the Bedouin one time? How would a fellow

who had the Bedouin recognise a traditional Irish fiddler from County Clare?'

Motoring along in Dessie's car Dessie said, 'Why half-six to half-seven anyway? What kind of a time is that for fiddlers?'

I said, 'It's part of Harry's exotica.'

'Fuck that for a game of soldiers. We had a centre once, just one guy to beat a few yards from the line with the winger outside him. Dummies, gets caught. Why the fuck didn't you pass the ball? I thought they'd be expecting me to do that. Simplicity is fucking beyond some people. You know Mike Moloney?'

'The window cleaner?'

'Yeah. He gets up at all hours on Monday morning, it's how he cures himself, works his bollox off. I met him at four on Monday afternoon when I was heading for the airport. He called me. He was like a guy who was stunned, like he was after being attacked. Which he was. Five past eight on Monday morning he was up on his stepladder doing O'Mahoney's, the bookshop window. He said the next thing he knew he was surrounded by Dunstan Tucker and his wife. Mike pulled out five hundred business cards wrapped in an elastic band. He never had a business card in his life. Whatever way they talked him into it they were back in a few hours with the job and it was a cash/no VAT/bargain price that had him breaking into his last twenty quid. I had to lend him a tenner.'

We rang the bell and asked for Harry, who came out and signed us in. There was a big long uncovered rough wooden table there, flanked by a long continuous wooden stool at each side of which were seated hearty types all squashed in together according to the rules of the club, and tonight the menu was Irish stew, tinned vegetables and onions and one large lump of a spud swimming around in a bowl of a packet of Oxo soup and what looked like the odd lump of Chum or

Pal bobbing to the top as the noshers were getting to the bottom. Fellows wearing short jackets and long scarves. The Daltons were fiddling by the fireplace facing the dinner mob and although I could read on the menu up on the wall TOPIC: HAMLET – OLIVIER VERSUS DEPARDIEU, the propositions were not anything as bear garden as one might have reasonably expected, because most of them were stamping their feet and banging their spoons on the table in communion with the Daltons.

'This is the real thing – ' Harry nudged us while he ordered three pints of bitter. I was afraid to look at Dessie. Instead I pretended to be absorbed by the complement not dining. Guys there wearing shirts with the collar a different colour. Young Japanese with the *FT* stuck in their suit pockets. The arts bunch, skinny guys combing their long hair back with their fingers, designer cords, birds hanging out of them. There was a full-size table just beyond the bar. Dessie had one swallow from his bitter, watched the crowd, listened for a few seconds to the Daltons. 'Aren't they,' Harry said, 'as they say, something else?'

'Be back in a minute, Harry. Can't resist a game.'

Dessie went in and soon he was playing snooker with what he claimed was an arse bandit wearing a cravat. But there was no doubt about it, the Daltons had most of the place by the balls. They were using the creased-forehead concentration style, the sacred art of the fiddle. When Dessie finished his game he rejoined us and listened for another few minutes. He had won on the yellow, the steamer hadn't even a bridge, Dessie shrugged. The Daltons had a couple of pints each on the mantelpiece and now another two were brought over by one of the Japanese aficionados. 'You're a horrid decent man,' Pat or Mike said, 'the blessings of Jasus on you.' Harry was beaming. Dessie said, 'Harry, let's sit down over here and talk business,' and to me Dessie muttered, 'They'd be stoned out of Kilburn.'

Dessie doesn't waste time. 'Harry, I'm the only one here to shout that the emperor has no clothes, but I don't do that because that's not how to take the money off the people. They're fiddlers from County Clare? Harry, whoever they are they're from Roscommon and the only way I recognised the Mason's Apron is because I've been listening to it since I was a baby.'

'They're not the real thing?'

'They're not even from County Clare.'

'But they're live. They're not disco. Look, the punters are happy.'

'I don't have music in my pubs as a rule, but I can tell you, Harry, I can tell you I'm not breaking my rule when I say I will hire them for my Dennison Arms. You see this shower of sophisticates? They're traditional Irish music *buffs* compared to my bunch in Belgravia, so if they go down here they'll go down there. But another thing, Harry, that Pat or Mick, the navvy with the big earring, he thanks the customers when a pint is put up in front of him. No genuine County Clare fiddler would do that. Tell him to spit on the floor.'

Harry was happy. He said, 'This calls for more drink.' But of course Dessie didn't let him buy the round. 'So,' Dessie said, 'what's the damage, how much do they draw?' Harry said what they got from the Fulham Arts Club. 'I'll throw another tenner on top of that. I wonder are they even from Roscommon.'

When Dessie went to the jacks and the Daltons took a break to murder a couple of the pints, I said to Harry, 'With Dessie I'm flying around morning, noon and night so tell me, how contactable are you in case of any hitch before we launch the lads next Monday?'

Harry gave me his business card.

'Fine. And Sunday, you available Sundays or is it your day off or dine out or anything?'

'Dine out, Junior? And miss mother's cooking?'

'It's just in case you took her out for a treat or . . .'

'I stay in with mother for a treat. We have our simple roast and we listen to Bing. Although we've just come from Aunt Sookie's and Aunt Sook has had that dreadful television in and mother's been hinting, saying, "It might be fun." Synthesisers! I've never let any of my stable appear.'

'You know, it's funny you should say simple roast. Of course I have it when I go home, I go with Uncle Budge to my pal Dunstan's, Dunstan's wife Peggy insists, but I'm so rarely at home. I have access to a kitchen in our flat, but you know how it is. I can't cook anyway. Still, what you're never used to you don't miss, I suppose.'

Fuckit. Am I talking to the wall? Of a bank? I get into places on Christmas Day by just saying casually in a pub: Thank God this day week is Christmas, the one day I look forward to, because you might think me mad now, but believe it or not it's the one day in the year I go out of my way not to eat anything, because a fella told me one time the body needs a day off from food . . . What? I insist you come to us . . .

Dessie came back and Harry suggested, 'Should I get them uniforms, do you think, Dessie?'

'No need, Harry. In that one respect they are ship-shape and Bristol fashion.'

Now that we had Harry's vote for the price of a couple of fiddlers, I could concentrate on my own business. I was hot with *The Second-hand Wardrobe* and ready to spring out of the traps on Monday. But with the bookstall job Friday, Saturday and Sunday I would be able to give the new novel only four days a week. Dessie went home as usual for the weekend and as Dessie's supposed front man where Harry was concerned – if he had been listening to me – I tried to think of a reason to ring Harry.

Harry had suggested to Dessie that he would of course provide the usual posters and leaflets to promote the Daltons, but Dessie said no, that class of razzle-dazzle was infra dig where genuine County Clare fiddlers were concerned and Dessie said to me afterwards in translation: Fuck, I'm letting them in Monday because it's the quietest night. But I rang Harry anyway on Sunday at around twelve o'clock and said: Just checking everything's going all right. Don't worry about a thing, Junior, remember, Harry Lamb delivers, that's his motto, no double-booking with Harry Lamb. Good, good, I said, see you tomorrow night then. Enjoy your dindin, Harry. And you too, Junior.

On Monday morning I went to the publishers and suggested to the secretary that maybe I should check with himself out of courtesy to confirm that it was all right again to use the basement. I had an unwarranted vision of himself down to the humblest of the house all called together to witness me taking my seat, stretching the fingers, as they backed out on tiptoes shushing each other and carefully closing the door. But the secretary said it was probably OK, he couldn't be disturbed, he was with an author.

So that Monday I wrote:

THE SECOND-HAND WARDROBE
by
Junior Nash

and the first sentence would not come because I could not help thinking all day long of roast beef.

There were about thirty customers in the Dennison Arms on Monday evening. It was Ingy's night off, but Dessie had him hanging around in case any undesirable Irish refugees who happened to be passing were lured in by the racket. 'Here he is,' Ingy roared when I opened the door, 'my old pal from the

Seaside.' Ingy put his arms around me and squeezed me and kissed me on the forehead. 'Your eye is grand, how's your bollix?' Dessie sat at the counter reading the evening paper, ignoring me. 'Give that man a pint,' Ingy said, 'because he's a poet that I hit by mistake and it's a terrible mistake to hit a poet and from here on any man who looks at Junior Nash crooked will have to deal with Ingy Casey.' I'm used to pubs and can fit into a scenario with the best, so before Ingy could show me off any further I said, 'Not a poet, Ingy. Writer.' Ingy gave the counter a thump with his fist. 'Writer, the man is. Better again. And what's more the man is a nephew of the great Budge Griffin, who taught Dessie how to play rugby.'

Ingy introduced me to a couple of his London Irish cronies, ex-bruisers of front row men, and Ingy told them our story and since they had met Ingy's sister sometime one of them said, 'I wouldn't mind waving my dong at Dolores.' Ingy said, 'Cut it. Respect my sister, OK?' But there was no real frisson in it as they were comfortable with each other and with me because in ten minutes I was included in the audience to a dozen dirty jokes before Dessie folded his paper and gave me the beckon.

'I was driving through town yesterday around five,' Dessie said. 'I see Dunstan's front door open, first thought it might be someone in the offices downstairs, but then I saw Dunstan's banger. So I went in. They were all above. Peggy and Warren were cleaning the place, you know how tidy Dunstan is. And Tom was there and Dunstan was training him on the machine. And they had a customer. Jimmy Flah. You know Jimmy Flah? Used to work in SPS? He got redundancy, bought a lathe that he has in the garage, going out on his own. He's just leaving with his goods. Five hundred two-coloured letterheads. Five hundred two-coloured invoices. Five hundred two-coloured quotation forms. Five hundred two-coloured business cards. Five hundred two-coloured With Compliments slips. Jimmy asks me to put the word out, if anyone wants whatever he does, tool bits or whatever it is. I go down the stairs with him, ask him how he's doing so far. Oh, he has no jobs yet but he's putting feelers out. I could forgive the business cards and maybe a few letterheads that could be used to act as invoices or quotations, but Jesus, With Compliments slips. I ask him for the crack what he needs With Compliments slips for. He'd met Dunstan in the street and there was an exchange of how's-it-goings and the minute Dunstan heard Jimmy was starting up, Dunstan hauled him in. The With Compliments slips are what Jimmy is going to attach to cheques when he's paying his bills.'

'Is Dunstan on the dry?'

'Not that I know of. Why?'

'He said he was.'

'Must be a Dunstan joke. I have a message for you myself. From Budge.' Dessie handed me a carrier bag. 'He said you left so fast he hadn't time to organise these black puddings. He said not to give any of them away until you had examined them properly.'

I glaumed at the bag until I found two hundred quid under the black puddings. Dessie said, 'I notice it doesn't bother you that he didn't attach a With Compliments slip.'

Harry Lamb came in alone. I thought he looked worried. 'Dessie, I forgot to tell you, have you announced them for nine? I don't know how it slipped my mind, they're always fifteen minutes late. I hope you won't be angry with me?'

'They sound more like West Clare fiddlers every minute. What are you having?'

Dessie had made no announcements. Only Ingy knew they were coming and how we knew they'd arrived was a sighting by one of Ingy's pals who faced the door: 'Oh, oh. Trouble, Ingy.'

'God bless, all,' Pat Dalton introduced the Daltons to the Dennison Arms.

Dessie said to his barman (former bus conductor with a gift for turning back the clock), 'Their drink is on the house.'

The Daltons were a big hit. Within half an hour they had five pints apiece growing flat beside them and Ingy's mates were coming over to Dessie: 'Jasus, Dessie, fair play to you.' Two of the ex-front rows had their jackets off, yahooing and trying to recapture the few Irish steps last practised at some long-forgotten ceili. What the Daltons did for a break was to rest their fiddles on their laps and Mick stared at the faraway corner of the ceiling and wailed out a woeful lament about a chap wrongly imprisoned in Van Diemen's Land for twenty-one years, and that prompted a volunteer from Ingy's gang to give us 'The Black Velvet Band', accompanied by Mick Dalton on the fiddle and Pat Dalton slapping the sole of his boot.

'Harry,' Dessie said – he told me later he just wanted to make sure he had Harry stitched in – 'Harry, OK, Mondays here and I could probably use them in the Dew Drop Inn in Camden on Thursdays – if they're not booked out.'

'They won't play any place on Thursdays.'

'Oh?'

'It's the night they do their own stuff. They go to a place in Hampstead where they play for nothing with other fiddlers. They won't play requests or play anything for the punter. They just play for themselves. But any other night . . .'

I added my bit to the stitching in stakes: 'Harry, I have a present for your mother.' Harry looked at the black puddings: 'Junior! Yum, *yum*! Mother will be delighted.' Fuck-all mention of roast beef.

'So,' I said to Dessie after hours, 'that's that. Job done. Back to my book in the morning.'

'I was on to my travel agent. I think it's better if I don't handle it myself. And you did a good job with Harry. Got you an eleven o'clock flight. And I've told them in future that any time you call up, they'll handle it, send me the bill. I want you to start with Maxie. Just wing it, watch his eyes, figure out how greedy he's going to be.'

CHAPTER 10

I RANG MAXIE MCMANUS from Dunstan's job. 'Of course I know you, Junior. How are you?'

'Dessie Dennison asked me to give you a shout. This election lark. When could I call and see you?'

'Marie. Appointment book. Who was talking about that the other day? Coleman. Francis Coleman. Hang on, today's Tuesday, tied up this afternoon. Morning gone. Lunch. Meeting two-thirty. Meeting four. Could be finished five. Thursday, gone all day Thursday. Golf classic Friday afternoon. Unless I could fit you in sometime Friday morning – say twelve-thirty?'

'I wouldn't keep you long, Maxie. If your meeting was finished at five tomorrow I could be there. I have to get back to London.'

'OK. Come out if you like, Junior, but I can't be a hundred per cent sure. With these guys I'm seeing at four, they're big hitters and you know I'm into conservatories now?'

'No.'

'No? Well, of course, you're away. I hope Dessie knows. Call out so tomorrow.'

I was smoking a fag, let it fall, put my foot on it. 'Christ,

Junior,' Dunstan said, picking up the butt, putting it in the ashtray. He was wearing a navy pinstripe suit. Any time I'd been in DT Offset before his uniform was jeans and jumper. The shelves were stacked with paper stock. There was a two thousand run going through, the covers off the machine, Tom Tucker at the controls, wallet of Allen keys open from which Tom made a judicious selection every now and then to adjust the blanket and plate cylinder pressures, Warren stacking up each completed ream, wrapping and Sellotaping and putting the good one on top. I'd missed Peggy. She and Dunstan had been out all morning beating the bushes.

I said, 'Tom, you copped on fast?'

'Ah, there isn't all that much to it, Junior. 'Tis only pressing buttons,' as he gave the water molleton roller a twirl, prodded the duct with the ink knife.

I hauled Dunstan out for coffee. He listened to me while I told him all about Harry Lamb and the Daltons. Listened. Just listened. Waiting for me to finish. As though I was distracting him from his business. So I said, 'But you told me you couldn't ask people for business, you couldn't take the rejection. And here you are, a hot shot at it.'

'I've Peggy with me. It's . . . different. I am good at it. But it's having Peggy with me.'

'Where'll you be tonight?'

'Didn't you get my message? I'm on the dry.'

'Why, Dunstan?'

'I've been thinking of it for a while. I don't like the idea of drink getting the better of me.'

'What are you talking about? I'd drink you under the table. When we're in rounds you fucking hold us all up. What kind of a bollix would give up the drink? Outside of someone like Budge and why he did it?'

'Junior, please. Don't give out to me. Give me a few months and then you'll understand.'

*

I got the half-four bus out to the industrial estate, apologised to Maxie's receptionist for being early. Maxie had started down a lane. Although it was never any of my business, I had heard some idle chat once in the Cove while I was basking about Maxie having some sleeping Japanese involvement that helped with the Industrial Development Authority grant. And another phrase wafted back from my subconscious, an indigenous business loner complaining, 'I said if I had slit eyes you'd give it to me.'

At five to six Maxie's receptionist offered me a second cup of coffee as she was putting on her coat to go home. I'd had nobody to drink with the night before. I like down town, where I always had Dunstan or at weekends sometimes Dessie if he was slumming. Tom drinks down the road from home, but that wasn't my patch. I'd got a couple of possible opening sentences for *The Second-hand Wardrobe* on the third pint and fuck this cunt keeping me waiting, I knew where I should be, in my basement, *staying out of it!*

But Maxie gave me the big welcome, arm round me into the office, like a banker in the old days, saying bring your coffee with you.

'You're representing Dessie, Junior? I like the way Dessie does business. When Dessie does business, there's no talk about the match yesterday and no asking after the families or the children. Until afterwards of course. There's no more concerned man than Dessie. He wants to know what way I'll vote, right? I'll be straight. I don't know. Next Good Friday is a million miles away.'

'Maxie, you don't want women in the Cove.'

'Of course I don't. It's what I said to Francis Coleman. Look at that brochure.' Maxie had the agency for the Uncle Sammy Sunshine Conservatory. 'Francis might be interested in the one showing the pool. He has a pool already. If Francis wasn't a barrister he'd be a good businessman. You know what he said? He said conservatories are for women to sit in while their husbands are out making the money to buy the conservatories. Francis said a man selling conservatories who gets the reputation for keeping women down has it harder than the next guy. I said: Fuck you Francis you're trying to bribe me, you sly cunt. Have a look at that one. What would you think? Eleven by fourteen. Do you know what's grigging me? If I'd only had the agency when Dessie was building the houses. The bay windows, a lot of the money went into those bay windows and what was all we had to do? We could have left a fucking hole where the bay windows are. You know how much a hole costs? Fuck all. Then we get our eleven by fourteen job, bring it in ready-made, assemble it, back it up to the goddamn hole and there you have Desiree with her mates, the little teacups and the biscuits, the wind and the rain howling outside and they chatting away about mastectomies. Junior, show Dessie the brochure and remember that's the shagging brochure price, Dessie will know how to read that. But I want him to understand one thing, and make sure you get it through to him, Dessie could decide to put a conservatory into the front of every one of his houses but I can't guarantee the Maxie McManus vote. I'm in business. I'm a good businessman because I have to be or I go to the wall. But I don't sell my soul for business. I'll do what's right on the day. It's what I told Francis Coleman. I said: Fuck off, Francis, you can't buy me.'

I was in the Dennison Arms with Dessie and Ingy was there listening in. Ingy said, 'You want me to go over and kick the fuck out of him?'

Dessie was working with his biro and notebook. He doesn't trust calculators. 'Take it per conservatory. Rent could go up fifty to sixty a week during the season. I know the guys who want to be one up. Make it easier then to let it out during the winter. And we're creating an asset. When he put in the windows I stretched him out with stage payments. This time I'll be the guy who has to go to the bank, he'll want the shillings up front. At the end of the day I wouldn't be out of pocket and we're talking about, say, three houses here. It's only a fucking vote that's for sale. The only thing is this vulgar shit would ruin the look of my houses. After they pay for themselves I can always tear them down again. We know where we are with Maxie. He's for sale up to twelve o'clock Good Friday. If we need him. But with a bit of luck we won't. I take it we have Harry. You, me, Dunstan, four. As long as Dollars doesn't get AIDS in America he's OK. Benny Bobinizer and Staff Cox. Benny eats Gold Flake, has to get it sooner or later. As long as he hangs on until Good Friday. Staff plays squash. Those guys go like that. OK, you tell Maxie, Dessie says we're in biz.'

'Will I ring him?'

'Ring him? No, no. I want you to look at him. Watch his mouth. Tell me if he lets it shape into a little smile.'

'When? Dessie, what about my book and my job?'

'I threw the Daltons into the Dew Drop last night. So do your job weekends. I go home weekends. You got me Harry, you got me Maxie if I need him. So we're going to go after Charlie Anka. The Fennessys. And even Shamey Flynn? Why not? They were a sensation in the Dew Drop,' Dessie said, the way a cultured man might observe an Australian soap go to the top of the ratings.

I called the publishers to let himself know that I was postponing *The Second-hand Wardrobe*. Out of courtesy. In case he was creeping about downstairs perhaps in search of something from the backlist and failed to hear the thunder of the typewriter. But it was after twelve o'clock and he had gone to lunch. So I told the secretary. I thought she might have said, 'Oh!' But instead she said, 'No problem.' Before I backed out I threw in the magnanimous, 'I wanted to let him know in case there might be someone else who might like to use the basement. For the time being.' Although I had to admit that the last four words were superfluous, as most of our list are top honchos and if any one of them managed to hack through the piles of books all over the floor and reach the card table I use for a desk, he would probably shake his head and decide to stay out of it.

My first weekend back at the bookstall was taken up as usual by sorting. I specialised in salvage among the three-for-a-pound baskets. Finding a *Catcher in the Rye* or *Gatsby* trapped in an elastic band by a Cookson and Cartland, giving it the kiss of life and marking it up to three quid. It was an aptitude appreciated by Tony, my gaffer, who also had jeans stalls, leather goods, jewellery (Tony's mantra: 'Women will hang shit from their ears') and racks of Donegal tweed jackets from the Caracas sweatshops.

On Monday I jet-setted home to meet the Fennessys.

Fred Fennessy was attending to a little boy's cut knee. Fred wore his official white coat over his grey suit trousers. The wine striped tie was that of one of our local boat clubs. His shirt was a muted pink and the shoes were black toecap. But it was his hands that attracted me the most. Spotless. Cuticles ordered to highlight the crescent moons at the base of the nails as he gingerly used the swab to absorb the little last drop of blood and then apply the white powder, gauze, and with a smooth flourish of his two thumbs flattened the Elastoplast into place. 'Now there's a good soldier.' The little boy was holding his mother's hand and the mother said, 'Thanks very much, Mr Fennessy. What do I owe you please?' But Fred was otherwise occupied, dipping two of his elegant fingers into the liquorice-stick jar. 'Here, my good man, and try not to run too much until that knee is better.' And when the mother tried again, Fred said, 'None of that talk, madam,' as he put his arm around her shoulder and held the boy's hand and escorted them to the door.

Down at the end of the shop in the optical department the identical twin, identically dressed, was backing away couturier-Pierre-fashion to bend his head and eye the glasses he had just looped on a lady's ears.

Fred didn't recognise me. I introduced myself and said, 'I was wondering, Mr Fennessy, if you and your brother would honour me by coming to lunch, courtesy of Dessie Dennison.'

'Dessie? That's bountiful of him. Please thank him but we stagger lunch here. Though we're both just off for coffee now to Hanratty's. Do you think Dessie's philanthropic lust would be sated by a pair of coffees?'

We had to wait until the lady selected from the range of tortoiseshell. Fred said, 'And to what do we owe such an honour?'

'It's about the Cove.'

'Pardon?'

He hadn't heard. I said, 'Can I tell you both together then?'

While we walked up the road to Hanratty's Hotel, Fred told Frank as much as I had told Fred and I was sharp on the look-out to detect a crack in the twinspeak. Frank said, 'About the Cove, you say? The one where we used to swim as kids at the Seaside, Fred?'

'Where we used to freeeeezzze, Frank.'

'And Dessie wanted to treat us to lunch. This should be interesting. I can't wait to hear it, Junior? You did say Junior?'

I got the coffees and a few scones, and Fred and Frank thanked me and said, 'And thank Dessie.' I said, 'Fred? I couldn't but admire the way you treated that child.'

'Ah, I have children myself. You married, Junior?'

They both had five children each. I said, 'Any twins?'

'No.' They both shook their heads and I could see they hadn't yet retired defeated. But they ushered me on with my story.

'That's interesting,' Fred said, 'it's still there, people still go there. And it's Men Only? But mightn't be and we have a part to play?'

'Wait,' Frank said, 'does it mean that to vote, we would actually have to go into that water again on a Good Friday?'

Hmmmm. 'What do you think, Fred?'

'Dessie is an old school pal. It doesn't affect us one way or the other. Except for that freezing water. Still, I'm game if you are, Frank.'

'We must note it in our diaries. So that we'll remember. There, it's done. Tell Dessie thanks for remembering us. And not to worry. We won't forget him. He can count on that.'

I saw the Fennessys Tuesday and called to Maxie McManus Wednesday. The receptionist said Maxie was tied up all day at meetings but she put me through to him. Maxie's upstairs offices overlook the factory floor like a prison tier. I told Maxie, 'Dessie says to say we're in business.' Maxie and I could see each other through the aluminium windows of our respective cells. He had the phone cradled between his ear and shoulder. He put up two thumbs.

I called in to DT Offset. Budge was there collating and numbering a quadruplicate NCR set. He told me, 'Junior, I made my first plate today. Did the whole lot. Photographed the artwork, dish-developed it and got it dead straight on the masking sheet and the plate came out perfect. It did a fifteen thousand run without breaking up. And Tom's promised to teach me the machine. Tom can't make a plate yet you know.'

In London on Thursday, Bill had a message for me. The message was taken by George, who hadn't a biro but thought he'd remembered it. Bill said, 'Bet George got it arseways. I wrote down what he told me but does it make sense?'

MOTHER SAYS COME TO DINNER SUNDAY ONE-THIRTY. BLACK PUDDINGS DELICIOUS. LOVELY NEW ADDITION TO STABLE. HARRY.

We had none of that prawn cocktail or baked Alaska nonsense. Our starter was roast beef, creamed potato, roast potato, gravy. After that we had mugs of offal and onion soup and then jelly and custard. I was only half-way down my fag, listening to 'Don't Fence Me In', when Harry insisted I bring my cup of tea upstairs.

What could Harry do with Four from Finsbury? By one of those flukes in a business notorious for its serendipity, Harry had gone from the theatre to a Fulham Broadway pub to clear the head with a beer. He was served his drink by an ex-Christian Brother. And it wasn't even a Dessie Dennison pub. Harry thought of sending them as they were, Four from Finsbury, to tour Ireland singing Negro spirituals. He toyed with calling them Lancashire Pud and keeping them in London doing Gracie Fields. The barman cut into Harry's crinkled brow with the amiable, 'You seem deep in thought, sir.'

Harry told everybody his business, because telling people his business was his business. The pub might need an act, who knew?

'I see,' said Brother Chuckey, 'why don't you dress them up as nuns and get them to sing hymns?'

I had the Baptista and the Blessed Virgins' photograph on my lap as Harry was telling me of his discovery. While Harry was going on, ' . . . the world première in the Dennison Arms . . .' my hand lost control of itself, lifting the cup of tea. I had to mop poor Baptista with the cuff of my shirt.

'Don't worry, Junior, we have lots of photographs and that's not the one we're using on the posters.' When I told him that Brother Chuckey was one of my old teachers, Harry said, 'Wonderful. Dessie will be all the more delighted.'

My business isn't fiction for nothing. 'It so happens, Harry, that Tony, that's my boss in the bookstall, Tony has a lorry load of stuff that he has to check out in Manchester. He wants me to go with him to vet the books, so I'll be away for a few days. You should go directly to Dessie yourself with this one.'

'You think so? I'll do it tomorrow night, when he's mellow after the Daltons.'

I asked Harry the name of the Fulham Broadway pub. I went to an afternoon picture and had a coffee and read the paper, waiting for opening time. Brother Chuckey did not seem to be on duty. I said to the barman, 'Excuse me, is Jim Chuckey on tonight?' The barman said, 'You know 'im?' I said, 'Friend of mine.'

''Ang on. I'll check.'

He went upstairs and came back down, followed by the guvnor, who spread his palms on the counter and eyed me. 'You the law?'

I laughed. 'No,' I said, 'but thanks. I'm flattered.'

'What are you then?'

I told the landlord my story. He said, 'You sure? He didn't look old enough to be your teacher.'

I explained that we had Brother Chuckey straight from the seminary. But the guvnor was still suspicious of me. I told him, honest, you want to check me out, a friend of mine has – I mentioned some of Dessie's pubs, I told him he could ring Ingy in the Dennison Arms or next day ring the publishers, I said as a matter of fact it was ironic that Brother Chuckey should be working here, as my friend Dessie was more likely than anyone to hire a Christian

Brother, although I believed Brother Chuckey wasn't a Christian Brother any more.

'He's an ex-Christian Brother and no mistake. Mrs Bowyer is the best cleaning lady I ever had and her husband said if I hadn't hired an ex-Christian Brother in the first place it wouldn't have happened. Mrs Bowyer fucked off with your friend Brother Chuckey. They lasted a full five days together. Mrs Bowyer would have run off with a barrow boy. I took Mrs Bowyer back and I had to settle Tom Bowyer for a hundred quid – he's probably been trying to get someone else to run off with her ever since. Your Brother Chuckey beat her up, called her names. How can a man hit a woman?'

How can a man beat the shit out of children? Where was Brother Chuckey now?

'Dunno, mate. Hasn't called for his cards. Can't blame him for what happened – except beatin' her. For that he gets no reference.'

I would not go near Dessie with the Baptista proposal and also my supposed Manchester lorry load would save being sent home again for at least a week. The waitress on the plane was already treating me like a commuter, coming around with an extra helping of black pudding. Late Monday night Dessie rang. I had stayed in the pub downstairs with Bill, and George took the call while I was around the corner getting chips. George is a sweet spoken man not given to language but he forced the message out:

FUCK YOU AND YOUR MANCHESTER LORRY. COME ROUND TOMORROW NIGHT.

'I had the feet up,' Dessie said, 'the Daltons were working up a lather on the fiddles and my bunch of yuppies holding back orgasms when Harry comes in and sees the great business I'm doing. Harry says: Dessie, I have a great new live act that I think you might like. I say: As much as I like the Daltons? You're some cunt with your Manchester lorry. You should have warned me. Harry says that he has a group that sings hymns. What kind of hymns? Like "Happy We Who Thus United", Harry explains. I say: Harry, how in the name of Jesus, Harry, did you hear of "Happy We Who Thus United", that's an Irish confraternity hymn, and also, this is the Dennison Arms, the Brompton Oratory is up the road. Harry told me about four birds he discovered at a barbershop singers' contest, a group called Four from Finsbury. I muse out loud: Where do they get the names for these pop groups? But Harry tells me that was their old name, that they're now called Baptista and the Blessed Virgins, but that in fact there is only one girl in the group and she dresses up as a nun. The parents of the other three girls wouldn't let their daughters do it. So naturally I nod with understanding. I say: Victorians, are they? Then I sum up. I say: Harry, have I got it right, you're offering me a group of one member called Baptista and the Blessed Virgins and she dresses up as a nun and sings hymns like "Happy We Who Thus United"? Harry says there are lots of collective names for individual singers and that he got the idea for the nun and the hymns from an old teacher of yours, a Brother Chuckey who works in a bar that's not one of my bars, Brother Chuckey provided the hymns, he gave Harry an old hymn book with the words and music. And now Harry has only just got the act together and he wanted me to be the first. I said: Fuck off, Harry, you're trying to ride me. But he has a bundle under his arm and he produces the poster. I have to believe him. Harry wouldn't spend money on a poster just to back up a joke. So there's Baptista all right, dressed as a nun, her head is dressed as a nun, the rest is a G-string, sequins and spangled high heels. Down at the bottom there's APPEARING with room to write where and when. I'm tired after a long day and flying over and back for the weekend – you know the old guy with the white beard who sits with the dog begging outside Hanratty's, I chucked a quid into his cap and he shouted the usual Jasus, God bless you, but he called me back and gave me one of Dunstan's own business cards – anyway, I'm on my fifth pint and just then the Daltons finish a number and the cheering and clapping are more grating than the fucking fiddling, so I look at my bunch and I reckon: They deserve it. I say: Harry, you're on. Because I still don't believe we have his vote till Ab says those for Dessie Dennison this side and Harry does his stuff. We talk figures. I know this is one where you go for shit or bust, so I tell Harry: We charge. We do it on a Tuesday night, we charge three quid a head. Call it a private function, member-ship wheeze, booking at the bar. Tell me, I didn't go to your school, what kind of perverts are they?'

'I tried to meet him.' I told Dessie about the bar on Fulham Broadway and Mrs Bowyer.

'He give up the Brothers to get his hole?'

'I don't know anything about him. He was transferred when we were doing our inter. I hadn't heard a thing about him since.'

'OK. I want you around. We're going to stick with this Harry until we're comfortable he's happy. We work on one at a time. What's the score on the Fennessys?'

' . . . actually,' I finished, 'they're nice people . . .'

'They're pricks! Can't waste any more time on them. You gave Maxie the word?'

The posters went up in the bar. Total cynicism. Buyer resis-tance. Blokes leaning on the counter riding Ingy: How are the sales? But the legs did it. A few nights staring at the legs and after a few pints, here, give me a ticket for the laugh, better be good, Ingy. The word reached Sunbury and a gang came down. I helped Harry go round Fulham and the King's

Road and Knightsbridge and Belgravia to any pub or shop that might take a poster. Harry announced Baptista at all his other gigs, even the Fulham Arts Club. Harry said we were aiming at the stars to hit the mountain. Dessie had a hundred and fifty-nine paid up on the night and maybe twenty more regulars who wouldn't pay but Dessie let in anyway, everyone swamping booze. Ingy had to conscript a half-dozen of the London Irish to help behind the bar. Harry had a backing guy for Baptista who was happy on a score and a few pints. He had one of those keyboard-cum-drums that a monkey could press the buttons and play. Baptista was getting sixty. After that Harry and Dessie were on fifty-fifty. Dessie was real cocky, his chest stuck out. He said to me and Harry, 'For somebody who doesn't go in for music in my bars, when you do it, Dessie, you do it right. A couple of ton each, Harry, plus the bar take thanks to a lunatic Christian Brother.'

Baptista kicked off with 'Happy we who thus united/Join in cheerful melody/Jesus, Mary, Joseph, help us/In the holy family'. Dessie said, 'Either Brother Chuckey didn't give you the right air, Harry, or it's the way Baptista is jazzing it up, that's not the same wail we had to learn in our day. That would go down in Old Trafford.' And it went a bomb in the Dennison Arms. There was wild cheering and whistling. Somebody came over and said, 'You never lost it, Dessie.' Baptista did 'Soul of My Saviour' and then 'Confraternity Men to the Fight'. The crowd were mad for it and I thought I could see why. Baptista stuck out the legs and gave the fanny a push and wobbled the diddies. A guy who was ribbing Ingy earlier in the week came up to him and said, 'I never thought a hymn could give me a horn.' And one ancient regular had tears in his eyes, slobbering to Dessie, 'It's just like the old songs are best, it's the same with the hymns.' Baptista started 'Immaculate, O Mother I/Could weep for Mirth'. And then . . .

He must have seen Harry's posters.

He was wearing his soutane. First he just stood inside the door where Dessie had a volunteer at the box office. He stood there like someone too polite to come up and order a drink while the entertainment was going on. No one took much notice of him because – as Dessie growled afterwards – you can't be seen to think anything unusual about a man wearing a soutane in a pub in case you might be suspected of being a closet Christian or have something like a set of values. Then again, with a nun on stage maybe he blended in.

Even when he moved up through the crowd, when I noticed him first, and stood in front of Baptista and said, 'What are you?' everyone thought it was part of the act. Except me. Dessie said, 'Harry, you never told me about this?' Suddenly Brother Chuckey shouts, 'You're a scut. What are you?' Baptista stops singing. 'You're a scut, what are you?' Brother Chuckey shouts again. The crowd start cheering him on, sure it's part of the act. One of Ingy's mates encouraged Brother Chuckey: Good on you, chief. 'You're a scut,' Brother Chuckey is roaring at her, but with the same icy cool of the schooldays. Baptista starts giggling and looks down at Harry, but Harry just shrugs at us, as he told us afterwards, when Harry sees a happy audience he's happy himself and also he's wondering if it isn't some sort of refinement that Brother Chuckey forgot to tell him about.

Then the backing guy and his one-man band gadget stops playing and the bar goes quiet. 'Impertinent scut,' Brother Chuckey hisses at Baptista, 'what are you?' Just then even Harry and Dessie cop on that this can't be part of any act, because they can see the poor girl doesn't know what's going on and is obviously frightened. But it's too late. Next thing Baptista is gone back on her arse and her legs shooting up in the air through the spangled beads and the veil fallen off her head after Brother Chuckey's given her the most unmerciful thump in the eyes.

And then he was gone.

How did Brother Chuckey get out, a man who hit a woman, I heard Dessie asking himself later. Dessie and Harry both rushed over to Baptista, while, as Dessie said, the same dickheads who are so with it mixing with soutanes suddenly discovered some old-fashioned respect for the cloth and parted to let Brother Chuckey pass. Then again I thought myself that a lot of them were London Irish after all and slow, accustomed out on the pitch to staring at a handful of their own teeth and asking, 'Who hit me?' When Dessie realised that Ingy too was bending over Baptista and that there was no sign of Brother Chuckey, Dessie gave the order, 'Ingy! Get after him.'

Dessie could not accept Ingy's excuse but I could. Ingy ran out of the door and turned into Eaton Place and after a couple of hundred yards doubled back and went left, headed for Knightsbridge. When Ingy caught up to maybe fifty yards of Brother Chuckey, Ingy stopped. He stopped, Ingy said, because Brother Chuckey wasn't running. Brother Chuckey was walking, with his hands behind his back, like Field Marshal Montgomery, Ingy said, as though he was architecturally window-shopping, inspecting the buildings. Ingy stopped, Ingy said, because the idea came to Ingy out of nowhere that Brother Chuckey was the Devil. Ingy claimed his legs would not move. It was only when Brother Chuckey put his finger up for a taxi that Ingy shook off the mesmerism and then it was too late.

Dessie, Harry, Ingy and myself were having a wind-down pint over two hours later. Dessie and Harry had taken Baptista home, collecting Doggie Byrnes, Dessie's London Irish solicitor on the way. There wasn't any damage done to Baptista, no broken nose or black eye or cut, no wound other than the indignity. While I was in the bar helping Ingy tidy up, Dessie and Harry and Doggie were letting Baptista herself tell the story to her mam and dad. They could not apologise enough, Dessie told me he told the parents, indicating himself and Harry, and went on that not being well up on legal matters, for all he knew there might be a case there to be taken against him as proprietor of the Dennison Arms but that in all honesty it was difficult to be responsible for a mad person coming in off the street, but if there was a case there it would involve the knock-on of Dessie having to pursue Brother Chuckey and that was not his style. It was obvious from what Dessie had since learned (supposedly from me) that the trauma of no longer being in orders had unhinged Brother Chuckey and it was not for Dessie to judge the poor man's actions. Dessie would of course abide by any course of action the parents were willing to pursue, but for what it was worth Dessie would be grateful if the parents would accept a token of two thousand pounds and sign this bit of a *nolle prosequi* so that they could all put the distasteful business behind them and also Harry would see to it that Baptista would have plenty of gigs but under her own name, Hazel, and definitely not dressed up as a nun or singing hymns, which in retrospect – though they had all thought it a good idea, Harry, Dessie and the parents themselves – was possibly pushing out the frontiers of pop too much too soon.

'Dessie,' Harry was saying, 'I must insist, at least let me pay half.'

'No. Not a chance, Harry. As long as you're sure you can fix up Hazel.'

'Done in my head already. I have a trio called the Conkers . . .'

We couldn't have but warmed to Harry even if we had never needed his vote. Dessie was in rare mood, having got another lock on Harry and maybe thinking himself lucky Hazel's parents weren't litigious. Even Ingy was tickled.

'What are you laughing at?' Dessie put on the anger. 'The Devil. You think, Ingy, I should spread the word at Sunbury that you saw the Devil?'

'Please, Dessie . . .'

We were having such a great crack that after Harry and Ingy left to share a taxi, Dessie held me back for another last pint. Dessie said, 'We'll lie low on Charlie Anka for a while. I don't want you to go near him until I figure out a strategy. I'd prefer not to go near him at all. I don't want to get into bed with a Charlie Anka or Maxie McManus if I can help it. But I've been thinking for the past couple of weeks: Do you know what I think we should do?'

I was able to respond to his proposal, 'I like it. I *love* it, Dessie.'

CHAPTER 11

I HAD NO excuse for a while but to go back to my book, dammit. Himself was abroad at a fair. The secretary assured me there should be no problem. After she hadn't shouted, 'Great!' So I mucked in, keeping my eye on the sign, and by December had completed Part 1. Dessie said of my other work, 'What is this business of Part 1, Part 2 and Part 3? The whole fucking thing is set in one room. I can smell the guy's dirty socks.'

While I played the anchorite, Dessie was over and back bringing news of Dunstan's thriving empire. He and Peggy had doubled the repayments to the credit union. Johnny O'Donnell told Dessie, 'I wish all our customers were like that.' Also, Dunstan and Peggy were lodging all their cheques – and cash – to the savings account in the credit union and drawing to pay bills.

While I was still early into *The Second-hand Wardrobe* and, after a productive day, supping the earned pint with Bill downstairs in the pub, George brought a message from Dessie:

BECAUSE OF THE CROWD MAD ABOUT THE BLESSED

I went to dinner to Harry and mother every second or
third Sunday, that is, whenever I was invited. According to
Harry, Hazel and the Conkers were doing very nicely thank
you, Junior. Dessie was in suspense waiting for the other
shoe to drop. I even suggested it myself to Harry. I said,
'Harry, how come you're not trying to push Hazel and the
Conkers into Dessie's chain?'

'Has he asked, Junior?'

'No.'

'Best not to then. No painful reminders. That's not to say
I'm not thinking of Dessie.'

And, I suppose inevitably, Brother Chuckey applied for a
job in the Corner Flag.

For three weeks after he clocked Baptista, Brother
Chuckey worked his way in from Fulham to Earls Court,
carrying his ball and chain of a reference. Brother Chuckey
had got the Fulham job through an agency which, having
had the balls chawed off them by the guvnor, wouldn't touch
Brother Chuckey now. Turned away again with a 'Sorry,
mate' from Little Australia, Brother Chuckey was inspired
to haul himself up to Little Ireland in Camden Town. In
some of his applications Brother Chuckey had tried a 'just
over, no experience' approach, but pubs were suspicious of a
man of his age without qualifications. But the truth hurt too.
The Stag's Head had a STAFF WANTED notice in the window
and the short-staffed proprietor, Joe Malone, gave him such
a welcome that suggested he might be shanghaied in over
the counter and started on the spot. Emboldened, Brother
Chuckey told his true story. 'The cleaning lady?' Malone
said. 'Do you know how hard they are to come by? But I
know a place where they'd be a sucker for you.'

Brother Chuckey had not seen Dessie Dennison on the

night of Baptista or heard of Dessie's chain. Dessie traded limited companywise under the banner Crescent Group. Malone said, 'Try the Crescent Group. They have one down the road, the Dew Drop Inn, but your best bet is the Corner Flag, off Old Street. A mate of mine who worked there's just left to go home.'

Jack Fagan (Non-Invested Investment Funds) ran the Corner Flag. Normally he would have had the discretion to hire Brother Chuckey on the strength of Brother Chuckey being an ex-Christian Brother or of having run off with Mrs Bowyer. But of course Fagan had heard of the Baptista fiasco and gave Brother Chuckey a cup of coffee while he rang Dessie. 'Hire him now,' Dessie said, 'tell him the boss will be along in an hour but that's a formality and don't mention my name.'

Dessie collected me. 'Why do I need you? I don't need you. But I thought you'd want to meet your old teacher.'

'I don't.'

'So just shake hands with the Devil, all right?'

The Corner Flag is one of Dessie's smaller pubs. It has a three-sided counter that can keep an eye on all the custom, which at seven o'clock midweek amounted to about ten or eleven. Brother Chuckey sat immediately inside the door with his back to the street, so unassumingly patient over his cold coffee that we passed him and were alerted by Jack Fagan nodding over our heads. When we turned, Brother Chuckey had the same confident cold stare that I could never forget. Dessie nudged me to open the bidding.

'How are you, Brother?'

He was unchanged but I was unrecognisable to him, not having been bald or worn a beard in class.

'Who have I?'

'Junior Nash.'

'Nash? Junior Nash? The rivers of Spain, Nash?'

'The Douro, the Tagus, the Ebro, the Guadiana, the Gua-dalquivir.'

'Russia.'

'The Don, the Dnieper, the Volga, Ural, Kama, Oka, Bug . . .'

'Sheffield . . .'

' . . . steel . . .'

'Cheltenham . . .'

Dessie jumped in: 'The Gold Cup.'

' . . . cheese . . .'

'Seventeen thirteen . . .'

'Utrecht . . .'

'Eighteen twenty-nine . . .'

'Catholic Emancipation . . .'

'The Act of . . .'

'Eighteen hundred and one . . .'

' . . . union.' Brother Chuckey stood up. 'How are you, Nash? I had to sit on you. Shake you up. You were inclined to backslide. Do you own pubs?'

'Not so lucky, Brother. My friend does. Dessie Dennison. He owns the Dennison Arms.'

After shaking my hand Brother Chuckey, about to shake Dessie's, stopped. 'Oh. Then I may as well move on. Nash, I hope you are doing well? Somebody told me years ago that you were getting on fine in England and that worried me, because that's a euphemism for down and out.' He was backing towards the door as he spoke.

'Here, don't you want the job?'

'You'd hire me after that incident?'

'You probably had a reason. How does he know Utrecht and all those rivers, and cheese – I never heard of it?'

'Nash wasn't educated. That's something children pick up after leaving school. I beat *learning* into Nash. So that he would remember it. Nash, how is Tucker?'

Dessie said, 'Have a drink?'

'Yes, thank you.'

We set in to catch up. I told him about myself. 'Good, Nash. Good. I must read them. You got on. I should never have doubted you. Doubted myself. Every one of you got on. And I know why. And you know why, Nash. And Tucker?'

Dessie subdued his body language while I put on the dog on Dunstan's behalf. Dunstan had his own printing business, a tidy operation that he had deliberately kept small so that he would always be in control. He could afford to send his wife and son and his father to the Seaside for two months every year, joining them for his own holidays and for long weekends.

'Good. Good. Good. Another success. Tell me, Nash, why did he cry? You remember?'

'I remember.'

'Can you tell me after all these years?'

'I suppose I don't see why not.'

'Tell me, Nash.'

But Dessie was too busy to listen to that. 'I'll leave you, Brother, or do I call you a name?'

'James.'

'James. My manager will show you your room and you'll be happy with our wages. We pay top. For good men. We don't have cleaning ladies. You're the cleaning lady. I'll make a deal with you. If you don't let me down, I won't let you down.'

They shook on it. 'Thank you,' Brother Chuckey said, 'Mr Dennison?'

'Dessie.'

Telling Brother Chuckey about Tom Tucker's visit to the bank, I poured it on from Dunstan's side.

'Why didn't he tell me?'

'In front of the class?'

'Why didn't you tell me privately, Nash? I beat you for your own good. But that problem, I could have dealt with that, Nash. No one had problems like that that I knew of. What was I there for? To prepare you for the world. At your age all that entailed was beating you. It worked. All of you that I've heard of are successful. Unlike – unlike a lot of the scuts that were allowed to slip through me in later years. When I couldn't beat them . . . but Tucker survived it anyway?'

With Dessie gone, I gave it to Brother Chuckey as though Dunstan was pulling the strings. 'He didn't survive it.' I brought Brother Chuckey through Dunstan's full banking history, how JFK's visit and assassination affected Dunstan only with reminders of his childhood trauma, brought Brother Chuckey up to date with my own recent business expansion appeal.

'But, Nash, he's had, you say, over twenty-five thousand pounds from them over the years. Shouldn't he be proud of that?'

'The pain's still there. He wants more even though it looks like he's finished. He knows twenty-five thousand doesn't matter to them. And he still hurts because he was only ten years old. It wasn't money. It was a child's holiday. I'm worried about him all my life. He's my best pal.'

I had to leave it at that for a few minutes because I could see Brother Chuckey was thinking, in the way he didn't like to be interrupted when he was looking out of the window at school. And I was thinking myself how he had shown me off in front of Dessie. How in God's name did I remember those rivers in Spain? Then all those quizzes on TV, even *University Challenge*, it came back to me, Bill saying one night: How did you know that?

'You're to tell Tucker, Nash. You're to say I'm asking for him. All my boys are a success and I won't let him be any different.'

Brother Chuckey let me get him another drink.

'So,' I said, 'can I ask you about yourself? How are you? How've you been?'

'In the end they decided I was mad.' Brother Chuckey smiled, shook his head. 'They didn't call it that. They suggested a rest. They diagnosed working too hard. That's a new illness. Working too hard. Cotton, Nash?'

'Blackburn, Bolton, Bury, Rochdale . . .'

'Font . . .'

'Seventeen forty-five . . .'

'There were fifty-two in your class. When I collected the essays on Monday, can you remember when I had them corrected?'

'Tuesday morning.'

'Isn't it curious, Nash, it wasn't noticed that I was working too hard then? That I was mad? Your parents wanted you to get exams. To get exams you needed facts. I beat them into you. Your exams got you jobs. My first failure came long after I was transferred up the country. He was fifteen, a Willie Walsh. I had him out at the line. And it was a line that he didn't know that had him out at the line, Nash. "Here where men sit and hear each other groan." Then he was stuck, began to chew his nails . . .'

' "And palsy shakes a few sad last grey hairs . . ." '

'All right, Nash. By the way, "Breathes . . ." '

' "There the man, with soul so dead, who never to himself hath said, this is my own, my native land . . ." '

' "I did learn it," Willie Walsh was whingeing. I clouted him. "I did learn it, Brother." I clouted him. "If you'd learned it you'd know it." And then the little scut said, "You can't do that. You're not allowed to hit us any more." The scut. I hit him. I said, "But I am hitting you, Walsh, you little scut." And the scut said, "I'll bring up my father." I didn't hit Walsh again. His father came up to see our superior, Brother Downing. Mr Walsh, Brother Downing suggested to me, was concerned that I might be using excessive zeal. A thick building contractor who could not spell excessive not to mind having heard of zeal. But you see, Nash, Brother Downing was cracking before I did, only Brother Downing didn't know it. The whole country was cracking, going soft. I let Walsh alone. It was near the inter anyway. Oh, he got his inter, like they all did. Do you know where he is now, Nash? Do you know where that boy is that I could have helped like I helped every one of my boys? He is in 5B – the mental wing of a hospital. They said in the end I was mad, but it's that poor boy is in 5B. A succession of jobs that his father got him and that he was no good at. The father had to take him into the business. Drink, nerves and 5B. Irremedial.'

Was he crying for Willie Walsh or himself? There was an old tear creeping down the face.

' . . . you're a writer, Nash. Observant, I take it? So you've seen it or read about it. Your lucky escape. Yours and all my boys. Your successors brought in notes from their parents that they were too sick to do their exercises. They had colds. Were you ever too sick to do your exercise, Nash?'

'No, Brother.'

'Most of them that I've heard of, their marriages are broken up. Or their sons take drugs. Some of them ended up working in factories, Nash.'

'I worked in a factory, Brother. So did Dunstan.'

'You were on the staff. In an office. I'm talking about operatives. And some of them, some of them were seen on television, telling the country about the brutality. Throwing in the sop that they were grateful to the Brothers and that of course there was the odd good one. The odd good one, Nash. They weren't thinking of me there. I lasted as long as I could, Nash. I fought. And I lost. My last battle was Killala.'

'Humbert. Seventeen ninety-eight.'

'At ease, Nash. My last school was fifteen miles from

Killala. And by then the educational tour had arrived. I wouldn't let them go, my class. Where would that end? It was all there in the history books. Nash, in the two-year inter cycle, did I cover the curriculum?'

'You had it covered in the first year.'

'And again and again and again in the second year. You couldn't wait to take the field on exam day. Now parents complain that the curriculum isn't properly covered, having sent their boys in with the money to go on tours. I could have beaten Killala into them free gratis and for nothing. No. Their parents came up. And I had an empty classroom . . . What was the name of our magazine, Nash?'

'*Our Boys.*'

'*Our* boys. They're not ours any more, Nash. God help them. What we gave them for nothing they thought they could buy and they can't. The Easter Teachers' Conference. Proposal: That teachers be allowed to opt out of teaching religion . . . The Church of Christ Scientist, Nash?'

'Mrs Mary Baker Eddy.'

'So. Here I am, Nash,' Brother Chuckey tried the perky, 'mad.' He was mad, but only like my pal Dunstan was mad. I wanted to know about Mrs Bowyer but didn't know how to ask. I said, 'Did . . .' and stopped.

'Yes, Nash.'

'No. I shouldn't ask.'

'Please do, Nash.'

I rambled on about how I was an unmarried man myself but that I must confess I'm not a virgin, that kind of approach, that it was none of my business, but presumably Mrs Bowyer was a new experience for him, and that I was just curious . . .

'I will tell you something, Nash, that I have never been in a position before and felt obliged to tell anybody. I'm human, Nash. Only human. Mrs Bowyer did her cleaning sometimes late at night after the bar closed and I was having my couple of pints. Drink is comparatively new to me too. I was working in the pub eight months. I had seen all the sights that I wanted to see on my days off and I began to get lonely. I should have seen it coming. Mrs Bowyer was inclined lately to do her cleaning more at night rather than the morning. Around the time your friend Harry Lamb came in, it was my father's anniversary. He was just two years dead and he had left me the house and the land he had leased out when he got too old to work it, I'm an only son, so I'm not short of money. I sold the house and land. But I was lonely, everything was gone, my vocation, my father. Your Harry Lamb, when he told me his problem, I was thinking of myself, my life taken away from me by fools, my mission, and here was a man with the problem of what to do with pop people. I said it to him as a bitter joke, like that's what the world was coming to anyway. He jumped at it, especially when I could give him the hymns. Ask him for my hymn book back, will you? But Mrs Bowyer. I have bad thoughts the same as everybody, Nash. And am used to controlling them. She's a coarse woman. I heard her talk to people in the bar. While she was cleaning this night she took a break and sat beside me. Knackered, I am, she said, and took a gin from the optics. Offered me one of her cigarettes. Fag, Jim, she said. I told her I didn't smoke. She said: Don't do much, does yer? Or whatever way those people talk here. Then she said: Fancy a fuck, Jim. I was embarrassed. I know I blushed. And I admit it, Nash. I experienced an erection. She said: 'Ere, want to see me tits? Do you understand my position, Nash?'

I had a horn myself listening to him. 'I understand, Brother.'

'She knew I was a Brother. As I say, I have money. We did it three times that first week and I was exhausted from her so much it was all I could think of, I wanted more. It was I suggested it – we go to a hotel. She said: Dirty weekend, Jim, eh? I always blushed when she said those things. We went to a hotel that we thought was far enough away in the Gloucester Road, booked in as Mr and Mrs. I hadn't much in my case but she saw my soutane. I was sick of what I was doing but I couldn't stop. One day she said: Jim, let's do it with this yoke on yer. I had to wear the soutane over my naked body. She had me in the bed putting her hand up underneath it . . .'

I think both of us had a horn.

'And yet, Nash, that's what saved me. My soutane. I sat on a chair near the window of the bedroom and I could see myself in the dresser mirror. My naked legs under my soutane. Mrs Bowyer was still lying on the bed smoking her cigarette. She said: 'Ere, Jim, take that bleedin' yoke off, give me the shivers, that do. Or I'm not sure what she said because I wasn't listening. I was looking at my soutane and all the other soutanes who beat the fight into me. Who trained me. Trained me to fight. To fight back, Nash. Like Dunstan Tucker did and will continue to do, I'll see to that. The robe of office, even with the *lèse-majesté* of my bare leg, it gave me back my strength. I went over to Mrs Bowyer and I said: You are a slut, what are you? Idiot woman giggled. 'Ere, listen to 'im. I clouted her. I said: You slut, what are you? And when the manager and his lackeys broke in the door to investigate her screams I was well back to myself. I hadn't given a good beating in such a long time. Mrs Bowyer was thrown out first, allowed to get dressed while their eyes were averted. Then I made them wait outside while I packed. In my soutane I ordered them out into the corridor. When I saw those Baptista posters, that was just another mission on the road back. I'm going to begin here, Nash, thanks to your friend. No more beatings, only bouncers can do that now. I'm on two years' sabbatical and I will go back and go through the motions. I'll educate, ask the pupils what it is they would like to learn, if anything. But while there's one out there who had the benefit of me when I was a full man, I'll be there for that boy. I'm there for Dunstan Tucker. You tell him, Nash. Will you do that, Nash?'

'I will.'

'You will what, Nash?'

'I will, Brother.'

Chapter 12

I'VE KNOWN DESSIE since that first Good Friday at the Seaside, through all the schoolboy summers and our adult life in London. The mordant streak could never cover how comfortable he was with his life. But now he broke out and wore his happiness openly. It was as if Dessie was a lepidopterist and Brother Chuckey a rare butterfly that Dessie had finally caught in his net. Dessie used to say, 'It's simply business. Give a man a second chance and he'll work better than any guy who hasn't been through it.' But I could always see through him to his good works and he knew it and he had to have been chuffed giving Brother Chuckey, my old teacher, the leg up. Dessie probably thought it was the same in my eyes as if he had given me the second chance. And he was right. For a while Dessie and I were warmer together than his hitherto crusty carapace would admit. It brimmed into his asking seriously about the book. Although I never wanted to talk about a work in progress, I felt obliged to return his serve with a little flesh on the gist. He wanted to understand, the way Tom Tucker did effortlessly, and he showed that he did have the key inside him, if possibly he only had the time, when he said, 'I flick through all those best-sellers on the racks at Heathrow. You should write a book that starts with, "It's three seventeen in Tokyo and a different time in New York." Or the flight number of a plane leaving Singapore.'

He wanted to embrace me into the contentment that he saw all round him. Brother Chuckey had submitted to the wing of Jack Fagan and Jack reported full marks to Dessie. Within a couple of months, Brother Chuckey could do the bank and order, and he was also the best cleaning lady Jack had known.

Dessie was also happy that Harry Lamb was sparing him Hazel and the Conkers, that Harry was keeping the head down, feeling indebted to Dessie.

After every weekend at home Dessie came back with better and better news from DT Offset. I wouldn't know the place, Dessie insisted. All the ink tins with the lids off that had you wondering what was stuck to the arse of your best trousers, they were now stacked on the INK shelf that Budge and Tom had put up. The outsides of the tins had been cleaned of overspill, you didn't have to wash your hands after a two-minute visit. The main paper merchants weren't yet dealing with Dunstan, but the Kodak man had put him on to a supplier who gave Dunstan credit after the first advance payment and the new supplier had access to most of the standard brands. Again, Dunstan's stock wasn't scattered around the floor. Budge and Tom had built PAPER shelves. They had even, Dessie claimed, bought a new can of three-in-one oil and the machine no longer sounded noisier than Dunstan's car, which he was hoping soon to replace with a six-year-old Fiesta that would be impressive when he was making his calls to the industrial estates. And it was a race in the credit union between his indebtedness coming down and his deposit account going up. Tom had switched to the darkroom and Budge to the machine and the all-round multi-purpose talent could not be fed enough orders, so adept was the dispatch. But, I couldn't help but worrying, was he still on the dry? Listen, Dessie said, touch wood, I don't think he has time to drink. As long as those banks aren't on his mind.

And then Dessie said to me, after hours in the Dennison Arms, 'I was thinking, Junior, again touch wood, but when I become president, and Ab's checked out Dollars, I let Ab know that I'd pay for Dollars to come over, just let my travel agent know, but Dollars has a parish in Oregon as fat as himself. They send him home every year, pelt him with presents Thanksgiving and Christmas, invite him into their homes for any excuse . . . but what do you think, I'm not thinking of myself here, but if we were to get a chain – of office – for the sake of, say, having a dinner sometime during the winter. Most of the people don't see each other from one summer to the next, it would keep the continuity going – the type of thing that would shorten the winter. What would you think?'

I said, 'Sounds a good idea to me,' my business being fiction.

At last Harry Lamb got a call from Francis Coleman. Would Harry by any chance be the Harry Lamb who had swum at the Seaside on Good Friday, '55 Yes. Francis had business in London every other week, could he call on Harry to have a chat? Harry said no, that he would be delighted to meet Francis next Good Friday, when he would be at the Seaside to vote for his good friend Dessie Dennison. And no, there was nothing Francis could do to change his mind.

Dessie said, 'You were right about Harry. Must be one of the few people who is what he seems. When it's all over and we do, if you think it might be a good idea what I suggested, and we do have our first reunion dinner, make damn sure that I don't forget to bring Harry over at my expense and treat him right. As a matter of fact, I should have Harry over on his holidays, stay in one of my houses. You can tell him that yourself. You still cadging the dinner off his mother?'

About Charlie Anka Dessie could not decide. He said, 'I think leave him until after Christmas. But maybe you should have a shot at hyphen's brother-in-law, Shamey Flynn. I can't see how you'd get him, but you might get a line on how they feel.'

Dessie himself had brought Benny Bobinizer and Staff Cox out for a few drinks. They got plastered together. They were his brokers and also, yearswise, Dessie had been sandwiched between them at school so they had a great night remembering their old Jesuits. Dessie said Benny smoked forty of his eighty-a-day Gold Flake while they were drinking and Staff had earlier played a murderous game of squash with Froggy Mack and had actually beaten Froggy, who from what Dessie said only lost a game when he failed to bite you in the neck. Next day Dessie went to see Dr Justin Devane, who was Dessie's, Benny's and Staff's doctor, Justin being another Jays' old boy. Devane said, 'Dessie, I can't give you a medical report on two of my patients. I could be disbarred.' But Dessie persisted, 'Just tell me will the two of them live till Good Friday?' Dr Devane could only offer, 'The people who sit with Benny in the pub are likely to go first. And if Staff beat Froggy then he could probably get a life policy from himself.'

I went over from Heathrow midday, Flight Number EI 347B, whatever time it was in Tokyo. I called into Dunstan straight away to use his phone and make an appointment with Shamey Flynn. They were on a quarter of a million run for the Halpin's Tea Company. It was a price overprint job with Halpin's supplying the labels. Peggy got the job through a pal of hers whose husband was the print buyer for the tea company. It was the only order the buyer could give Peggy as Halpin's had a nineteenth-hole contractual arrangement with another print shop that went back over thirty years. But the overprint run was a headache job at a cut price that tied up an otherwise lucrative machine and that Halpin's printers looked on as almost a Christmas gift to the tea company. But for Dunstan, no raw materials bar ink and plates and slave labour, the price of one pound ninety pence per thousand was a bonus. They were bringing in the run averaging almost six thousand an hour with eight-hour shifts shared by Tom, Budge and Dunstan himself, now in his jeans again and Peggy doing the wrapping.

'Four hundred and seventy-five quid for two days' work, Junior.'

And no, neither Budge nor Tom would take a penny.

'There's the order book,' Peggy said. I'd never seen her so happy. From my knowledge of the game there was the best part of a month's work in the book. I said, 'Dunstan, Dessie told me he got one of your business cards from the fella with the dog who rattles the can outside Hanratty's.'

'You can laugh. We got three jobs out of him, didn't we, Peggy? One was a painter, a hundred wet paint signs, the guy with the garage at the back of here, he got two hundred business cards and Hanratty's itself gave me a shot at their menu.'

'Dunstan,' I said, having planned it that way, to see if I'd catch him out, 'the Seven Deadly Sins?'

'Pride, covetousness, lust, anger . . .' He stopped only for a second but it would have been enough to get a puck from Brother Chuckey in the old days. ' . . . gluttony, envy, sloth. Why?'

'Brother Chuckey's asking for you.'

'Yeh, Dessie had some story about him in the Dennison Arms. You meet him?'

I didn't want to talk about Brother Chuckey and Mrs Bowyer while Peggy was there, so I said, 'Why don't I tell you about him over a pint tonight?'

'I told you. I don't drink now.'

That sounded much worse than on the dry. Peggy was concentrating so much on the wrapping with an 'I'm here but I'm not here' detachment – staying out of it – that I held back. I said, 'We have a coffee someplace?'

'I'll be finished the run in an hour, hour and a half. I'll have a coffee with you then.' But he had no enthusiasm for hearing about Brother Chuckey. He was indifferent, as he was more and more to everything now except the business, as he had been one-track when the banks consumed him. So I rang Shamey Flynn.

'Flynn Consultancy?' Shamey Flynn himself answered. Of course, he would be delighted to see me. Come round straight away.

He was a financial consultant, Dessie had marked the card, because that is what they call themselves who are too proud to drive a taxi or work in a Dessie Dennison bar when those are the only realistic options. Shamey had been a clerk in Ranks flour mill since he was fifteen, until the mill closed and he came out at forty with a no-pension fifteen-grand lump-sum redundancy. His principal expertise now was finding mortgages for those with not too much of a stain on their records. But, Dessie also warned me, Shamey's a nice guy.

He had a tiny office in a low-rent street and had an answering machine instead of a secretary. He did have a second chair, and no sooner was I seated than he said, 'I bet I can guess why you're here,' and then he guessed correctly. 'I've actually been thinking about it. If there was some way I could vote for Dessie I would. But I can't. I just can't. I like Dessie. I'd love to vote for him.'

'Don't you like your brother-in-law?'

'Like him? I hate the slimy bastard. I *hate* him. I'm cheering for your side. But I can't vote for you. I really wish I could. I really do.'

I said, 'Is there anything we can do? You're honest with me, I'll be honest with you. Can you be bought?'

'I'm telling you, I'd sell myself for nothing. I'd pay to vote for Dessie. The problem is my wife. She just wouldn't wear it. I tried her. She told me not to even dream of it.'

'What would she do if you voted against Tommy Ryan-O'Brien?'

'Tommy O'Brien. Fuck him and his fucking hyphen. Jennie, my wife, Jennie, whenever she had to fill in a form with her maiden name, it's Jennie O'Brien. She knows the hyphen is a heap of shit too and she cried harder when her mother died than bollix. He was looking at a coffin and all he saw was a hyphen. What she'd do is she'd probably go out of the house for a few days in a huff.'

'Just a few days and come back?'

'I know what you're thinking. It sounds fast, a few days. Look, Jennie's a most unbelievable beautiful person. We're mad about each other. But the madder people are about each other, the madder the rows, you know? When we do have a row she goes off and stays with hyphen. And I get dizzy. I could be sitting on a bar stool and I feel I'm going to fall off. At mass in a cathedral I feel I'm in a telephone box. I've often had to cling to a bus stop afraid I'd fall down on the street. That's why I hate that bollix, he takes her in. Instead of shutting the door on her face and saying go home to your husband.'

I said, 'I take it then you were never unfaithful? We can't get you another woman?' Of course I laughed and said it as a joke. But I meant it.

'Thanks anyway. I must tell Dessie you tried. No, Jennie doesn't like the hyphen part of him but he's, you know, her brother. That's it. Her brother. But listen. Dessie mightn't need me anyway. I hear what's going on. I talk to Francis Coleman. Francis doesn't like the prick either. But this is a game to Francis. He's tickled by it. And Tommy hyphen is shit hot with compo briefs. But they're only sure of me and the Fennessys – the Fennessys would leap into that water on Christmas morning and piss down Dessie's throat. Maxie McManus is holding tough but they're reasonably sure of Charlie Anka – but then you haven't yet tried Charlie – they feel they're sure of Charlie because Charlie's intellectual bent is, you know, glass of wine at receptions, liberal functions, he goes to all the Protestant things, the ecumenical stuff, himself and his phoney of a wife, you know, leading from the front, you could hardly even get him to talk rugby any more. Francis feeds him bait like an opportunity not to be the laughing stock of Europe. Francis even dangles posterity: In years to come, Charlie . . . but that doesn't mean Dessie can't try him. Your best bet though is to buy Maxie. Then you don't need me, and please invite me to the celebrations after ye win, as long as Jennie doesn't find out.'

We went to Hanratty's for the coffee. The old man with the dog was not on duty outside, but a few of Dunstan's business cards were tucked in amid the hotel's brochures and the stuff advertising all the castles and lakes for the tourists. Dunstan said, 'You should have a business card. You need only put down on it Junior Nash, Writer and your address and telephone number.'

'Let me tell you about Brother Chuckey.'

I began again with Baptista because I thought he could not have listened properly to Dessie telling it. Every so often Dunstan looked around the hotel lounge, while I was talking. I didn't even engage him when I came to Mrs Bowyer. I've a dirty mind, like anyone who has to live without a regular woman. I said, 'Just imagine Mrs Bowyer putting the hand up under the soutane and pulling his langer.'

'Sounds gas all right,' Dunstan said, looking at his watch.

'He's very interested in you. He asked me why you cried that day. I told him the whole story. He was very sympathetic. He gave out to me for not telling him at the time. He sends you his best regards and says if you ever need him he'll be there for you. His exact words.'

'He was straight. He never bothered me, Junior, like he bothered the rest of you. If he had been a banker and Dad went in looking for the money, Brother Chuckey would have said you're a navvy, Tucker, what are you? He'd hit you and then it would be over and you could get on with your life . . . not like that cunt Butler, half-one Dad was in there, half-one to half-six, five hours I was in heaven, then I get kicked in the teeth, two weeks of my life plucked out of me, when I'm ten and two weeks is a hundred years. The cunt. If there's still a fucking hell I hope he's in it. The whole lot of them, Junior, you hear me, everyone of those *cunts* should be in a special hell. Bastards . . .'

It was great to have the old Dunstan back.

'OK, Dunstan, fuck them is right. But you're coining it now. You don't need them. I know, I know, don't hit me now, I know it's not the money, I said it to Brother Chuckey. I mean, you're flying it, why should you give them the power to get you down? Why should you even let them into your mind? Fuck 'em! Those people are beneath you. You're a giant and they're pygmies and you're letting them bother you? When you're proving you can do without them?'

'I've something coming up. I'm not sure when yet. But I'll want you to come over. What did you say that Harry fellow cost Dessie over Brother Chuckey, two grand? See if Dessie would pay the flight. If he doesn't you pay it – have you it? And I'll give it back to you.'

'What are you talking about?'

'I can't tell you yet. Anyway even if I could, I wouldn't, I want it to be a surprise. I'm hoping it could be good news, Junior.'

'Is it another go at a bank?'

'Don't ask me any more. I better be getting back.'

Chapter 13

It was actually the night I finished Part 1. I went to the bar downstairs to celebrate. I was in early, before Bill's time, and was waiting to treat him and George too, though George at the moment was on some sort of duty, collecting glasses. George collected glasses in the old-fashioned way. He went to a table where there was an empty glass and carried it up to the counter. Sometimes he stretched himself, the lazy man's load, and brought up two glasses together, one in each hand. Every time he brought up a glass he stood by the glass until the guvnor was free to accept it, acknowledge that George had brought up the glass. Tonight was a comparatively quiet night. On busy nights the young barman interrupted the service for all of a full minute to dash out and collect two palmfuls of Leaning Towers of Pisa.

Bill took the call but came down to tell me Dunstan wanted to give me the message directly.

'Junior,' Dunstan said and his excitement came through the wire, 'can you get here for Wednesday night?'

'Day after tomorrow, I'll see, I'll ask Dessie. He hasn't come up with anything for Charlie Anka yet.'

'Who? Oh, that. Ring him and ring me back.'

'You're at work?'

'Where the fuck do you think I am?'

We were travelling executive class. 'Pretend,' Dessie said, 'that it's part of the celebrations for your having finished Part 1. What third of the room is it set in?'

He'd decided to come with me, suspicious that Dunstan or anybody else might be up to something that Dessie didn't know about.

I said, 'If you had to get fucking executive class, why didn't you get a smoking seat for me?'

'You may as well get used to it. They've done a survey. They've found that even among smokers themselves sixty-two and a half per cent favour a ban on smoking on the domestic flights.'

'That's not true.'

'Oh. Isn't it? Here, read it.' It was there in the in-flight magazine.

'That is fucking horseshit. No smoker wants a ban on smoking anyplace, let alone up in a plane.'

'It helps people who can't give them up.'

'People who want to give them up aren't smokers.'

'I don't believe it either. But it's coming. They have to fall into line with Europe. We can't just take all the agri-money and not have to give them something.'

'You mean it's some cunt in Brussels with rimless glasses and a slide-rule mentality . . .'

We were having a stew in the executive but now I understood why on my last afternoon flight from Heathrow, sitting in the back with the pariahs, the hostess brought down packets of peanuts. We were being set up.

'It shows Ab was right,' Dessie said, 'he was dead on. What would you think, when I'm president, we should get a plaque, we could put it up inside the shelter with some sort of weather-resistant protection for it, something that would say By the Freely Arrived at Democratic Decision of the Majority, the Presidency of, Myself, Ordained, Men Only, you could make up the words for it, what you think?'

'Dessie, I'm gasping for a fucking cigarette.'

'Toots Toomey is back there in a smoker, he doesn't smoke, I'll get him to swap with you for a while.'

Good old Toots, whoever he was. I smoked three on the trot.

We landed twenty to six, checked out half an hour later and got a taxi to DT Offset.

'I didn't know you were coming,' Dunstan said to Dessie, 'you don't have to come with us.'

'It's no problem.'

'You'll cramp my style. I know it.'

'Where are we going? What's the mystery?'

The town was twenty-four miles away.

Dessie said, 'I haven't my car with me.'

'We'll go in mine. We have to be there by half-seven.'

'I'm wearing a good suit.'

I sat in the back and let them talk business, now that Dunstan was a businessman. Again, Dessie offered to put his own printing business through Dunstan but Dunstan again wouldn't have it.

The town's name and the words SOCIAL SERVICES CENTRE were Letrasigned on the glass of the front door. Dunstan said to us in the hall, 'Hang on here for a few minutes. I have permission from the main guy but he said to observe the form I should explain it to the rest first. Just in case they might be uncomfortable with the two of you.'

'What the fuck is he up to?' Dessie said, indicating the posters. 'What are we doing in a place like this?'

CONQUER CANCER, I was reading myself, and IF YOU SMOKE I SMOKE.

'What to do about headlice.' Dessie shook his own head.

FOSTERING – KNOW YOUR RIGHTS.

'Thinking of suicide? Ring day or night. What do they do, give a guy a rope?'

EATING DISORDERS/ANOREXICS.

'Do you suffer from shyness, depression, anxiety, phobias, antisocial habits. That's one for you with your fags. Anti-social. Join GROW.'

SCHIZOPHRENIA. AWARE: Defeat Depression.

'Cot Death Victims Monthly Meeting. Do they hold it in Limbo?'

IF YOU WANT TO DRINK THAT'S YOUR BUSINESS. IF YOU WANT TO STOP THAT'S OUR BUSINESS.

'Battered wives. Ring ADAPT HOUSE . . . Junior, this is your country, I don't belong here. I don't belong in this, this underbelly, RUBELLA, fuck . . . here he is . . .'

'It's OK, you can come up.'

'What . . .'

'Shut up, just come up and sit at the back and listen. And don't put me off.'

I can give the speech verbatim because I have a copy of it still, the copy prepared by the committee of the Kodak man, the Kodak man's brother in Dublin and Dunstan himself. There were about twenty of them there, sitting on the tubular seats and as the head man said, 'Welcome, Junior. Welcome, Desmond,' they all turned to give us the friendly nods and Dunstan showed us where we were to slide into the back row. Then the head man said, 'And *welcome, Dunstan*!'

That brought applause as Dunstan went to the top of the room, turned, held up his hands for order and began.

'My name is Dunstan . . .'

'Jesus . . .'

'Let me begin with a frank admission that I wouldn't have the courage to make if I hadn't had the benefit in the past few months of listening to, say, Eugene there, or Martin over there and all the rest of you. Appearances, they say, are deceptive. I stopped drinking three months before I ever came here. My goal then was vanity. In my innocence I thought that would be enough. You see, I was one of the people who always laughed long and loud at the very idea of AA. It was for people who didn't have will-power. During the three months before I came here, while the weight was coming off me, I was sixteen stone when I looked at myself in the bathroom, and shame, vanity, nothing more, said to me . . .'

I didn't notice any NO SMOKING signs so I lit up. I never needed a fag more. Dessie was already folding and unfolding his arms and crossing and recrossing his legs.

' . . . even when I got down to, I mean especially when I got down to the slim, svelte male model you see before you (*pause for laughs*) I despised AA all the more, and to prove it I went back on the drink. I drank seven nights a week but I always could prove that I hadn't a drink problem by saying I only drank eight or nine pints a night, never shorts, and that I never even thought of drink during the day . . .'

Dunstan's speech was eleven pages long. The first two paragraphs contained the planned incoherence of sincerity crafted by the Kodak man's brother. The speeches given at rugby or boat club dinners or debating societies by those with a casual thumb sticking out of the blazer pocket were not necessarily guaranteed to pacify a roomful of aspirant alcoholics, the Kodak man's brother had divined. A speech in a social services centre painted hospital green could in fact not be too long as no one in the audience would look at his watch as closing time sped through the tunnel. No. The key-note demanded was an admission of guilt, as long as it took, and it did not matter whether it came from the tongue-tied or Demosthenes as the audience to a man would have previously taken to the rostrum to tell long tales of twenty years of wife-beating.

I know I had a pain in my head as Dunstan stuttered through his opening. Dunstan at sixteen stone I just could not visualise but the collection of Christian names all sat leaning forward with the chin erect. When Dunstan lapsed into the fluency of his school debating days it emerged that his smugness had been punctured by a fellow jogger who was in AA and who had said: But, Dunstan, how much weight did your wife lose? And Dunstan was puzzled. And Dunstan said to his fellow jogger: What do you mean? And Dunstan learned that he had given up drink to benefit himself and had had no thought for his wife, as he had had no thought for his wife in all his drinking. But the audience knew all that since they had written the script. They leaned forward all the more because they knew the big picture was about to start. The admissions department. Blood. Emotion. Dunstan recovered the faltering style to present dollops of Dunstan's past held up by finger and thumb and polished by the cuff of his committee.

The Kodak man's brother's preface to the speech admonished Dunstan: *Nothing wrong with going all over the place until you get to the target in the end – then slip it in almost by accident with your eye on the guy you're going to hit.*

Dunstan created a sixteen-stone fat father who never once gave his boy a piggyback up to bed or sat with Warren while the boy moved his finger across the page in the steps of Noddy and Big Ears. The mob could recognise that one even though the truth was that Dunstan demanded the prerogative of putting Warren to bed Monday to Friday, though insisting: Fuck Noddy and Big Ears, I'll read him *Oliver Twist*. But the Dunstan regurgitating the propaganda said he was never in the house at the child's bedtime because he always had a reason to go back to work after tea for all of fifteen minutes and then to the pub to 'unwind'. When Warren had his birthday parties Dunstan discovered that he 'would be in the way' and self-sacrificially absented himself to the pub. School parent briefings, the pictures, the carnival, snap apple, anything that took place at night conducive to Warren's growth inspired Dunstan to just remember another appointment. I could, Dunstan claimed, holding up a hand to stem his own torrent, go on all night about the damage I did to my son. Need I say, said Dunstan, who was the last boy in his class to bring in the money for the books? And so Dunstan went on all night, slipping in: I'll put it mildly, my business was in trouble and I had to resort to borrowings . . . *Dunstan, important not to give money own section. Slip bits of the money in under different headings like little bombs to go off as one big bomb when you're going for it in the end.*

I couldn't help but remember calling for Dunstan to go drinking when I was home. 'Not tonight, Junior, Warren's taking me to *Jungle Book*.'

While he pissed his money down the drain, Dunstan had Peggy performing domestic miracles, running all over the town to bazaars and second-hand shops to tog herself out. It was seven years since they'd had a holiday. Warren couldn't even swim. And the rows! Even within the context of the gyp he was trying to pull, Dunstan stopped short of battering Peggy. *Dunstan: OK if you can't bring yourself to say you used to clobber her, remember there's mental anguish.* So poor Peggy sitting at home eating cigarettes until Dunstan comes in from pub and watches last ten minutes of programme with her and observes: Some heap of rubbish.

I copped on quickly and so didn't have to listen to most of the tripe. I knew for instance that Dunstan loved to surprise Peggy with a hundred-pound voucher for Helene Modes. The tax, the VAT man, the paper suppliers, the banks, they could all go fuck – the publicans could stay home from the Bahamas – the preferred creditors for Dunstan's bobs were Peggy and Warren. He would have divorced Peggy if she walked on the same side of the street as a second-hand shop. But to the Sanhedrin, Dunstan presented a man who was the opposite of Dunstan. He turned his virtues upside-down. Where he was loving, considerate, tactile, he admitted to being morose, testy, without the time to fondle his son's hair, preoccupied with the dash to the pub. He trotted out a litany of his boorishness. I stopped listening because it hurt me to imagine Peggy being so treated – even in fiction.

' . . . that was your old Dunstan,' Dunstan turned into the straight, 'before – thank God – he learned humility. And now funnily enough I ask you all to let me boast. We hope to go on holiday next summer to the Seaside. Thanks to AA, thanks to God and above all thanks to my wife.' Dunstan didn't mention the slave labour camp of Budge and Tom but he did more or less tell the truth about Peggy and Warren pitching in, how they were as united as the Holy Family, Peggy giving him the courage to become the best foot-in-the-door man who never drove from a tee. 'I won't bore you with the technicalities of the printing business except to say that in any business you must grow or shrink. You can't stay still. My printing machine is the same machine I had since the day I started. I could never keep up with the latest developments. I'll give you an idea. Typesetting: I must be the only printer in the country still using Letraset, and type I have to farm out. And now I'm nearly enough on my feet not alone to plan a holiday, but seriously hoping to buy an almost new Mac for typesetting. None of you might know what that is, but compare it to having a bike and rising to a car. It mightn't be much to other people but to me it means we're going up, we've reversed the direction. I've been turned round and for that I thank my wife, as I said, AA, God and his Blessed Mother.'

Pause with head bent.

One or two, unfamiliar with the play, tried to start up a round of applause, but Dunstan stayed the mob with a Mark

Antony outstretched palm. 'One last boast. Why am I here in AA rather than in AA back at home? Shame. I couldn't join at home in case people saw me going in and out of the AA meetings. I said: I'll try it, to the man who saved me as it turned out. Was I sceptical! I said: I'll try it but not where people can see me. He said: Whatever you like. Because of course he knew. He knew I would see it. Thanks to you. Thanks to all of you. Ashamed. Of gathering my family around me again? Of seeing clearly? Of being able to hold my head up? Of not having to duck around corners to avoid people I owe? Why am I here? Rather why am I still here? I'm not. Not from a couple of weeks on. Then, I'm going to stand up again, as I have tonight, in front of those who know me, friends, neighbours, whatever, perhaps even somebody who may have a grudge against me, perhaps a creditor. I hope so. And let me tell you why. I live ten miles out the road from where I work. It's just a little village.' *Dunstan, use the dew story if the weather has been appropriate – nobody will know where you live or care less.* 'What I'm going to tell you now is possibly what some people might laugh at, might think me mad. But I hope you will understand. In helping to lose weight I've taken to the bike again. That few days of frost we had a week ago, I was cycling in to work in the morning and I noticed something. I cross a little hump-backed bridge above a stream that splits the fields and I stopped to lean on it because I saw something that I must have seen a million times without noticing it. I saw the field wearing a light frost that the early sun was just about to act on. Hoar or dew whatever is the right word, I got off my bike and vaulted in over the ditch, went into the middle of that field and knelt down. There's usually a traffic build-up near the bridge and some of the cars were high enough to see me. See me kneeling down and scooping the dew and rubbing it into my face. I rubbed it in my face, I kissed it, I drank it. Where has that moment been all my life?' *Dunstan: it's not as hard as you might think. Actors do it all the time. Swallow. Practise swallowing. If it doesn't come, fake it. Swallow, put your thumb and finger to the bridge of your nose.* 'I . . . I'm sorry . . . *Dunstan: sniff* . . . I can't . . . I didn't intend . . . forgive me . . . thank you, thank you and thank you again . . .'

Dunstan was given a fair hand, myself and Dessie excessively, for camouflage. *Dunstan: best reception is usually given to those who don't top tales told previously so don't make yourself out to have been too much of a bollix.* Dunstan came straight down the hall to us. 'You'll have to leave now,' Dunstan said, 'I'll have to hang on to listen to the next guy. There's a pub second next door on the left as you go out, I'll meet ye there when I can get away.' We stood up and to the heads turned round and smiling at us I assembled a thank-you wave. Dessie was already clattering down the stairs.

It is unusual for Dessie to take a short but he threw back a whiskey at the counter, watching the pints settle. I like to take a sup out of the pint myself before I light up but I had already been puffing before I left the social services building. 'Well?' Dessie said.

'I thought he was good.'

'One of those guys back there is a banker.'

'You think so?'

'I'll bet on it. Usually they're made treasurer. I'd say it was the guy top of the right, the balding guy with the few strands going across . . .'

'With the button-down grey shirt and wine tie,' I said. 'If it is Dunstan might be in luck. That guy was beaming all the time.'

We picked out bits of Dunstan's speech to amuse ourselves while we were waiting. We'd just got the second pint when Dunstan came in.

'Sorry about that. The decorum. I couldn't just leave

without listening to somebody but then I explained ye were waiting. Christ, last guy in there's done everything bar bugger his grandfather. Whose round is it? Someone get me a coffee.'

'Get your own fucking coffee,' Dessie said, 'you mad fucking lunatic, dragging us over here. What were we supposed to be doing there anyway?'

'Ye're trying to pluck up the courage to take the step. Normally you'd have to go to an open meeting but I told them if you saw me in action . . .'

'OK,' Dessie said, 'who's the banker? Where did you get the idea? What's going on?'

'Day I left the Seaside. Went straight out with Peggy Saturday morning to get business. Kodak man was passing through town coming back from his holiday. Saw us. I told him how Junior got the knock from the bank the day before. He said he thought there was only one thing left. Told me about the AA. Said there was no need to even go on the dry. Could go to one out of town. He said there was a banker at every one of those meetings, the odds were on it. But to make sure he'd get on to his brother, scout around, they came up with here . . .'

' . . . baldy guy with the grey shirt, wine tie . . .'

'On the ball, Junior. He's retired . . .'

'Hang on,' Dessie said, 'you didn't have to go on the dry. Why did you go on the dry?'

'If it's down to this I said I'd give it everything. You know, get the feel of the part? They say he's a gentleman. Sandy's his name. Sandy Symington. He's settled here. You know the way all those bankers fuck off back to where they came from? Sandy's made his home here and's staying here. He was manager of the Southern. We've had a lot of coffees in here, which reminds me we'll fuck off before the mad cunts come in, but I've let little things slip out, softening him up, things like as a bank manager you'll understand business. So do devil's advocate on me, how'd I do in there?'

' . . . you did fine,' I said. 'What way do you intend . . .'

'For fuck's sake, not you, Junior. Dessie, you try and trip me up.'

'How much are you trying to hit him for?'

'Five.'

'For what?'

'Buy a Mac.'

'He'll recommend you lease it.'

'No. It's second-hand.'

'Where are you buying it?'

'The Kodak man's brother.'

'But it doesn't exist?'

'It doesn't exist. That's not a problem. He'll make up an invoice if that's necessary, I could even have the cheque paid to him.'

'You're managing fine without a Mac.'

'No. Every week I pay out on average fifty quid for typesetting.'

'That's not true. There's a setter in the Quay Printing Works who gets forty a week on top of his dole and he can tom at night using the firm's equipment and he does your stuff for peanuts.'

'Sandy Symington doesn't know that.'

'Sandy Symington's retired.'

'He's here. He lives in the town. He's respected. He'd represent me. They'd have to listen to him. This is money to help a man pull himself up by his bootstraps. They're giving it for fucking foreign holidays. He knows priests and people. It's like I'm a member of a flock, a prodigal son. It can be done, they can say you must help this man, this family man, his record was bad in the past but look at him now, fighting to regain his self-respect . . .'

'What if the bank wants to see the Mac?'

'The Kodak man can get a loan of one from someplace and we can have it in DT Offset until the cheque is cashed and then give it back. If anyone ever called to have another look at it after that it's gone back for maintenance.'

'I can't see them interested in a tuppenny ha'penny bit of equipment worth five grand – they'd just give it to you as a personal loan – it might as well be the attic, but just suppose, because you walk yourself into it and they did make a cheque out to the Kodak man's brother, how do you know he won't hang on to the money?'

'He won't. I've never met him but he hates the banks as much as I do. Even if he did, so what? The thing is the bank loses its five grand, it doesn't matter where it goes. I don't need it. I can make money now.'

'You won't be paying the money back? The new Dunstan isn't that new?'

'Say I get the money before Christmas. I'll make two months' repayments. Then I hit the bottle. When I find out Peggy's screwing somebody, say Junior, I crack up. And I'll do all that part because I like Sandy Symington – if he can swing it for me, I like him, I mean. So that when whoever it is says: Sandy, you cunt, you walked us into it with that Dunstan Tucker, Sandy can show the extenuating circumstances. Although two seconds after I cash that cheque I'm going to get maggoty and fuck those crazy wife-beaters back there.'

'What will you do if you get the money? And I think you might get it.'

'Do you? D'you think I was good tonight?'

'You might get it because for once in your life you don't need it. And that's when they're always likely to part. But what will you do when you get it?'

'I just told you. Get pissed and fuck them.'

'I mean what will you do with the money?'

'It'll pay for the Seaside for the next two years.'

'Then what?'

'That'll be it. It's what I said to you, Junior, when you got the knock, one last shot and I retire. I mean, Jesus, what's left after the AA route? I talked it over with Peggy. I promised her. This is it. Then I retire.'

Chapter 14

On the next Sunday, the second last before Christmas, Harry Lamb rang. I answered the phone, barefoot, wearing the porter-polluted pair of frayed corduroys and the ash-, egg- and sweat-stained button-abandoned shirt that is my uniform when I sleep. We're not dressing-gown people. Whenever I meet Bill on the landing, both of us up for the six in the morning drinker's leak, he has nothing on but the long johns. 'Junior, mother says can you come to dinner on Sunday?'

'Today, Harry?'

'No, no. Mother gives better notice than that. Next week. Mother wants it to be our Christmas dinner. We'll pull crackers, Junior. And I have a surprise. I know you'll love it, Junior.'

I went to the Dennison Arms on Monday night to get the Dunstan news from home. I was in time for the last half-hour of the Daltons. Dessie said, 'Wait till that racket is over.'

Dunstan had telephoned Sandy Symington the day after the AA meeting. A 'your advice on a business matter' call. Sandy would be only too delighted. Come this afternoon, the town hotel for coffee. When Dunstan arrived Sandy was already in a discreet corner of the lounge, notepad and a goodbye Parker on the table. Sandy stood up and gave Dunstan the big shake hands and ordered another pot. Do you miss it? Sandy asked Dunstan by way of not being so ungentlemanly as to jump to business without a courtesy. Not any more, Dunstan said, not with the help of the AA. I certainly don't miss the man I used to be. I know, Sandy nodded, but I must admit I miss it myself sometimes, but it was a case of when the liver speaks Symington listens. Had to listen to my doctor. One of us had to go. Sandy Symington or the drink. But how can I help you, Dunstan?

If I didn't put you to sleep last night, I don't know do you remember I mentioned this problem I have with typesetting? Yes, yes. And Dunstan, according to Dunstan telling Dessie, even pushed his luck: I could do it by maybe scraping up everything I've saved since thank God I got sense at last.

No, no, Sandy Symington said, not the way. PAYGA-BAA. That's what a bank is for. First we'll clear our heads and write down what we have. Dunstan could see on the notepad that Sandy had already written down: PAYGABAA. Now, name and address – Dunstan Tucker, address? Dunstan told Dessie it was the fastest thinking he had ever done in his life. They had all slipped up, Dunstan, the Kodak man, the Kodak man's brother. I told a little white lie last night, Dunstan said to Sandy, and swore to Dessie that he smiled confidently. I don't live ten miles outside the city, Dunstan confessed, but it's where Peggy and me dream of living. It's my wife's dream for years but I didn't want to say it last night because I thought it might seem too . . . sentimental. I do cycle out there before I go to work every morning, that's ten miles out and ten miles back, just to look at the village and in particular there's a cottage with whitewashed little walls in front around a rose garden, OK, by the time I make enough, added to the sale of our own house, that particular cottage mightn't be for sale but something will or we can buy a site and build, but that's what I hold in front of me, that's the ideal, that day I went into the frosty fields, that day I was on fire with the dream. And to himself, Dunstan told Dessie, Dunstan said: Fuck us all, why didn't we realise I'd be asked for my address? Of course. Understand perfectly, Sandy said, but we would have been only too delighted to hear that. Sentimental? Not at all. As Dunstan gave the address of his beloved inner city home built for the poor. And this Quay Printing Works, you're paying them how much a week to buy in your typesetting? Madness. Dead money. PAYGABAA, Dunstan. Dunstan said: Pardon? Ironic, Sandy pointed out, the last two letters, AA. Motto of mine while I was in harness. Pay As You Go And Build An Asset. That's what you must do and that's what a bank is for. Dunstan said to Dessie that he was so over the moon he pushed his luck further: I don't want to go to the credit union, because I'd prefer to clear them first to re-establish myself, to prove I'm not just talk. Quite right, Sandy said. And on with Dunstan: I know it will take a long time but I want to address, I want to face up to my other debts, I want to pay back, every penny eventually, but the banks won't believe me and I can't blame them, I've been a bad boy, a very bad boy, and Mr Symington, (Sandy interrupting to say Sandy, Sandy), Sandy I'll understand, there'll be no hard feelings if you wouldn't be comfortable putting the case for me . . . Sandy: 'Dunstan, another motto of mine: Even the Rock of Cashel can be moved. Leave it with me. You'll have your Mac.'

By Wednesday I'd sped through the short opening chapter of Part 2. I got tanked up with Bill in the bar downstairs. Because we live overhead the guvnor lets us drink on a bit as though we're staff and it was after twelve when we went up to the flat. Bill said, 'Have a cup of tea, Junior?' Happy with the way the work was going, wanting to prolong the night, I said yes, thanks, as the phone rang.

'Junior?' Dunstan said and I could hear the drunkenness.

'Dunstan, how are you?'

'Scuttered, Dunstan's scuttered, Junior.'

'D'you get it?'

'Junior, they're only a shower of cunts. Know what they are, Junior, shower of cunts. What are they, Junior, say it for me, shower of cunts.'

'You sound like Chuckey. What happened?'

'Junior, I want you to do me a favour, we're like brothers, we are brothers, Junior, I love you. Junior, you're the only one who understands, you an' Peggy, my lovely wife, she'll do it for me, I know she'll do it for me, Jesus, Junior, I'm crying. Fuck 'em, I'm cryin' my fuckin' eyes out again. Say to me they're cunts, Junior, please. Say the cunts are cunts, Junior, just say it, just let me hear you say it . . .'

'They're cunts, Dunstan. What happened?'

'What happened? What happened is my father, my lovely father . . .' He was bawling and sobbing. I wanted to hop the phone off the wall because it was only a phone, that I couldn't use to go through and put my arms around him. I said, 'Dunstan, look, whatever happened, you'll be OK, I'll be over Christmas, I'll be with you, OK?'

' . . . my lovely father, that gentle man, that wouldn't hurt a fly, he dressed himself up, that's what happened, he dressed himself up, because his little boy asked him for a holiday . . .'

He was crying so much that the tears came all the way to my side of the phone and ran down my face. 'That lovely man, that laughing man with a pint in his hand, that was all he ever wanted, that lovely man dressed himself up and he asked cunts for a holiday for his little boy, the bravest thing he could have ever done . . . for me . . . oh, Jesus Christ, Junior, I was only a little boy, oh, Jesus Christ did they need to keep the thirty pound so badly, was there not enough of it in all the vaults without them locking away my fucking holiday . . . oh, Jesus, Jesus, Jesus, fuck 'em, oh, fuck the cunts, Junior, say it, what are they, say it for me . . .'

'They're cunts, Dunstan.'

'Junior, shout it out. Roar it out at the top of your voice for me. My pal. Do it for your pal. Shout it out, Junior, at the top of your voice . . .'

'They're cunts!'

'No Junior, please. Shout it. Shout it for me, please.'

'They're *cunts*!'

'You all right, mate?' Bill said, looking out, with the teapot in his hand.

I said, 'Dunstan, what happened? Why didn't you get it? I thought Sandy . . .'

'Sandy's the loveliest man. The loveliest man. When I tell you what that lovely man wanted to do for me . . . Junior, do you ever pray? Do you ever pray now? Will you do something for me? Will you say one prayer for me? I've been three months in a room full of perverts. They drove me to that. People who beat their wives. I was only, you were with me, I was only lying on the bank of the river, I wasn't near anyone, I wasn't doing anything, those cunts, those *cunts*, I end up in a room with perverts, Junior, say one prayer for me, any one you like, say it that I'll be all right, will you do that, Junior?'

'I'm saying it now, Dunstan. Of course I will. But I want you to do something for me. Where are you? In the job? Peggy at home? Who has a phone, that'd be up? Crick O'Neill. Ring Crick O'Neill. Tell him you're delayed back at the job, could he give Peggy a message, you need her there for something. Dunstan? Dunstan, you hear me? I'm not there, I can't be, but Peggy is. And you need her now. You get Peggy and you put your arms around her. OK? OK, Dunstan?'

I could hear him blow his nose.

'Junior?'

'Yes, Dunstan.'

'You're right. My old pal, you're always right. I love you, Junior. You're right. I don't need to ring Crick. I'll leave the car. I'll walk, I can walk. You're right. I need her to hold me. I knew I was right to ring you. Who else is there? Say it one last time for me and I'll leave you go. What are these people, Junior. Say it one last time and shout it so loud that you nearly lose your voice. Just once more and I'll put down the phone. Please.'

'CUNTS!!!!!!!'

I stayed up for an hour smoking and drinking tea with Bill and telling him about my pal Dunstan. George slept through it, next day asking did we hear anyone shouting or was he dreaming. Bill said, 'You tell your mate from me, he ever rings and you're not here and Bill answers, your mate needs someone to call those cunts cunts, tell him just ask Bill. 'Cos cunts is what those cunts always were and always will be.'

We had the turkey and ham and prunes and custard and Bing sang 'White Christmas'. Now that I was comparatively used to a Sunday dinner I had my old appetite back. I'm only a bit of a picker, but I worked hard to gobble the lot down because mother said, 'Harry always cleans his plate.' Harry is a great eater, but maybe that's because he wants to get the damn thing over with and haul the victim upstairs to the stable. Out of respect for mother, I tried to hold Harry for a while over the tea. I gave him Dessie's invitation for both of them to holiday in one of Dessie's houses. Harry said, 'Do you hear that, mother? I've been telling mother, Junior, what a trouper Dessie is. Wonderful man.'

'Harry,' mother said, 'what about Aunt Sookie and Herne Bay?'

'We can go to Aunt Sook as well.'

I said, 'Why don't you bring your Aunt Sookie with you to the Seaside? I can speak for Dessie. You'll have the house to yourselves. All on Dessie – air tickets, the lot.'

'Oh, not air, Junior. We don't fly.'

I said, 'You mean all those times you've been over and back with your groups, you went by boat?'

'I haven't been over since that time I was ten. There's a chap in Dublin, he handles things at that end and I look after his people here. Now let me show you what I have for Dessie. Excuse us, mother.'

'No,' Dessie said. 'No. No. No. No. No, no, no. Tell Harry to shove his vote up his hole. Fuck Harry. Under no circumstances. No, no, no.'

'Dessie, Butch Frawley owes me five bob.'

'If he could owe you five bob, Fort Knox wouldn't pay his debts. When did you have five bob to lend anyone? How come you didn't get it back?'

'I was to meet him outside the Banba next day but he never showed up.'

'And he's not showing up here. Tell Harry no.'

'It's only for one night. They're just farewell gigs. They're retired, just coming together to celebrate twenty-five years since their foundation.'

'They were planned? They're not the result of a big bang?'

'Dessie, Harry sees this as practically a gift to you. He thinks, because they're from our home town, you know. It would be like throwing a present back in his face.'

'I'm putting up with a terrible time in the club since Baptista. Now the Bedouin. My neighbours here in Belgravia, they're not exactly Jews? You tell Harry they're to show up dressed as humans, they can tog off down at the back. And no publicity. Ingy will get the crowd. But no publicity.'

'You'll do it? Good man, Dessie. D'you meet Dunstan?'

I hadn't told him about Dunstan's phone call. I'm thick with Dessie and I'm thick with Dunstan but they're goalposts and I'm the crossbar.

'I'd a good few scoops with him. He's off the dry. The banks won't be fighting for each other for a while yet to see who gives him the gold watch. He got shot down again.'

'How? I thought Sandy . . .'

'Sandy rang him Wednesday to get him to come an hour before the meeting. Sandy said to hear the good news. Dunstan said he nearly put his foot through the rusty floor of the car he drove so fast. Found Sandy with the big smile and the coffee pot ready in the hotel. Now, Dunstan, Sandy said, what would you like to hear first, the good news or the better news? Dunstan laughed and said: I won't be greedy, I'll settle for the good news. So Sandy said: The bank has turned you down. Dunstan's face fell so far that Sandy spat out the better news that Dunstan only half heard because what would it matter if he was told he won the sweep? Anyway, here's what happened. First, Sandy Symington, I did a bit of checking out myself, Sandy is what Dunstan says he is, though whether Dunstan still believes it now is another matter, Sandy's a gentleman, one of the best that was known in the business, like Roger Egleston and Billy Bowman when Dunstan was starting out. Sandy is possibly the last of the gentlemen. Sandy went to the guy who replaced him. Now in the old days, take the manager that Sandy replaced, if that ex-manager rang Sandy up and said: Sandy, sending a friend of mine into you, needs five, he's sound, Sandy would have said: Of course, does he like fig rolls? Now this was Sandy's first time going to the guy who replaced Sandy and Sandy thought it would be a breeze. But guess who appointed Sandy's replacement? Joe the Boss . . . Now leaving aside that what Dunstan did to Joe the Boss is known to the young Turks in a way that they would not admit to themselves that they know it in case Joe the Boss found out, leaving that aside, what type do you think Joe the Boss appoints anyway? Not gentlemen. And as I said to you before, if it wasn't for Dunstan and that Kodak man's brother, the criminal, we might still have gentlemen in the manager's seat instead of what we have, including that cunt Timmie Frawley in my thirteenth house. So this guy who isn't yet forty told Sandy: Certainly I'll be happy to process the application. Now Sandy hardly knows the guy, a blow-in from Dublin, and Sandy laughs, knowing the manager has only to reach for his biro and write the cheque for a miserable five. But your man tells Sandy there's been a tightening up and all the other lingo that Sandy knows can't be true. Except if you're a manager that could be pulled by the hair by your Brother Chuckey saying: Robbers? And you're a manager who will come straight out with: James, Briggs, Dick Turpin, Dunstan Tucker, Bonnie and Clyde. Sandy gets indignant. Says to bollix: Come, come, I'm personally recommending Mr Tucker. Sorry, Mr Symington, not without security. Look at the track record. Sandy points out he knows all that but Dunstan now a new man, in AA. Cites precedents of a whole heap of AA converts who got new credit ratings having all but gone in with guns in their heyday. Bollix won't budge and can't tell Sandy that Joe the Boss would fire him if he did because, as I say, bollix knows but isn't supposed to know about Dunstan and Joe the Boss. Says: All I can do is do it with security or guarantor. Dammit, Sandy says, if that's the way then I'll go guarantor myself. But Mr Tucker is not to know that. Sorry, Mr Symington, but you know that can't be done, Mr Tucker must know that he has a guarantor, you'll both sign the same form. Oh, very well then, says Sandy, if you must, you must. Make out the cheque, I'll sign now, let me use your phone and see if Dunstan can get here before you close. According to Sandy, bollix hesitated, almost afraid to say it, afraid Sandy would hit him, which is what Sandy admits he almost did, bollix says it, that Sandy will have to deposit the five and leave it there till Dunstan comes good. Sandy explodes. Are you telling me my name isn't good enough? and so on, dropping a few names that he thought might frighten the shit out of your man. But no go. Sandy forces himself to calm down and says: Good day to you. Goes home and gets on the telephone and rings round a few places where he knows guys he can trust who still have an ear to the ground and finds out about Dunstan and Joe the Boss and has to accept the situation. So over the coffee he tells Dunstan that the better news is that Sandy himself is only too happy to put up the five grand but insists on giving it to Dunstan direct and let Dunstan lob in monthly whatever he can afford until it's paid off. Dunstan, according to himself, did a better job than any Sydney Carton. Mr Symington, I will never forget your decency. Sandy, Sandy, Dunstan, call me Sandy. And Dunstan goes on with a no, incredibly grateful to you but no, I'm sorry but I'm definite, no. I'll get the Mac myself and if it means we have to postpone the holiday then so be it. The reason I had hoped for the bank wasn't so much a matter of the money itself, it was more a vote of confidence I was looking for, just like AA has given me the belief in myself, but I've come this far so I'll just have to go another bit down the road on my own. Dunstan keeping his sea legs as the tumbril trundles along. Poor Sandy stretching out his hand to grab Dunstan's wrist: Promise me, Dunstan, promise me, if you buy your Mac, and next summer you're short, then at least let me lend you whatever it will cost to give your family the holiday they must deserve more than anybody. Dunstan says can't promise that, Sandy, but will bear it in mind and thank you again and would appreciate it if convey to meeting unable to be present tonight as need solitude to absorb disappointment as hopes having been high and as joining AA at home next week best wishes to all. Hope, Sandy says worried, not tempted to . . . Have no fear, Dunstan assures Sandy, and drives home at a hundred miles an hour to make up for lost time and get pissed. He said he rang you.'

'I didn't understand what he was saying. Just that he'd got the knock. I didn't get the details.'

'At least he knows now, I said it to him, he'll never, never get another bob off them. And he's better off. He's shown himself how he doesn't need them. You agree?'

I didn't say anything. Dessie went on, 'Now, Charlie Anka. I've figured out your approach. And you have to do it. If I take the Bedouins, then you have to do this for me.'

'Hold it. If it's a *quid pro quo* for the Bedouins, then the answer is no.'

'It's up your alley. Charlie's now a member of the Sunday Poets' Broadsheet . . .'

'No. Fuck off. Tell Harry to shove his vote up his hole.'

CHAPTER 15

I WENT OVER on Christmas Eve and stayed until the fourth of January, the third being the night of the Sunday Poets' Broadsheet launch. Say you're born within the silence of the Rock of Cashel. You're knock-kneed, asthmatic, myopic and seven stone in your hobnail-booted feet. You win a holiday in Buenos Aires. You're on the high stool in the Hotel Junta when some reprobate of a hidalgo sashays in and within a second of his having discovered you're from Tipperary you become a temporary missing person, having been hauled off to his ranch to play full back for his peons in the All-Argentina Hurling Final.

I have had it all happen to me. When *Hand Me Down* was published and I went home to what turned out not to be bunting across the streets, cheering crowds and a civic reception, I was stopped by a curate hitherto unknown to me. I was the very man, he told me. He was bringing out a history of the parish. I might dash off something for him. He would leave it up to myself. Whatever I thought best. He must read my book. Is it in the library?

A man introduced himself to me in a pub as the compiler of the programme for the Annual Over 40s Soccer Competition, the proceeds from which were in aid of the Friends of the Elderly. I might make a contribution. You know the type of thing. Something on the lines of my own playing days maybe, before gear bags and all, togging off on a dry stone. Or maybe I might prefer to do a crossword, not too difficult, with a soccer theme running through it. Or whatever I thought myself, whatever suited me, leave it up to yourself. For a good cause.

Budge handed me a letter. Both of us puzzled. Who would write to me at my home address, so long gone. It was from the Pinky Downey Art Gallery. I was invited to an exhibition of watercolours and sketches by Mary Anne Walsh.

The Black Teapot Theatre Company sent one ticket for the Monday paper night production of *The House of Bernarda Alba*.

How it is for the big hitters I don't know. Here I was, despite my success in remaining a man alone, bullied by the old school bully himself, Dessie Dennison, into attending the launch of the Sunday Poets' Broadsheet. I couldn't enjoy my Christmas thinking of it. I didn't even get any sympathy from Dunstan when we were drinking after the races on St Stephen's Day.

Charlie Anka had been on the straight road before he got lost in all directions. He was a six foot three No. 8 at a time when that was not considered too small for the position. He did not play for our club, that is Budge's old club, yet I must be fair to Charlie, he was no more dirty on the field than anyone else and could hold his own with our crowd – so he was just another one of the filthiest bastards of all time and respected for it. He made his money out of cars, wangling the dealership for a make whose cheapest model gleams in the showrooms at around thirty grand. Charlie's club are the nobs of our town. They get jobs for each other and circulate the business among themselves, where we might use our influence to lean on someone in the labour exchange to switch a dole signing day if it clashed with the nixer of papering the grandmother's bedroom. Even I can accept Charlie joining the golf club. Business is business for those thick enough to believe it. And as for that business under Charlie's captaincy of his having initiated the wives' attendance at the dinner in his honour, I can think of no greater pox on golfers than to force them to look at each other's wives.

The first cancerous fork on Charlie's road was his abandoning the Seaside in favour of Spain, the type of growth that logically led to his turning up at fashion shows with his wife and her pal Desiree. And Charlie had already made his first million when the hormonal imbalance led him away from the locker room. Once Dessie had made me agree to go to the Sunday Poets' Broadsheet launch, he amused himself by cutting me into the grizzly details of Charlie's non-arrested development. Charlie had grown out of Frankie Cowhey the barber and experimented with the various soccer and pop-star styles, from the shoulder length to the layered, and had now settled, or so it seemed, Dessie said, for the ponytail. At that I said: Fuck you, I won't. But Dessie said: Too late, you promised. Anyway, blame Flood's Family Crests. Charlie's wife belonged to the Crypt Crossword Society and it was at one of their table crosswords that she won a voucher donated by Raoul Joseph Flood, a local but national authority on lineage. For his birthday she gave Charlie a present of his family's crest and history. Charlie was descended from the hunchback Ankas, who were the hereditary ollaves to the O'Briens of Thomond, whose name is never absent from the pages of Irish history, certainly not since the High King Brian Boru himself. Chuffed, Charlie did not put his hand over his shoulder to feel for an incipient lump. He looked up ollaves in the dictionary and overnight became a poet.

I was drinking with Dunstan after the races and giving

him an ear while he bewailed the loss of over three good drinking months undercover in the AA. I said, 'At least, as Dessie said, you know now. It can never be there for you. No more hopping your head off a stone wall.'

'Fuck Dessie.'

'Brother Chuckey will think of you as the one that got away.'

'What? What are you talking about?'

I reminded him.

'If I ever needed him he'd be there for me? Tell him I need him then, will you?'

'For what?'

'What the fuck do you think? Sometimes I think you don't listen to me. Tell him I want to rob a bank. Just one more time.'

'Seriously. Will I tell him that?'

'Are you deaf?'

'Don't jump down my throat. Now you can do me a favour. Small favour.'

'What?'

I told him.

'I will in my bollix.'

'Just come in with me. Hang around for ten minutes. To give me confidence.'

'I can't. I'll be busy on the fourth.'

'How do you know?'

'If I have to do nothing on the third I'll be busy on the fourth. Or I might jump in off the bridge. But I'm not going to that fucking thing.'

'I won't tell you a secret so.'

'What secret?'

When Dessie said to me the night Brother Chuckey clocked Baptista: Do you know what I think we should do? And I said: I like it, I like it, Dessie added that we should keep it just between the two of us since if it got out it would ruin the whole surprise. But I had never kept anything from Dunstan. So I told him now. Dunstan said, 'Jesus, big deal. I thought it was going to be something important. Don't forget. Tell Brother Chuckey.'

'You won't oblige me?'

'Junior, you don't need me. It's right up your alley. Just be yourself.'

I have worked hard in the interest of my craft at nurturing a catholic taste and now in the mellow years shun only golf, basketball, tennis, classical music, painting, fine art, symphony concerts, opera, sculpture and poetry. This launch of the Sunday Poets' Broadsheet was held in the Pinky Downey Art Gallery, where an exhibition of visual art was yet showing. There were a few enamel buckets hanging from ropes. A Coca-Cola bottle was embedded at the base in a mound of sand. On my way in I had to skirt a sculpture of two holes joined together that the uninitiated might identify as a figure of eight but had, I have no doubt, a much more profound significance. There was nothing Sunday about the paintings. A squiggle of spaghetti or maybe intestines was titled *Labyrinth of the Soul*. I was about to study a self-portrait of Cyclopean angst when I spotted the saddle of a bicycle swanning on a ledge and beside it the most exotic exhibit in the whole hall, Maxie McManus. He was almost hidden by the broadsheet that he held open with his right hand on top and his left at the bottom. The Sunday Poets did not skimp. The broadsheet was an imperial twenty-two by thirty inches. I went straight to Maxie for comfort, to establish our mutual philistinic bona fides.

I said, 'Did you get lost?'

'Junior Nash. How are you? How's Dessie?'

'We're all fine.' I pointed to the saddle of the bicycle. 'What are we supposed to make of that?'

'What?'

'That. That there.'

'That's mine. To keep in shape, I've a three hundred quid bike chained to the railings, why make it comfortable for the fucking thieves.'

'What are you doing here anyway?'

'I'm reading.'

'You are? Whose?'

'The young fella there selling the things. Are you buying one? Let me bring you over, make me look good.'

The poet selling the broadsheets – at a fiver a go – wore a fedora hat to shade his beard. Maxie introduced me, just my name. It didn't mean anything to the lad. Maxie said, 'He's unwaged.' So I got the broadsheet for three quid. Maxie asked him, 'How do you pronounce your man's name again?' I opened my broadsheet to read where Maxie had put his finger. 'O Euripides, lib of long ago . . .'

I chose the white wine because that's the colour Maxie was drinking. The Sunday Poets suffer from an attack of collective modesty. They do not read their own work. The tradition is that each poet has his or her offering read by a celebrity. Like Maxie McManus is a celebrity. Our town is not London. Or New York. Or Japan. I said to Maxie, 'Come over here while I'm getting my bearings. How did you get hauled in?' He explained, with only the saddle of a bicycle eavesdropping, 'I have his mother interested in a conservatory. That's her over there with Charlie Anka's wife and Desiree. I volunteered. How's Dessie?'

'What way is Charlie voting?'

'Who knows? That's years off. Do you know him?'

'No. I saw him playing.'

'Come on. I'll introduce you to him.'

There was a tape going someplace in the background, something I'd heard before, sure of it. On our way over to Charlie, we were stopped by Desiree, who gave me such a welcome that made me feel the entire congregation was infected. 'Ah, Junior. It's nice to see you being sociable at last. Miriam, my friend, Junior Nash, the writer.'

Miriam was Charlie's wife so I gave my best, kept my dinner down. Did I have any particular time when I wrote or did I wait for inspiration? I couldn't help overhearing Maxie rubbing his knee up between the poet's mother's legs: ' . . . conservatory . . . bet . . . young Thomas, . . . conducive to writing his poetry . . .'

Miriam knew, she told me, that I must be driven mad by people coming up to me and asking, and then asked me herself. She didn't say how much money do you make from your books. She asked how much of a print run was the norm and how many copies did my last book sell and what percentage of the price did a writer usually receive. Even as I slide the frayed cuffs of the shirt up the jacket sleeve I have a way of dealing with that inquiry – inflate the print run, the sales and the author's percentage. Then Miriam grasshopped on to the observation, 'There's Francis. You know he was to do it but Charlie stood him down.'

I said, 'Pardon?'

'Francis Coleman.'

'Oh,' I said, pretending to have received clarification.

She went on, 'When Dessie rang, Charlie was tickled pink. Francis didn't mind. Francis, your ears must be red. We're just talking about you. You know Junior Nash, the writer?'

We shook hands. 'Course I do,' Francis said, 'I should sue him for doing me out of the brief. But it's more up his alley. Charlie will see justice done to his opus.'

I held the broadsheet under my arm and the wine and fag in my other hand. I was looking for someplace other than the floor to put the glass down and see what bilge that bollix Dessie had doomed me to deliver. But Maxie pushed me on towards the next knot of luminaries, which included Charlie Anka and Pinky Downey himself, Maxie saying, 'Slyboots, you didn't tell me you were reading. What chance have I with a professional like you?'

Pinky Downey was dressed as an art gallery proprietor should be. Like a queer. He wore a frilled Scaramouche shirt and a cummerbund. But he had the flabby handshake of the heterosexual. 'Welcome,' Pinky said to me. 'My gallery is honoured.' Since I had wallowed in fifteen years of anonymity in my home town, I could only deduce that Pinky was saying any reader of Charlie's I'll lick his arse too, because Charlie has big bucks. To go with his ponytail Charlie had one of those jackets that motor-rally groupies wear, with a logo of his agency. What else goes with a ponytail? A paisley cravat, obviously, lumberjack shirt, blue jeans with a belt with a big buckle and cowboy boots. As if I wasn't dwarfed enough as it was.

'I know Dessie's game,' Charlie said, wagging a finger, 'ye're after my vote.' But I could spot his crazed ambition that Junior Nash would proclaim: This is Poetry!

I said, 'You're on the ball, Mr Anka. We certainly are. But that's for another day. Tonight, I even said it to Dessie, I told Dessie I wouldn't come here tonight if he came himself too. I said: Dessie, you haven't a poetic feeling in your whole body.' I tapped the broadsheet: 'Art has its own agenda.' Charlie nodded sacramentally. He said, 'I know that. You must come to one of our at homes. Well, Pinky – ' Charlie looked at his watch.

'Yes, I think so. We will.'

Tinkling a pound coin against the side of his wine glass, Pinky Downey shushed the throng. He welcomed us all to the monthly launch of the Sunday Poets' Broadsheet. It was perfunctory stuff. I looked around the gallery to try and identify my fellow surrogates. Francis Coleman was the only one who stood out as having any stature and he had been dropped in my favour. After all, where would the Sunday Poets go to find victims? The first poet up introduced his poem. It was a simple landscape, he claimed. He got the inspiration in this very art gallery, for which he owed a debt of gratitude to Pinky Downey himself, just looking at a painting of the Falls of Doonass – it was so vivid that he knew he must capture it in words. And without further ado he would now call on Miss Mitchell, who taught him at infant school, taught him his first poems, the ball is in the hall, the cat is on the mat. A big hand please, for Miss Mitchell.

The poor old dear unfolded the monstrous broadsheet and began:

Incessant drops of spectrum wonder . . .

Why didn't I faint? Or clutch my chest and gasp for air? Or something? Because I didn't think of it. I watched the landscape poet listening hard to his old teacher to make sure she caught every nuance of his brushstrokes. She did read well. And it was her pupil the poet who led the applause, proclaiming with every loud clap that he was content with the background and would ever acknowledge Miss Mitchell as the true fount of his talent.

Maxie was up next. It is one of the great pleasures of life to watch someone make a bollix of himself. Maxie was brutal. 'O Euripides, lib of long ago,' Maxie began, saying the first two words as though he was writing to a mate of his. He ran one line into another where that was unintended by the poet with the fedora hat, the beard and the mother who might fall for a conservatory. Maxie paused only for breath and the odds were against a station being where the train stopped. For Maxie confidence equalled speed and his ordeal was over so fast that he was lucky not to include the first line of the next poem. I joined in the big hand but noticed that the poet did not contribute. Yet he looked happy. I realised after a few more readings that some poets applauded and others didn't. Apparently the protocol of the Sunday Poets' Broadsheet Launch was *à la carte*.

We had a 'Lament for a Cot Death' read by a counsellor, without whose comfort the poet would not have come through. It brought the house down, while the stricken mother sat quietly in a far corner of the gallery, crying softly. I forget what the next two offerings were because I felt entitled to unfold the broadsheet to prepare for my own stage entrance and divined that I was third next. Reading the shite that would have to come out of my own mouth, I asked God to forgive my gloating over Maxie and to help me get through and I would never sin again.

It seemed that a second passed and Charlie Anka was at the rostrum introducing his 'Nihil'. Asked us all to bear with him. New to this business. Consider it an honour if the well-known writer Mr Junior Nash could convey some sense – or should he say senses? – of what he was aiming for, put it all straight down without thinking, thinking one night, couldn't sleep, where would we all be without God, if there was no one up there? Without further ado, ladies and gentlemen, Mr Junior Nash.

I folded the broadsheet as tenderly as I could so as not to put a crease in the parchment and I was distracted by Charlie's car logo at the bottom, where he was prominently thanked as the sole sponsor. The delay, I fancied, might have been interpreted by the gallery as my indulgence in osmosis to ensure I did justice to the work, as might reasonably have been expected from someone in the business, from one whose alley it was right up.

' "Nihil",' I began, 'by Charles Anka.'

In my delivery I paused after every line or word, whichever was the longer. Or shorter.

Nihil
To know

> Knowing
> That
> In the knowing
> There
> Is
> No
> Knowing.

I looked up from the broadsheet and around the room at the attentive faces and I knew. I knew what was going to happen. I knew it in an instant. I knew it would happen in an instant. I had read so far brilliantly. Where there had been the odd uncontainable polite cough during the earlier readings, now all was so quiet I could hear Charlie Anka's heart beat. I could certainly hear it from the look on his face.

I ploughed on.

> To feel
> Feeling
> That
> In the feeling
> There
> Is
> No
> Feeling.

I felt. I felt a tear plop out of my eye. And I knew. I knew it was going to happen any second. It took only a second for me to tell myself that it was going to happen any second, but it took much longer to explain it to Dessie afterwards, because then it sounded like an *ex post-facto apologia*. Which it is. The tear was not for the shite as the mob surmised. It was for myself. Nobody had the right to tell me what was right up my alley. What was right up my alley was me down in a basement, writing. I owed it to myself now to defend my alley.

I tried to go on.

> To love
> Knowing
> That
> In
> The
> Loving
> There is the taste
> Of touch.

I owed it to Brother Chuckey, who beat *The Golden Treasury* into me. I owed it to the world.

> Not to hate
> Loving
> In the not hating.

And there I stopped. Cannily fingering the tear to buy time. The time to be seemingly overcome and roll up the broadsheet and carry it, walking slowly, through the attendance, as Brother Chuckey had melted out of the Dennison Arms until I turned and had my back to the near exit and positioned the broadsheet before my toe and executed a drop-kick that was successful in its soar and I roared, 'FUCK THIS SHITE,' and added, because I had the floor, 'and FUCK THE BANKS.' Then I ran.

Before I reached the pub I, too, had been so infected that I composed:

> Sportsmen all
> They kept their eye on the ball
> As I ducked out the hall.

*

The rugby pub was a safe house, no danger of an invasion by poets or the AA. I was out of breath as I shouldered the door. I'd run all the way in case Charlie had become quick-witted and followed me.

'Well?' Dessie said.

'Someone get me a pint.' I sat down and started to eat a cigarette while Dunstan held up his finger to the barman.

'Well?' Dessie repeated. 'How did you get on?'

I wouldn't talk until I had my drink. And then I told them. Dessie had been with me all the way until the sudden unhappy ending. Dunstan listened with more interest than usual – the banks must have climbed out of his head for the night. And as Dessie said, 'You what?' Dunstan slapped my shoulder. 'You did? Good man, Junior.' Dunstan was so happy that he reput my case to Dessie.

'Dessie, he had no other choice. We're talking here about something you wouldn't understand. We're talking here of what's not money. It's everything that money isn't. He had to stand up for it. Right, Junior? Another thing, look at this election. There's the three of us. You're sure of those broker fuckers whoever they are. And this Father Dollars character, he won't let you down. That leaves Harry Lamb. From what you've both told me, he sounds like a lamb. He couldn't possibly let you down after all you're doing for him. So what's the point in crawling after the Charlies and Maxies. There has to be some depth that even someone as low as yourself wouldn't sink to. You don't need to.'

'Listen, you were half asleep until Junior said he said: Fuck the banks. Junior, it was self-indulgence. You could have said the few more lines, swallowed your wine and your pride for a minute. As for his at homes, you wouldn't have had to go. D'you think I haven't been invited? It's accepted, I don't go any place like that. Desiree goes. She represents me. And what's supposed to be the big difference between Charlie's poetry and the bed-sit shite you write?'

But Dunstan was laughing. He made me laugh. We were laughing at Dessie because Dessie was right and of course it was self-indulgence. I had given myself a holiday. It isn't only poetry that is infectious. Dessie had an attack. And when we laughed ourselves out, Dessie said, 'You didn't get a chance to see his face, did you?'

'I'm telling you. Ronnie Delaney wouldn't have caught up with me.'

I had to go over it again and again now that Dessie was making the best of it. I was telling them about Maxie and his saddle of a bicycle when Maxie came in carrying his saddle of a bicycle. Pointing to our table, Maxie called four pints from the barman but it was a few minutes before he came over. There was a rugby mob just inside the door and Maxie had a word here, a word there, and pressed a lot of biceps.

Maxie said, to Dessie, jutting his thumb at me, 'You've some friend.'

'I know. Takes all sorts, Maxie. You ever write a poem, Maxie, I'll read it for you. And I'll do a good job on it.'

'Dessie, let's talk business.'

'Shoot.'

'You've thirteen houses . . .'

'Twelve. There's the cunt in the thirteenth, remember?'

'Who? Oh, Timmie Frawley. All right. Twelve. I think it would be a good idea if you put a conservatory in all twelve houses.'

'That was never on.'

'You don't know the mood back there, Dessie. Charlie isn't acting the poet at the moment. He's back in the days when he'd bite your bollix off. They were all around him. Everybody wanted to know what it was all about. The election came up. The mood back there, there's no sympathy for a man who'd keep women down. There's an awful lot goes into selling one fucking conservatory, Dessie. I can't ring bells like Charlie with his agency, I have to crawl in under

214

doors. Dessie, I had to read poetry tonight. Something about a yoorippycunt. Tough world out there, Dessie. Look, conservatories, they have only a shelf life. Like the freezers when they came in. People bought a full sheep to put into the things. Then suddenly you open it up and there's one fucking tomato in there and a bit of chicken and ham spread. It's conservatory time now, but it won't last. Like the women in the Cove, that's been coming, you know that yourself. The time is here now for it. The women will have their bite at the Cove and then they'll get fed up of it and we'll all be grand again. But for now I got to sell people conservatories. If I could flog twelve conservatories now and wait for the thing to blow over, I know I'll do all right when we're all scratching our bollix again in the Cove and those crazy cunts back there turn their time to looking for divorce and abortion and women priests – bless me, mother, for I have sinned watching your knockers while you were giving me communion. What I'm saying, Dessie, is I'm willing to take a risk on you, on us all, that we'll eventually come out on top. Just say the word, or rather, if you don't mind, you're the one man I trust, but just for this time, if we got it down on paper, reasonable deposit, that I can go to work a minute after the election, after I've delivered. Excuse me two minutes, I see Donal Brock down there, he's putting in an extension . . .'

'Junior,' Dessie said, 'suppose Staff Cox or Benny Bobinizer or Father Dollars, suppose one of them, something happens, they die, the vote is six all . . .'

'If it's a draw after twelve rounds, the heavyweight champ retains his title. Status quo prevails unless there's a chairman's casting vote, which is normally for the status quo, and in this case that's Ab.'

'That's Cove-free of women you're talking about. But what about the election? I'm not an outgoing president. Me and the hyphen are challengers. Who gets it? They might object if Ab voted for me, whereas they couldn't with the other business.'

'What the fuck does it matter? We won't have women in the Cove. Let Joe O'Connor do another year. If his wife lets him.'

'No. I have to beat Tommy Ryan-O'Brien. It's a personal thing. Pride.'

I knew what it was. He wanted to become president. Full stop.

'Junior, there's no need for you to come over again until the day of the election. You're neglecting your book. I'll drive you home to Budge. I'll pick you up in the morning for the airport. Hold it. I want everyone over the day before. Dollars. Harry. Yourself. Ingy will come with you. Stay with you until after the vote. You know what I'm saying?'

I did. He wasn't worried about Staff Cox or Benny Bobinizer. It was probably an outside chance, but just in case Charlie Anka set the dogs on me and I was lying in hospital with one foot up in the air and being fed through a hole in my throat, Dessie was considering how he could still become president, and he cared less of a fuck if Two-Ton Tess was bellyflopping in the Cove while he flaunted his chain of office.

Maxie came back.

'Maxie, why should I plunge on twelve conservatories if they're going to go out of fashion?'

'No, no. They're not. They're a good product. I wouldn't offer you something unless it was gilt-edged. No, it's the crowd on the other side. They'll buy from me only because conservatories will be the in thing for a while. You'll be buying because you'll be making your usual independent business decision. You think for yourself. It's the fickle people, I don't want to be forced into doing business with them.'

'You're good, Maxie. Thinking independently, I think

you should think for yourself on this one. Thanks for the drink. This is one, Maxie, where you must follow your fanny.'

Dessie drove us home. On the way Dunstan said, 'Junior, don't forget Brother Chuckey.'

'What's he talking about?'

'None of your business. I just want him to give my regards to our old teacher.'

PART 3

Chapter 16

I DID NOT forget about Brother Chuckey as Dunstan was to accuse me. No. Charlie Anka did me a favour. Told by Dessie that I would not be needed back home until election day and that I could attack my book, I stayed in bed in the morning waiting for inspiration. Freedom to write is a curse. Having to scratch to find the time is a better system. But after a couple of days and nights sitting downstairs in the pub over the unearned lifeless drink, I remembered the big shot at the poetry reading drop-kicking the broadsheet. I had a choice: I could look back in shame or I could get off my arse and down to the basement and wring the drops of blood on to the blank page. Before the end of January I'd completed Part 2.

I thought of Brother Chuckey every night for the first week and said: Not tonight. The Corner Flag was out of the way, off Old Street. I can swear that I decided to definitely call at the weekend, but on Friday night when I joined Bill, he told me George had taken the message which was eloquent in its brevity: PRICK! I rang back.

'I was going to do it tomorrow.'

'I don't believe you. But forget it. Give me his number.'

*

I called into the Dennison Arms on Monday night for a passing pint and to hear the latest from the Daltons. And I asked Dessie what news from home.

'All leave is cancelled in Dunstan's sweatshop. They were on three hundred triplicate NCR books, hundred in each, for Hanratty's, perforated twice and numbered twice on each copy. Budge was nursing the paper through the machine, Tom had this perforating strip Sellotaped to a board and he was using an old penny to rub the two copies over it. Warren was numbering and Peggy collating, stapling and binding. Dunstan was out canvassing. If he can go out and get business on his own – like I've been telling the stupid dickhead for years – if he can do it on his own now without Peggy, then I hereby pronounce him cured.'

Once I had finished Part 2, I went to Harry's every other Sunday. The Bedouin were rehearsing, shaking off the rust. Coming over second week in March. Beginning in London. Wanted Dessie to be the first to get them this side of the water. Then going on to Birmingham and Liverpool.

Some nights when I heard a step behind me, and other nights when I didn't hear a step behind me, I turned quickly.

I worked at my book. I worked on the bookstall. I looked forward to the Bedouin. I investigated what Dessie thought might be a good idea, the secret, that only myself, Dessie and Dunstan knew about.

After every weekend Dessie came back with more news of DT Offset. That beehive would never know another poor day.

I was flying it through Part 3. Dessie was working on the travel arrangements. The Bedouin were almost on top of us.

Just look at this litany of gratification that presaged their arrival. On the Saturday morning before they were to appear, I rescued Sherwood Anderson from the three for a pound basket. I showed it to Tony, marked it up to three quid and said, 'The only safe place for this is that I buy it myself. Here.' Tony took the money. He said, 'I think I know how you feel. Come over to the clothes stall.' In the manner of a matador, he held up a Donegal tweed jacket that was Made in Donegal. 'There was only a fiver tag on it, mate. It's yours. My treat.'

It was possibly around the time that I was trying on the perfect-fit jacket in the market that Dunstan rang Bill and left the message: 'Peace at last. Thanks to Brother Chuckey. Don't bother to ring back.'

Appropriately, having the Sunday roast with Harry and his mother, we were serenaded by 'Pennies from Heaven'. Harry savaged the dinner and even picked bits off my plate to rush me upstairs. He tried again: 'Junior, it's not too late. We have tomorrow, Tuesday and all day Wednesday. Look at them, it's sinful that Dessie won't let us put them up.'

'No, Harry, he's right there. If one of those posters appeared and someone saw them and the word got through to Dessie's neighbours, he'd be bought up and kicked into the road.'

'They deserve a full house. After twenty-five years . . .'

'Harry, for the same reason, he wouldn't let you print tickets. They'll pay at the door. Ingy's been to Sunbury, the quiet word is gone out to the select from Dessie's other pubs. You'll have a crowd. That's a promise. Has Dessie let you down yet?'

Of course Harry knew by now that if there was one man in the world whose word could be trusted it was Dessie's. But to Harry the impresario not being able to distribute posters, flog tickets, it was like telling a priest: It's OK, someone else will say mass.

Dessie was over at home, checking with Butch Frawley that they would be circumspect and get in and out of the Dennison Arms with the finesse of hoodlums. Also, Dessie was meeting Staff Cox and Benny Bobinizer to make sure they would be in the Seaside on Holy Thursday night. He talked to Ab, who confirmed that Father Dollars was to arrive from Oregon three days before the election and Ab himself would drive Father Dollars down on Thursday. 'But,' Dessie said while we were waiting for the Bedouins, 'that prick Dunstan. He insists he won't go down until Friday morning. You know what his excuse is? Peggy isn't coming down and he doesn't want to sleep in a bed without her. And – it's the only reason I let him off with it – he says he's going to get up at five to re-create the day he came down by bike. I checked it with Budge and Tom. If they're not in the Seaside by half-seven I'll have Ingy drive back along the road in case of punctures or whatever.'

Dessie was going to arrange to get Harry over by boat, to arrive in the country at eleven o'clock on the Thursday morning, and then by train and bus so that Harry would be tucked in at the Seaview that night. I would fly over with Dessie himself and Ingy Thursday morning. Dessie was happy.

I had almost to put my foot on the horse's neck of *The Second-hand Wardrobe* to stop it running away with me. I mention it only to complete the all-pervasive contentment that attended my reception of the Bedouin Showband.

Ingy's riding instructions were to round up as many as possible without telling them anything at all about the nature of the treat other than that they would be under pain of excommunication from Dessie's favour if they laughed at the performance or didn't at least find a curtain to hide behind. Admission was a fiver. They could bring their wives or steady girlfriends. No scrubbers. The limited licence – Dessie's was a man's pub apart from a handful of old dears who lived in the neighbourhood – muted speculation that it would surely be mud-wrestling on the menu. A comedian was suggested. Chris the Cap mentioned. But you were expected to laugh at comedians sometimes. Baptista had been ADVERTISED. At only three pound a skull compared to a fiver for this mystery man or whatever. Hearing 'mystery man', one slow-witted quick-thinking beefcake from Sunbury flashed a tenner on at evens that it had to be Josef Locke himself and that the wives and steady girlfriends would never forgive the men responsible if they missed another comeback. Then, pocketing the tenner, the bookie pointed out: Who'd have the balls to laugh at Josef Locke?

The logicians went to work. It was a fiver. Wives and girlfriends. Used for cooking, cleaning and going to bed with. Scraping the muck off the gear. Dancing! U2? Did people dance to U2? Nobody knew. Could they be got for a fiver? Dessie knew everybody, probably their manager, a token charge, proceeds going to charity, the secrecy explicable on the grounds that the group might be using the occasion to make a major political statement. But why the injunction not to laugh? You haven't heard any of their political statements, have you? But it would explain wives and girlfriends. Feminism. No. Not on Dessie's side of the street. All right. Try again. Fiver. Wives and girlfriends. Dancing. Stick with dancing. No scrubbers. Strauss Ball? No, Ingy didn't say anything about monkey suits. Baffled. Hang on! What's Dessie famous for? Against Harlequins . . . No, no. The leg up to anyone in need of the second chance! Hey, why should we pay a fiver for a crowd like that that we're not supposed to laugh at, here, Dessie, Dessie, 't isn't one of your charity cases, is it?

Later, Dessie said to me, 'Why didn't I think of it. That's it. I'm giving them a second chance. I can wash my hands of it. Anyone comes up to me, I can say I gave you a second chance, didn't I?'

One hundred and thirteen paid at the door. The Sunbury mob and those press-ganged from Dessie's other pubs were augmented by representatives of Dessie's suppliers, from the Paki who provided the continental quilts to the Cockney who had the franchise for the Scotch eggs. The crowd were a comfort to each other, speculating that it had to be a star attraction. Or a dog's dinner all together to provide a flourish to Dessie's career as a philanthropist. There was a crane of necks at the window when the van pulled up. When Harry Lamb jumped down, somebody told the crowd, 'It's your man, the guy who gave us Baptista.'

Harry led the Bedouin through the hall door to the barmen's lounge at the back of the pub. They were professionals, didn't have a drink before or during a gig. They went straight to work. They were not fiddlers from West Clare. They weren't the Daltons. The word went round the crowd. There were six of them. All carrying bags. Heavy bags. After five minutes, Harry came out of the barmen's lounge carrying two kitchen chairs and seated them on the mini-stage. Back in for two more. And another two. Arranged in two rows of three. Harry spoke into the microphone. Testing: one, two, three. Then he switched it off. And on. And looked to the togging-out room. And announced, 'Good evening, ladies and gentlemen, and all those who got in for nothing.'

As instructed, nobody laughed.

'Tonight, a big welcome, please, for the All-Ireland Champion Accordion Ceili Band, celebrating their silver jubilee, the one and only, the Bedouin Showband.'

The crowd gave the big hand. Harry put out the palm, like those boxing hyperbolists before the big fight: 'Butch Frawley.' Butch came from the wings dressed in the Arab robes, unrecognisable under cowl and behind yashmak. Butch, with the box strapped on his back, bowed and sat in the middle of the front row.

'Ghosty Collopy!'

Harry may as well have been announcing John Wayne

or Cassius Clay. Nobody could yet tell one Bedouin from another. Ghosty sat one side of Butch.

'Divine Dickie!'

Completed the front row.

'Lexie Hayes!

'Fats Flynn!

'And the man with a sob in his voice, the one and only, Simon Quinn!'

Everyone laughed that night as on every occasion the Bedouin had played, at just the sight of them. That never bothered a Bedouin. Harry left the stage and came down to join Dessie, said, 'Great crowd, Dessie. Well done,' as Butch was rising, saying into the microphone, 'We can do without this for a start,' and moved the microphone to the side of the stage. I said to Ingy and a few of his bruisers from the club, 'The Rose of San Antone.' Though billed as a ceili band, the Bedouin played no Irish music at all other than, say, what Butch sang now, 'The Rose of San Antone'.

The dust settled. There was a man up there on that stage dressed as an Arab, playing the accordion, singing 'The Rose of San Antone', accompanied by five other Arabian accordionists. People almost looked under beermats for the gimmick. Butch finished to puzzled applause and straight away sang 'The fox went out on a chilly night/Prayed for the moon to give him light'. The singing and the accompaniment po-faced. The number was greeted with the applause of the cheated. A Dessie charity case. No mistake now, as Butch ordered, 'Ladies and gentlemen, please take your partners for an old-time waltz.'

' "The Streets of Laredo",' I said, just before Butch began to sing 'The Streets of Laredo'. Ingy and the mob looked at me. 'You mean,' Ingy said, 'they sing the same – '

'Yeah. They have their repertoire. And that's it.'

'Some gimmick!'

The Bedouin did have a gimmick. But it wasn't the Arab

dress. They had to wear something. Back in the early days all the showbands wore uniforms. Unaffected Italian suits and winklepicker shoes, say. White sports coats and black satin trousers. Ties, with maybe the band leader in a cravat. It was the age of respect for the uniform, an age coming to an end as the Bedouin were trying to emerge. Postmen, bus conductors, bellboys; cinema usherettes, the girls selling ice cream in the foyer or from the kiosk; the front-of-house man with his arm stretched out to check the fourpenny rush, he had a uniform; the police, the army, the Red Cross, priests, Chuckey in his soutane; painters wore white overalls, not a dirty black colour to camouflage the drops from the brush, no, white to proclaim the pride in the trade; the ticket checker on the train; spivs wore velvet collars. Everybody knew who the other fella was. There was some order. Even the Beatles. After whom confusion took root. The authorities shed the apparel that proclaimed the office and soon the only definite recognisable uniform was worn by the man and woman in the street, every one of them. Jeans. Then the next group of four appeared and not only were they wearing no uniform at all, apart from the uniformity of the guitars, they were each distinctly maggoty in their calculated individual scruffiness. With the chalice of conformity passed to the punters, the musicians shook off the strait-jacket. The musicians, the lunatics, took over the asylum. They stole tramps' clothes and had themselves photographed without their instruments, the guitars, in anarchic stances in grave-yards, used-car lots, city dumps. But it was early in the evolution from the Italian suits to the sweaty vests that the Bedouin Showband were born.

The six were playing in the once jammed ceili halls pro-moted by the Pioneer Total Abstinence Association. And it seemed the next day the take on the door wasn't enough for a round in the nearest pub, if they could have found room, jammed as the pub was with those pissed out of their tender minds celebrating the junior cert results. In their ceili days they traded under the prosaic St Patrick's Ceili Band. They had a meeting to discuss their survival. They accepted that their only hope was to become a showband. To become a showband they recognised that they would first have to decide on a uniform as there was no such thing as a showband without one, Butch explained to me the night he borrowed the five bob in the Banba. They were selling out and they knew it. The meeting was held in the pub and with every pint they flirted with one item of the agenda after another. Once committed to abandoning their standards, they savoured every possible debauch. Without coming near agreeing a uniform, Lexie Hayes pointed to Simon Quinn and said, 'And he'll have to get a wig.' Simon Quinn said, 'Fuck off.' But Lexie Hayes persisted: 'Or play a guitar. You can't have a bald man in a showband.' Simon Quinn said, 'Whatever I do, I'll never play a guitar.' They were having a bit of a ball about the bald Simon when Lexie Hayes said, 'Problem is, a toupee would cost the same price as three sets of uniforms.' They were diverted back then to the first item on the agenda and the price of uniforms. Again in drunken jest, Ghosty Collopy said, 'If we've to pay all that money for a hair-piece for Simon, we'll end up bollix naked unless we wrap a sheet around us.' And that led to a suggestion of togas and calling themselves the Senators. But there was already a showband called the Senators, even if those original Senators wore cowboy gear. As though frustrated by the cheek of those Senators and stuck with sheets, Butch himself, Butch was to boast to me, came up with, 'We could be Arabs.' They were by now seduced by the notion of uniforms for a song – even the humble Italian suits cost a bomb – that they saw themselves dressed like Arabs and they liked what they saw. Suddenly Divine Dickie said, 'The Bedouins.' So after two hours, within two minutes, they had the uniform and the name. Such was their innocence in selling a soul, they thought they were going over the cliff altogether in plunging for what they thought of as a country and western repertoire. They were almost there. Only to decide on a gimmick. They pawed over the precedents. When the Jack Dillon Orchestra came out of the closet, big Jack Dillon himself put little Joe Lowney up on his shoulders. Jack danced a hornpipe while Joe accompanied him on the flute. It was a breeze for big Jack, but little Joe Lowney always complained that his arse felt as though he had just ridden a bicycle over a mile of pot-holes. With a ton of accordion on your lap, Butch explained, a box player likes to sit down. Everything was in place. It had been as easy as sin. Then Simon Quinn said, 'All right, but I want a good one.' Puzzled, the other members of the former St Patrick's Ceili Band said, 'What?' Simon said, 'The wig.' And they had a great laugh. Until they realised he was serious. They said to Simon, 'Fuck off.' And Simon said, 'Fine. You fuck off. I'm not joining any band unless I get a toupee. And a proper one.'

Dessie said, 'Ingy, get someone up dancing.'

I had twelve and sixpence that night, fifteen years before. I saw the posters for the Banba Ballroom in the Kilburn High Road. The posters claimed that the Bedouin Showband were Fresh from Their Successful Tour of the Middle East. I went to the Banba to borrow a quid off Butch Frawley. I persuaded the guy on the door that I was only going in for five minutes to say hello to one of the band. The attendance in the Banba was the largest of the entire tour, over three hundred, more than double the previous bumper in such exotic parts of the Middle East as Liverpool and Birmingham. The Banba audience was almost a hundred per cent displaced rural Irish from the country's western seaboard, culchies without street-smart irony who accepted the

Bedouin Showband for what they were, six accordion players dressed as Arabs who though armed only with accordions played no ceili music at all.

I was in time that night to catch Butch on 'The Streets of Laredo'. Second in the line-up was Ghosty Collopy. All six were top-class accordionists but Ghosty was such a wizard with the box that he had the only instrumental solo spot of their gigs. Back home, fending under their own ensemble management when they toured the west, where the aficionados knew a box player from a box player, the band was sometimes billed as Ghosty Collopy and the Bedouin Showband. Apart from such as the 'National Anthem' and 'The Yellow Rose of Texas', when they all sang together, everyone in the band was also a solo singer and Ghosty's standards were 'Red River Valley' and 'There's a Bridle Hanging on the Wall' and 'Pal of My Cradle Days'.

Ingy managed to get about twenty up on the floor for 'The Streets of Laredo', those who didn't need to be drunk to dance. The rest were attentive – that is, not rowdy, yet maybe a little mesmerised. When Butch announced Ghosty, I said, 'Red River Valley'. Mostly the same twenty got up again plus maybe another ten or twelve. The night was going all right.

Back in the Banba, in justification of their showband appellation, Butch Frawley had introduced Divine Dickie. He had been Richard Divine in the St Patrick's Ceili Band. On the night of the inaugural Bedouin meeting, Simon Quinn, flush with the scalp of his toupee, said, 'And if I'm willing to wear it, he should change his name.' Richard Divine said, 'What's wrong with my name?' They were drunk by then. Simon said, 'I just don't like it.' The inversion of Christian and surname was appropriate considering the gimmick, as Butch continued in the Banba: 'Ladies and gentlemen, the world champion back-to-front box player.' Divine Dickie un-saddled the piano accordion and strapped a button job to his back. He stretched his hands behind until he could reach the buttons and that had the effect of his head jutting forward like a face in the stocks as he laboured to play and sing 'I Was Dancin' with My Darlin' to the Tennessee Waltz'. It was, to a city slicker like myself, like watching somebody having a musical toilet.

Before the band had a break and I got the chance to try and tap Butch, Lexie Hayes did a Tauber medley of 'Girls Were Made to Love and Kiss' and 'You Are My Heart's Delight', the latter to the sole accompaniment of Ghosty Collopy, who alone had the wit at his fingertips to provide the unintrusive complement. Then after Lexie, Fats Flynn had leapt upon 'It Was an Itsy-Bitsy Teenie-Weenie Yellow Polka-Dot Bikini' that goaded the Banba quickstep to burst from its chrysalis into a fully-fledged frenzied jive, a most ungainly sight when performed by sunburnt lads and lasses reared swinging scythes through fields of Irish wheat. Then came Simon Quinn, the oldest and first to need a toupee, who had the gift of putting the slow maudlin into 'Why Did I Leave My Little Back Room in Bloomsbury?'. When told the first time he sang it that it was not country and western, Simon said, 'I don't care. My mother used to sing it.' That opened the floodgates to Fats Flynn's 'Itsy-Bitsy'. But there was a debate all over the world as to what was true country and western.

I had seen the Bedouin often back home and, I admit it, with only their Arab uniforms keeping pace with the musical evolution, we townies used to break our bollix laughing at them. But that night in the Banba among the less sophistic-ated, the Bedouins had their own integrity and plugged away so that you stopped laughing the way you stop laughing half-way through a *Laugh* magazine. The dancers got down to the main business of the dance hall, which, whether you are born in the Yemen, Ballydehob or within the sound of Bow Bells, is native to clodhopper and Fred Astaire alike and it doesn't matter what horse is up there having bolted from a stable.

Butch had seen me standing at the back of the hall in the Banba and at the break he came down through the crowd and unloosened his yashmak and cowl.

'Junior Nash. Of all people. I'll take one of your fags.'

'I have a fag. It's about all I have. How are you, Butch? How's the tour?'

'It's coming to the best part. We don't get paid for the whole tour until tomorrow. This is our last gig but we have a couple of days before we go back to live it up. Jesus Christ, I'm going to eat the biggest fucking steak tomorrow. The only thing keeping us going. Simon poled a groupie in Birmingham and got a fiver off her, she thinks we're passing back that way. Only for Simon's Arab langer and his hairpiece, we wouldn't have lasted this far in fags. How are you doing? You couldn't lend me five bob till tomorrow?'

' "There's a Bridle Hanging on the Wall",' I said to the lads.

I counted them. When Ghosty eased into 'Pal of My Cradle Days' there were forty-eight up. And they danced just as po-faced as the band played. Dessie's Cockney was up gliding around with the trouble and strife. The rest of us lounged about in passive acquiescence to the languid foxtrots. It was so respectable. Dessie said, 'Ingy, is that really Slats Slattery out there or are we seeing things?'

A word about my drinking. I do not get truculent when I am drunk and that has nothing to do with my being a weakling. The dust jackets might claim that I was a builder's labourer, but that is not true. It is part of the selling-out process that a writer must embrace if he ever hopes to get a royalty cheque for five hundred and thirty-four pounds. No. I am more likely to become sentimental. Even now, with

Ghosty coming to the end of the pal of his cradle days, with only a few pints inside me, the hairs on the back of the neck were acting up. But I have one drunken fault. When I'm right, I have to prove I'm right. I can get cranky. If somebody says it was William Holden and I say: No, it was Robert Mitchum, and I know I'm right and somebody insists William Holden, then nothing will do but to put the bets on and run to a library for a film book or ring Hollywood if necessary. The score of a match. Who wrote what book. When I'm right I can't take it when I'm called wrong. It's just a lack of self-confidence bolstered by drink and I get cranky. As though I was the emcee and not Butch, I said, 'Divine Dickie next. Watch this, Ingy. He plays the button accordion behind his back.' I said it as I took a gulp out of my fourth pint. And Butch said, 'Ladies and gentlemen, everyone now please, the one and only Fats Flynn, to get you rockin' and a-boppin'.'

'It was an itsy-bitsy teenie-weenie . . .' I didn't count them but there must have been over half the mob up. The women went mad for it. The Sunbury heavies abandoned the jackets and loosened the ties. There was a lot of sweat. Ingy himself got up. He was a bit awkward, just missed taking the head off a woman with his elbow. The Bedouins, once they got the crowd going, got going themselves, quickened the beat, Fats rising, slipping out of the accordion and leaving the box on the seat, one hand in the air, the other sawing back and forth across his midriff as he slithered inside his robes.

'He does a slow one now,' I said when Fats finished 'Itsy-Bitsy' and the crowd stayed on the floor and clapped and whistled through their fingers and then waited with their hands around the ladies' waists. ' "Put Your Sweet Lips a Little Closer to the Phone",' I elaborated. Ingy was still out on the floor and the couple of guys beside me nodded. I didn't like their lack of enthusiasm for my prescience, as the

Dennison Arms became electrified with 'Went to a party in the county jail – ' the Bedouin Fats becoming a Dervish – 'Everybody, let's rock.' I could feel the crankiness getting a grip on me. The couple of guys grabbed two of the regular old dears and went rockin', deserting me. I was a wallflower. I never could dance. I had space at the counter. Dessie and Harry were separated from me by a few dedicated barflies. I was about to move towards them, interrupt their salivating over the take, when they too found a couple of the Sunbury steadies and joined the wildest and most successful night so far that the Dennison Arms would remember. I said, 'He'll definitely do "Put Your Sweet Lips" now, he can take off Jim Reeves . . .' I think I thought I was forecasting to one of the barmen, but he flew away from me carrying two sloppy pints to the end of the counter. I bit my nails while they were cheering Fats again. It was the cheering and the whistling, I was sure, that put Fats on the wrong track as out of the unknown repertoire came 'Shake, Rattle and Roll'.

The sweaty mob came back to the bar. At least I had an audience. Butch announced, 'And now, ladies and gentlemen, the one and only Divine Dickie . . .' I grabbed Ingy. 'This is it, Ingy, "I Was Dancin' with My Darlin' to the Tennessee Waltz", he plays it behind his back.' Butch carried on: 'Take your partners for a slow waltz to the soothing "I Was Dancin' with My Darlin' to the Tennessee Waltz".' I said to Ingy, 'See? Watch this. He'll change the accordion first.'

But there was no sign of the piano accordion being unharnessed. Divine Dickie played and sang it straight and half the crowd got up to take a rest, crawling around the floor, joining in the song.

'He always plays it back to front, Ingy,' I insisted, but Ingy said, 'Hm? There's Slats. I must talk to Slats.'

'But do you know another thing?' I said. 'Before you go I must tell you this one, Ingy. And lads, the best thing of all is they're supposed to be the All-Ireland Champion Accordion Ceili Band, but get this, they play no Irish music at all!'

'Slats!'

'. . . and he always plays that behind his back up to now . . .'

My fourth pint was gone. Someone drank it. Me. I grabbed another that I knew wasn't mine and gulped it, and when a heavy came from the jacks, puzzled, saying he could have sworn he had a full pint, I sang dumb.

'And now, ladies and gentlemen, take your partners for "The Siege of Ennis".'

'But they never . . .' I tried, as I was nearly knocked down by the rush to the floor. Half-way down my stolen pint, I ordered another. I was talking to myself. They were famous for their fucking repertoire that never changed. They were making me look like a liar, a bluffer. I sulked sitting at the counter.

'. . . the one and only Lexie Hayes . . .'

'. . . he does Richard Tauber, "Girls Were Made to Love and Kiss" and "You Are My Heart's Delight", only the guy in the front accompanies him, Ghosty Collopy . . .'

'. . . Ireland's Richard Tauber . . .'

'. . . I knew it . . .'

And I forecast Simon Quinn's 'Why Did I Leave My Little Back Room in Bloomsbury?' and Simon Quinn sang 'Why Did I Leave My Little Back Room in Bloomsbury?' and I said, 'Always. Always sings that. And Divine Dickie, it's his name back to front and he always plays the box back to front when he's doing "The Tennessee Waltz", I can't understand what happened to him tonight . . .'

At the break Butch came over to me and we had the big reunion. Butch said, 'Give me one of your fags.'

'Don't tell me you're skint?'

'No, no. Forgot to buy them. What do you think? I can't believe it, we're goin' a bomb.'

'Why didn't Divine Dickie play it back to front?'

'What?'

' "The Tennessee Waltz", he always played it back to front. On the button.'

'It's just a one-off tour. We're just sticking to being ourselves. No gimmicks. People have to take us as we are.'

'But your articles of faith were country and western, Arab gear, accordions, you had Fats doin' rock and roll. And you did a "Siege of Ennis". That's St Patrick's Ceili Band stuff, Butch. I'm boostin' you up here telling people what you play and you fuck it up playing everything and anything.'

'We're not young any more. There's three of us on the dole. Ghosty's the only one makin' a livin' out of weddings. Even at that they throw him out at twelve and a fucking disco comes on. Divine Dickie is on two weekend twelve-hour shifts in a computer factory, Lexie has his sweet shop. We haven't time to be fucking well organised. 'Twas my own mad idea, this twenty-five years' caper, so I said we'd just be ourselves, but it's funny, I know how to work a crowd, we're doin' well here, Junior, the rock, they like the bit of the rock, and then "The Siege of Ennis", we could be on to something, if it works here. I have to go to community health clinics for help with my mortgage. Jesus, if this could be our break, we're not too old – you don't think we're too old?'

'You're fine. Look, I told everyone about Divine Dickie, just get him to do it once, behind his back . . .'

'He could only ever do it to "The Tennessee Waltz" and he sang that already.'

'He could sing it again, no one would mind. I've been telling them, they're all looking forward to it.'

'Naw. Dickie's fucked from arthritis. He doesn't even use the button any more, just the piano.'

'He could borrow Simon's, Simon's on the button.'

'I don't know. I couldn't ask him. We said no gimmicks. This was our chance to be ourselves . . .'

'Butch, listen, it could be the very thing to top it all off. You're right. Ye're doin' fantastic. Everyone used to look forward to it before, remember?'

'Everyone used to laugh at it.'

'Is there someone laughing tonight? Apart from the start. Until they got used to the gear. They're eating out of the palm of your hand. You announce it. I promise you, Butch. I'm working the crowd too, I hear them. They'll go for anything, they're in love with you. You have this crowd. Do it for me, Butch. Look, some guys back there don't believe it can be done. I told them. I said, "Just you watch." And then Dickie doesn't do it.'

'I dunno. I'll ask him. We'll see. I better get back. If I do, you'll buy me a pint after.'

'By popular demand,' Butch roared, looking down at me, letting his eyes shoot up at our in-joke . . .

'Ingy! Now. This is it. What I'm telling you all night . . .'

I'd watched Butch confab with Divine Dickie, saw them get the button accordion from Simon Quinn.

'The world champion back-to-front box player, Divine Dickie! Stay in your seats, ladies and gentlemen, sit back and hear "The Tennessee Waltz" like you've never heard it before.'

I edged over to Dessie and Harry. 'Ye can thank me. I had to make him do it. I had to persuade Butch.' But I seemed to be getting shit for thanks. Anyway I was right. I said he played it back to front and now he was going to do it. And I would have had all the other calls right too, if Butch hadn't fucked around with their famous repertoire.

It was all over in ten minutes.

It was warm in the Dennison Arms and most of the band were red in the face anyway. So just because Divine Dickie was a little redder than the rest of them, that was natural.

Playing back to front takes more out of a player. 'I Was Dancin' with My Darlin'' was as far as he got. I don't believe a man's face can turn blue that quickly, but that is what those at the front claimed afterwards. The Dennison Arms stage is only a foot above ground level and Divine Dickie's chair, what, another foot and a half? He hadn't that far to fall as he came toppling forward. It was a slump more than anything, he didn't hit his face off the ground. Even though the Dennison Arms clientele might have been excused for thinking it part of the act – after Baptista – due credit to them for the lightning action stations. Particularly the Sunbury people, who probably had practice from the thirds matches, where they were usually overweight and past it.

Dessie barely breathed, 'Jesus Christ. Ingy, quick!' Dessie turned to the barman. 'Gimme the phone.' He dialled three times. Emergency Services. The Dennison Arms, Belgravia. Heart attack.

Ingy was already at work. I saw him put his left hand palm down on Divine Dickie's chest and give it a thump with his right fist. And then go mouth to mouth. Then my view was blocked. Slats Slattery and the Sunbury lot stood with their backs to the resuscitation, Slats ordering, 'Everybody back, please. Thank you. Don't anybody come any closer, please.' There were screams from the ladies and the Bedouins were on their feet on the stage, all accordions unsaddled, all looking down at Divine Dickie except Butch, who was looking towards me as I slid behind a second row, even though I was fucked if I was going to take the blame – if they were a proper band they would have rehearsed properly and Divine Dickie would have breezed through. Although I prayed: Jesus, please God, don't let him be dead. We could hear the ambulance. Some of the crowd rushed outside to wave them in with the stretcher. Within a minute Divine Dickie was on his way to St Thomas's, Butch going with him in the ambulance, the rest of the Bedouins following in the van, Dessie and Harry and Ingy about to go in Dessie's car. I said to Dessie, 'Is there anything I can do?' The thanks I got for that was, 'You mad prick!'

Before he ran out of the door Dessie told the barmen to lock up right on time. I was always an exception to that exceptional command and I kept the barmen busy for an hour while the crowd dwindled on into after hours, until we heard Dessie's car and Dessie, Harry, Butch and Ingy came back.

I said, 'How is he? Is he . . . is he all right?'

But the four of them almost knocked me down going to the counter, before Ingy said, 'He's OK. He'll be fine, a mild one.'

'Yeh, he'll be OK, if you hadn't broken his ribs, Ingy,' Dessie said, but I could see there was relief all round in all their faces. Dessie had ordered four pints, forgetting to order for me, or just not ordering for me.

'I barely tapped him. Has he a weak chest, Butch?'

'We all have weak chests.'

While I had the chance to listen before they turned on me, I took in that Ghosty and the rest of the Bedouins were still at the hospital, satisfying themselves that Divine Dickie was definitely sound, even though Dessie got it from the ambulance men and the doctor that there was no need to worry, they would keep him just a few days to help the ribs and recommended that Divine Dickie have a full medical at home. They went over the whole night again and again, like people do after such a happening. And it was only Dessie who gave me a bollicking. Called me names. You stupid this. You mad that. Then Harry hit the counter: 'Never, never, never double-booked. Never in my life. But this. Never ever failed to fulfil a fixture. Never put my people on television, never double-booked, never failed to show.'

Butch said, 'Where's the jacks?' asking me and then giving me the nod to go with him.

'What's the score on your friend?' Butch asked me after tapping another fag – 'keep forgetting to buy them'.

'Who?'

'Dennison. Is he loaded?'

'He eats. Why?'

'The tour is cancelled. You know that. We can't go to Birmingham tomorrow and Liverpool on Friday and leave Divine Dickie. It wouldn't be right.'

'What about the show must go on?'

'That's Hollywood. Harry Lamb is like you. He said couldn't we play with five, he'd sit by Divine Dickie's bedside himself. But I said no. We were always one for all and all for one. It's a mark of respect. Those Irish slobs in Birmingham and Liverpool can live without us. But your friend has scratch?'

'I don't get it. What're you on about, Butch?'

'Don't get me wrong. The Bedouin are used to the hard road. Tonight, a customer in here hounds me to make a sick man play the accordion behind his back. A customer of this, your friend's place. And then another guy jumps on Divine Dickie and breaks his ribs. We're not complaining about that. That goes with the territory. Harry would probably fix everything up, but all that's bothering him is two gigs in Birmingham and Liverpool and no band. Harry's a showmust-go-on believer. Look, Ghosty and the lads, there'll be no acting up from them. We came over in the van, on the boat, but I don't want to go back that way. If I could get back tomorrow on the plane, I've a wedding Friday. That's a fair few bob for me, Junior, these days. If we all were able to get paid for the Birmingham and Liverpool nights, that'd be one thing. But if I could go home ahead of the lads and fit in the wedding, it could smooth everything over. What you think?'

'Butch, how could you have a wedding Friday when if this hadn't happened you'd be playing in Liverpool Friday?'

'I was booked before we ever decided to come together for the twenty-fifth.'

'But didn't you tell the people, the people getting married, didn't you cancel?'

'No.'

'Isn't that what Harry calls double-booking?'

'Do you know what life is like out there in this business? They cancel me. You know? Ring up a couple of weeks before a wedding and tell me, the boyfriend says sorry about this but I never knew that the girlfriend had another band booked already. What happens is they book me because they heard I was great at another wedding, me on my own with just the box coming cheaply they think, the box and that fucking object I have to play these days with my foot to pretend I have drums, and then they all get talking and they hear about three shitheads with guitars that come cheaper than me, they're getting three performers instead of one for less money and even if they don't cancel me, they're young, they laugh all night at their fathers and uncles dancing to me and then can't fuck me out the door fast enough to get the disco going, and if they can't wait and get rid of me half an hour before time, they try and knock a half-hour's money off my bill. I don't get many bookings, Junior, and the odd time I double-book, if I cancelled one the other might cancel me and I'd end up with fuck all. People have no honour any more.'

'But what would they do Friday if you were in Liverpool? They wouldn't know you weren't coming until – until you didn't come. How do they manage then?'

'You think I give a fuck? Now, you're wide. Just our wages for the two gigs and a plane ticket home for me tomorrow. And there'll be no fuss. He can have my word on that.'

When I came out of the jacks with Butch I was ready to give Dessie the nod and a have a quiet word, but Dessie gave me the nod first and brought me away from the counter. 'Listen,' Dessie said, 'we got a big problem with Harry now . . .'

'We got a problem with Butch.'

'What? What problem?'

I told him.

'All right. Fix the fucker up. Get the money off Ingy and give it to him. Get Ingy to ring my travel agent and organise Butch out of the country pronto. OK. Now fuck Butch. Harry. He's demented over there. He's never failed to deliver, which I respect. He thinks he can get Hazel and the Conkers for Liverpool. Ingy's ringing some numbers, trying to make contact. But I'd figure something out for Liverpool myself, with the time, but Birmingham tomorrow night, Harry's gone through everyone, they're already booked or so scattered they can't be contacted. I'm telling you, look at him – don't let him see you – you ever see his face like that?'

Harry was like a dog all right. 'But,' I said, 'what about the Daltons, would they do it? Could they do it?'

'Good man. Come on. Get Ingy to get that mad cunt out of here, get him his plane ticket, give him his money.'

Dessie's people are efficient. Ingy found Hazel. The job was oxo for Liverpool. He got the travel agent. No problem. They forked out the money. There was great acting from all concerned, wishing Butch all the best, Dessie insisting on an immediate taxi to take Butch to his kip hotel north of Kilburn. Overriding Butch's protestations that he was grand, felt like a two-year-old. No, no, Dessie was saying, feeling responsible for Butch, could be delayed reaction, a good night's sleep, right, Ingy? Ingy knew of instances . . .

After the door closed on Butch, Dessie said, 'Junior here has come up with it, Harry. The Daltons. Birmingham doesn't know how lucky it is.'

Well, we made Harry smile. At my innocence.

'I thought of them,' Harry said, gloomy again. 'You

forget. It's Thursday. That's the night they play in Hampstead with other fiddlers. Doing their own thing. It's their sacred night.'

'I forgot,' Dessie said. 'Shit. Of all nights.' This sounded a bit lame to me, coming from Dessie. It didn't sound like Never Take No for an Answer.

'And,' Harry said, 'I also thought of switching them with Hazel but I've Hazel booked for tomorrow night.'

I watched Dessie looking at Harry for a minute and then I watched Dessie looking at Ingy. 'Suppose,' Dessie said, struck with an idea that he then rejected. 'No. I couldn't ask them. And I couldn't expect them to do it for me. Unless . . . Ingy. You're the Daltons' best mate since they came here . . .' This was Ingy's first time hearing that he was a pal of the Daltons. 'Actually it's amazing the way they took to you, you big slob. You're always laughing and joking with them. What if Ingy asked them, Harry? It would be just one night they'd miss in Hampstead. What do you think, Ingy? You think it's worth trying?'

CHAPTER 17

I DO NOT know how film stars handle it. Having to have a
bodyguard. By teatime on Holy Thursday I was weary of
Ingy. It was different coming over on the plane with Dessie.
Ingy and I were staying in the house Dunstan rented from
Dessie. The three of us reached the Seaside at two o'clock
and had lunch in the Seaview. Then I brought Ingy over to
show him the house and to freshen up and then we walked
all over the Seaside from Gilligan Point to the hot rocks,
across the beach, past the boathouse and golf club and on
out to the Cove. And in the Cove Ingy admitted, 'That fucks
the Forty-Foot.' The Seaside was almost empty, only a few
lame-brains playing golf, hope for the world. I was only
used to Ingy in a pub and when I'm not in a pub myself
I'm used to just being by myself, edgy. We didn't have too
much to talk about. I was uneasy in Ingy's sole company. For
the couple of weeks after the Bedouin Showband I'd stayed
away from the Dennison Arms, having set myself the target
of finishing *The Second-hand Wardrobe* before the election.
And on Holy Thursday morning, on our way to the airport,
I had delivered the manuscript, missing my publisher by a
day. He'd gone away for Easter.

We had orders from Dessie that both of us were to stay

out of the pub until night-time. Dessie was not worried about Ingy. He was afraid that I might get cranky. Back again at the house with an hour to pass before tea and not being able to find a deck of cards, Ingy said, 'What about a swim?' I said, 'You're on your own, Ingy.' I went across the road with him to Gilligan Point and sat with my legs dangling as Ingy threw himself in, Ingy the Christmas Day veteran of the Forty-Foot. Ingy's screams could probably have been heard in the Forty-Foot. Still, I envied him his appetite for the tea.

Dessie joined us for the fry in the Seaview. Dessie said, 'Harry Lamb isn't here yet.' Dessie had been on the phone. The ferry had sailed on time, a calm crossing. But the train out of Dublin was delayed in the midlands for almost two hours because of a dead cow on the line. The secret of Fatima is less well cherished than the true cause of a train breakdown. Dessie was worried about Harry. There had been only a couple of weeks in it since the Bedouins, but Dessie was worried because I had not been invited to Sunday dinner, and when Dessie had to telephone Harry to complete Harry's travelling arrangements, Dessie thought he sounded cold. While we were still at the tea, Harry rang the Seaview to assure all that he was on his way, ringing from where the bus made a ten-minute stop. So we accepted that Harry's frost had been due to the terror of having narrowly avoided failing to deliver an act.

I went back again with Ingy to the house to have our shaves before we went for the few scoops in Mick O'Mara's, where our side was to have its Holy Thursday night headquarters. We left Dessie to complete his mother-hen scouting act.

'Sure, good God, look in. Junior Nash. And is it Ingy? It is the bastard. Mary, 'tis Ingy back. Welcome, lads. Have ye eaten? Is Dessie here, and Dunstan? Is Budge and Tom down, lads? What'll ye have?'

Dessie came in. 'Sure, good God, 'tis Dessie himself. Welcome.'

Dessie said, 'Father Dollars is playing poker with Ab's crowd in the Albert. Benny and Staff are in the Seaview. Harry has just arrived. Knackered. He's gone straight to bed. The only thing I got out of him was he asked me did I think he was too old to learn how to fly. I looked into Scott's. Charlie Anka, the hyphen, the Fennessys, Maxie. Maxie gave me a hungry look. Fuck him. Coming down the road I bumped into Shamey Flynn. He asked me could he join our celebrations here tomorrow night. I said Fuck off, Shamey, some people will do anything for a drink on Good Friday, but then I said I was only kidding. I know he hates the hyphen. I said he'd be more than welcome. I said Francis Coleman can come too if he wants.'

Mick O'Mara came out to us. Spoke softly, ''Tis all set, lads. I spoke to Kerr the Cop. We can be open but we must be closed. Come in around the back. Can't let Batsy out. Batsy, in around the back tomorrow. Kerr said no singing. Even if we sing in whispers, I said, but Kerr said no. Scott's tried him, you see. Kerr gave out to them. On the day the Lord died, Kerr said. So 'tis only in here will be open. Invitation only. Tell everyone yourself, Dessie.'

Batsy sat by the fire, the tea-cosy on his head, his elbows on his knees and the palms toasting. It was odd to be in Mick O'Mara's on a Holy Thursday night with just Batsy there and Mick himself and the three of us – me, Dessie and Ingy. The holiday atmosphere was missing. Up to date with each other in London, we didn't have too much to talk about now with just about everyone here, all ready for the election. Dessie did mention the token prick Dunstan for not coming until Good Friday morning, but otherwise he was relaxed and methodically lowering the drink. I missed Dunstan, Budge and Tom in the pub. We were like three who might fall asleep, only that Mick O'Mara's ministrations kept us awake: Ye're sure ye won't have anything, lads? Ye're sure ye're fed now? Will we see you no more Dessie? Or will you still talk to us when you're a president? Is there any news from over, lads? I hear things is very bad. There's talk there's men left behind on the footpath outside the Crown every mornin'. Will it ever end, the recession? Sure, God be with the days. The subby used to wait outside the door for Monty. Knock him up and get him out of bed. 'Twas what they had to do for good men. And those that they do pick up outside the Crown now, they say the rate is something shocking altogether. That 'tis no better than what's given out in a factory. And there's nothin' no one can do about it. 'Tis take it or leave it. Are you writin', Junior? Did you? Sure, good God gimme yere glasses, lads, we'll have to celebrate that. And Batsy, you have to be in on this, Batsy. Mary, Junior's written another book. Sure, there's nothin' better to cheer us up than great news. And Ingy, how's that lovely sister of yours, is she fine? And ye tellin' me yarns about yere poor mother that was only all made up? Is she grand, your mother, Ingy?

We had only five pints. Dessie drove us back to the house after Ingy and I collected sausage and chips and a pint of milk. 'Lock him in,' Dessie ordered Ingy. I was sleeping in Dunstan's and Peggy's bedroom, *en suite*. I said, 'Dessie, this is ridiculous. You think Charlie Anka is going to bust in and break my legs? What happens after the election? Do I still have a bodyguard?'

'After the election Charlie Anka can cut your bollix off, prima donna. No. You needn't worry. Ingy is going to look him in the eye before we go back.'

Dessie knocked us up in the morning as though he was the subby and I was Monty Gleeson. We went to the Seaview for breakfast. Dunstan's car was outside. Himself, Budge and Tom were nibbling at a penitential portion of scrambled eggs. They had left at half-seven not five. We had ours and sat around until quarter to ten. Dessie said to me, 'Find Harry's room and go up and wake him.' When I knocked on Harry's door he called out, 'Just up, Junior. Be down soon. Tell them in the kitchen to fill the frying pan.'

Some things had changed since that '55 Good Friday. The three-hour agony doesn't last three hours any more. The congregation wouldn't stand for it. Or sit for it. It's more like three-quarters of an hour. What hasn't changed is that there are no rashers or sausages being chucked on the pan in the Seaview. It was dull and cold out. Harry came down in all his cavalry twill and tweed, waistcoat and one of those sleeveless driving jackets. We introduced him to Dunstan, Tom and Budge. Harry slapped his hands. 'What's for nosh, chaps?' And before he was answered he noticed the sign: LAST BREAKFAST NINE-THIRTY. 'Oh,' Harry said.

'That's all right,' Dessie said. 'We'll get her to fix you something. What would you like?'

'I'll have the lot, please, Dessie. One of your famous fries.'

I think the explanation is shame. I have seen something like it before in other Englishmen. In Harry's case it was probably shame in front of Dunstan, Tom and Budge. Dessie told Harry how traditional they were in the Seaview. Not people who would want to convert you to their religion, but at the same time steadfast in not having rashers and sausages on the menu on Good Friday. 'Of course, of course,' Harry said, 'I understand. As a matter of fact, I think I only think I'm hungry.' He was a bit red in the face, humble in the company of Catholics who cling to their mortification, not realising that for most of us, to break the fast would be to court the third leg of a treble getting beaten by a nose. 'I'll eat after my swim,' Harry blustered. 'What time do we plunge, Dessie? Can I fit in a walk around the Seaside?'

'We have to be in the water by twelve, but I want us all

there before half-eleven. Have your walk and meet us here and I'll drive you out.'

'Isn't that it?' Harry said, pointing to his right out of the Seaview porch. 'I remember it. That's the Cove out there, am I right?'

'That's it.'

'Couldn't I walk there? How long would it take me?'

'Suit yourself. Fifteen, twenty minutes at the outside.'

'I'll get my towel . . .'

'I've a car full of towels, Harry.'

'Right. Then I'll see everybody before half-eleven.'

We sat on in the Seaview porch drinking coffee and smoking. Harry walked straight down to the prom wall and stood for a while looking out at the bay and then he went left along the seafront. Benny Bobinizer and Staff Cox came by. They had slept in their mobile homes. They were heading to the golf club for coffee. Father Ab and Father Dollars Mulcahy drove up from the Albert and called in for us to welcome Father Dollars. 'Well,' said Dessie, 'here's one man won't feel the cold,' shaking Dollars' hand and slapping the paunch. 'What do you do in America besides eat, Dollars?' Ab and Dollars went on to the golf club too.

Any car going to the Cove had to pass by one road or another that was visible from the Seaview porch. 'The Fennessys,' Dessie said. Then, 'Look at that for vulgarity.' It was Charlie Anka in a stretch limo with Maxie in the passenger seat. Francis Coleman drove up the road with Ryan-O'Brien and Shamey Flynn as passengers. Francis stopped and turned down the window. Dessie opened the porch door.

'May the best man win, Dessie,' Francis said.

'See you, Francis.'

Joe O'Connor was the first day-tripper to call in.

'She let you out?' Dessie said.

'Now, now, less of it. A thought occurred to me on the way down. What's my position? I was elected in July and a new president comes in today. Do I lose office today or do I hold on till July?'

'It depends. If Ryan-O'Brien wins you stay on till July. If I win I'll take over immediately, relieve you of the burden of office. I dunno. Ask Ab.'

'Where is Ab?'

'The golf club with Dollars.'

'I'll see you later, men.'

At eleven Dessie said, 'Let's go.'

Dunstan drove Budge and Tom out in front of us. On the way Dessie said, 'Look out for Harry. Or I'd say he's probably there already.' He wasn't. All the opposition were sitting on the rocks at the far side, stripping. Father Ab, Father Dollars and Joe O'Connor were chatting in a group. We stayed on the steps side of the Cove and Staff Cox and Benny Bobinizer came within a few minutes. The usual Cove banter passed the time, sizing up the water, some of us claiming to be wrecked from the night before. Ingy said, 'I'm going to try this famous Cove. I see the other crowd going in, Dessie, maybe the best place to talk to Charlie Anka is in the water.' Outside of the principals, there were about thirty there altogether – those who came down for the day in support of either side and some of the dregs from the golf club who had an early nine holes and came just to get the full of their mouths. The only one to arrive by bicycle was Kerr the Cop. Dessie said, 'What are you doing here, Kerr?'

'A request from that bollix over there that's standing against you in case there might be trouble.'

'Here's the cunt in my thirteenth house,' Dessie said. Timmie Frawley was at the top of the steps with Ryan-O'Brien's wife. They stayed at the top of the steps. The opposition were now in the water, Francis Coleman, hands in his anorak pockets, standing on the rocks watching them. Ingy went down our side and dived in, treading water near Charlie Anka; and said, as Ingy told us afterwards, 'Hey, look at that Junior Nash up there. I won't drown you now if you don't ever even think of looking at him again.'

'Dessie,' I said, 'it's quarter-past eleven and I don't see a sign of Harry.' Between the cliff walk and the road back to the prom there were hardly a dozen out walking and they were all couples. We could see the road as it wound and we couldn't see Harry. If the walk took twenty minutes, then Harry was at least twenty minutes away. 'Come on,' Dessie said.

We ran to Dessie's car and drove madly along the road past the golf club, the boat club, and when we turned into the prom we saw him. Harry was walking with one hand leaning for support on the prom wall. Hardly walking, dragging one leg after the other. Dessie stopped the car. 'Get out.' I ran over to Harry, while Dessie did a three-point turn.

Harry had had his gaze out over the bay and turned left to walk the prom. He went as far as the Dessie Dennison houses and then turned back and strolled up the main street, where he was kidnapped. Or, to put it another way, he met a man leaning against a doorway who said to Harry: God save you. As we reconstructed it afterwards, the man shook hands with Harry and said: Welcome, you're a stranger here I'd say. Politely, Harry Lamb gave his name. Sure, good God man, isn't the talk all about you here last night. Harry said he could get the smell of onions. And you're here for the election, aren't you the great man to come all the way to vote for Dessie, and did you stay in the Seaview and have their famous breakfast? Actually, Harry said ... It was at that point, Harry said, that he was kidnapped. What? Sure, good God man, hold on till I look up and down, the coast is clear, hop in fast till I close the door in case Batsy's around and he'd duck in under my arm.

Mick O'Mara, according to Harry, was indignant with hospitality. Sure, don't mind that crowd up in the Seaview, we're not Arabs that cut the hand off you for liftin' the pint I'm goin' to fill for you now after I put on the pan. Mary's gone off sayin' her prayers, even Eugene and Michael and Siobhan herself won't touch a bit on Good Friday, and all the bad things being said about young people. 'Twill be the first time I'll have company eatin' since long ago with Monty. Were you ever in the Crown or did you ever come across a man called Monty Gleeson? Eighteen hundred bricks he could do in a day, Monty, and 'twas Monty himself gave me the dispensation. Ah, we were off our heads in those days, young blood, and 'twas a case of often givin' all our money to the bookies outside of what we left in the Crown. I remember, 'twas one bad Holy Week with every day waitin' day till Good Friday came along and we got the brown envelopes, and I said to Monty: My God, what I wouldn't give for a steak, and Monty said: Did we eat Monday? and I said no, and he said: Did we eat Tuesday? and I said no, we didn't. Monty said: We didn't because we hadn't the price of it, but we have it now so let Monday, Tuesday, Wednesday and Thursday be four Good Fridays and we'll make today another day, and Christ if I didn't agree with him. Drink up that now to start you off.

Harry said, 'I don't think I should. Before a swim . . .'

What swim. Sure, good God, 'tis only fallin' in and two strokes and out again to say I vote for Dessie, and if you got a cramp itself, will you look at the men around you to pull you out. Sure, that Ingy could drink the Cove so fast you'd be on dry land. Hang on one minute till I turn the steaks – I've no spuds on, 'twould take too long.

The odd time Harry did have Guinness in London, a half-pint was his measure, yet he couldn't resist the exhibit that

Mick O'Mara put up in front of him. One sup from the creamy top mingling with the smell of the onions and Harry almost ran in after Mick O'Mara to the kitchen to kick the pan and tell it hurry up. Mick O'Mara shouted out to him: As Monty always said, 'tis enough to have one side tender, hunger will finish off the other side if 'twas only half done.

Mick O'Mara brought out two huge oval plates with steaks that would satisfy a Texan, oozing onions. Harry waded in with his knife and fork even before Mick O'Mara went back to the kitchen to bring out the salt and the brown vinegar. By Jasus, Mick O'Mara said, good man yourself, lep on top of it. Did you ever work on the buildin's? Harry had almost gobbled up the steak and drunk half the pint when Mick O'Mara said: 'Tis the first race I've lost in years, and went back to the kitchen and came out with a third steak on his fork, dripping grease along the pub floor. The spare man that Monty said should always be put on in case of emergencies, we'll halve it. Mick O'Mara cut a quarter for himself and forked the rest on to Harry's plate. Are you sure you never worked on the buildin's?

Harry was trying to reach the public toilet between the end of the prom and the boathouse, but once we had Harry in the car Dessie wouldn't stop. Dessie said, 'You'll have four thousand miles of lavatory in a minute.' Harry slowed us down walking on the cliff as far as the Cove, but once down the steps he stripped quickly and dived in. Harry had a beautiful stroke. Instead of just going across to the far ladder he snaked gracefully far out enough to float and break the second rule of the Cove.

The rest of our crowd went in, just a quick statutory dip. Dressed, both sides and the hangers-on came together and Joe O'Connor called for order. Joe O'Connor said a few words that I have good reason not to remember and Father Ab, a priest with a captive audience, made a witty speech in which he referred to a milestone in thwarting or anticipating

European legislation as the case may turn out to be, again a speech most of which I can no longer remember, before Father Ab said, 'All those for Dessie Dennison, that side.' Tommy Ryan-O'Brien led us across the Cove, as was always the custom of protagonists voting for each other.

Dessie, the Fennessys, Shamey Flynn, Maxie and Charlie Anka remained behind to vote for Tommy Ryan-O'Brien.

And so did Dunstan.

CHAPTER 18

I DON'T KNOW why everybody got on to me afterwards as though I was some legendary frontiersman who had failed to read the broken twigs leading us into a trap. They thought writers were supposed to be observant. We're not. We only see what's not there. I'd as much blame Harry as myself for not being a prophet. And Harry in fact is the only one I'd exempt. He'd met Dunstan for the first time that morning. When I knocked at Harry's bedroom, he had been about to go to the toilet, having some load yet to shed that he had taken aboard in the form of fish, chips and mushy peas and tea and bread and butter in a Harry Ramsden's on a coach stop. I'd distracted him and the call subsided until he staggered out of Mick O'Mara's. Dunstan had been himself that morning, apparently uninterested in the election, as he had always been apparently uninterested in everything other than the banks and his wife and latterly his business. And looking back, Budge and Tom must have played a blinder, or more likely the rest of us, me and Dessie, we were just off guard.

When I turned around after following Tommy Ryan-O'Brien over I assumed Dunstan was in dreamland. I called, 'Dunstan!' And Dessie, in position to vote for hyphen, thumped Dunstan on the shoulder and said, 'Wake up.' Dunstan didn't move. And then, suspicious for the first time, I went back over to Dunstan. I said, 'Dunstan, come on.' He looked straight out behind my head. 'Junior, go away.' I tried to pull Dunstan by the arm. 'Dunstan. Come on. Our side.' He wouldn't budge. I had to face it now. I said, 'Dunstan, please, I beg of you. Whatever you're thinking about, please, don't do it. Come on now, come over with me.'

Dessie said, 'Junior, go back.' I let go of Dunstan's arm and yet remained standing in front of him, trying to get him to look me in the eye. I said one last, 'Please, Dunstan,' and then I had to back away. Father Ab announced the result of the election. Dessie went over and shook hands with Tommy Ryan-O'Brien and Francis Coleman, and then said, 'Ingy,' and both of them went up the steps and out of the Cove.

Cranky? I was crazed. I grabbed Budge and Tom. Tom said, 'Junior, he's my son. I can say no more.' I said, 'Budge?' All he would give me was, 'It has nothing to do with me.' I went to Dunstan. I said: 'You cunt!'

'Call into the job,' Dunstan said and went up the steps.

I could guess what had happened but I couldn't believe it, didn't want to believe it. I sat down on the rocks. Harry, Staff Cox and Benny Bobinizer, Father Dollars and Ab came round me, asking, 'What happened?' I said, 'I don't know.' Budge and Tom went up the steps after Dunstan. Timmie Frawley and Tommy Ryan-O'Brien's wife came down to join the crowd congratulating hyphen. Kerr the Cop came over and said to Ab, 'Is it safe for me to go back to my business?'

I stood up, never so sick in my whole life, feeling slimy, tainted, besmirched by that cunt, that fucker, that low animal. As Dessie had disappeared in the car with Ingy, I had to walk back. Harry came with me. My last sight of the Cove that day was hyphen's wife coming out of the shelter in her bathing costume, and that ponytailed prick poet sniggering up at me.

I walked back in with Harry. 'But what went wrong, Junior?' Harry asked me. I said, 'Harry, I'm sorry. I don't want to talk about it.' When we got to the Seaview, Dessie and Ingy were waiting. I went to Dessie. I said, 'Dessie . . .' but he cut me off. Ingy was due to fly back on Saturday morning to run the Dennison Arms over the weekend. Dessie said, 'Junior, forget it. It's over. That guy's finished, gone, doesn't exist. Don't mention his name again. Harry, Ingy's going back in the morning. I can arrange it if you want to risk flying. We're leaving now. I can put you up in my house at home. What do you want to do, Junior?'

So the four of us left the Seaside, routed.

For the first thirty miles nobody spoke. It was obvious from the speed at which he was driving that Dessie was eaten up with murderous disappointment, hatred. Then he eased his angry foot off the accelerator slightly and started to talk to Ingy about some of their day-to-day problems in the Crescent Group of pubs, business they normally dealt with in the office but that Dessie adopted now to try and shut Dunstan out of his heart. Who needed to be switched where to cover holidays. Harry and I sat in the back and didn't speak. When we got home Dessie said, looking at me in the mirror, 'Where do you want me to drop you, Junior?'

'Dunstan's.'

I had hardly got my second foot out of the back of the car when Dessie engaged first gear, but I had time to say, 'Dessie, I can't tell you how . . .'

'Junior, you did everything I asked you to do. You might be a nutcase but you're straight. You're a guy I wouldn't like to lose. And Harry. Harry, your summer holiday stands. It'll be there for you always. Now Junior, it's good to have you around. But it can only be this way. You can't mention the name again, the name of that thing across the road. Now fuck off, I'm busy.'

I stood outside Dunstan's, looking after the car, sweaty with shame. Then I was in a hurry. I wanted to get into that building, listen to the shit and forget about him just as much as Dessie. I went up the seventy-eight steps so fast that I was out of breath when I opened the door. I stood there, still holding the knob, taking in Dunstan, sitting at his desk, his feet up on another chair, tapping one of those paper boxes that holds a ream and that he uses to keep his odds and ends. He was grinning.

'Junior, get a load of this.'

He took out a cheque book and flicked it like a dealer thumbing a deck of cards. He held it out to me. It had DT OFFSET printed on it.

'From the Provincial. Where it all started, Junior. That's what makes it sweet. And here.'

A second cheque book. In his own name.

'There's two grand of an overdraft with DT OFFSET. And five hundred on the personal account. But! Wait for it, Junior. Look at this.'

A term loan document. Five thousand. Written after PURPOSE OF LOAN was ATTIC CONVERSION.

'Well?' Dunstan said, still grinning but impatient, wanting me to do a jig. We think we can act. I tried to be exaggeratedly composed. I let the two cheque books and the term-loan document slip from my fingers on to the floor and started to walk about the room. 'For fuck's sake,' Dunstan said to my back. I could hear him getting up from the chair to gather up his booty. 'What's the matter with you?'

I walked around like an inspector, hands behind the back, stopping to read the outside sheets on the packed parcels of finished jobs. I looked into the darkroom. The double-drainer sink was gleaming when before all you noticed was rust. The stocked shelves, quality paper and board. The whole range of inks. The Gestetner itself had been attacked with white spirit. The whole prosperous gleaming well-oiled operation making his treachery so much worse. I stopped on the far side of the Gestetner and leaned on the machine.

'And you got it all for just a little vote.' I tried the jaunty, the sarcastic. But then I couldn't act any more. 'You cunt! You slimy heap of shit!'

'Hold it. Hold it there kid. Jesus. You were the guy who was supposed to have understood. But *you* weren't through it. *You* hadn't a holiday robbed from in front of your eyes. Now you just listen, let me explain . . .'

'*Shut up*! Shut up, you low fucking animal, you. I don't know what anything means! No. I'm some ape! Your holiday was robbed and I don't understand it? Because it didn't happen to me? Listen to me, you fuckpig, you. Did I have parents? I had fuck-all parents. Did I live with it? *I lived with it*. I was brought up by Budge, right? Great man, the finest, but how shall we put it, prick, Budge was . . . a bit unschooled? Tom Tucker mightn't have gone to school much, but he had a feeling for literature. I had to be alone all my life – my greatest hopes, my longings, I had to keep them to myself, the only one I had for family wouldn't understand. I lived through you. You had everything that I wanted, but all I ever got in my fucking life was my name on a book and a fuck once in the blue moon from some decent drunken woman in a pub. But you were always there, I had you and Peggy and Warren, like I was split in two and you were the part of me that got all the normal things, the best things. And I could be happy because you were more than a brother to me, I loved you because you were my pal, I cheered you from the sidelines when the banks were at you, I worried, I never met Dessie but I asked about you. I loved you like I loved Budge, your father, Peggy, Warren . . .'

'I love you too, Junior . . .'

'Shut up, you, you . . . you smell. What you did to me was to pour stink over me. You suffered, you say. You don't suffer when you sell out to cure it. You gave in to it. Dessie Dennison never refused you a bank loan. Budge didn't. Nor Peggy. Nor your own son. Or Tom. I didn't. But you covered us all in shame. You're a weakling. What are you? You're blind, you're . . . you're characterless, you're shit. That's it. That's what you are. What are you, Tucker? You're shit, Tucker. What are you?'

'I'll try again.' Dunstan came opposite me to the other side of the machine. 'Because I want you to remember, Junior . . .'

'I'll help *your* memory. You shit. In case the pain might ever be tempted to go away and you might forget what the big bold banks did to the poor little boy on his mother's lap, in case in a moment of weakness you might ever forget Joe the Boss. You remember Joe the Boss? In case you might ever be tempted to forget Joe the Boss. Here . . .' I spat across the machine into his face.

His eyes closed but not from the spit. He gripped the side of the machine and the tears came with the old facility of his interviews with Billy Bowman. But I just said, 'Hey, don't waste your tears. I'm not a bank manager. You cunt!'

Deranged as I was with hatred – not the old fly-off-the-handle anger, the real, nasty business – still I didn't run down the stairs. Holding the banister, I clumped down carrying the gut hope that he might appear on the top landing and shout come back, I can explain.

I'd left my bag in the Dessie Dennison house. So, I realised now, had Ingy. But all we had brought were toilet things. I had my plane ticket and my money. I couldn't face going home, walking up the street past Dunstan's house. There were traffic jams heading out to the suburban shopping centres and the town itself was wide open except for the pubs and picture houses. Penance now was confined to movie buffs and drinkers. Me. But the good news was that the travel agent was open. I had enough to switch my ticket to the midday Saturday flight – Ingy and Harry were going out early – and to get the bus and stay in the airport hotel and bribe the porter to feed me the drink that helped me cry through the night.

CHAPTER 19

I WAS NOW able to tell Tony that I wouldn't need any more time off from the bookstall. Harry didn't ring to invite me to Sunday dinner, but then he didn't know I was back. And I didn't ring Harry because I didn't want to meet him, didn't want to meet anyone connected with the Cove. I did my weekend drinking downstairs, my Sherwood Anderson on the table, not wanting to talk even with Bill. But I didn't read. I stared through the book and beyond it into my misery, trying not to cry.

On Monday night I went to the Corner Flag to confront the cunt who must have put the other cunt up to it. 'He's not here,' Jack Fagan said. 'I was going to ask you if you knew where he was. He was due on Saturday morning. He didn't show. I've just been on to Dessie. He cut the nose off me. He said: Forget him. Carry on yourself till I arrange things. What happened over, Junior? Dessie lost, some mate of yours shopped him?'

'He's no mate of mine, Jack.'

I left and went to the Dennison Arms. Dessie was drinking one of his quiet pints away in a corner, away from the Daltons, reading the weekend sales figures from all his pubs. I said, 'I was in the Corner Flag, Jack told me about Chuckey. It fits. It was probably his idea that Dunstan . . .'

'What did I tell you? What was the last thing I said to you?'

'I was just . . .'

'Don't. It's over. We won't talk about it again. And don't mention the thing's name.'

'I fucked him out of it . . .'

'Junior, please. I don't want to hear. You want something to do, go back to work on our secret.'

CHAPTER 20

AN APPARITION HASN'T been seen like it since Barry Fitzgerald's mother appeared from nowhere in the last half-minute of *Going My Way*. But this was no *deus ex machina*. As far back as the night Brother Chuckey clocked Baptista, Dessie said to me: Do you know what I think we should do? And I had agreed: I like it. I like it, Dessie.

I went to the Crown just on opening time on a Wednesday morning. The barman on duty was young, a lively, talkative guy, in love with barwork, knowing that he was passing through, taking a sabbatical before he went back home to do medicine at Trinity.

'How, sir, may I help you this dreadful morning, thank God, as half the lunatics who come in here are always saying?'

'Coffee, please.'

'Super. You ever notice that? You go into a shop or a pub and no matter what you buy, they either never say thanks at all or they go overboard and say: Super. Or: Magic. You pay someone for a box of matches and they say: That's great. I prefer the "there you go" animals. They're honest. All they mean is it's terrible to have to work in this bollix of a place. Cream?'

'Please.'

'There you go. Magic. Super. Fifty pence. Thank you.'

'I wonder, can you help me . . .'

'Shoot. We're here to serve.'

'I'm looking for a chap . . .'

'With a beard?'

'I don't know, I doubt it . . .'

'I've been here for the past two summers. Now I'm just doing a year before I go to college. They figure I'm a year young. Not too young to kill myself getting the points. But before I came here first I worked for a couple of weeks in the West End. Guy comes in. Excuse me, I'm looking for a chap named whatever he was named. I say: I'm new here. Guy says: He has a black beard. I look around me. I'm the only one in the whole pub who owns a razor. So you're not looking for a beard? Pity. Because no beards come in here. Except the odd one.'

'The man I'm looking for, his name is Monty Gleeson. He would have worked on the buildings . . .'

'The buildings? A guy who worked on the buildings? In the Crown? Now he'd stick out in here. I mean, among all the ex-prime ministers.'

'The name mean anything to you?'

'What you say, Gleeson. I can't think of anyone this year. By the law of averages there must be a Gleeson. The two summers I was here, I'm going to shock you now, I was shy. You wouldn't know I was here. I was afraid to talk to people. God, I used to blush and everything if you just looked at me. Gas. Look at me now. But I didn't get to know the people much the way I do now. What'd he look like, your friend?'

'I don't know. He could be anything – sixty, sixty-five – but he was famous on the buildings in his day. He used to sing a song, before your time, you ever hear of "South of the Border" . . .'

'I have him! Jesus, that man! Fuck! Such laughin'. *Up Mexico Way*. The old English fiver. The old penny. He could do eighteen thousand bricks a day?'

'Eighteen hundred.'

'Whatever. I'd swear that guy said eighteen thousand. I spoke to him once. No. I listened to him. A morning just like this, like you, he was first in, called a pint, he got talking to me about the old days. Gas. The old days. Fucking gas. Did you ever see an old English fiver yourself?'

'When I was a kid, yeah.'

'Big?'

'Yeah, I think so. I think it was white.'

'Well, according to your friend the thing was as big as a bedspread. He was paying for the pint with one of the new fivers and he said he could remember when money was money. In the old days. He was an outlandish liar. The old penny, you know what size that was? You could use it for the wheel of a cart. They're all like that in here. They'll be in in a minute. Now that you mention him, I haven't seen him this year or last summer. I'd say he's dead.'

A man wearing a cap, frayed donkey jacket and using a walking stick came in. 'Vincent will know,' the barman said. 'Morning, Mr Byrnes. Usual?'

'I'll water it meself.'

'Vincent, gentleman here is looking for Monty Gleeson.'

Vincent said, 'Aye.' He fumbled out the price of the whiskey. 'Is that so? Monty'll be here no more.'

'Is he dead, Vincent?'

'No. This man isn't a tax man?'

'I'd say not, Vincent. Are you?'

'No. A friend of mine who knew Monty asked me to look him up and give him his best wishes.'

'No matter anyway. He's in that nursing home they have in Kilburn. I can't go there, I'm no good to visit hospitals or places like that. Or the mortuaries. They found him on the floor. And the hospital wouldn't let him out unless he had someone to go to. He's like myself, he had no one. That's where he is. He could do eighteen hundred bricks a day. If you see him, tell him Vincent was asking for him. Tell him I'll go to see him when I can. I know I can't, but don't tell him that.'

I waited until the afternoon to go to the Marian Nursing Home, to coincide with visiting hours. But even as I rang the bell I read: VISITING ALL DAY. I was answered by a pleasant old skivvy to whom I think I almost gave a heart attack when I said: May I see Mr Monty Gleeson, please. She spoke to two people at the same time, to me, pulling me by the sleeve, 'Come in, come in, sir. Nurse Fidelma! Nurse Fidelma, it's a visitor. To see Mr Gleeson.' A starched bosom and white hat framed the happy, smiling, healthy face as Nurse Fidelma looked out from what was an office no bigger than an under the stairs closet.

'You're very welcome,' Nurse Fidelma said. 'Margaret, put on the kettle. Are you a relative, Mr . . .'

'Nash. Junior Nash. No. I have never actually met him. A friend of mine back home asked me to look him up.'

'Oh.'

The Marian Nursing Home is run by the parish. Two adjoining houses knocked together and bought on mortgage. It had ten bedrooms and a television lounge, kitchen, dining room and a mass room that doubled as a reception for the hard to please who did not like to visit in a television lounge. A blackmailed roster of doctors gave their free time to check on the health of the patients. As did the nurses nurse for nothing. The only people who were paid were Margaret and another skivvy who cooked, cleaned and made the beds. Their wages, running expenses and the mortgage were funded from cans rattled outside mass and in the Sunday morning Crown.

Nurse Fidelma said, 'Come into the kitchen, we'll be more private.' She showed me where to sit at the table and then hauled a chair for herself almost up on top of me, put an ashtray between us, pulled out her fags. I said I'd stay with my own brand. Margaret ran around like a blue-arsed fly, flinging assorted biscuits on a plate and trying to encourage the kettle.

'Your friend, is he related to Monty?'

'No. He was his greatest friend – worked with him on the buildings. A long time ago.'

'Oh.'

Margaret poured the tea and sat with us, again almost on top of me at the other side of the table. She took out her own fags.

'He's very difficult,' Nurse Fidelma said, and Margaret agreed by just lifting her eyes. 'We've only six here at the moment. Monty won't talk to John because John was only a barman. He won't talk to Paddy because he says Paddy was a tapper. Martin and Paul he thinks are the worst, because they worked in factories. Sometimes he'll talk to old Donal, but old Donal can't talk back, he's all gone down one side from strokes and he can only grunt.'

Monty was found on the floor. Almost on closing time the third night in a row that he was missing from the Crown, they investigated his doss. He'd fallen against the cooker, broken ribs. He'd lost his balance. He had never been to a doctor. In the hospital they saw that his blood pressure was gone through the roof. Monty's kip was on a top floor. Without anybody to care for him, the authorities would release Monty only to the Marian. But he was lucky there in that the Marian did not commandeer anybody's pension, funded as it was by the can. That was almost two years ago. In the early days he did get a few visitors, not many, but they were old men, had died.

'He can walk,' Nurse Fidelma said. 'Ask Margaret.

Sometimes he leaves the bathroom door half open. He doesn't have to put his hands on the toilet seat and heave himself out of the wheelchair like people like him should have to do. He justs stands up and walks. No, I'm wronging Monty – we can trust you, Mr Nash? He doesn't leave the bathroom door open, it's not fair to say he's forgetful when he's not. I look in the keyhole. As a nurse that's permitted, and because I can trust Margaret to be able for it, I let Margaret look. But we say Monty leaves the door open because we don't want the other girl who works in the kitchen to look in keyholes. Monty won't let us into the bathroom when he's having a bath. It's a big bathroom because sometimes you have to have room for two strong nurses and a wheelchair and the patient. Monty gets out of the wheelchair and walks to the bath and has no bother walking in over the side. But for spite he spends all day in the wheelchair and we can just about get him to use the walker, right, Margaret?'

Margaret let the smoke out through her nose, snorting nostrils of agreement.

Nurse Fidelma and Margaret escorted me to the television room to see the lion king with the thorn in his paw. Two were in wheelchairs, Monty and old Donal. John the ex-barman, Paddy the tapper and Martin and Paul who only worked in factories were sunk into armchairs. They all seemed to be nodding off while the televised cricket watched them.

'Monty.' Nurse Fidelma smiled at Monty, giving him a little shake. 'A visitor, Monty.'

He was wearing a rumpled brown striped suit, the Sunday uniform of the old days. And a jumper, shirt without a tie and a scuffed pair of brand-name runners. There was a tray attached to the wheelchair, on it an ashtray and roll your own tobacco. He was shrunken, unless Mick O'Mara was the greatest liar in the world, didn't look now like he could do eighteen hundred breaths a day. The hair, what was left of it, was a natural dirty oiled grey, brushed back.

'Who's that?' Monty said to Nurse Fidelma after looking at me and showing no love.

'He's come all the way from home to see you, Monty. Junior Nash, Monty. Now, we'll talk better in the mass room.'

Nurse Fidelma began to wheel him as Monty said, 'I know no Nash.'

Nurse Fidelma and Margaret ranged three chairs in a semicircle around Monty, seating me in the middle. 'Who are you?' Monty barked at me.

'Now, Monty, be nice. You have a visitor, right, Margaret?'

'That's right, Nurse Fidelma. Be good now, Monty.'

I pulled out my nervous fags.

'Gold Flake,' Monty said, staring at the box.

I offered him one. 'I haven't seen Gold Flake since . . . I don't know you.'

'That's right, Mr Gleeson. But a great friend of yours asked me to see you. A man who's always talking about you. Mick O'Mara . . .'

'Who?'

'Mick O'Mara.'

'I don't know him.'

'You must. He's always boasting that you taught him to sing "South of the Border – " I was becoming confident, with the backing of Nurse Fidelma and Margaret, so I added, 'Up Mexico Way.'

'That could be anyone. That could be hundreds.'

'Mick O'Mara says you could do eighteen hundred bricks a day . . .'

Monty shifted a bit, gave a little cough. 'That's well known.'

'Monty,' Nurse Fidelma said, 'why don't you sit on the armchair? You'll be more comfortable, stretch your legs.'

'I can't walk.'

'Yes, you can. If you try. If you want to. Margaret, get the walker there. Now. Come on. Up with you.' Nurse Fidelma unlatched the tray from over Monty's lap while Margaret pushed the walker in front of him. He made a big effort getting out of the wheelchair and holding the walker as he dragged himself a few paces into the armchair. 'Now. That's better, Monty. Go on, Mr Nash.'

'And you had steak on Good Friday. Mick O'Mara said you yourself gave him permission to eat steak on Good Friday because things were tight early in the week.'

That puzzled him into trying to remember. 'Mick O'Mara. Mick O'Mara. Won't come. But I only gave permission to good men. Some I'd have on hunger strike for their whole lives if I had my way. The likes of Byrnes. Mick O'Mara. Mick O'Mara . . .'

'I met a Byrnes this morning, asking for you. In the Crown. A Vincent Byrnes. He said he's going to call to see you.'

'Latchiko. Tea boy. Worse. Tea boy who never earned it. Poured porter into foremen. Lazy fucker . . . Sorry, nurse. Sorry, Margaret. I gave that bollix a quid and he was late and the horse won at a hundred to seven. Call to see me. 'Twould be like what would happen to me. All the good men dead and only the likes of him left. The Crown now, in the old days I wouldn't be lying there for three – ' Monty started to cry – 'three fuckin' days and nights on the floor . . . an' I'm here now . . . my room gone that I had for thirty years . . .'

He fumbled out a brown handkerchief that had been born white.

'Monty, give me that. Use this tissue. Margaret, take that out to the laundry basket. You bold boy, Monty.' Nurse

Fidelma went on to distract us all from the man who was crying into a tissue, crying and lamenting. 'All gone . . . no one left . . . room and all gone . . . wouldn't let me home to my room . . . gone . . . 'cos I get dizzy . . . you can't even get dizzy when you get old now . . . in a house with factory workers . . .'

He was a pitiful sight. Shrunken as he was, yet the old strength of the man fought not to cry. Fought and lost.

'Mick O'Mara,' I said.

'I don't know him! I've no one. I'm crucified!'

'He knew you in the Crown . . .'

Monty trapped the end of a tear with the tissue and wiped it back up his face. 'The Crown.' He spat the name of the pub. 'They don't talk any more, they don't sing. They don't listen. It's all Manchester United, it's all they care about. They're hopin' to be left behind when the van calls in the mornin'. Some of 'em. So they can be all day in the pub. They'll watch anything. Runners. They're glued to lunatics throwin' spears up in the air to see how far they would land. And cricket and golf and tennis and madmen driving cars around bends and crashin' and all burstin' out in flames. The barmen only humour you . . .'

'Quick.' Margaret rushed back. 'It's Sister Josephina.' Margaret put her own cigarette out in the ashtray. Nurse Fidelma had a long last pull and did the same. 'You're all right, Mr Nash. You're keeping Monty company with your Gold Flake. Monty, try and remember this man Mr Nash is come from. Mick O'Mara. Concentrate on the name: Mick O'Mara.'

The doorbell rang. Margaret went to admit Sister Josephina.

I said, 'He's in the Seaside. He has a pub and a farm.'

'How would I know him. One of those fly-by-nights that passed through here. All the good men ended up with nothin'. The best of 'em. Old Paddy Mackessy. On the floor like me. 'Twas only half-past eight in the Crown an' he used to come in at eight, an' I said: Somethin's up, an' I led everyone out to find him an' the doctor could prove he was only dead an hour. Pubs. Farms. My arse.'

'Monty,' Sister Josephina said, 'Monty you have a visitor!'

I stood up and shook hands with Sister Josephina, a Medical Missionary of Mary, in full habit. No bicycle clips or crash helmets. She folded her arms inside her sleeves. 'And you're up and in your armchair. Good. That's good, Monty. Are you ready for our game?'

Monty said, ' . . . no change, a latchiko said when we collected for Paddy Mackessy. That's good, I said, and tore his wages out of his arse pocket. Because if you tried to give me change I'd stuff your mouth with half-crowns till you choked . . .'

'Now Monty, you can play where you sit. Ah, Martin. John. Paul. Margaret, bring in old Donal. And wake up Paddy if he's asleep.'

The factory workers and the ex-barman shuffled in and Margaret wheeled old Donal and Paddy walked beside her, holding the wheelchair and yawning and chewing his gummy lips. 'Give out the books now, Margaret.'

Martin, John, Paul and Paddy moved their chairs close to Monty and old Donal in his wheelchair. Margaret gave them their books and a stunted bookie's biro each. Nurse Fidelma got the table tennis ball from the drawer of the dresser, from behind which Sister Josephina pulled out a topless and bottomless wooden set of squares. 'We'll begin,' Sister Josephina breezed, lobbing the table tennis ball to bob before it settled in a square. 'Hmm. On its own. Number four. And, today, two Scots Clan for a line and three York-shire Toffees for a house.'

Nurse Fidelma and Margaret came with me to the front

door. Nurse Fidelma had to use a key from the inside. 'In case they get wanderlust,' she explained. We stood in the hall, Margaret already again puffing. I joined Nurse Fidelma in one more fag. Both of them looked at me as though I was some sort of exotic visitor. Which I was. Nurse Fidelma said, 'Will you come again? He might remember.'

I said, 'It depends on my instructions. After I make my report.'

'Mick O'Mara might know something that will remind Monty.'

I couldn't tell her that my report was to Dessie. Not yet. I said, 'I'll see.' I shook hands with them both. Half-way down the street, a penetration in the back of my neck impelled me to turn round. They were still at the door. They waved. I waved back.

CHAPTER 21

THERE HAD BEEN only three people in Mick O'Mara's on Good Friday night, Kerr the Cop, Batsy and Mick O'Mara. Dessie heard that from Mick O'Mara himself when Dessie was home for a weekend and saw Mick O'Mara in town to buy a suit, wandering the main street and looking up at the two-storey buildings, having by now forgotten the big buildings of London, where in the old days they probably had rarely looked up. Only sang up. Dessie was in a hurry someplace but stopped the car and got out to say hello out of politeness. Isn't there great changes, Dessie, Mick O'Mara said, but Dunstan let you down they say. Dessie said he didn't want to talk about it. I understand, Mick O'Mara said, sure we could hardly talk about it ourselves when Kerr the Cop brought in the news, only Batsy there with us guardin' the fire. 'Twas so dead we closed at closin' time even though there was supposed to be no openin' time.

But the celebrations that were to have taken place on Good Friday were nothing to the night Dessie had planned for July, when he hoped to spring Monty on Mick O'Mara. Everybody would be there. Now, when I mentioned Monty, Dessie said, 'OK, we know where he is. Leave it. We'll see when the time comes.'

One night, almost two weeks after Good Friday, I was drinking with Bill when Bill said, 'How's your writing going?' I had forgotten about my book. Next morning I was around to the publishers at opening time. Himself was in New York but he'd left a letter for me only two days ago before he left, puzzled that I hadn't called.

Very much afraid this latest will do nothing to add to your reputation. Thank God. Congratulations. Usual advance.

Even at that, celebrating with Bill, the drink was tasteless. Not being able to ring and say, 'Dunstan . . .'

April, May, June, and the pain of his treachery would not go away. Now that I wasn't writing, Tony got me Monday and Tuesday work on the stall of a mate of his in Camden. That helped to get through the days.

Harry rang, but I told him that I didn't know when I would be able to go again on Sunday, that Tony was extending the market to a full day. I couldn't face Harry and mother at Sunday dinner. No matter who I was with now – Bill in the pub, a customer at the bookstall – I could think of nothing but Dunstan. Or 'thing', as Dessie would only refer to him. I thought Dessie would skimp on the Monty mission, an extension as it was to be of Dessie's presidential celebrations. But no. In the end Dessie honoured his promise.

The first Saturday in July is traditionally the official opening of the Seaside – when the primary school children start their holidays. But the June weekends bring a crowd. And the heatwave began in the middle of June and lasted until mid-October. Those with small babies too young even for that excrescence, the pre-school, they come in June. As do those just finished the leaving cert. And the retired. Idle. And those too poor to be able to afford the July and August rates. But not too poor that they have to go abroad.

Dessie would not mention the 'thing' but gradually he began to talk about the Seaside again. Yes, the women had arrived. Even in June, with the heatwave, the Cove was a crowded place now. Charlie Anka was back this year. And Francis Coleman was there. Tommy Ryan-O'Brien's wife did all but send a maid down early to book a flat rock for her rug and she had a gang of cronies who were an awful sight in bathing costumes. But against that there were also the younger crowd, in bikinis, and the men of course, gentlemen, true to the gentlemanly spirit of defeat, had to wear trunks that could not be voluminous enough to cloak the perpetual erections. There was a claim that someone swam far out into the Cove to wank, but nobody believed that it could be done.

Despite the sun, the bulging tits and tight bums, the colour, the crowd, – the month before the season officially began – the Cove was a gloomy place. Not a decent joke heard. By which was meant indecent.

Dunstan had not been seen there once. That was hardly a surprise. But neither had Tom Tucker. Nobody knew if Budge would come. Every year he booked his holiday when leaving the Seaview on the last day in August by saying: See you next year.

I used to wonder how parents survived the early tragic death of young children. Now I knew. They didn't. I was alive myself, could see the reflection in the mirror. I carried on like those parents did, a little of them dead. Possibly like them I had so much to be happy about now, were it not for the death. Downstairs with Bill, in the sweltering heat, letting my pint go flat, having Bill observe, 'Not in good form tonight, mate,' I had to lie.

Bill said after a few weeks, 'How's your friend that those bank cunts were botherin'? Haven't heard him phone you in a while, unless that George takes messages and forgets.'

I said, 'He's fine. He's a booming business now.' That was

still true. Dessie had reported, his only reference to Dunstan, 'I met Maxie. He's trying to snake back into my good books. Gave me a business card in case I ever needed to contact him. Wrote his ex-directory home number on it like he does with every dog in the road that he gives a card to. He said he'd had this batch printed at DT Offset. Maxie said: you know how it is, Dessie? We gotta survive. He gave the thing a bit of business because *it* had helped him to be on a winning team, businesswise. Then Maxie said: what happened though on Good Friday, Charlie says he doesn't know, hyphen won't tell me, says he doesn't know either. I said, Maxie, you're just a heap of shit.'

If I could only have talked it through with Bill. But I couldn't. Couldn't say: You mean Dunstan? That's the Dunstan I grew up with since we were babies. Made our First Communion together and all that. That Dunstan? Oh, he just turned out to be a heap of shit. A dead baby.

I sweated through the heatwave, unable to look forward to the plunge on the first Saturday in July. But it did come, the first Saturday in July. I went over with Dessie on the plane Saturday morning. Dessie had got Ingy to hire a mini-bus to bring Harry and mother, Monty, Nurse Fidelma and Margaret and the Daltons. They arrived at the Seaside early Saturday morning, put Monty to bed in Dessie's own Dessie Dennison house, to be fit for the night. We met Ingy in the Cove. Nurse Fidelma and Margaret took turns minding Monty and walking the prom. The Daltons hit the pub.

Dessie and I reached the Cove at just after two. Ingy was there before us. We had a lucky dip, lucky because by half-three there wasn't room to dive in between ladder and ladder, you would have had to walk far out on the rocks to where the Cove gaped into the ocean. So early after lunch, there was still a fair crowd when we arrived, maybe thirty – I counted four of them women, two together and one each on her own. And they were there as calmly as they might have been found in a coffee shop. As though it was natural. Already. Yet they didn't bother me. Having to swim with the trunks on was an irritant but, cooled down, sitting on the rocks, the ladies – only four of them there yet – seemed a horde carrying barbarian banners, in huge letters: THE ONE TRUE PAL OF YOUR LIFE IS A SHIT. On a day that should have been the most joyous: Monty in Mick O'Mara's.

The Cove began to fill up. Every now and then I looked to the top of the steps to see if Budge would come. The hyphen, Charlie Anka and the hyphen's wife came, the wife carrying a transistor and the hyphen carrying the wife's rug. 'There it is,' one of the old-timers noted, 'a transistor. What was I always saying?' Father Ab arrived with Father Dollars, home again from the fat parish in Oregon. All was as it used to be in the Cove except the weather was wonderful and all greetings had to include some comment on the mixed status now, like, from Ab, 'Afternoon boys. And girls. Good boys now, all togs on.'

Some women who came down were happy simply to have a dip on a beautiful day in this famous Cove that their husbands or boyfriends had told them about. And soon we had our own gang together – Joe O'Connor, who said, 'I had a row with my wife. I said: No, I will not bring you down, until I get proper permission when the time comes', Staff Cox and Benny Bobinizer, and Maxie, who togged off on his own, spoke to everybody, both factions, and to the women, not bothered in his bollix whether anybody spoke back to him or not. And on the subject of bollix, Charlie Anka went into the water at the same time as hyphen's wife. Showing a form of leadership.

By half-three the Cove was packed. It seemed that everyone who had ever been there before was here now, plus the women of both sexes, everybody except . . . I looked up and saw the procession.

Warren, as you would expect impatient youngsters to be,

was in the vanguard. Followed by a stranger. Then Budge and Tom. Then Dunstan and Peggy, Dunstan carrying two small folding chairs. And Brother Chuckey and the Kodak man. Brother Chuckey wore his black pants, black socks and black sandals and his black shirt, though without the constricting collar. They went over to the rocks on the far side, had to pass us first. I could figure Dunstan. Brazen-it-out department. Like those guys who fiddle funds, name on the papers, but without the balls to fuck off and emigrate and hide all over the world, too homesick without ever having been away, they hang in, salute you to death, with bounce-back determination to put shame behind them, hang in until it fades into: Wasn't there something once about that fellow and missing money years ago? Until people die and others are born and in the middle some grow up and the brazen balls has air to breathe that doesn't cling any more. Survivors, they're called. I said to myself, you can survive to be a thousand, Dunstan, you cunt, but the day it's forgotten I'll never forget to remind you, and I'm fucked if I'm saluting any of that crowd coming down now, except Warren. And Budge. I have to salute Tom too. Fuck that Kodak man, he was in on it somehow, and whoever that other guy is and bollix Chuckey. And no, I will not salute Peggy either, because she knows. She knows he was wrong. If it's her job to stand by him, tough shit. She's wrong.

None of them saluted me or any of us. They filed past, heads set, until they were all together on the far rocks, like some odd outing.

They stripped immediately, the men wriggling into the trunks under cover of a towel. Peggy had hers on already under the shorts and T-shirt. Women are crafty like that. There were yelps from the Kodak man and the stranger when they dived in, strangers to the Cove, not inured to the cold water. But once they stayed in a while they got used to it and we could hear them yapping happily to each other as we just sat there in the gloom. I thought it was Babylonian the way they enjoyed themselves, splashing about and floating and agreeing: Isn't it brilliant? No wonder you kept it to yourselves, Budge, I heard Peggy trill. The sparkle of the sea, the sun, the purity of the water, the air, the Cove had never looked so beautiful and I wished to God it was all over and we had done our business with Monty so that I could escape from this paradise full of serpents and back to cold baths in London to get through the day. Away from Budge and Tom and Peggy and Warren. And Dunstan. I don't think anybody noticed that I was crying, intent as they were watching traitors making love to the Cove nectar.

That was wonderful, they said to each other as they dried and then smuggled themselves back into their clothes. I watched Dunstan light his post-swim cigarette, thought of how he used to squat beside me. He unfolded his little chairs for himself and Peggy. Brother Chuckey, carrying his black short coat over his arm, led the rest away, Budge, Tom, the Kodak man, the stranger. It was odd that they were leaving and Dunstan, Peggy and Warren staying on. Odder that Brother Chuckey led them straight towards us as he waved in the direction of the top of the steps at the descending Francis Coleman.

'You first,' Brother Chuckey said to Dessie as everybody sat down to encircle our circle. 'If I was to say to you, Mr Dennison, that Dunstan Tucker was at a stage in his life when he was down, couldn't fall further, and his good wife helped him to stand up and whip his business into a healthy shape with the confidence she gave him, would it not be the act of an ingrate to vote to keep such a woman out of the Cove? Sit down, Francis.'

Dessie said to Brother Chuckey, 'Fuck off.'

'As for you, Nash. Are you listening, Nash? Do I need to shake you up? It was Francis Coleman's idea . . .'

'Who are these people?' Dessie said.

'I'm the Kodak man,' the Kodak man smiled at me. 'This is my brother.'

I said to Dessie, 'The Kodak man. And the Kodak man's brother.'

' . . . right, Francis?'

Francis Coleman nodded.

'Francis went to Dunstan and offered him the bank facilities through Timmie Frawley. What did Dunstan say, Francis?'

'He laughed,' Francis said. 'He said: So you know my weak spot? He said if it was anybody else but Dessie, if it was Junior, he'd grab the bank money because Junior would understand and that personally Dunstan got itchy when he wasn't near women, but sorry, no can do, Dunstan said. He said if it was Joe O'Connor standing, or Budge or even his own father, Tom Tucker, he'd vote against them to grab the money but no, not Dessie Dennison. So I said: Why? What's so special about Dessie? Dunstan said that what's so special about Dessie Dennison was that Dessie was the only one in the world he wouldn't do it to. And that there was no one more special than that. I did my best. I tried to persuade him that Dessie would understand. Dunstan said no, Dessie would not understand, and that he wouldn't respect Dessie any more if Dessie did understand. Every man to his own honour, Dunstan said. He said: Sorry, Francis, you have no idea how sorry I am. I made him promise he'd think about it for a week.'

'Nash,' Brother Chuckey resumed, 'the night Dunstan rang me in the Corner Flag, next day was Saturday. I wasn't due on until the afternoon. I met Dunstan at Heathrow, we had a two-hour coffee between his flight over and back. He hadn't mentioned it to his wife. You know about his mother's lap, Nash? For the whole week after Francis Coleman propositioned him, Dunstan was on his mother's lap. He said he was demented again. With pain. He was afraid.

He'd seen it in the AA, heard people confessing how they could rationalise and justify all sorts of low behaviour when they were besotted. He was afraid that would happen to him. He begged me to cure him. I said: Cure you of what, Tucker? Of trying to get money from banks, he said. I said I would certainly do that. I said: Will you be happy then, Tucker? He said no. Then, I said, I won't cure you. We talked for the two hours. We met next in Dublin Airport with our friends here, after Dunstan, as I instructed him, asked Francis for another week.'

I had never met the Kodak man's brother before but I had an image of someone with a velvet collar and drainpipes. He was wearing a bookie's Bahamas shirt and shorts that reached below the knees. He spoke.

'Never met Dunstan until now but I liked his form. When the Kodak kid here used to tell me Dunstan had made another hit, I'd go on the brandy for a night. I liked his style, his what'll I call it, his innocence, 'cos that's the way I used to be one time myself. Didn't confuse the bankers with human beings or anything, but I used to think they were just poor dopes who had a job to do who wouldn't be capable of getting a job any place else. Until this time that something went wrong for me and I had to lease a car, because I needed a car in a hurry and it was before I could get back on my feet and the banks were pushing leasing and wouldn't part with the spondulix so that I could go to Mannie Manifold Motors and do a deal for cash. Never could get to like that car. I had to open this account that the money would come out of every month and I filled it up for three months. Then it was in April, I think, they started sending me letters that probably started We Note Your Account, but I don't know, I didn't open them. June I was well back in action myself and could have gone to Mannie and got a good deal, but I said: I may as well run this heap into the ground first and give it to my wife to go into town for coffee with her pals. The letters start to come registered – you know the bank logo that they spend millions on, they just print it in black when it's their legal people writing to you. Never get angry with a banker. Never. I rang up and oiled the guy over the phone, big deal coming through, asked him what's your best deposit rate over a hundred grand one year. I thought they were happy enough, certainly would have been in the old days, because they always knew I was going nowhere, they knew where to find me in Foxrock, where I've always rented from my son since he was old enough not to have me rent it from my aunt, who's frail and frightened when I ask her to sign things. I dragged on until second week in September, but you can imagine, business or no business, my mind was on nothing but the Dubs in the final. I'd to go to the airport to pick up our cousin Father Cyril – he was coming from New York with the tickets. Driving to the airport to collect him, I actually said to myself: This is no heap to be picking Father Cyril up in, I'll give it to the wife tomorrow and see Mannie. Father Cyril had six tickets for the Hogan Stand, five rows behind where Dev was sitting. We just had a couple of pints. Then we went to the car park. I kissed the tickets, put 'em in the glove compartment, Father Cyril realises he's left a duty-free bag or something back in the bar. I go with him. That's when the car is stolen. Rang the cops immediately from the airport. Hardly slept that night, to be told in the morning the car was repossessed. Well, I could hardly crib. Went to the bank, told my man about the tickets in the glove compartment. He said of course he'd check into it, give him an hour. Was I sure? he asked me when I went back. He spoke to his men and both of them swore that there was nothing in the glove compartment except a rattling biro, and a heap of stuff that he now had for me, plus a few anoraks from the boot. I said: Where's the car? He couldn't tell me. Bank policy. I said: Where's the two guys? Couldn't tell me that either. They were part of a sort of special branch who send in their souls with their CVs. I ended up having to watch that match with Father Cyril in the Nally Stand – you had to go to the Hill, right, kid, with the lads. I couldn't do anything about the car, didn't want to. At least I could drive Father Cyril around in something decent from Mannie's. But the other business niggled me, even with all the celebrations going on, so I got on to a tout that I sometimes had to buy from and he had it checked out easy enough with the seats just five rows behind Dev – a mate of my guy in the same racket had made a killing buying the tickets from a guy who came up to him and only looked for a tenner each over the odds, the whole six tickets. 'Twas then it really hit me that you're dealing with low people who'd sell tickets to touts with the Dubs themselves in the final. Ever after, when I'd hear of Dunstan, I knew 'twas only his innocence was keeping him winning and I'd root for him. When Brother Chuckey here came over and Dunstan and we had a conference, I was only too happy to be there. And the first thing I said was: Dunstan, how can these guys trust you to vote with them after they've given you the money? Dunstan said he wouldn't get the money until after the vote. So I said: How can you trust them to cough up after you've voted? Dunstan hadn't thought of that, because he hadn't thought of voting against Dessie anyway. I said: You got to clear that up or there's no point in talking. And then I said, because we had a conference and nothing to talk about and Brother Chuckey here after flying over, I said, just for something to say and to pass the time, I said: Dunstan, when I think of what you did with the money you got from the bank down through the years, I said, you're . . . what's that word again kid?'

'Philanthropist.'

'I said: Dunstan, you're a philanthropist. All you ever did was give it to your pal Dessie to stay in his house. To give a holiday to your kid and your wife. I said: If you got the money, what would you do with it this time? Dunstan said: it's irrelevant. He wasn't going to vote against Dessie full stop. But I went on, because we had to kill time until Brother Chuckey went back, I said: Dunstan, suppose just for the sake of supposing, you could vote against Dessie and you got the money, Dessie'd hardly rent you the house, what would you do? Rent someplace else? Dunstan said no, but it was stupid talking about it because he'd never vote against Dessie, but for the sake of supposing just to satisfy me, he wouldn't go to the Seaside at all. Well, this was all talk for talk's sake. I said: What good would the money be to you then if you couldn't go to the Seaside. Then Dunstan said something that I'd like to have on a parchment and framed and put over the mantelpiece and see it every day. Dunstan said: I could burn it. I said: The money, burn the money? Dunstan said: Yes, as long as I took it off them. I'm a long time knocking around. And I've never seen a class act like that. He had to be helped. It hit me, he had to be helped. However it could be done. No one could ever be so true to the faith. I took Brother Chuckey aside. I said: First we have to be sure these people who want his vote, that they can deliver. And then I said: It's up to you and me to persuade him he's got to vote against Dessie and to hell with Dessie because this Dunstan is an artist.'

The baton was passed to Francis Coleman.

'Dessie, I'm speaking for myself here but also for my profession. Barristers are a busy people. We get just about as bad a press as the banks themselves, but we have to accept it as the law is arcane. Whereas with the banks, a half-blind widow with an ear trumpet can figure out she's being gypped by the banks. Anyway, I'm a busy man but this election is light relief from a stressful career. Dunstan comes to me and asks how can he trust me. I said: Dunstan, you have my word on it. It's true, there is an innocence about this Dunstan, you can see it shines out of him, as I suppose you'd expect from a person with a one-track attitude to life, like Mother Teresa. So I suppose it was from mixing with you thieves that I see all round me that emboldened him to employ the trenchant and come out with the back alley: Can I wrap this word of yours up and show it to my people? I was going to throw him out. I'll do a lot for hyphen, but I won't sit in an office and listen to my word being impugned. As though it was Maxie I was doing business with. Which made me think of the dirty half-dozen on our side already. So I looked at this innocent who was trying to be street smart and I showed him. How it could be done. We decide to give it another week.'

'Hold on now there, Francis,' the Kodak man's brother insisted, 'you take Brother Chuckey. Brother Chuckey had to fly over again, this time to Dunstan's home town, because Dunstan decided to dig in, almost didn't want to discuss it any more, his mind was made up, nothing would persuade him to vote against Dessie. Brother Chuckey paid for the flights himself and our meetings had to coincide with his weekly day and a half off that big-hearted publicans give their staff. And the kid here and myself, we had to travel down. Even when we came up with what we came up with and persuaded Dunstan to nibble at it, that's all he would do – backed away like a dog to have a slash against a tree. It wasn't until we got Budge here, and Tom Tucker and Dunstan's wife herself, to come in with us that we finally got him to agree. And on top of that we all had to meet you, Francis, again and bring in that Johnny O'Donnell fellow from the credit union. Is that right, Budge?'

'That's the truth.'

'And on top of all that again we had to go to Dr Justin Devane, who's not Dunstan's doctor but a friend of yours, Dessie, as Dunstan knew, and could be depended upon here. I think that's about it. No, one more thing from a personal angle, and this is for you, kid, to remember. I wanted to nail

Francis down on this, I suggested that we be allowed to bring Mannie Manifold's solicitor in to tie it up that we wouldn't all have to be sweating on your word, Francis, when it came for you to fulfil your end. You wouldn't have that. But I went to Mannie's solicitor behind your back anyway and his advice was that we shouldn't push it, that your word was good enough. As I say, it's a personal angle, but I couldn't sleep until Francis did deliver. I don't think I could ever use Mannie's solicitor again. And I think that's that. That's it, Dessie. That's the whole story.'

'That's *what*?' Dessie said.

'That,' Brother Chuckey said. He turned his black coat to pull out a rectangular long brown envelope.

It was the deeds to Dessie's thirteenth house. In Dessie's name.

I conducted a quick contentment count, beginning with Dessie himself. He needed only to glance at the deeds. Then he surveyed Brother Chuckey, the Kodak man, the Kodak man's brother, Budge and Tom. Dessie gave himself away by looking at the deeds again. He was familiar with deeds. He looked again as he might look again at his own flattering photo. Everybody else watched Dessie to see if they were winning. Dessie turned his head for a second to take in Dunstan and Peggy sitting on their little unfolded chairs on the far rocks.

'Go on. Drop the other shoe,' Dessie said, to the Kodak man's brother.

'Dunstan knew more about his own standing with the banks than Francis could possibly know and Dunstan told us the only reason he agreed to go back to Francis was to find out, out of curiosity, how Francis could swing it, in case some other time Dunstan could use it, after of course voting for Dessie. Francis could do it because Timmie Frawley was retiring. Frawley had the say no bother for five grand and an overdraft. Frawley's retirement package was already in place, he was only seeing out the days. And he agreed because this hyphen fellow, Frawley actually liked him, good friends. And because he was also moving back up the country where he came from, and where his wife came from and where both their mothers were still alive. Frawley wasn't worried about shit hitting fans. And another bonus was that Frawley himself hated banks for making him not able to be a human being all his life. Dunstan would have his cheque books and loan before he voted, so that part was tied up. Dunstan cashed the five-grand loan, raided the overdraft and the personal – that came to seven and a half. Dunstan put another five hundred to that. He gave four thousand each to Budge and Tom and told them to join the credit union and feed the four grand each into the account over the last three months. All the DT Offset money was already in Peggy's credit union account. Peggy took four thousand out of that and opened a number two credit union deposit. All this was after Francis sitting in with Budge, Tom and Peggy – no Dunstan – and Johnny O'Donnell. It was agreed. Budge, Tom and Peggy would be able to borrow eight thousand each after three months to buy a holiday home. But the holiday home was on the market immediately. Francis was to buy it in trust for Budge, Tom and Peggy. Except he bought it in trust for Dessie and parted with the deeds when Dunstan got Tom, Budge and Peggy's money from the credit union and gave it to Francis. And if Brother Chuckey will forgive me, on behalf of Dunstan, fuck the banks.'

'No,' Dessie said. 'Not this time. They'll go after him for the lot. Five and a half is personal and the two overdraft on DT Offset, he's doing well now, they'll go after him, examination order, and this time they'll do it after the second missed payment.'

'Oh,' the Kodak man's brother said, 'you didn't hear what happened to Dunstan? You're away a lot, you're out of touch – you didn't hear? A tragic case. His wife is under

counselling. It's probably something that the banks themselves would understand. They'd know that he was carrying
a chip on his shoulder against them since he was a small boy.
He's the only type of person that you could believe would do
it. He has a little business that he got two thousand pounds'
overdraft for and five hundred personal. And he also got five
thousand pounds to convert the attic of his home. The poor
boy snapped. She told Dr Justin Devane, Peggy did, they
were sitting at home just like a normal night when Dunstan
said: Watch this, Peggy, and he burned seven and a half
thousand in the fire. Budge or Tom will tell you, they were
the first people Peggy ran up the street for. They found that
poor boy laughing at all that money burnt in the fire. Dr
Justin Devane has been prescribing tablets. Dr Devane is
hopeful. But Dunstan can't work in his condition. DT Offset
was only hanging on, Dunstan working there all by himself
with nobody to help him. I hear that his wife may try to keep
the business alive, or a new start-up-again business that she
might call O'Neill Offset. But what chance has a woman?
That poor broken boy had to apply for the dole. But there
they told him he couldn't unless he was fit for work and they
would have to investigate him anyway first. But with Dr
Justin Devane's certificates in the meantime he can draw
from the community welfare. And he has the medical card
that helps him get the tablets free, so that's one cross off his
back when he's putting the tablets in the dustbin, or letting
them fall in over the bridge to be on the safe side. Dunstan
had all his old bank statements, judgements, *Stubbs Gazette*
back numbers to show the welfare officer while the welfare
officer was declining a cup of tea from a man who burned
seven and a half thousand. Vincent de Paul paid the last light
bill and they have a, what's that word again, kid, I can never
pronounce it . . .'

'Indebtedness . . .'

'Indebtedness officer trying to sort out their problems.

He's working closely with Dr Justin Devane. But Dr Devane told the indebtedness officer that it may be years, if ever, before Dunstan recovers, although some days Dr Devane is more hopeful and tells Peggy that he knows of extraordinary cases where people who did the Novena to Our Mother of Perpetual Succour . . . that if he thinks he sees an improvement, and Peggy can keep the bit of a business alive, that he might, just might, not promising anything now, let Dunstan go into O'Neill Offset for an hour now and then for therapeutic reasons, while the indebtedness officer is writing angry letters to the Provincial, offering two pounds a week if they persist in being so heartless as not to write it off. All of us who love that poor boy are keeping our fingers crossed that he'll get well. Even Mannie Manifold, who was good enough to give advice based on his experience of some of the customers he's known down through the years.'

Dessie continued with his own examination order. 'Peggy's four, Tom's four and Budge's four, that's twelve on deposit. Against twenty-four for the house, what about legal fees, stamp duty?'

' . . . that's all covered,' Francis Coleman said. 'Dunstan even had two hundred out of it just to buy chips . . .'

'The credit union is owed twelve thousand net . . .'

'Don't worry there,' the Kodak man's brother said. 'Dunstan will pay that. Nobody yet has figured out a way not to pay the credit union and still go to mass. It's sad though. Dunstan is having his last look at the Seaside today. The two to two and a half thousand that he used to pay to rent a house from you, he has that earmarked to pay off the credit union.'

'I almost forgot,' Brother Chuckey said, 'what good are deeds if you can't open your door. Here.' He tossed Dessie the keys. 'And I think you should reconsider what I said to you earlier, about Dunstan voting to allow his good wife and women like her into the Cove? Now that he won't be able to come here any more because he's poor, paying back the credit union, it would be nice if the ladies here could remember their liberator.'

What to do? Dessie didn't have a problem. He gave Ingy the deeds. 'Mind that. And get dressed, we've work to do.' He stood up and slipped into his runners to pad over the stones to Dunstan. Dessie is no man for the maudlin. As I was to learn, all he said was, 'Hi, Peggy', handed Dunstan the keys and squatted in front of both of them for a minute. 'I have to move fast, it's a big night tonight. Check the thirteenth house, tell me what's needed. I can't send Ingy home tomorrow after the night he's going to have. I'm going to get him to ring the Dennison Arms, arrange staff movements. You, Peggy, Warren and Tom, stay in the thirteenth . . .'

'And Junior.'

'And Junior. I have this Monty staying in my house with a couple of women who're looking after him. Ingy and the Daltons and the rest can stay in . . . what we'll call your old house. Right? You lunatic.'

Dessie came back and said to Brother Chuckey, the Kodak man and the Kodak man's brother, 'Where are you all staying?'

'We were thinking of the Albert,' Brother Chuckey said.

'No. Ingy, look after them. Let's go, Ingy.' Dessie had only one leg in his shorts, under the now obligatory towel. 'Well,' he snapped at me, 'what are you waiting for?' I was miserable. I knew when I was blushing. 'Go on, Junior,' Tom Tucker encouraged me.

They knew I was coming over, yet they affected to look out at the sea. I almost turned back, did look back, and saw Dessie and Ingy watching from the top of the steps, to see, before I could think of what to say, in the once manly Men Only Cove, Dunstan clasp my two ears and kiss me on the lips.

CHAPTER 22

THERE IS A half-curtain across Mick O'Mara's front window over which a tall man or someone like me craning his neck can see out. For the arrival of one who sang *Up*. Because of the heatwave, the front door was open and I had been able to smell the onions twenty yards down the street. I was in early, the first of our crowd, but Mick O'Mara was already on top of the news. Junior. Mary, Junior's here. She'll pay no attention to me now while she's over the pan with Eugene and Michael due in after another great day at the hay. Isn't it great, Junior? He did it all for Dessie. Ye're all friends again, the way it should be. Did you get the chance to eat? Are you sure? And Harry's here, Dessie says, he brought his mother. He told me he never worked in the buildings and 'tis hard to credit. That Harry could ate for two good men. Whist, is it musicians we have . . . The Daltons were a bit sunburnt for having had to use the street going from pub to pub. God save all, they said. Mick O'Mara said: God save ye yereselves. I introduced them. Pat and Mick Dalton, Mick O'Mara. Please to meet you boss, the Daltons said. Ye're welcome. Any man with a fiddle is always welcome here, what'll ye have? Ye're from Roscommon, I see. Oh, Mick Dalton said, you're a horrid quick man. Sure, why wouldn't I be? Pints, lads, is it? Didn't I know them from all over in my time. In the old days. Roscommon. Did ye know Bernie Oates at all? Ye'd be too young, I'd say. Ye didn't. A good man, Bernie was. I paid for the Daltons' drink. While Mick O'Mara was throwing the money in the drawer, concerned because I could see they were half pissed, I muttered to them to keep their mouths shut about Monty.

The Kodak man and the Kodak man's brother and Brother Chuckey came in, having luckily eaten at the Seaview, as the first thing the Kodak man's brother said was, 'Listen to that smell.' I ordered their drinks as I introduced them to Mick O'Mara. I heard all about ye, lads. From Dessie. Ye're welcome. Can I get ye anything? Ye're sure? You taught Dunstan, Brother, and Junior too, but you came all the way back to help Dunstan. You're a mighty man. We don't have bad language here, Brother, I won't allow it, but we'll especially go easy on it tonight now that you've honoured us. You'll get that, Junior, aren't you great? The English shilling, 'tis still mighty. We'll have a good crowd tonight so. Batsy'll be rubbing his hands. Hoping for the fallout. Are they going to play now, I wonder, or is it early? They can be temperamental you know.

The Daltons had taken seats at either side of the empty fireplace, as genuine Irish traditional fiddlers from West Clare would, or even sometimes optimistic guitarists, near to the convenient mantelpiece, to hold the pints that would come appreciatively off the assembly line. Brother Chuckey thumped me on the shoulder. 'What are you, Nash?'

'Asleep . . . Brother?'

'Did you think I would fail one of my boys, Nash? But you were a backslider, I remember. Good luck, Nash.'

'Good luck,' the Kodak man and the Kodak man's brother joined in.

Sure, good God, I better go down and talk to those artists in case they'd think they weren't gettin' attention and go out in a huff and leave us without their talent, excuse me lads.

I said, 'You cured him, Brother. Well, all of you. You can consider me as much in your debt as Dunstan is.'

The Kodak man looked at the floor with great modesty, I thought. 'I was talking to Mannie Manifold about it before we came down. Mannie said: Nothing will stop him thinking of Dunstan only as Bonny Prince Charlie. What's that word, kid . . .'

'Moratorium.'

'Right. It's a moratorium on lending that we see in operation here. The banks can advertise all they want on the radio and television and in the papers, but Dunstan won't let them lend until the credit union is clear. We're all agreed on that . . .'

' . . . speed bonny boat, Nash?'

'Like a bird on the wing, Over the sea to Skye.'

Ye're not ready yet, lads? Sure, I know. Take yere time. Sure, when ye're right just give the signal.

'Mannie swears he'll keep his eyes and ears open. We have years to be patient. Not ourselves, we have to do our best on a day-to-day basis. But for Dunstan. There could be a flood of foreign banks coming into the country with this European lark. Mannie says the building societies as well are already moving into the personal loans, OK, they might be doing it only as agents in cahoots with the banks, but it doesn't matter, there'll be so many all trying to lend money, fighting with each other and all of them trying to beat off the credit union, what Mannie claims is there could be confusion, that one way or another one of his customers will figure it out, because Mannie says Dunstan is the talk of the garage. Mannie says that when Dunstan comes back from his exile, Mannie will raise an army for him.'

Sure, good God, 'tis Harry at last.

Harry linked mother into the bar. Dessie had them

booked into the Seaview for the night while he had some of the local help in to get a house ready for them. I welcomed Harry and mother and introduced them first to Mick O'Mara, who overwhelmed the dear lady asking her did she know what a son she had at all, comparing Harry to masons, hod-carriers, bricklayers and tug-of-war champions. From the old days. I continued with mother, introducing her to Brother Chuckey and the Kodak man and the Kodak man's brother. Harry had just time to tell us that he had heard of the Cove developments from Budge, with whom they had dined. And Mick O'Mara had not yet found one of his few bottles of sherry to tempt mother when the Daltons started in second gear.

Sufferin' Lord God Jesus Christ, I beg your pardon, Brother, I'll be back to you in one second, missus. Mick O'Mara was quickly out from behind the counter, picking up a couple of empties from the tables to use as a diplomatic shield while he stopped the runaway horse. Lads, lads, he calmed the Daltons, sure 'tisn't time at all yet, wait till we have the house full. When they're too comfortable and settled in for the night. Enjoy yereselves there now meantime and there's two pints coming up now from me in a minute. Mick O'Mara shook his head when back behind the bar. They can't be blamed, Mick O'Mara said to us, those poor lads. Sure they're from Roscommon.

I had to go to the jacks. When I came back, Dunstan and Peggy had arrived. Everybody wanted to be in the bar on time for the main event. Dessie came next. He was fed. He was sure he was fed.

Batsy came in the back door, shifty, the eyes darting and sensing a good night on the way. Good-night, Batsy, Mick O'Mara said, 'tis only right you should be here, a survivor from Good Friday, and Kerr the Cop is coming too. Your seat is taken by those Roscommon lads, but find someplace to hide down there near them and if you see them likely to have a go at them fiddles, alert me or keep them talkin' about the stories of their travels. A pint, is it? Don't tell me Budge and Tom are fightin' now.

'. . . you're bein' ridiculous, Budge.' Tom and Budge were stopped at the door, in some argument.

'I'll get this,' Brother Chuckey was saying, but he was shouted down, a polite row ensuing, everyone from Harry and even mother to Budge himself the abstainer laying claim to be entitled to buy next.

'Wait till I tell you about him,' Tom Tucker said, but he had to hold off because Harry was saying, 'I'd like you to meet my mother.'

The pub was already hot with happiness.

'What about Budge?' Peggy said. She was sitting with mother, the way ladies like to be with each other. 'What about him, Tom?'

'He won't talk to the two Miss Shines.'

'I didn't say I wouldn't ever talk to them.'

'Twice they went past him tonight when I called for him and they said: Hello, Budge, and he wouldn't answer them.'

'I'll talk to them when they've done their penance.'

Ah, Kerr the Cop. We're all to be arrested now, lads. Give yere wrong names. Good night, Kerr. Batsy's down there. 'Twill be no Good Friday wake tonight, Kerr. Lads, let me just keep fillin', ye can tell me who won the fight to pay when ye're sorted out.

The arrivals and the introductions went on. And on. Father Ab and Father Dollars. Sure, good God man, the world and his wife is here tonight. Ye're welcome, fathers, we're honoured. Brother, isn't that grand company arrived now for you?

I wondered. Writers shun each other. But at least as men of the cloth Brother Chuckey and Father Dollars had in common Dollars being expelled for fucking and Brother Chuckey having been fucked in his soutane by Mrs Bowyer.

A cigarette came in the door next followed by Benny Bobinizer and Staff Cox.

A sort of impatience began to settle on the bar. We were getting itchy for Monty. Dessie went to the door and looked down the street. 'Any sign?' I said.

'No. Go round the back and see if you see anyone.'

'Why would they come in the back?'

'Is this question time? Do what I told you.'

I didn't see anybody round the back.

'No sign,' I said.

'I'll break his fucking neck.'

'Who?'

'Nothing.'

I began to talk to myself. A sure sign. I said: Do not get cranky. That fucker Dessie, I asked him a simple, polite question and he bites the head off me. Don't get cranky. Don't do anything to steal the limelight from Monty's big night.

The Lord save us and guard us, is it an invasion, have they come for our rain?

Now I understood Dessie, but I was still cranky that he'd had to keep it a secret from me. The Bedouin came in the back door as ordered to by Dessie. The Seaside is a sensitive place. A few make a few bob during a Seaside heatwave, but outside of what is usually a short wet summer the Seaside is a small fishing community trying to make a humble living catching mackerel for a country addicted to burgers and Kentucky chicken. A parade of Arabs down the main street would have led to great expectations, Dessie understood. The owner of the Albert had been trying to find a buyer for twenty-five years.

The Bedouin stopped inside the back door and put their accordions on the ground and Mick O'Mara was enlightened when the head Bedouin, Butch Frawley, came over to me and Harry and there was a huge round of introductions.

Fiddlers, Mick O'Mara said. From Roscommon. Arabs with melodeons. A heatwave. Should we look up Nostradamus, lads? Is it Russia is to be converted next?

After I gave him a cigarette and the counter was fighting behind his back for the honour of buying the Bedouin a drink, Butch said, 'I hope Dessie Dennison appreciates this. Divine Dickie had to lose this weekend's two twelve-hour shifts in the computer factory. Lexie had to hire a nephew to mind his sweet shop. Ghosty passed up a wedding and I even lost a wedding myself. Try and get your friend to think of it that way, will you?'

That sounded fair enough to me. But when I did mention it to him, Dessie said, 'I told him to try and think of it as a charity gig. I said everyone, and I mentioned everyone involved, I explained to him the sacrifices they were making, I said I could have picked another group, but that I wanted to give the Bedouin the opportunity to show their better nature. I said: Try and think of it that way, Butch, you'll find you'll feel good. See if you can turn up. And if you can't, no harm done. Except to you when I get Ingy to kick your bollix in.'

Francis Coleman and Shamey Flynn came in and were taken in charge by Dessie. Dessie introduced them first to Mick O'Mara. From the other side, Mick O'Mara said: You're welcome. 'Tis great today, lads. Teams never met each other off the field in the old days, d'ye realise that? 'Twas straight home and never see each other again until the next time. Now they have golf outings. But 'twould make you wonder. All sorts of distractions. Were they better men long ago when you think of it? But do you know what while we're on the subject, everybody here, Arab musicians and Roscommon fiddlers, 'tis a night cryin' out for singin', lads. Who'll start? But there's Eugene and Michael. And look, Siobhan's with them now, somethin's up. Go in to yere dinner, lads, and come out when ye're ready. I'll need help.

'Hi, Dad. I was working too, Dad. I went out to the farm and brought them the buttermilk.'

Aren't you a great girl, how did you get out?

'I got a lift out.'

From who? Who gave you the lift?

'Mickey Crann.'

Oh. That's all right so. You'll be hungry too. Go on down.

'Can I go to the amusements, Dad?'

Sure, I wouldn't want to be Nostradamus to know that was comin'. Where were we lads? Will we start? Who'll sing? Butch, is that your name, are ye ready? Will ye play before the Roscommon lads or what?

Butch interrupted Dessie and Francis Coleman. 'Charity or no charity, we're not playing relief. Put those other fellas on first.'

He might be right. If we could slip 'em on, sure, they might have another pub they're intendin' to see. But get somebody to block the door in case they do too much damage.

'Mick,' Dessie said, 'give it another while.'

You think so, Dessie?

Dessie went to the door, looked down the road. I watched him. He turned, gave me the nod.

They were on their way.

Nurse Fidelma and Margaret walked on either side of the wheelchair, Ingy pushing. Dessie had sent a cheque to Nurse Fidelma, asking her could she have it subsumed into the Marian funds, from which Monty might be togged out appropriate to the heatwave? Monty wore cream slacks and a short-sleeved shirt and a good pair of laced brown leather shoes. He might have been anybody during the old days for whom there had been a whip-round. I introduced Dessie to Nurse Fidelma and Margaret. Of course, Nurse Fidelma and Margaret knew the truth but Monty, because it was the way

Dessie wanted it, Monty believed he was here at the Seaside courtesy of the Marian Nursing Home.

'A friend of mine,' I said to Monty, 'Dessie Dennison.'

Monty was grumpy. 'I'm not goin' in there unless I know him.'

Dessie and I stood in the doorway to hide Monty from Mick O'Mara possibly looking out, with me moving slightly away from the jamb to let Monty lean forward from the wheelchair to look in. Monty reversed the wheelchair, turned so that his back was to the wall.

'I know him. He was a great man. I can't go in like this. Somebody help me up.'

Ingy held Monty's hands and eased him to his feet.

'I must see if I can walk. I've no practice.'

Ingy linked him while Monty took a few steps away from the bar. Monty put his hand on a windowledge, shook off Ingy. He walked by himself just to the edge of the footpath. He walked back and he walked up and down and around in a circle. He stopped and lifted his legs, one after the other. 'I'm after pushing him the whole way in from Dessie's house,' Ingy complained.

'I know him,' Monty said again, 'a good one. I'll go in. I'll go in by myself. Everybody stay behind.'

Monty had long since lost the raw building site tan. He was a stooped figure using a frail shuffle to get through the big bodies blocking the door. We let Nurse Fidelma and Margaret in after him and then we followed, me looking at Dunstan and pointing ahead to Monty. With little shoves of fists into sides and knees nudging knees, the word spread silently and there was all but silence itself in the bar, so much so that Mick O'Mara said: It's gone grand and quiet all of a sudden, but sure, we'll all be livened up in a minute. Good night to you, Mick O'Mara said to Monty, and what can I get you?

'I'll have a pint,' Monty said. 'And how are you, Kevin?'

'Ah,' Mick O'Mara said, 'good to see you again.' He put his hand out over the counter. They shook. It's a bit high, Mick O'Mara said, pointing to the tap, you won't mind if I let it settle. And what for your company? These ladies are with you, are they? Nurse Fidelma and Margaret were behind Monty on either side of him. While Monty decided whether they were with him or not, Mick O'Mara didn't wait for an answer. He said: Excuse me a minute now while that's settlin'. I see Junior Nash there that I have a message for. He came out from behind the counter and called me aside to say: We're in right trouble now, Junior. There's only one people knows me as Kevin. Sure, it happens often in here now and again, 'twas my name on the buildin's for six months of the year as well as Dermot for the other six months. That old lad now, I can't place him for the life of me, but he's with those two lassies, I think, so while I'm playin' the cards close to the chest, you be movin' in on those females and see if you can get the name out of them.

Everybody at the bar had copped on that Mick O'Mara didn't recognise Monty. And nobody would have copped on faster than Monty himself. I asked Dessie what I should do. 'If he was a steak, he'd recognise him. Don't do anything. Let them at it. That Monty looks like he's enjoying himself.'

Nurse Fidelma and Margaret had whiskeys. They didn't say please Monty when he asked them what they'd like. They were on the ball.

What Mick O'Mara did was to bluff on behind the counter holding the two whiskeys. 'And tell me, are you here or over these days?'

'Oh, I'm over, Kevin.'

Now, ladies. Mick O'Mara put the whiskeys on the counter and topped off the pint.

'How much is that, Kevin?'

Sure, good God man, keep your hand in your pocket. There's fights all over the place with people trying to buy drink all night and why wouldn't I join in myself? Good luck. And don't let those Arabs frighten any of ye, they're only musicians dressed up. We'll have great crack now in a minute. But are things quiet over, I hear shockin' stories . . .

'I'm a bit out of touch, Kevin.'

I know. We all are, I suppose. Do you know what I can't remember, I can't remember now, would you have known Bernie Oates? There's lads down there from Roscommon reminded me of him only just now. Did you know Bernie?

'Did I know Bernie Oates, Kevin? Of course I knew him.'

You did. What am I talkin' about? 'Tis so long ago I've it all forgotten. And there was the great Paddy Mackessy. And the one and only Monty Gleeson himself. But they'd be after your time, I'd say, you wouldn't have known them men now.

'Indeed, I did, Kevin.'

Did you? Tell me, have you any news of him? Monty. I can get no word. Is he alive? You know him? Have you seen him?

'He's alive. I know him well, Kevin. But I've never seen him.'

Thank God. Monty's alive. You know him well, you say? But you say you've never seen him?

'That's right. I know Monty better than anybody knows him. But I've never seen him, Kevin.'

Did I let somethin' fall into your porter by mistake by any chance . . . and look at everyone laughin' . . . am I bein' set up or what, lads . . . know him but never see . . . 'tis . . . oh, thank the Sacred Heart of Jesus . . . 'tis . . . it is you, Monty . . . you latchiko, you . . . let me out.

We cheered. We laughed. We slapped the counter. We nearly fell off stools. And we were respectful while they had their arms around each other, two good men crying, Mick O'Mara holding Monty at arms' length. But, Monty, you're gone weak. Are you eatin'? Will you have somethin' now?

304

No wonder I couldn't place you there for a second, and these lovely ladies?

Mick O'Mara made Monty sit down at a table. Take the weight off your feet, Monty. Look at the bar. Half the pub dry and no one to serve them. Eugene. Michael. Come up out of that. Mary. D'you know who's here, Mary? 'Tis Monty. Eugene, Michael, d'ye hear me? Come up fast and serve. What shower? Clean dirt is no poison. Good lads. Batsy. Come over here till I introduce you to Monty.

The whole bar was introduced to Monty. We were like people queuing up to sign a visitors' book. This is Junior Nash, Monty. Oh, ye met? Tell me. Go way. A home, Monty? A home? In Kilburn. Three days. That's all wrong, Monty. That shouldn't happen. That can't be right, that's a terrible thing. Oh, I'm sure they're very good. Nurse Fidelma, sure, can't I see she's good? And Margaret. I agree with you, Monty. She must be a topper. Let me thank you too, Margaret. And you, Nurse Fidelma. Saints. Sure, I know. And 'tis Junior went to see you. And 'twas Dessie started it. Dessie, come up here to the top of the queue. Will you eat, Monty? You're sure. What about the girls? Ye did. A salad. That's not what you had, Monty, is it? Salad. Sure, Monty that's not eatin'. You'll have it later? You will. There's Mary. Here he is, Mary. She never comes up, Monty. She's too busy. That's true for you, Mary, he is lookin' well. Although he's shook, Mary. I know. What's that, Nurse Fidelma? To be sure 'tis a grand smell. Will ye go down, yourself and Margaret? Do. Go with Mary, sure, when does she have female company. Do. Go on. What'll we do? Eugene. Eugene, run. Let Michael hold the fort. Run out to the butchers, Eugene, and get a hundred-weight of sausages. For everyone. And run back. Tell Siobhan to put on more pans. We'll have no little sticks to stick in 'em or baskets to hand 'em round in, we'll use plates. Or saucers, what matter? Hurry, Eugene. Start up the musicians, lads. We'll have a night first, Monty, and we can talk after. Harry, this is Monty. That man can ate as good as Paddy Mackessy, Monty. Look at the clergy I have for you, Monty, even from America. And Christian Brothers. What's that, Junior? They won't? Not before the fiddlers, you say? I know. But I can't welcome Monty with those fiddlers from Roscommon. Even if Bernie Oates came from there itself. What, Dessie? You'll ask Ingy to ask them? Will you? Good man, Dessie. And you behind everything. You're great. This is Harry's mother, Monty. Eugene, run in. Help Siobhan put them all on as fast as you can. Tell Siobhan the amusements will wait. Are you all right, Michael? Batsy, keep the glasses comin'. He's a good lad, Monty. Michael. They've put in long hard hours at the hay since seven this mornin'. These lads are from Dublin, Monty, they came here Good Friday to help Dessie in the election. But sure you don't know about that. How could you? I'll tell you all later. Kerr the Cop, Monty. We were to have celebrations Good Friday but they fell through, Monty. 'Twas only myself, Kerr the Cop and Batsy in here by ourselves. We could make no fist of it. But by God we'll do it tonight. Whist, they're agreein' to Ingy. They're goin' to play, Monty. Francis Coleman, Monty. You're shakin' hands with a barrister, he was on the other side, but he's welcome. Monty, a great friend of mine, Budge. Budge Griffin. He's an uncle of Junior now that visited you. 'Twas Junior called to see him, Budge. Tom Tucker, Monty. When you see Budge, you know Tom is somewhere around. Wasn't it like we used to be ourselves one time God bless us? Peggy, where are my manners gone. Monty, this is Peggy, Dunstan's lovely wife, and Dunstan himself – oh, he's a boyo I'll tell you about when I'm explainin' everything. Quick, one of those Roscommon lads is reachin' for the fiddle. Excuse me, Monty, I must stand up. No more introductions till later. They're ready, Ingy. Let 'em start fast. 'Tis good Mary came up, Monty, she did it for you. I knew she would, Monty.

I was sitting at the counter beside the Kodak man's brother. The Bedouin were arranging the chairs. I said, 'That one, Butch, he'll start with "The Rose of San Antone".' Before they sat down Butch announced, 'Ladies and gentlemen, the St Patrick's Ceili Band is honoured to be invited to play for Mr Monty Gleeson – ' Butch indicating Monty, for whom Butch suggested we all put our hands together. Then the Bedouin all took off their robes and threw them in a heap on the floor. They were all wearing green shorts and a white T-shirt with the St Patrick's Ceili Band printed in green. They played and Butch sang 'Tis maybe someday I'll go back again to Ireland. Maybe at the closing of my day.'

Fuck that langer, Butch, I said to myself, but you will not spoil Monty's night, you will not get cranky. Butch and the St Patrick's Ceili Band made a marvellous job of 'Galway Bay,' while everyone in the bar stole a look at Monty, who was obviously choked. Butch worked the audience with soul and sincerity, Nurse Fidelma, Margaret, Siobhan and Eugene, waiting out of respect, holding the plates of jumbo sausages until Butch finished, with the tear in his voice, 'I will ask my God to let me make my Heaven in that dear isle across the Irish Sea.'

Butch bowed in the direction of Monty Gleeson. The applause was for Monty, led by Mick O'Mara. Great stuff, lads. That's the real thing. That brings back the old days; Monty. Here's the sausages now. Hold on. Butch had squeezed straight into 'I'll Take You Home Again Kathleen'. Hold off a while, Eugene. I abandoned all forecasts. The crankiness eased out of me. I spotted that Mick O'Mara was subdued, his chin on his chest, eyes wide, flicking from the St Patrick's Ceili Band to Monty. 'The roses all have left your cheek. I've watched them fade away and die.' You either ran out into the street with your hands over your ears to get away from this new St Patrick's Ceili Band or you sat there and listened to them, resisting even a polite cough into a closed fist. The songs our fathers loved. When our fathers were only our own age now. 'Take you home again – ' I hadn't known Butch to put such feeling into a song. However, I said to him later, You faked it. 'To where your heart will feel no pain.' I could hear Dunstan strike a match. He lifted the flame up to the cigarette in his lips and held it there until it almost burned his fingers, his eyes fixed on Butch and the St Patrick's Ceili Band. Dunstan was gently jolted out of his satisfaction and possible contemplation of another last comeback in a few years' time, his foot on the prow of the boat, hand held to his eyes, the Kodak man's brother and Mannie Manifold holding the Welcome Home banner on the beach. More, more, we shouted after we clapped and held the tears shining in our loving eyes.

'Now, ladies and gentlemen, what about a song from one of yourselves?'

Bring out the sausages, Eugene.

The names flew, everybody in the bar volunteered by his nearest neighbour. Give me a chance. That's only my third pint. No, not now, I might later. Here, the Kodak man called, like a winner at bingo, pointing to the back of the Kodak man's brother's head, here. The volunteered protested but was pushed and encouraged and clapped on his way to Butch, where the Kodak man's brother spoke into Butch's ear and Butch drew back and shook his head, consulted the St Patrick's Ceili Band, who shook theirs to a man. Butch pointed at the Daltons.

As Butch said to me later: Waxie's fucking Dargle. Jesus Christ.

Eat up, lads. Make sure everyone gets some now, Eugene. Siobhan, those people over there. And then go back and keep them comin'. The Dublin man is goin' to sing, Monty, by the looks. But it's the Roscommon lads that's goin' to be backin' him. Sure, mightn't it be the best way out. While the people are atin'. Nurse Fidelma, Margaret, see to those musical Arabs there while they're idle. Maybe he'd be a strong singer now, and that the backin' might be kept down. Sure, everyone looks happy. You all right in there, Michael? Good lad.

They can't help it, the Dubs. They know only Dub songs that can be appreciated only by fellow Dubs. Mick O'Mara drew sharp air in through his closed teeth when the fiddles were on their own between verses. They're from Roscommon, Monty. But 'tis all right, the people seem to be able for it.

A lone voice, that of the Kodak man, shouted: More! But the applause was not for an encore as the Kodak man's brother came back to us and Butch was on his feet to announce Richard Divine, now no longer known as Divine Dickie, and 'The Old Rustic Bridge'. It was as well I retired. Heatwave or no heatwave, we would not hear 'It's an Itsy-Bitsy Teenie-Weenie Yellow Polka-Dot Bikini' tonight. Mick O'Mara had forecast that it was a night cryin' out for singing. He couldn't have known that Butch would turn his prediction back to front.

The music lured more would-be passers-by in off the street. Tend to those people, Michael. Run in for more sausages, Eugene, everyone is to be fed. The newcomers brought their own conversational noise until they heard the silence, the choked cough reception afforded to Richard Divine. After whom Butch surprised us, calling by popular request – his own – for a song from Harry Lamb.

Butch told me he had never heard Harry sing. Butch did it because Harry had allowed them to appear without getting paid and also Butch desperately needed a leak and he was afraid the Daltons might not stay dormant while he was in the jacks. I think Butch was trying to hide his new good heart.

Harry hadn't a chance. The dumb can be cajoled to sing in Mick O'Mara's. The tone deaf. I sang there myself. No, no, Harry said, firm, almost indignant, blushing. But mother was smiling at Harry. Butch insisted: 'Come on now, Harry, don't play hard to get.' Honestly, Harry protested, I don't sing. I swear. But we went into action as we had once known how to do in the Cove, repelling intruders. We Want Harry. We Want Harry. He was too civilised, Harry, surrounded by barbarians. And once mother said: Do, Harry, that was enough. For us. Mother had to go further: We'll sing together, Harry. Yes, we all agreed, mother and Harry, clapping them into action.

Harry cleared the old throat. Ghosty came over to their table with the accordion.

Suntanned, Harry sang, Ghosty softly on the box.

> Wind blown.
> Honeymooners
> At last alone.
> Feeling
> Way above par.
> Oh how lucky we are.

Harry was Bing and mother was Grace. Dunstan moved beside me to get a better view. Mother is now your mother, Harry had said to me the first day I met him. Now if none of us there ever had a mother, mother was all our mothers. She was an English Rose. An Irish Colleen. She was apple pie. Dunstan leaned his elbow on my shoulder. Peggy winked at me. Harry and mother sang And I'll give to you. And you'll give to me. True love. True love. Two shy soft tiny voices. Harry looking into mother's smiling eyes. What could we do? It was a night singing out for crying. And on and on it will always be. True love . . .

Ghosty soothing them along.

Have you had enough?

That was what Mick O'Mara said, his own personal

trademark distraction from his tears. Talking to Monty. Referring to sausages. While Harry blushed at the applause, with delight. And the English Rose remained motherly pale and fragile, surrounded by our true love.

The problem for all of us when our applause finished was that nobody was able to speak. Maybe it was only a few seconds of incapacitating sentiment, but it seemed for ever, the embarrassed silence. Butch was still trying to think of How to Follow That when we were all saved by the Daltons, and grateful to them for backing our renewed conversation. Butch and the band had an early break. He came over to me.

'What's going on, Butch?'

'What? Oh, this – ?' pointing to his T-shirt. 'We talked about it. By the way, how're we doing?'

'You want the truth, Butch?'

'Of course. Cunt.'

'No. The truth is, Butch, I think ye're brilliant. I'm not happy with those shorts. You've all got white skinny legs.'

'It's a heatwave, Junior, you know. We only brought the robes just to surprise you. We'll never wear them again. The Bedouin are finished. No more gimmicks. There's no one else doing it. We're going to go back to being ourselves. We'll wear slacks in the winter.'

Butch looked around at the crowd in Mick O'Mara's. He asked me who they were. I told him. 'He's an American priest, Irish American, that guy? A Christian Brother? That Monty, a broken-down navvy. There's Harry's mother. English. He's a barrister? Look, Junior, keep this to yourself. I have to give credit to Ghosty for it. Emigration's coming into its own again. You know the way the politicians say we have a grand educated workforce – they don't say anything about it being a pity there's fuck all work – but you know how they like to go on, no longer sending uneducated labourers out into the world to live in a cheap room. Now, vibrant, confident, third-level talent going abroad to gain valuable experience to build up the country when they return with further skills. Ghosty says that's all horseshit. Ghosty's just back from seeing his brother in Boston. It's the same as it ever was, Junior, only there's more of them. The politicians are right about the cheap rooms. Except the cheap rooms cost a bomb now. And they're all crying into their beer the way they always did. And Junior, it's going to get better. I mean worse, there'll be more and more emigrants. All crying, Junior. We have to prepare for the leisure age, the politicians are saying. That's a euphemism for there's going to be fuck all more work in any country if you're depending on us. So we decided. We're going to give it a go. We'll sing no song unless a mother dies in it or some poor bollix is dreaming of a last glimpse of the old sod before St Patrick says hello. Dead mothers, Junior. Graveyards. Rustic bridges. Noreen Bawn. The lot.'

A year later, interviewed on *The Late Late Show*, Butch admitted humbly that he was at a loss to account for the popularity of the St Patrick's Ceili Band. We're just people who like to play songs we heard our mothers sing. He was plugging their new album that included one new single written by Ghosty: 'When I Go Mother, Be There at the Foot of the Bed'.

Butch went to talk to Harry. I was able to catch a bit of Mick O'Mara.

You have to admit though, Monty, they work hard at it, those fiddlers. Sure, isn't it the Roscommon way? Was there a better man, Monty, than Bernie Oates to work off a hang-over? Paddy Mackessy, Monty, 'twas you found him. Sure, I knew 'twould be you. You only missed him five minutes in the Crown and 'twas you led the search. God rest Paddy. And poor Bernie, gone too you say, he lived with a sister, he was all right so in the end. Is there anyone alive at all, Monty? But three days, you say. I'm sorry to hear it. Things are way worse than I heard. They wouldn't let you out. Over a bit of dizziness. Monty, how often we were high up and dizzy of a Monday mornin' and we survived. I'm not happy, Monty. How could I recognise you? Sure, you're not the same man at all. They should have let you back to your room. It wasn't right. I'm not happy, Monty. A home. In Kilburn. That wasn't there in our day. Old Harry Beegan that had no one, didn't we all call and take turns to have a look in, weren't you one of the people yourself that stayed up all night after the Crown closed to supervise Harry dyin'? You're not eatin', Monty. Don't tell me a lie. I know you. I'll have to talk straight to you later. There's them Daltons stoppin', we'll have to get the melodeons on fast.

Butch was talking seriously to Harry. Harry would never lose the faith. He was listening with innocent belief to Butch as though Harry could already see a year down the line. See Lexie leasing the sweet shop to his nephew. Ghosty only now available for society weddings. Butch treble-booking and not turning up for any of them just to keep his hand in. Simon Quinn and Fats Flynn had to be pulled by the leg off the dole. Divine Dickie, chucking in his two twelve-hour weekend shifts, telling the supervisor: You can shove this shite up your hole, I'm an artist.

Eugene, fill those fiddlers' hands with sausages to keep 'em occupied.

The band played on. Faithful to their new repertoire. There was no Elvis, Tauber or 'Why Did I Leave My Little Back Room in Bloomsbury?' which Monty might or might not have appreciated. 'Shall I ever see my granny's face again?' There was a bottomless cache of lament that catered for the extended family. 'My feet are here on Broadway . . . O the ache that's in them for the place where I was born.' As Butch was to elaborate: We could make enough out of the jukeboxes of New Jersey alone . . .

Father Ab did a recitation.

Father Dollars sang 'The Little Shirt Me Mother Made for Me', a favourite with out-of-touch Irish Americans.

The night had a long way to go. There was no shortage of singers, conscripts or volunteers. Everyone's hat was thrown into the ring. There was much support for Tom Tucker next. I would have bet on Tom. And lost. Dessie went over to Butch and the next announcement demanded Mick O'Mara.

Mick O'Mara was drinking steadily now, only taking the pint from his mouth to direct more food to any guilty empty hand and to talk while he was listening to Monty. Not now, lads, later, sure I can't neglect Monty. We want 'South of the Border'. We want 'South of the Border'. Sure, good Lord God, that's Monty's song. Do ye want me to be shot? Sing it together. Sing a duet. They want us, Monty. But we never sang together. 'Twas your song. Will you sing it yourself for them the way only you know how? We Want Mick and Monty. We want Mick and Monty.

Will you come up to the counter so, Monty, because 'tis in there I like to stand. Mick O'Mara went behind the counter and held the pump with his left hand. Use the other barrel there for a minute, Michael.

Monty stood up and rested his arm on the bar. Are you ready, Monty. Will we start so? Will I start and you join in or will you start and I'll join in or will we both start together? Will I count three?

South of the Border. *Up* Mexico Way.

We cheered already.

Mick O'Mara clutched the pump and from the second verse to tomorrow never comes they held hands like arm wrestlers.

And you knew. You could see what would happen. Mick O'Mara would stand at the open kitchen door, with one eye on the bar, as he put it to Mary: It's not right, Mary. That was never meant by God. He could do with another three stone. I knew all the good men and they never went down like that. 'Tis no way for a man to end. And couldn't he be there with Batsy helpin' to populate the pub when 'tis quiet? And when you come out yourself to sit by the fire in winter with only Batsy here and Kerr the Cop and myself, he'd be good to talk about the old days. There was never a dirty word came out of his mouth. You'd like him, Mary, I could promise you. And think when the odd old soldier drops in, think of the welcome Monty'd have for them, their eyes would light up. But 'tis for you to say, Mary. I've said nothin' to Monty, I wouldn't dream of it. How long more can we hold Eugene and Michael. They're good men already. But while they're here, in summer, if he had his strength back, couldn't I drive him out to the farm for the day, and he could bring the buttermilk out to the men at the hay. Not to have Siobhan gettin' lifts from Mickey Crann. Sure, I knew you would, Mary. Sure I wouldn't have asked you. I knew you would. You're a good woman. And Monty will know that. With all the talkin' I do be doin', I don't tell you that enough. I was a lucky man the day I met you, Mary. I won't. I won't go on away out of that. I mean what I say. What? It is not now. That's somethin' got into my eye.

Have you had enough?

Budge, Tom, Dessie, Peggy and Dunstan. All together at the Seaside. The St Patrick's Ceili Band that used to play in the Pioneer Total Abstinence Society halls, where we went when we were innocent. Brother Chuckey who said we'll all miss each other some day, Tucker.

And the *deus ex machina*.

It's not my doing. Mick O'Mara came out of the kitchen. Stood at the open door. Shouted at me: Junior! A shocked Mick O'Mara. Making the music stop and everyone looking at me, Dessie suspiciously. I had disobeyed Dessie. But this is not my doing now. I blame Mick O'Mara. After I had seen Monty in the Marian Nursing Home, Dessie said: OK, we know where he is. Leave it. We'll see when the time comes. But I didn't obey him. VISITING ALL DAY, the sign said.

You wouldn't find it in *The Second-hand Wardrobe*. There's nothing like it in my first, *Hand Me Down*, when I was green. But not that green.

Junior! Mick O'Mara accused me in the quiet bar. Mary, Nurse Fidelma, Margaret, trying to look out over his shoulders. You never told us. And 'tis Margaret, that minded Monty, 'tis Margaret that's to be yere bridesmaid.

'*The Cove Shivering Club* is sparkling and hilarious, full of characters and lines that lovers of Michael Curtin expect. Curtin is one of Ireland's very best writers. His books are marvellous achievements, very funny and very, very human. He has also created some of the best barmen in modern literature.' – *Roddy Doyle*

It all began on Good Friday, 1955, when, aged ten, Junior Nash and Dunstan Tucker swam each way across the bay, defying the freshness of the Atlantic in spring, and thereby became full members of the Cove Shivering Club. The rules were simple: you don't piss in the water and you don't bring a woman.

Membership of the club marks a step into manhood but, even at ten, manhood brings its trials. Dunstan, deprived of a summer holiday at the cove, develops a demented financial obsession. Junior, disturbed by the arrival of a rule-busting woman, finds the ceiling swapping places with the floor as he is clattered around by the benignly violent Ingy. Junior never really gets to grips with women; Dunstan never gets to grips with credit.

The other members of the Cove Shivering Club – the scheming Dessie, the bluff and the loyal Budge and Tom, the slippery Tommy Ryan-O'Brien, Father Ab Sheehy and Dollars Mulcahy, English impresario Harry Lamb – are linked in a farcical election minuet of their own, contesting the presidency of the Cove Shivering Club, their votes sliding uncertainly from one side to the other in a knot of inducement, strong-arm tactics, deviousness and raw emotional blackmail.

With its maze of comic twists and turns, *The Cove Shivering Club* brilliantly demonstrates Michael Curtin's wicked sense of the humorous absurd and his deeply affectionate understanding of the most human of moral frailties.

'Michael Curtin could be called the Irishman's Julian Barnes. Good on modern dialogue, clever with ticklish set pieces and screamingly funny about male eccentricities.' *Daily Mail*

ISBN 1-85702-473-7

9 781857 024739

£8.99
Fiction
A Paperback Original